For Rachel Caine, always.
As long as birds sing and stars shine.

CHAPTER 1

IF DANICA WATERHOUSE EVER DECIDED to write a how-to guide for other witches, the first rule would be: *Do not cast when you're hungover.*

It would be right up there with *harm none* for important tenets. Unfortunately, she was known for having great ideas but not so fantastic about following her own good advice. Which was why she was unlocking the door to the Fix-It Witches shop at 8:57 a.m. when it opened at nine, though a thousand angry goblins were kicking her brain stem.

Despite the gargantuan headache, the shop's logo always made her smile—two witches on broomsticks, both wearing tool belts. Her cousin Clementine had said the design was too risky, considering their nature, but Danica enjoyed the irony. Plus, people in the Midwest were too pragmatic to take such things seriously. The first Waterhouse witches had fled the Old World due to the persecution of poor Agnes, and then with that dustup in Salem, they had quietly slid a bit farther west to settle in and keep a low profile. At this juncture, the chance of discovery was minimal.

Clementine usually took the early shift, but she was out of town, and they had a backlog of work orders. Danica had promised herself she wouldn't drink too much at the bachelorette party last night, but she had been trying altogether too hard to prove she didn't care about the wedding.

With a groan, she got the door open and stumbled in, flicking lights on as she went. Not magically, although the light switches might've responded. The alarm system did, disarming with a flick of her fingers.

Danica had a knack with all machines, and sometimes it extended to various modern conveniences. Not reliably, however, and it was best not to get in the habit of leaning on small magics. Otherwise, she might slip up when she was surrounded by mundanes. And while she didn't think they would dunk her in a pond or tie her to a pyre before the council could intervene, it was still best to be cautious.

Before she tackled the gadgets waiting for her attention, she got a bottle of water and two strong painkillers. This hangover might scramble her ability to magically repair malfunctioning machines, and it wouldn't do to give someone back a toaster oven that now served as a shortwave radio. That would raise entirely too many questions, and it wouldn't help the business either. She could imagine the reviews online already.

When some of the goblin noise subsided in her head and she could see without a corona of light, Danica flipped the sign on the front door to open and settled in back at the workbench. In films, they always showed witches working around cauldrons, dressed fully in black, sacrificing small animals and whatnot, whereas she was wearing a pair of ripped jeans, ratty sneakers, and a fleece sweatshirt with cat ears on the hood. Not because cats were her familiars; she just thought they were cute.

Sadly, she also had a terrible allergy to them. Which didn't stop cats from sticking to her everywhere she went. Danica had no idea if that was witch-related or if cats were just assholes with a tendency to gravitate toward those who would rather pass. But the minute she set foot on the street, if there was a cat within five blocks, it would present itself, rub all over her legs, and follow her home sometimes too. It was bad enough with strays, but it got awkward when she had to call people to inform them that their beloved pets were on her porch and wouldn't leave.

She took another sip of water, and it stayed down. Good—she figured she was only *slightly* hungover, so it should be fine to get to work, as she was only breaking the *no casting while impaired* rule a little bit. So many inventions designed to make life easier, so many gizmos that needed fixing—Danica couldn't throw fireballs or heal the sick, but she *could* fix a television pretty damn quick. Tech magic had run in the Waterhouse family for generations, but she and Clementine were the only ones with real power these days.

Gram had poured her magic into a precious gift—a spellbook that would help her when she needed it most—to Danica when Gram retired, and her mother... Danica sighed. Minerva was married to a mundane, and she had squandered her magic, let it trickle away as she led a trivial life in Normal, Illinois, of all places. Sometimes Danica thought the name of the town where she'd grown up was a little on the nose.

Before Danica could get to work, the phone rang, and she

grabbed the extension in the work room. "Fix-It Witches, this is Danica. How can I help you?"

"Just calling to make sure you made it to work on time. Raquel posted some pictures of the party, and I saw enough to wonder if you'd even hear the alarm." Clementine's cheerful voice came across with a hint of reverb, indicating she was on Bluetooth and probably driving.

"You don't need to worry. I'm on it! I'll get half of these done before lunch."

"Big promises. Are you feeling okay?"

"Not great, but I'll recover." She wondered what pics Raquel had posted. *How embarrassed should I be?*

Normally, Danica didn't drink much, and it hadn't been the spirit of Bacchus that had motivated her to get crazy either. Nor was it a pure desire to celebrate Raquel's happiness. Fact was, Raquel was marrying Danica's ex, and Danica wasn't 100 percent cool with it. But she'd experienced an extremely prideful need to prove that she was totally, completely fine with Raquel's nuptial plans—not at all upset over the fact that Danica had dated Darryl Kenwood for two years and the entire time he'd talked about how neither of them needed to make things official to be happy.

To exacerbate matters, four months after Darryl hooked up with Raquel, he proposed to her. And Raquel was as mundane as they came. *No need to be official, my ass, Darryl. Hard not to take that personally.* If Danica was an evil sort of witch, she would've hexed his cell phone to spam all his contacts with a link to the last porn video he watched. *You still could,* a little voice whispered.

Since Clem knew the whole backstory and had even broken

up with her boyfriend in solidarity, it was no wonder she was worried. A thread of concern persisted in Clem's voice. "Why in the world did you go to Raquel's bachelorette party anyway? You've barely spoken since college."

"I was proving a point."

"The fact that you're pointlessly nice? Or that you're over him?"

"Maybe both? Look, she didn't steal him from me. *I* broke up with him, remember? I was tired of his crap, and I couldn't put up with it anymore, not even for Gram."

"Still—"

"Don't worry about me," she cut in. "I'm at work. The business is fine, and you can poke at my emotions when you get back."

"If you're sure. Darryl is a loser. I know why you were with him, but we're better off sticking to the pact. Don't let Gram pressure you into dating some random gene packet again, okay?"

She clenched her teeth, too grumpy for lectures at this hour. "I hear you."

"And don't get worked up," Clem added, like she needed that caution.

A witch with serious emotional issues trying to cast? All the machines might explode—extra bad for business.

"Drive safely," Danica muttered.

"Eat something! I'm off to learn how to make better use of our marketing dollars. Have a great day." With that, her cousin hung up.

Clementine—nicknamed Clem—was always looking to increase

profits and get more customers. While their abilities were awesome, they couldn't pay the bills without money coming in. She and her cousin were better off than most because they lived in the family home, sold to them for a song when Gram relocated to the retirement community in Citrus Hills. Where she had—unfortunately—practiced using social media on the smartphone Danica had bought her. Now instead of appearing in water bowls, Gram sent messages like a mundane, attaching photos of respectable witches. That was the beginning of dark days, the great Bindr (the only pure witch dating app) plague. With a shiver, she recalled the endless nagging.

"Did you fill out the profile yet? Did you take a nice selfie?" It had been so wrong when Gram used the word "selfie."

She sighed. On the other end of the spectrum, her mother asked Danica if she was happy and fulfilled, if she was following her heart. Three generations of witches, with her sandwiched in the middle, being tugged in opposite directions.

"Don't worry about what my mother says," Minerva had said the last time she'd called. "Just pick the person you love. Pedigree doesn't matter, that's old-fashioned talk."

Funny how Gram said the exact opposite, that Minerva ruined her life by marrying a mundane. Just remembering those conversations made Danica's head throb. Small wonder that she and Clem were determined to have fun, keep their hearts private, and guard their power like dragons.

Taking a deep breath to calm down, she inspected the fancy juice machine, scanning the issue neatly summarized on the card. Clem had beautiful handwriting, and she had left detailed notes.

"You won't make juice, huh?" Closing her eyes, she set a

hand on the top of the machine and, with an extra sense that she could never explain, sifted through the connections and parts until she could *feel* the broken piece. A different sort of repair shop would need to disassemble this machine, order a new part, and then put all the pieces back together, but Danica whispered sweet little words until the metal sighed and smoothed, the jagged edges whole once more.

Time for a field test. She had gotten some cut pineapple from the fridge and dropped it in the machine when a deep voice from the doorway startled her. "I'm sorry, are you open?"

Danica whirled to face the tallest, most delicious man she'd ever seen, a walking panty-peril. He had dark hair, a well-trimmed beard hugging a strong jaw, and eyes like butter toffee. She suppressed a weird noise in response to his improbable hotness.

Then her magic surged and the blender powered on, covering her in fruity froth.

Titus tried not to laugh, but it was impossible to stifle his amusement entirely. He turned the chuckle into a cough and said, "I don't think that's quite fixed yet. Seems to have a short or something."

"Yes, I can see that." With remarkable poise, the woman reached for a hand towel and cleaned her face; then she smoothed the pineapple chunks from her hair as well.

His sister had recommended the Fix-It Witches, and since the repair shop was only six blocks from his bakery, he'd decided to scope the place out in person. With only one working oven, it was hell meeting the demand for pastries daily. He'd heard that the cousins who ran this shop could fix anything, but nobody had mentioned how cute they were. The one he was looking at anyway—curly russet hair, soulful brown eyes, freckles dusted like a sprinkle of cinnamon on golden skin, and *yeah, better stop there.*

"Sorry, I called out in front and rang the bell. I heard you moving back here, but it didn't seem like you knew I was in the shop."

"I might have been on the phone when you came in. I'm the one who should apologize. Presumably you have something in need of fixing, and I made you wait." With a gracious gesture, she indicated that he should precede her.

Titus retraced his steps down the short hallway that led to the front of the shop. They had small appliances for sale, probably items they had refurbished; it made sense to augment their income since people probably dropped things off and either forgot about them or decided to buy something new instead. For a repair shop, everything was astonishingly clean, no hint of grease or dust.

"No problem. Sorry that I—"

She cut in, "I know it's a Midwestern tradition to apologize repeatedly when nobody is really at fault, but let's call it even."

Her eyes twinkled at him, and Titus found himself responding, charmed by her warm smile and her candor. "Thank goodness you stopped me. I was prepared to apologize six more times. I might have resorted to inventing offenses."

"Such as being responsible for my smoothie malfunction?" she suggested.

"That's probably my fault. I startle small appliances all the time. It's likely because I'm so tall and blenders are easily intimidated."

Most people found his sense of humor a bit odd, but she laughed, making his day 50 percent better, and then she joked back in the same silly vein. "Don't worry, all of ours have been inoculated against tallness."

Titus immediately wanted to marry her. Or maybe find out her name and buy her dinner. Either way. Maybe all of the above, in a more sensible order. But it would make sense if he started with an introduction, wouldn't it? "I'm Titus Winnaker, by the way. Sugar Daddy's down the block is my—"

"Oh my God," she breathed. "You're *him*."

He blinked. "Him who?"

"The CinnaMan. Your cinnamon rolls are famous!"

What?

She gushed onward, as if he were a rock star and she might soon ask him to sign her chest. "I buy a dozen *every* month to take to book club, and there are never any leftovers. It's devastating, but they're so huge and gooey and delicious—*and* I'm still talking, aren't I?"

"I'm afraid so. People don't really call me that, do they?"

"Well, we do. At book club. Clem says that your cherry Danishes are to die for, so she was in favor of the Great Dane, and Margie loves your cream puffs, so she wanted to call you DreamPuff, but I lobbied for CinnaMan since those are my favorites. At the risk of tooting my own horn, I'm pretty influential, hence—"

"I'm the CinnaMan," he said, desperately amused. "I've never seen you in the shop, but I mostly work in the back."

"Yes, you have *people* for that. Today I have none, alas.

There's only me, doing customer service and repairs. And speaking of which, Clem—short for Clementine—would be mortified that I still haven't asked how I can help you."

"Clementine is your cousin?"

"Cousin, housemate, and business partner. It's a wonder that we're not sick of each other by now, but we were raised as sisters, so that elevates our tolerance."

"When you see Clementine, you can reassure her that I'm perfectly satisfied with your service." *Oh, why did I put it like that?*

Her eyes widened. "Are you? You must have a soft spot for chaos and inefficiency."

"Normally, no, but in your case, I'm making an exception."

She leaned forward over the counter, propping her chin on her hands. "How interesting. Would you care to tell me why?"

"Would you care to tell me your name?" He suspected it was too soon to declare that he'd decided to marry her and was already christening their babies in his brain. Two at least, no more than five. He had to act fast before his curse kicked in.

Or maybe he shouldn't. The last time he'd tried to get with someone, she'd moved to Iceland and married a biologist who studied puffins. Attraction still tweaked him now and then, but failure made him wary, and he usually ignored any twinges of romantic interest. This woman must be special indeed.

"Certainly. I'm Danica Waterhouse, co-owner of Fix-It Witches, far less glamorous than it sounds. We've established that you've something in need of repair?"

"Have we?"

"Haven't we? Hmm. Is this like the endless apologies? It feels like you're prolonging this conversation."

Uh-oh, she's onto me.

"I could apologize for that, but I'm afraid our progress would reset to zero." When her eyes narrowed, he hurried on. "In fact, I do need someone to look at my oven."

"What seems to be the problem?"

"Well, it doesn't turn on." *And I did it again.*

He could tell by the flicker of a smile that tugged at the corners of her mouth that she'd heard it too. "How long have you been having this issue?"

There was nothing for it but to play along. "Two days now, but I suspect the situation will improve soon."

To his relief, she donned some semblance of professionalism and picked up an order pad from the counter. "Definitely, you've come to the right place. Are there any buns currently in your oven?"

Wait, is she asking if I'm married and my wife is pregnant? Or are we still talking about actual ovens?

Titus decided to answer as if the latter was true. "No, I've got two ovens, but I really need both of them working."

"Understood. Can you write down the address and phone number? I'll swing by this afternoon."

"That would be fantastic." He took the pen from her and filled in the requested info, barely restraining himself from writing his cell number next to the bakery one. With considerable self-control, he didn't add a heart either.

"I'll give you an estimate before I start any actual repairs. See you around one?"

"Sounds perfect."

Now he really had no reason to linger, so he headed out with the irrational fear that if he didn't ask her out *right now,* the next time he saw her there would be a ring on her finger. Today, she hadn't worn one, and she lived with her cousin, so that probably meant she was single. *Why is it so hard to confirm these things?*

This was why he was a disaster at dating. Asking personal questions was awkward and possibly intrusive, and what if he made someone feel uncomfortable? Better to stay in the kitchen and bake delicious food—something he was skilled at. Unlike social interaction. Plus, his abysmal track record made him gun-shy. It was hard to hope when your love life inevitably crashed like an oversized ship into an iceberg.

Titus savored the six-block walk back to the bakery. He loved downtown St. Claire, full of historic buildings that had been restored with loving care. Shops and small restaurants lined the streets around the old courthouse, built in 1873 in Romanesque Revival style, red brick and cream stone. There had been a minor kerfuffle when Titus had wanted to paint his shop mint green, but eventually, he had gotten approval, and a few other shops had followed suit, offering a splash of color amid somber tones.

His logo was a line drawing of a man holding a plate of cupcakes with red letters that read YOUR CAKE IS DONE. When he stepped inside, the bakery smelled of sugar and cinnamon, hints of fruit with a touch of cream. For a moment, he studied his younger sister, Maya, dressed in mint green and chocolate brown with a white apron over polo and slacks, as she boxed up a selection of pastries.

Their mother had picked out the staff uniforms, helped him secure the bank loan, and been pushy about the decorative touches, including the fancy white-iron bistro tables. This business wouldn't exist without her, and she'd been tireless in helping him achieve his dream. Even the bakery name had been her idea, as Titus had planned to call it Best Buns. Thankfully she'd talked him out of that.

Not a day went by that he didn't miss her.

Once the customer left, Maya said, "You're finally back. What took you so long?"

Titus smiled. "I met the woman I'm going to marry."

CHAPTER 2

AS PROMISED, DANICA FINISHED HALF of the work orders by lunchtime.

She changed the sign on the front door to one that read BACK BY and set the time to two. That was long enough to eat, tidy up, and check out the CinnaMan's oven. *Still can't believe I acted like such a dork.* Fortunately, her babbling didn't seem to put him off the notion of hiring them. It had been an act of supreme self-control not to run and hide after the juicer went Fruit Vesuvius on her.

Her bike was parked out front, seafoam green in vintage style with a basket on the front complete with fake flowers. It was ridiculous, and she loved it, especially since they lived just under a mile away, close enough to commute without a car, and right now, Clem had the one they shared for longer trips. Riding back and forth qualified as exercise. Just as well, because Danica wasn't prone to working out otherwise.

She waved to people as she pedaled home to the jonquil-yellow craftsman house that she and Clem had bought from Gram for a song. Danica adored it from top to bottom, from the covered porch to the deep dormer to the wooden swing on copper chains. She wasn't prepared for the slender, silver-haired woman perched on said swing. Honestly, Gram was age goals; she had on white linen slacks and a sky-blue twin set, and she made porch lurking stylish.

Danica's grandmother was a snowbird who lived in a retirement community in Citrus Hills, Florida, for most of the year, but she spent July and August catching up with old friends and spending quality time with her granddaughters in St. Claire. Since she had still had lots of former coven sisters in town, one of them was always willing to rent her a room for the summer. Gram could afford her own place, but she was always trying to help, so she stayed with someone who was struggling with bills or on a fixed income.

While Danica wasn't prepared for a chat and didn't have much time either, she was glad to see her grandmother. She leaned in for a hug, closing her eyes at the familiar smell of lavender and mint. "You have a key. Why didn't you let yourself in?"

"That would be rude, sweetheart. When you two bought the place, it ceased being mine and became yours. Love what you've done with the flower beds."

"That's all Kerry and Priya," she admitted. "I don't have much time. I need to shower and grab lunch, then I have—"

"Yes, yes. You're busy." Gram took her hands to soften the interruption. "And I'm on my way to lunch as well. Meeting some old friends. But I wanted to touch base. I saw some photos online…" The pause indicated that she didn't quite know how to put this. "Again, I'm so sorry. I've said this before, but I genuinely thought Darryl was a fine young man—that he'd make you happy. I had no idea things would end up like this."

"It's fine." It really wasn't.

In all honesty, she had only been dating Darryl because he fit the profile. He came from a pure witch family, and Gram approved. It had been two blissful years of Gram asking how her "young man" was and otherwise staying out of Danica's business. A few weeks after Danica and Darryl broke up, Darryl and Raquel happened, which started Gram on a campaign to get Danica to set up a profile on Bindr to find a "proper" mate. She rued the day she'd taught Gram how to use a smartphone.

"With all the filters on Bindr, I've found better candidates this time," Gram promised. She stood and gave Danica a warm hug, patting her back. "I'm relieved to see that you look well, if a trifle harried. I'll let you go about your business. The ladies are expecting me for food and gossip, and then I'm helping Gladys with the Lughnasadh."

"We'll visit soon," Danica promised.

Gram headed out with a flutter of her fingers, and within moments, a rideshare appeared at the curb.

Whew. Gram meant well, but Danica was in no mood to talk about dating with her.

Danica left her bike out front and let herself in with a flick of her wrist. This was her home ground, and the place was warded against intruders, acclimated to Waterhouse magic for three generations. Mostly she didn't need to worry about spell malfunctions here.

She and Clem had updated the decor, and the place was clean and modern now. They'd bickered about the cream walls; Danica had gotten her way about that, but Clem had won the argument about painting the woodwork, so it was still dark and natural, and Danica had grown to appreciate the contrast.

She took her shoes off just inside the front door to protect the floors and jogged upstairs to wash off the pineapple residue. *I've smelled like a damn piña colada all day.* Danica made it quick and dressed in a better outfit than the one Titus had already seen. This time, she chose her clothes with care in well-fitted shorts and a red-gauze top; then she hurried downstairs to make a sandwich. The fact that he was a mundane didn't eliminate her appreciation of his hotness and his awkward humor; flirting was chicken soup for the witch's soul. Or whatever. At any rate, her ego could use the boost.

At least the hangover is gone.

Checking the time, Danica dashed out the door and found a lanky ginger cat lounging on her front porch. First Gram, now this. "Go home, Goliath."

The cat flashed her a supercilious look, then sashayed pointedly away and hopped up on the swing as if to say, *You can't make me.* This jerk practically lived at their house; she even had his owner in her contacts. With a sigh, she made the call.

"Hello?" Hazel Jeffords answered on the first ring.

"Goliath is on my porch again, if you were looking for him."

"If you'd stop feeding him—"

"We don't," Danica said with faint exasperation, as the old woman who lived four houses down seemed convinced they were plotting to lure away her feline companion. "We have never once fed this cat."

"Well, I didn't even know he'd gotten out. Can you wait for me to come after him?"

Sighing, she counted to ten. "Yes, I'll wait."

The cat stared at her accusingly once she disconnected the call, green eyes wounded.

"What?" Danica demanded. Lowering her voice, she added, "You're not my familiar. I don't need one, and even if I did, it wouldn't be a cat."

Goliath seemed to shrug and started grooming himself, the cat equivalent of *Suit yourself.* It was more like twenty minutes before Hazel showed up, and she barely said two words to Danica while baby-talking the hell out of Goliath, who stared longingly over Hazel's shoulder as she carried him off.

Awesome, now I'm late. People will be cranky if I'm not back by two, like the sign says.

Quickly Danica got on her bike and headed for Sugar Daddy's. It was a gorgeous day, great weather for late July, and the heat wasn't sweltering. Sometimes the humidity made it worse, but not today. The bakery was dead cute, a bright spot amid earth tones, and inside, there was a queue of people waiting to clean out the pastry case. A young woman flashed her a cheerful smile as the bell rang, signaling her entry.

"Have a look and I'll be with you presently," she said.

"I'm here to check your oven, actually." Danica didn't rule out buying baked goods afterward, if the line thinned while she was working.

"Oh!" For some reason, the clerk studied her closely before breaking into an overly wide smile. "Go on back. Titus has been waiting for you."

I'm missing something here.

She wondered if she'd get to see him all geared up in his baker's outfit, kneading dough with strong hands, flexing forearms—okay, enough of that—but nah. It seemed like the baking happened much earlier, maybe before the shop opened. Sugar Daddy's only stayed open until everything was sold, and some days, that was amazingly early. People queued for the cinnamon rolls before the doors were even unlocked.

He was perched on a stool, reading, and the whole kitchen sparkled. She'd never seen so much gleaming stainless steel; no health code violations here. Which was a weird thing to find sexy. But the smell—even without anything delicious in the industrial ovens, the space still held hints of sweetness: cinnamon and sugar, butter and vanilla.

"What're you reading?" she asked.

Startled, he juggled the book and then dropped it, so it landed with the pink cover up, showing a cute cartoon-style drawing of a man and woman locked together in an embrace. She read the title with awe.

Okay, this is a setup. If it's not, then he's the perfect man.

Color tinged his cheekbones. "Err, um..."

"We read this last month for book club. It's so fun! Have you gotten to the part when—wait, no, that's a spoiler, I can't ask you that."

Crap, I'm babbling again. What is it about this guy that

opens my trap like I'm a dang boa constrictor? That thought prompted a whole bunch of disturbing oral sex ideas, and she locked that avenue of thought down like the Canadian prime minister was visiting.

Be professional, dammit.

"You're not going to make fun of me?"

"For what?"

"Reading romance novels."

"Of *course* not. I don't know any guys in real life who do, but I have male friends online who occasionally Skype into book club to chat, and they're really cool."

"The book club or your online friends?"

"Uh, both? Anyway, I'm being inefficient again. Is that still working for you?"

"More than you might expect," he said with a smile so powerful that she almost shielded her face from the glow.

"Awesome. Which oven is giving you trouble?" If she concentrated, she'd be able to sense the flaw on her own, but she couldn't do that in front of witnesses. In fact, she needed him out of the room for a while.

"This one. It doesn't even turn on." Titus led the way over to the recalcitrant appliance and showed her. "The damn thing is just out of warranty, and I'd prefer not to pay to replace it."

"I'm sure I can get it working," Danica said, "but it would help me if you could find your owner's manual, just in case I have a question. If I have to call the manufacturer's support line, you get charged for my time while I'm on hold, and that's not fair."

It was also an errand she could send him on that made perfect sense.

Titus nodded, already headed toward what she guessed was an office or maybe a storage room. "I'm not sure where I put it, but I know it's around here somewhere. If I can't find the hard copy, I'll download it and email you the file."

"Perfect." She closed the distance between them and put her business card in his hand. "This has my email on it."

It also has the business phone on the front and my cell number written on the back.

This was the perfect test, a way to discover if he was flirting or if he just enjoyed bantering with awkward witches. Once he disappeared from her line of sight, she got to work, setting a hand on the oven to see what was going on. Ah, there was a short deep inside. Danica closed her eyes and imagined the wire smoothing out, the copper whole, the casing sealed, and the familiar buzz passed through her arm, resulting in a soft spark.

Perfect.

By the time Titus returned with the requested documentation, she had the oven on and was checking the functionality. He regarded her with amazement. "You fixed it already? But you didn't even bring any tools."

Oh, crap.

Normally, she was more together than this, but between the hangover, the smoothie shower, his improbable hotness, Gram's visit, and her wannabe familiar, her head was a bowl of Jell-O salad, wobbly and full of random bits. Quickly she said,

"You'd be surprised how often that's the case. It just needed a hard reset. Was there a power outage recently?"

Please, please, please.

"It's possible. The refrigerators are on a generator so my perishables won't spoil in that case, but I didn't know it could impact the ovens."

"Oh, sure," she said airily, hoping that was true.

———————

She's like an oven whisperer. Competence is so sexy.

"How much do I owe you?" Titus asked.

"I'll invoice you by email if that's okay." She paused with an air of expectation, and he remembered her card, safely tucked away in his pocket.

"Sure, let me get you one of my cards." He didn't know if she realized she'd given him her personal number, but in case she did know...in the office, he scrawled his cell number on the back and rushed to offer it. "Here you go."

His fingers brushed hers in the exchange, and a zing went through him. Not a static shock, something else, a buzz that made him want to find out what would happen if they touched more and for longer. Danica wrapped her hand around the card and withdrew from contact a little slower than seemed normal, as if she'd felt it too. That was another question he couldn't ask without coming off strange. No wonder he kept failing at love.

"Thanks. Oh, just so you're not shocked, we charge a minimum of one hour labor along with the service call."

"I'm not worried about it. No matter what your minimums are, I guarantee that they're less than the cost of a new oven."

"I wish all our customers were so reasonable. Look for my email later, okay? Have a great day!" With a cheerful wave, Danica headed out.

Damn if he didn't like watching her go.

"How was it?" Maya stuck her head in a few minutes later. "Did you pop the question yet?"

"Very funny. I didn't even ask her out."

"That's just as well. You only met her a few hours ago. Did you at least get her contact info?"

Folding his arms, Titus glared at his younger sister. "Do I meddle in your life?"

"Constantly."

He sensed that this conversation wouldn't go anywhere good, so he cleared his throat and changed the subject. "Did we sell out yet?"

"Almost. Just a few madeleines and we'll be out of stock. When will the oven be ready, by the way? This is *really* cutting into our profits, and as a major shareholder—"

"It's done," he cut in, amused at Maya's description of herself as a "shareholder."

"Wow, really? Mrs. Carminian swore that the Fix-It Witches could repair anything faster than everyone else. I guess for once she wasn't exaggerating."

"Give her some free crullers the next time she comes in."

"Will do," Maya said cheerfully.

"Are you coming home for dinner?"

"Please. I have plans. I'm not the one who has to be up at 4:00 a.m."

"You make a good point. Then I'll leave you to sell everything and lock up. Have fun tonight and stay out of trouble."

She rolled her eyes, and he knew that was such a big brother thing to say, but he couldn't help it. To him, Maya would always be the kid who constantly had peanut butter smeared on her face because she ate it from the jar.

The baking assistant had already gone home since the kitchen was clean, and there wasn't much left to do for closing. Titus had already prepped all the ingredients for the morning rush, and thanks to Danica Waterhouse, he could get back to baking the usual number of batches. It wasn't like he was leaving his little sister with tons of manual labor.

"Go eat your oatmeal, and get to bed by eight," she said, waving him toward the door.

"Excuse me? I'm only four years older than you."

Maya made a dismissive gesture. "Okay, boomer." At his look, she added, "What, you already live like an old man, though maybe the cute repairwoman will liven you up."

Pensive when he left the bakery, he tried to decide if Maya was right. Since their mom had died and he'd taken a break from dating after one too many failures, it *did* seem like all he did was work, go home, eat, exercise, watch something, then go to sleep. And if he was honest, he didn't always work out, rationalizing that kitchen labor ticked that box. Those big-ass bags of flour were heavy, dammit.

For people who lived in town, commuting on a bike was

doable in good weather, but he and Maya shared a place in the country, only fifteen minutes by car but roughly twice that on a bike, and country roads didn't have bike lanes. Titus hadn't grown up in St. Claire, but he liked the town enough to stay, even after his mom passed away and his dad remarried.

Still not over that.

In his view, six months was altogether too fast to move on after thirty years. And it wasn't even like he'd been aware of any problems. Unlike many, his parents had always seemed happy, but six months later, Dad was marrying Susan and moving to Arizona. Now he was raising stepkids and barely seemed to remember his actual offspring.

Great, now I'm in a shitty mood.

Titus got into his blue Nissan Leaf, purchased used last year. His friends made fun of him, especially when he had the charging station installed at his house. St. Claire didn't have public infrastructure for electric cars yet, but he liked knowing that he wasn't making the world worse when he drove to work at 4:30 a.m.

It was a little embarrassing, but Maya was right. Bowling night was the center of his social life, and he'd gotten complacent. *Danica gave you her cell number, so she probably wanted you to text her, right?* Unless that was an oversight. Maybe she didn't know that was written on the back, and if he contacted her, it might be creepy. Why was he even considering this?

Stop overthinking.

Before he could talk himself out of the impulse, he added Danica's info to his contacts and sent a message. What did the baker say to the millennial?

Part of him couldn't believe he was sitting in his car, waiting for the adorable fix-it person to message him back. But she did, and not with *who is this?!* either. She seemed ready for the joke: IDK, what?

You can't have your cake and yeet it too.

Silence.

And there *goes any chance you might have had. Just because she laughed at one of your jokes doesn't mean she'd get all of them. Ah well, it was a pipe dream anyway.*

Then, before he could kick himself for even bothering in the first place, Danica sent a goofy emoji and a laughing one.

Nice.

Titus decided it was too soon to respond, so he drove home, plugged the Leaf in to charge, and then went to play with Doris. She bounded into the fenced backyard to do her business, and while she did, Titus dug up her tennis ball. For about an hour, he played fetch with the dog. When she'd burned some excess energy, he snapped on her leash; otherwise, she'd try to drag him into the fields to chase rabbits.

Living in the country, his closest neighbors were half a mile away. It also meant that there were no sidewalks for Doris. Luckily, at this time of day, there were few cars too. Most people worked a bit later in the afternoon, so he and Doris jogged along the road, yielding for the rare cars that also swerved wide, often with drivers waving or calling out the window as they rolled by, because St. Claire was like that.

He moved to make way when he heard the engine rumble of a vintage truck, but the driver stopped on the road like Titus and his dog were an area attraction. Mr. Stevewell, the old man from the farm at the end of the road, called out to Titus's dog like she might answer. "You're looking good today, Doris!"

And, of course, she did—with a woof and a tail wag. Titus had adopted her a month after his mom died, and now it felt like Doris had always been with him.

"What breed is she anyway?" Mr. Stevewell asked.

"They weren't sure, but they're guessing Labrador and something else. I found a picture that makes me think maybe Bernese mountain dog. Look..." He paused, realizing he was like a PTA parent showing off his kid's report card. "Sorry, you probably don't want—"

"To see cute pictures of dogs on the internet? I've always got time for that!" Mr. Stevewell got out of his truck and came around to look. "Check out the ears on that girl. I agree, our Doris could be related."

The dog had floppy ears, black fur with a white chest, a white stripe down the face, white tips on the paws, and a fantastic fluffy tail, similar enough to be Doris's doppelganger. Puppelganger? Whatever. "They have DNA tests, but I haven't gone that route."

"DNA tests for dogs? Now I've heard everything." Mr. Stevewell got back in his truck with a wave.

Titus continued his run. *I can probably text Danica when I get home, right?*

CHAPTER 3

DANICA INVOICED SUGAR DADDY'S FOR the repair work, and Titus paid at once.

That concluded the professional portion of their relationship, but five days later, they were still texting. And she *still* wasn't sure if he was flirting. The uncertainty didn't stop her from swapping memes with him and sending the worst jokes she could find since he seemed to have a taste for them. She decided it was totally cool to flirt with a mundane; flirting wouldn't impact her magic or ruin her life. Whatever they were doing, it boosted her mood like good medicine and made her disregard Darryl's noncommittal ass as if she hadn't even dated him.

With Clem back, the shop operated like a well-oiled machine. Not that they oiled any machines. They just had to pretend they did.

Tonight, it was their turn to host book club—the cover for their coven—which meant Danica had a reason to be outside the bakery at 7:57 a.m., queuing for cinnamon rolls like a fangirl. The funny part was, she wasn't even first in line. There were two women ahead of her, four behind, and the ones in front were nudging one another and giggling.

"Do you think we'll see him today?"

"Probably not. But God, he's so..." The older woman pantomimed biting her knuckles, and the other one shushed her.

She suspected they were mother and daughter, judging by the resemblance. Theory confirmed—the popularity of Sugar Daddy's wasn't simply because the pastries were delicious. Customers also came hoping for a glimpse of the elusive CinnaMan.

Can't believe I told him about that nickname. What was I thinking?

She wallowed in that embarrassment for two minutes, and then promptly at eight, the same clerk as always unlocked the doors with a bright smile. Today, Danica made a point of reading her name tag, faintly embarrassed that she hadn't done so before.

Maya, her name is Maya.

"Good morning, everyone. Come on in!"

As the first two women went inside, Danica asked, "Don't you think we're ridiculous, doing this for pastries?"

Maya shook her head. "Definitely not. When Titus got his driver's license, we road tripped to Terre Haute to try those famous square donuts. And oh my *God*, they are so good. The lady told me that they often sell out of the glazed ones by 9:00 a.m."

Surreptitiously, Danica entered "Terre Haute" and "square donuts" into her phone's browser and read things like "best donuts in the world" and "best I've ever had." *Huh. I should try those.* As she headed for the counter, other customers looked at the display case, but she was ready to pay. She even had her wallet out.

"A dozen cinnamon rolls?" Maya guessed.

"You know me so well." She paid in cash and waited while the clerk boxed her order.

As Maya handed over the mint-green bakery box, she lowered her voice. "I'm overstepping here, but my brother is *so* awkward. Titus wants to ask you out, but he can't decide if you'd be receptive. Since I'm a good person, I'll help. Green or red light?"

"Green," Danica said at once, as if her mouth weren't connected to her brain.

Slow your roll, he's a mundane. Gram will end you. And she's here. *Nothing gets past her. Just imagine how disappointed she'll be.*

Danica waffled mentally, trying to decide if she should change her answer. But...one date would be harmless, right? No risk. Just a little fun. Self-indulgence was good for the soul every now and then. But Gram...and the promise Danica had made with Clem...

By the time Danica decided to retract her response, Maya was saying, "I'll clue him in. Have a great day, and don't forget us for all your sweet needs!"

She managed a casual smile, hoping she hadn't made a mistake. "Does he make you say that?"

"Nah, the slogan is just something I'm trying out. I don't think it's going to stick."

"Pun intended?"

"I'm on a roll," Maya tried.

"Well, I knead you to stop."

"That's a pun too, right? It's hard to tell verbally, but I'm like 95 percent positive you said that with a silent K."

"You would be right. I'll get out of your way now." Danica turned to go.

"*Psst.* You didn't hear it from me, but when the weather's nice, Titus likes to eat lunch on the memorial bench by the courthouse."

"Interesting," she said. "And what time does this usually take place?"

"Around one."

Already on the way out, she smiled at the whispered response. Maya was full-on meddling in her brother's love life, and Danica didn't know how she felt about it. On one hand, she liked him. It was impossible *not* to. But things weren't as simple as she wished they were. Not for her.

The bakery box didn't fit in the basket of her bike, so she was on foot today, and she walked home to stow the cinnamon rolls. She didn't have to be at work until two, a thank-you for covering while Clem was at the marketing seminar, so she cleaned the house in preparation for guests and then took a bath. At half past noon, she made lunch—a turkey sandwich, an apple, and a bottle of juice. *Maybe I should eat here? Ignore what Maya said.* The desire to see Titus again overwhelmed caution, and Danica headed for the square.

That meant walking by the shop, and she hurried past in case Clem saw her. Her cousin would wonder what she was up to, and Danica didn't feel like explaining. This wasn't anything to worry about. Even Gram couldn't complain about her making new friends, right?

She had settled on the bench dedicated to Robert Andrew Langley beneath the elm tree and just taken the second bite of her sandwich when she glimpsed Titus in her peripheral vision. A zing zipped through her, like when her magic went haywire. *Dammit, this can't be happening already.* Today, he wore the baker's outfit without an apron, and it was a wonder more people weren't intruding on his lunchtime peace.

Be cool. You didn't know this is his spot. You're not waiting for him.

Surreptitiously, Danica checked to be sure there was room on her other side. Normally, she'd sit square in the center and dare anyone to encroach on her space. Titus slowed, and then he seemed to make up his mind, walking toward her swiftly.

"Hey, mind if I join you?"

"Please do." She made a show of gathering her supplies as if she hadn't been lurking like a paparazzo.

Titus sat next to her, leaving enough space between them to put down his nylon lunch bag, bright blue with a happy yellow duck printed on it. "What's on the menu today?"

"Turkey on rye, Gala apple, and orange-carrot juice." She took a sip.

Titus made a face. "I was with you until the last item."

"It's better than it sounds, fresh ginger for an interesting zing." But she didn't offer him a taste because she hated when people foisted things on her that she'd already expressed disinterest in.

"That doesn't look like a commercial bottle," he noted.

"We make our own juices and use glass bottles that other stuff comes in. In the early days of Fix-It Witches, we had a fair amount of small appliances go unclaimed after they were dropped off. Some of them we kept."

"I guess that means you have a fancy juicer?"

"Precisely. Got it for free, fixed it, and now I can make all the strangely delicious combinations my heart desires."

"Like what?"

"Are we really having this conversation? You can't be interested in my juices." *Oh God. I said that, didn't I? I actually said it.*

Titus made eye contact, keeping a straight face somehow. "I assure you that I am."

"Oh. I see. Well then. Kale, lemon, and pear is a bit odd but surprisingly delicious. I also like grapefruit, lime, and mint together. There's also my proprietary apple, cucumber, and celery blend."

"I've never had any of that."

"You look like you're fine with continuing that streak. Don't you ever want to walk on the wild side? It might be refreshing."

"When you put it that way, maybe I *am* too prone to playing it safe." He held out a hand. "Would you let me try some?"

It felt strangely intimate to pass him the juice, considering they hadn't known each other for that long, almost like a precursor to a kiss. Danica watched his throat work as he swallowed, and she imagined how lovely it must be for the bottle. He downed a quarter of her drink, and he was smiling when he handed it back.

"Good?"

"Excellent. Now I'm curious about your other creations."

That was an opening if she'd ever heard one. The words

rushed out before she considered them properly. "We could meet again tomorrow? I'll bring some for you too."

Oh no. I have to stop doing this. Bad idea, so bad.

His dazzling smile nearly melted her into a pool of warm oil—perfect for a massage, and his hands must be wonderfully strong. "I'd love that. Same time?"

So bad it's good. Despite her misgivings, Danica didn't recant.

"I'll be waiting." *This is a date, right?* Not a high-end one, but the first step in a romantic direction. *Don't do this,* Gram's voice scolded in her head. *Don't be like your mother.*

"Since you're bringing drinks, I'll cover dessert. I'll whip up something extra special." Those words, delivered in a husky tone, made her toes curl. Plus, he was promising to bake. For her. And considering the products at Sugar Daddy's, it would be amazing.

Okay, I can't resist. I'll just have a little *fun with him. I can quit anytime.*

———————

As soon as Titus got back to work, he had to brag. "Guess what?"

"Your dream girl proposed," Maya said, as she wiped down the front counter.

"Now see, when you go that big, it makes my actual news look small. But never mind. I ran into Danica at lunch, and we agreed to meet tomorrow. This is destiny, right?" He rambled on, knowing he sounded overeager and maybe even desperate. "She was just randomly sitting at my usual lunch spot. What are the chances? Maybe this time..." He couldn't bear to speak that hope out loud, not even to Maya.

Maybe this time I'll be lucky in love. I wonder if Danica likes dogs.

His sister smirked, but that was her default expression, so he ignored it and headed to the back to get started on prep for tomorrow. Stan, the baking assistant, had already gotten a head start, and they had a part-time cleaner who came a couple of times a week to assist with deep scrubbing. When they first opened, he'd run the place on a shoestring, making do with only Maya's help.

"You look chipper," Stan said.

"I guess I am."

"Something good happen?"

While they were friendly, Titus wasn't about to get into his personal life when the development barely counted as anything. "Maybe. Too soon to call."

By three, the kitchen was gleaming, and everything was ready for his 4:30 a.m. bake-a-thon. Stan waved as he pulled off his apron. "See you tomorrow, boss."

At first, it was weird hearing that from a man twice his age, but Stan was working because he wanted to. The man had retired as a Realtor and took a baking class because he was bored. Surprisingly, he had a knack for it, and he said he enjoyed staying busy. That was fine with Titus because Stan was prompt, hardworking, and reliable.

He didn't bother asking Maya about dinner. These days, she wasn't home a lot, and he suspected she was dating someone she hadn't introduced yet. He was content to wait while she figured things out, especially if it meant she wouldn't give him a hard time about Danica. God, even the name was cute.

Wonder if anyone calls her Dani.

It was straight-up embarrassing how hard he was crushing, worse than high school. If anything, he had even less game than he'd had then because he'd managed to ask Melissa Beck to the prom without embarrassing himself, but there had been plenty of humiliation on the date; he recalled how he'd caught her making out with someone else that night.

We're meeting up tomorrow. I'm still in this, even after all my goofy jokes.

"Are you good?" he asked Maya.

"Let me run to the bathroom, then you can take off."

"No problem."

After his sister returned to the counter, he waved and headed out. Outside, the day was bright and warm, edging toward eighty-five. People wore shorts and tank tops, soaking in the sun, and he spotted a few familiar faces, couples holding hands as they walked around the square. The old courthouse didn't serve gubernatorial functions anymore; instead, it housed quaint shops full of original art, pottery, and hand-sewn quilts. There was also a local interest museum run by volunteers.

When he was a senior in high school, his family had moved here from Chicago, and he'd hated it at first. No clubs to sneak into; only one theater, and it wasn't even a multiplex. A stupid bowling alley. No art museums, no Museum of Science and Industry. Fondly, he recalled running on a human-sized hamster wheel. *I wasn't even a little kid.* And the Shedd Aquarium. There used to be a worker who spoke in a monotone while extolling the virtues of fish. *This is a lake sturgeon. Do not touch the sturgeon.*

The guy had said "sturgeon" like forty times in his monologue and pronounced it with odd emphasis, cracking up everyone in Titus's group.

When they first moved here, he couldn't wait to get out of St. Claire. He'd started at Loyola; then his mom had gotten sick, and he'd come back to help. She'd always enjoyed baking, and it became something for them to do together. She hung on and fought while he went to culinary school nearby and got his degree in baking and pastry arts, and she helped him get started with Sugar Daddy's. He had been so convinced that she'd pull through. Once she was gone, he could've sold the business, but he didn't want to anymore. For him and Maya, St. Claire was home. Small-town life with reasonable access to city culture had grown on him.

His phone rang as he got in the car, odd enough that he checked the number. His friends would text, as voice calls were retro. *Ugh. I should have known.* Titus forced a smile, hoping the expression would infuse his voice with a semblance of warmth.

"Hi, Dad. How's it going?"

"I have some great news!"

While he suspected their definitions of "great" weren't at all the same, he still asked, "Oh yeah? What's up?"

"I wanted you to be the first to know. Susan is pregnant!"

At forty-two, Susan was only ten years older than Titus. She had a couple of teenagers from a previous marriage, but he had no idea they were even thinking about...this. His silence went on too long.

"You there?" Dad prompted.

Finally, he said, "Congratulations," because that was the

polite response and he'd been raised to react that way, even when anger was about to blow out the back of his head.

Luckily, his dad was too drunk on delight to notice Titus's lack of enthusiasm. "It's such a surprise! We weren't even trying. In fact, funny story, Susan went in because she thought maybe it was perimenopause and bam! The doctor tells us that we're two months along. She's due around Valentine's Day, if you can believe it. Both Susan and I are hoping for a little girl. She's already picked a name, Aubrey, and I guess it can go either way. That's supposed to be popular these days. That gender-neutral thing. Or is it nonbinary? I'm too old to keep up with this stuff, but I'm trying."

His dad was fifty-seven. Having a kid. Starting over.

Maybe Titus should be happy for him, but he couldn't bring himself to say the right words. He held silent, listening. Seething. Didn't matter since the old man kept talking.

"Anyway, you and Maya *have* to come for the holidays this year. Lucy and Jared want to see their older brother and sister."

Bullshit. Susan's kids didn't consider Titus and Maya family. In fact, he'd caught Jared hitting on Maya the last time everyone got together. *God, this sucks. She'll be heartbroken.* Maya would certainly take the whole "I hope it's a girl" as a sign that she was being replaced. *I have to tell her before Dad calls.*

"Uh-huh," he said, the most evasive response possible. "Look, I was about to get in my car. We'll talk more later, okay? My best to Susan and the family." Those words stuck in his throat, tasted like ash on the way out.

Without waiting for a reply, he tapped the screen to end the call and sprinted back to the bakery. When he burst through the front door, Maya was already picking up her phone. *That asshole.* Unlike his, her smile was real at first when she heard Dad's voice, but as she listened, the smile faded, and soon there were silent tears standing in her eyes.

Titus closed his briefly; then he signaled for her to hang up with a curt gesture. But she listened to whatever crap Dad was spouting for another five minutes. Finally she said in a too-soft voice, "Okay, but it's time to lock up, and I have to get to the bank before it closes."

As she rounded the counter, Titus flipped the sign to closed and turned the bolt. Maya was full-on crying when she got to him, and he wrapped his arms around her, wishing he could punch his dad in the face. Not filial, definitely not polite. But the bastard deserved it. He patted her back the way he did Doris's, but Maya didn't seem to mind.

"Sorry. I should've gotten here faster."

"That's why you ran in like your shoes were on fire? Trying to break the news first."

"Yeah."

She let out a shuddering sigh and stepped back to wipe a hand across her face. "You're a good brother. I'm glad I did you that favor."

"What favor?"

"Never mind. I think...I don't feel like going out tonight after all. If you don't already have plans, let's make dinner together at home. It's been a while, and it seems like..." She let out a shaky breath and bit her lip.

"What?" he prompted gently.

"You're the only family I have left."

Smiling, he tousled her hair, knowing it would irritate her, but he also took care not to rumple her style too much. "I'm thinking…pizza tonight. With my famous homemade crust, six types of cheese, and your choice of toppings. What do you say?"

Despite the evidence of recent tears, her smile brightened to a level he'd call blissful. "You're the best."

CHAPTER 4

DANICA'S CELL PHONE RANG AS she opened the front door.

Margie Bower always arrived first, and she held a plate of pimento cheese sandwiches with the crusts cut off. Danica waved the other witch inside, taking the call on the porch. "Gram, is everything okay?"

She heard furniture being dragged in the background as her grandmother replied, "Fine, darling. I wish I could attend your meeting tonight, but Gladys has something special in mind for the Lughnasadh, and we're having our own get-together."

On Gram's end, someone called, "Angelica, where do you want the chocolate fountain? The ice sculpture is melting. Can you look for Gladys? She needs to cast a chilling spell on it."

Danica grinned. "Sounds like fun. Remember, if you need it, I've got bail money."

Her grandmother laughed. "Understood, and I appreciate it. Right back at you...and I won't even tell your mother."

Danica laughed as she was meant to, as Gram enjoyed being part of her circle of trust, enjoying confidences she didn't even share with her own mom. "I feel safer already."

Then came the probable purpose for the call. "By the way, I've flagged two excellent prospects for you on Bindr. Check your email, all right?"

She stifled a sigh. "Yes, Gram."

"Talk to you soon, my dear!"

As Danica disconnected, Leanne Vanderpol climbed the front steps carrying a box of wine—unsurprising, as she didn't cook. Danica followed Leanne into the house, mildly annoyed that she couldn't have *one* night with her coven sisters without Gram nagging about Bindr. Soon after, Vanessa Jackson and Ethel Murray came together, as Vanessa was Ethel's ride. The older woman didn't drive, but she did bake delicious mini quiches. Vanessa contributed a Greek salad to the potluck, and as Danica arranged the food on the kitchen island, the last two members dashed in. Priya Banik and Kerry Quarles were inseparable, as they had been dating for the last four months and were talking about moving in together.

Once everyone had exchanged greetings, filled their plates, and settled in the living room, Danica held up a hand for attention. Gradually, the separate conversations quieted.

"You've gathered us here to thank us for our support, and you'd like to announce your candidacy," Margie joked.

"Run for mayor," said Leanne. "Then I can work for you instead of that asshole."

Leanne did PR work for St. Claire, though her official title was director of communications, and she was damn good at her job. If Danica was seriously considering getting involved in politics, she'd want Leanne on her team.

"We haven't even opened the wine yet, and you're already fierce," Clem said to Leanne.

Dammit, I'm losing them.

Since they got together to drink, eat, perform group spells, and act up, talking about books was usually the last thing on the agenda. Eventually, they *did* get there, but they vented about personal stuff, shared good news, and complained about work crap first. Then anyone who needed help with spellcraft spoke up. And then they got around to chatting about what they had been reading, and sometimes they let online friends Skype in, as she'd mentioned to Titus.

Danica cleared her throat. "So Gram's in town, and she just called me to harp about finding my perfect witchy match."

"Again?" Vanessa laughed, doubtless thinking that only popcorn would make this family drama better.

"Yeah. I'm so tired of hearing about our bloodline," Danica muttered.

Clem said softly, "Gram can be...a lot. She pushed me into dating Spencer and pestered you until you went out with Darryl."

For our own good. Somehow, Danica swallowed the instinctive defense. She didn't need to shield Gram, not here, not with her coven. They all understood, even if they teased.

"Such a jackass," Leanne said.

Ethel nodded. "I never liked him. At least you didn't marry the lummox. Your grandmother would never approve of you divorcing a 'pure witch,' and now you're not stuck with a partner you'd prefer to poison."

Priya grinned as she popped a mini quiche in her mouth. "Are you trying to tell us something, Ethel?"

"I'll never talk," the old woman answered. "Even if the statute of limitations is up."

"You know it's easier to get a divorce these days, right?" Leanne ate a pimento cheese triangle. "I should know, I've done it twice."

Clem settled onto the couch next to Danica, eyeing her with concern. "I'm worried about where you're going with this."

"Don't worry, I'm not getting married or anything." Danica touched her cousin's arm in reassurance.

"Oh shit!" Suddenly, Clem sat forward and clutched her hands. "You're pregnant, aren't you? You got drunk and made a bad decision at Raquel's bachelorette party. It's not Darryl, right? Tell me the father isn't Darryl."

Kerry had been on her phone, and she snapped to attention. "Are you serious?"

"Think about what you're saying right now. It's only been a week. How would I even know?" Danica sighed because her actual news would seem small in comparison.

"Oh. Right." Embarrassed, Clem ate a bite of the Greek salad. "Sorry, go ahead. I didn't mean to steal your spotlight."

"Anyway. I'm just excited because I've found the *perfect* rebound—the ideal guy for a fling and...he's a mundane. Nobody tell my grandmother," she added, though that was probably unnecessary.

Everyone started talking at once, asking questions about her rebound plans, and Danica ignored her friends for a bit. Satisfied with their reactions, she nibbled a chunk of pineapple and remembered how the blender had frothed all over her the first time Titus set foot in their shop. She followed that with a crustless sandwich and some salad.

Finally, Leanne won the floor by talking the loudest. "Hey, I fully support rebound sex, but after a few dates, talk to him to make sure you're on the same page. If he thinks you're dating seriously and you're just in it for some thrills, it could—"

"Break his heart," Vanessa supplied.

"Who cares?" Clem muttered. "They do it to us all the time."

Priya nodded. "Your grandmother doesn't hold mundanes in high regard, but they have feelings, just like we do."

"And they're not soulless either," Ethel said cheerfully. "Though they used to be prone to accusing us of all sort of things back in the day."

True. And that history of persecution was part of why Gram loathed mundanes, wanted nothing to do with them. If a cow got sick, it must be a witch. Trouble with wireworms devouring a farmer's corn? Witchcraft. The husband was cheating? Definitely witches. Because Aradia knew, none of that could happen on its own.

"Relax, if we have a fling, it will be because he's into it," Danica assured them. "I'll make sure he knows I'm not looking for anything deep or meaningful." Then the impact of that hit her. "Oh crap, I sound like Darryl. Should I...not?"

"Yes, you do sound like him," Clem said. "And maybe keep an eye on that. Just...be careful, okay?"

Clem hated seeing people she cared about get hurt. And she'd watched her mother suffer through a bad marriage, seen what Darryl put Danica through, then she'd witnessed how Margie had been thoroughly screwed by her ex. Her cousin nursed a lot of bitterness from seeing those she loved get stepped on.

"Sometimes relationships don't work out," Vanessa said thoughtfully. "But that's no reason to stop trying."

Leanne finished her drink. "I didn't mean to discourage you. You deserve some fun, and none of us will say a word to Madam Waterhouse."

The rest of the coven offered solemn nods, promising to keep Danica's walk on the mundane side a secret. There had been kisses, sure, but this was the first time she'd ever been tempted to go all the way with a mundie, and maybe Titus was so appealing because of the lure of the forbidden? There was just something irresistibly adorkable about him.

But Kerry had questions. "Who is this guy? Tell us what makes him so perfect!"

"He's local." But if she told them all about Titus, they would descend on the bakery to scope him out.

"Just don't fall for him," Clem warned. "Remember our promise."

Somberly, Danica nodded. After their breakups, the cousins got drunk on too many margaritas and swore to stay single. When they sobered up, it still seemed like the best plan, the path least likely to offer unnecessary conflict and heartbreak.

Vanessa sighed, visibly bored with the current topic. "Maybe we're overthinking this. Having a fling with a mundane just *isn't* a big deal, no matter how Mrs. Waterhouse feels. That's unnecessary family drama."

Margie nodded. "If we can all agree that Vanessa's right, I'd like to move on. Because I have some news as well."

Ethel leaned forward in her chair. "Well? Spit it out!"

"My ex finally paid the child support he owes. I was able to catch up on my mortgage payments, and in August, I can send Chris to the iD Tech camp robotics session he's been begging for!" Margie had been trying to get that money for years, and none of the spells they had tried as a coven had done the trick. Unlike in the movies, magic didn't solve every problem with a snap of the fingers.

"Congratulations!" Danica said.

The others echoed the sentiment, and Clem hugged Margie. When things quieted a bit, Kerry said, "They garnished the asshole's wages, didn't they?"

Margie grinned. "He finally took a job where that was possible. He's been working off the books, so I couldn't 'get my hands on his money,' but I guess those jobs are harder to find these days."

"I will never understand," Ethel said. "Doesn't that fool realize the money is for his child? You didn't make that baby alone."

Priya and Kerry swapped looks, and then Priya said, "One, we're breaking our rules about not talking about men the whole time. It counts even if you're complaining and not gushing over them. Two, we have news too!"

Leaning over, Kerry kissed Priya on the cheek. "That we do. I sold my house, and I'm moving in with Priya."

After another round of congrats and hugs, Leanne said, "Time to open that big box of wine!"

She poured for everyone, and they did a toast—to Danica's potential rebound fling, the end of Margie's money woes, and Kerry's cohabitation with Priya. They drank quite a bit, ate even more, and eventually got around to talking about books.

First, they discussed the one they had agreed to read as a group and then, as usual, ended with recommendations of what they had been enjoying separately. Danica couldn't shut up about *Empire of Sand* by Tasha Suri, and she got recs for authors she'd never tried. Most of them bought books on their phones as the recommendations piled up, and Ethel wrote the titles down to look for them at the library.

"Does anyone need help with a ritual?" Clem asked.

Everyone shook their heads—a quiet meeting then, witchery-wise.

"Is everything set for Lughnasadh?" Danica asked Ethel, who was organizing the rite along with Gram and Gladys.

"All good. This isn't my first rodeo," the older witch assured her.

"Damn, it's past eleven. I should get home. Chris will be wondering where I am." Margie got up, and her move signaled everyone else.

Vanessa and Kerry had stopped drinking a while ago so they could drive. Danica walked the guests to the door; Clem just waved as she started tidying up. But the minute Danica closed the door, her cousin put the plates down and folded her arms, wearing the sternest look ever.

"Are you out of your mind? Gram's here. It's not a matter of us keeping your secret. The minute you fool around with a mundane, she'll find out. And we'll never hear the end of it. Is a bit of fun *really* worth so much drama?"

———————

After the pizza feast, Titus watched *Thor: Ragnarok* with Maya.

Though their movie tastes didn't always overlap, they agreed that this one was sheer perfection, and they owned it because they tended to watch it whenever one of them was bummed or had had a shitty day. The news from Dad qualified on both counts.

"Thanks," Maya said, as the credits ran. She got up and hugged him. "I'm going to play some Sims before bed."

"Night, Mini."

"Don't call me that." But she didn't sound as grumpy about the nickname as she had been twenty years ago.

Normally, he'd get ready for bed at this hour since he had to be up early. He had played fetch with Doris and then taken her for a run before making pizza with Maya. Now, Doris was snoring, sprawled out on her bed in front of the fireplace. In July, there was no fire burning, but the dog loved that spot best because she could see all through the house, the best vantage for guarding. All told, it had been a full day, but he still needed to bake something special for lunch tomorrow. He wouldn't have time in the morning.

But what would suit Danica's tastes? She liked turkey sandwiches, apples, and strange juice combinations. That wasn't a deep profile to design the perfect dessert. *A tart of some kind would be best, and I have Fuji apples...* Without pondering too much, he pulled puff pastry sheets from the freezer, made fresh last week, and put together some beautiful apple date tarts that he rolled to look like roses; they came out gorgeous, all pink and gold. These were best eaten fresh, but they would still be delicious tomorrow at lunch.

After packing the tarts, he whistled for Doris. "Outside!"

He rapped on the back door, and she raced through the house into the backyard, which was fenced. A pet door let Doris come and go as she pleased, but Titus made her pee before going to bed. He stepped onto the back patio to wait for her to finish sniffing everything and do her business. When she trotted back, he rubbed her head and gave her a cookie.

"Good girl. Ready for bed?"

Doris cocked her head and then followed him into the kitchen. As he went, he switched off lights and made sure the front door was locked; then he headed to his room. Doris took up most of his queen-size bed because she sprawled. Sometimes she'd go sideways across the mattress and kick him with her back paws like he should find somewhere else to sleep.

Living with Maya meant that he never invited anyone to spend the night; hell, he'd never slept with anyone before. It always went catastrophically wrong before he sealed the deal. So not only was he a virgin, even if by some miracle he got to that point with Danica, Doris would fight about yielding her spot in the bed.

"Don't get ahead of yourself," he told his reflection as he brushed his teeth.

Titus had the master bedroom along with a private bath—not a big one, and there was only a shower stall. Maya had the bigger bath, a Jack and Jill design that gave equal access from both her room and the guest bedroom. Typically, he didn't go in there, and he didn't touch her stuff. They'd argued a fair amount when they were kids, but these days, they shared the house well and seldom bickered about the chores. Maya had written up a rotating schedule, and as long as they stuck to it, there was no question of whose turn it was to do something.

He got in bed and checked the alarm on his phone. *All set.* On impulse, he opened the messaging app, though he knew Danica hadn't contacted him. Technically, it was her turn, but since she'd taken the initiative about lunch, maybe he could relax the rigid rules he had been following in regard to not contacting her too much or too often, not spamming her with stuff when she was busy or disinclined to chat.

Looking forward to tomorrow. Night! He added a smile emoji, wishing he had the nerve to use the heart-eyes one, but that was too soon. *Is it normal to worry about this stuff too much? It's not like an emoji is a marriage proposal.* Too bad his past relationships hadn't ended with exit interviews. *Before you go,* Titus might've asked, *can I ask precisely how I drove you away? I'll take notes.*

Since getting up early was exhausting—and it was later than usual—he fell asleep without trouble. Doris woke him with a lick on the forehead two minutes before his alarm went off. Really, it was amazing how well the dog could tell time, considering that dogs couldn't tell time. *Or can they? Maybe I should Google it.*

Groaning, he rolled out of his warm bed and got in the shower. If Doris needed to go badly enough, she'd see herself out. Otherwise, Titus would shoo her out as he was leaving.

He raced through his morning routine and checked to see if his beard needed trimming, but it still looked tidy. Then he went to the kitchen to have cereal. People would probably be shocked if they knew what he ate, left to his own devices. But Titus had met a lot of people like that in culinary school. They cooked fancy food all day for other people, then they went home and ate ramen.

"Not yet," he told Doris as she bounded in the pet door. "It's too early."

The dog gave him a soulful look, licked her chops, and then stared pointedly at her food bowl. Knowing he was a soft touch, he fed her a cookie and then filled two compartments in her dish and set the timers. This was a fancy food-giving device. One side opened at eight in the morning, and the other popped open at two. Titus was always home early enough to give Doris her dinner. He'd read so much about dog care before adopting her, and it was supposed to be better to give them smaller meals more often. Her water fountain was full, but he plopped some ice in it because he spoiled this pup rotten.

"Go back to bed," he told her.

Of course, she didn't listen. Instead, she watched him make a sandwich and even begged in classic Doris style. She rolled over and showed her belly, head lolled to the side like she was literally dying from lack of lunch meat. Laughing, he gave her a slice and put everything away.

Titus got to the bakery five minutes later than usual, so Stan was sitting in his car, listening to some audiobook. Titus could hear that it was about unleashing your inner potential as he went by. The older man got out of his car and waited for Titus to unlock the door and turn off the alarm. Then he came inside and headed straight to the kitchen without even a "good morning." That was typical, as Stan wasn't the chatty type this early.

The morning passed in a flurry of baking, and before Titus

knew it, lunchtime finally rolled around. He sent Stan and Maya to eat at noon because he had to go at one. Titus didn't like working the front because the minute Maya left, there was always a swarm of customers. One of them was a cute guy, unmistakably flirting, and if Titus didn't have plans, he might see where that went. But today, Danica was waiting for him, and he didn't want to mess it up. He was cranky when he finally got to leave at 1:05, and he wanted to sprint for the park bench, but rattling around the box might destroy the tarts.

What if she already left? He was only ten minutes late, but he never did this. When he got together with Dante, Miguel, Trevor, and Calvin, he was always first to show up and would sometimes end up holding down a table for half an hour while everyone else trickled in. Some of the friends he'd made in high school had moved, but at least he still had the core group. Miguel had married his high school sweetheart, and Dante had tied the knot after college, so he'd lost touch with them a little, though it was better now that Dante was divorced. Well, not better for Dante. Trev and Cal were single like him, and they made up the larger part of his social circle.

I'm trying to expand my horizons. Taking a chance on Danica.

Nerves insisted that she'd bail if he was late. He settled for speed walking, but worry tugged at him until he saw her, waiting for him on the bench.

Thank goodness.

His chest eased. Already, she had become important to him, although really, he didn't know if they could even be considered friends, let alone anything else. She stood and took a few steps toward him, and the apparently reflexive response reassured him.

"I thought maybe something came up."

"Just the usual run on sweets as soon as Maya went to lunch. It's like they know I'm not great on the customer service end. I would've texted you if an emergency called for a sudden change in plans."

Amusement glittered in her eyes, her mouth curved in a private smile, but she didn't let him in on the joke. "You're here now. That's what matters."

CHAPTER 5

DANICA COULDN'T STAND HOW FREAKING adorable it was that Titus had *no* idea that half the people who worked downtown waited until Maya went to lunch to storm the bakery, hoping for a glimpse of him. Normally, she'd suspect false modesty, but he truly seemed clueless about the connection. It absolutely wasn't a coincidence.

"Thanks for waiting. I'm the punctual one normally."

"Not a problem. Here, I made the lemon kale pear juice I told you about yesterday. I hope you're feeling brave."

"It's very...green. That probably means it's good for me, huh?" He didn't look enthusiastic as he took the bottle and sat beside her, closer than yesterday. Not near enough to touch, but there wasn't room for their lunches between them this time.

"Yes. But it's also delicious, I promise." Unwrapping her cheese-and-lettuce sandwich, Danica stole a glance at Titus, wondering if he was up for a fling.

With Gram in town, even casual dates would be...challenging. She'd watched *Chilling Adventures of Sabrina* with Clem when it first came out, and they'd laughed at the stuff the writers had gotten wrong. One thing they had right was that the mundane population could *never* know about witches, a policy instituted after the Great Purge. Now, all babies were ensorcelled, and if they communicated "I am a witch" via any medium to a mundane, it triggered an alert, and the council descended. There was no hidden witch school, and the elders were casual about most things, but they enforced that rule strictly. Witches who broke that tenet had their minds wiped, and the mundane was usually transmuted into an animal so the secret could never get out.

That was why it was so difficult for a witch to marry a mundane and why Gram felt that it was a terrible life, and it sapped magic too, at least for the Waterhouse witches.

Such strict enforcement had kept them safe for years. People thought the world had gotten more logical, more rational, so mundanes imagined they'd grown out of the witch hunts. *We're better than that,* they wanted to believe. *Not prone to mass hysteria or putting stock in superstitious nonsense.* Truth was, witches had simply gotten better at hiding.

We don't serve the Dark Lord either. Such nonsense.

In fact, they were descended from Aradia, a goddess who gave magic to her followers, different gifts for different lines. Mundanes had managed to get a glimmer of the truth, but they always dragged Lucifer into it, possibly because the idea that a goddess could have accomplished anything on her own troubled them.

Sighing, Danica took a bite and stole a look at Titus's unbelievably perfect profile. The slope of his nose was a thing of beauty, such a weird trait for her to notice.

"Something wrong?" he asked.

Danica nodded. To keep from lying to him, she chose an alternate truth. "Remember the day we met?"

"It would be hard to forget. The blender you were working on betrayed you."

That was my magic. But yeah.

"Probably because I was a bit hungover." Quickly she explained the circumstances—about Raquel and Darryl and the bachelorette party. "It's not that I *wanted* a future with him, but he spent two years telling me how much of a free spirit he was. A few months later, he proposes to someone else? Yikes."

Titus had been eating silently, listening. "Are you...not over him?"

"I was never under him," Danica said quickly. "I mean, I *was*, but—"

"Why don't I stop you there? I'm asking if your heart still belongs to him and that's why you were upset to hear he's marrying someone else."

She laughed. "Oh hell no. It's a hundred percent a smudge on my pride."

"Okay, but you were frowning hard just now, when I asked what was bothering you. And if you're still thinking about this—"

"Mostly, I wish I wasn't this petty. A truly enlightened person would've skipped the bachelorette party entirely."

"Whereas you went and drank too much to prove how little you care," he guessed.

"You already know me so well." That was alarming.

Titus smiled, an expression so sweet that it made her breath catch. That look was irresistible; she wanted to kiss the hell out of him. Instead, she held eye contact a little too long, felt heat in her cheeks, and ducked her head to finish her sandwich in embarrassed bites.

"I'd like to know you better," he said, low.

Yes. No.

That was a wonderful, terrible idea. All the reasons she shouldn't go further raced through her head. Gram's disapproval and Clem's disappointment, not to mention risking her magic… Then she recalled how the coven seemed to support some low-key rebound action. *Don't I deserve a reward? Something just for me.*

Her mouth went off like a fire alarm. "I'd love that. What did you have in mind?"

Titus shotgunned the green juice as if it were tequila to give him liquid courage, and then he said in a rush, "Would you go out with me? On a proper date."

"How proper are we talking? Do I need a corset? Stockings with lines on the back?"

His nervous look eased into genuine amusement. "Wear whatever you want. The important bit is that you agree to have dinner with me. Or a movie. Or bowling. Or—"

"Dinner and bowling," she cut in.

Oh crap, I'm really doing this. Why aren't you from a witch family? But even knowing that this had to end couldn't keep Danica from wading into dangerous waters. The heart had no common sense at all.

"Friday night?"

That was in two days, long enough for her to fret over the decision but not back out. *Hell, it's one date. I should worry less and live in the moment.*

Belatedly, she realized Titus was waiting for a response. "Yes, I think I'm free. I'll text you my address. How was the juice?"

"Good," he said so quickly that she suspected he hadn't tasted it at all, just swallowed it like medicine.

She peeled the orange she had brought with her today, focused on keeping the skin in one piece. She had read that if she did this, it would make her lucky in love. The peeling ripped before she got it off entirely, and she tried not to take it as a dire omen.

"Here." Danica split the orange into segments and passed him a few. Their fingers brushed, and the same sensation from the day before sizzled through her.

His eyes went hot as he slid the orange slice into his mouth, gazing at her with the sort of longing she'd only read about. Unable to help herself, Danica licked her lips, and Titus closed his eyes briefly, as if she presented too much temptation.

Hello, chemistry.

"Thanks." Clearing his throat, he produced a Tupperware container and offered it to her. "The dessert I promised."

Ridiculously excited, she removed the top and beheld the most beautiful apple tarts ever. The slices were folded into puff pastry to resemble a rose. The light dusting of glittering sugar gave them a magical glimmer, like something out of a fairy tale. She hesitated to devour such delicate beauty. Maybe it was ridiculous, but she snapped a picture with her phone, wanting to treasure this memory. In the end she couldn't resist—and it was all buttery sweetness, brightened with the bite of the apple and an underlying fruity spice she couldn't place.

Dammit. Now I want to kiss him even more.

"These are the most beautiful flowers I've ever received," she said softly.

————————

It's too soon. It's definitely *too soon.*

But watching Danica eat the tart he'd baked especially for her, savoring each tiny, delectable bite, Titus desperately wanted a taste as well, right from her soft mouth. Before he could stop this terrible decision, he was leaning in. And oh God, she came toward him as well, head angled, and her eyes were closing.

She's so pretty.

From out of nowhere, a cat leaped between them, making a horrendous yowl. It was a huge ginger, bristling like mad, claws out, and Titus scrambled away. "What the hell? Where did you come from?"

Danica sneezed. "Go home, Goliath. Stop stalking me."

"You know this cat?" It seemed like a weird thing for her to say to her own pet.

"Unfortunately, yes. He's utterly obsessed with me, and I'm allergic." As she spoke, the orange tabby crawled on her lap and glared at Titus with fierce green eyes, hissing when he reached out a hand to rub the cat's head.

"Is he a stray?" Even as he asked that, he guessed not because the animal had glossy fur and was extremely clean and well fed.

And on second look, he was also wearing a black collar with a tag on it. "Silly question, never mind."

"He belongs to a lady who lives on my street."

"And you said he's stalking you?" That was weird and hilarious but entirely appropriate, considering his own levels of interest so early on. Titus already had something in common with this lovesick cat.

"I mean, what would *you* call it? He's constantly running away from home. Goliath shows up on my porch like four times a week, and now he's chased me all the way downtown. His house is almost a mile away!" She lifted the cat to stare into his eyes. "Stop it, okay? Hazel will be super worried about you, you jerk!"

Titus couldn't help it. He cracked up over her calling the cat a jerk right to his face. Many cats *were* jerks, but he'd never witnessed a scene quite like this because the cat almost seemed to understand her. His head went down, and his tail curled in. The formerly aggro feline went boneless with disappointment, it seemed like.

Danica sneezed again, wedging the cat beneath her arm as she delved for her phone. "Hazel, it's me."

He couldn't hear what the other woman said in reply, but it sounded cranky.

"Yes, he's with me. I'm outside the courthouse eating on the bench beneath the elm tree. You have half an hour to get here. So help me, if he follows me to work—" Another pause. "I'm telling you, we *never* feed him!" She hung up and squinched her eyes shut as if she might be counting; then she flailed her free hand. "I've only used a pay phone once, but I was arguing with my mother, and it was *so* satisfying to bang that receiver down. How am I supposed to angrily end a cell call? And oh my God, I hate that Hazel doesn't know how to text. Voice calls are the worst."

"Especially with Hazel," he said, feeling like he'd stumbled into a mystic portal where everything was weirder and more interesting and infinitely better.

"You have no idea," she muttered. "Would you feed me another tart? I *deserve* an extra dessert for cat sitting. Hazel will scold me for luring Goliath, which I assuredly did not, and then Clem will yell at me for getting back late from lunch." Her sad eyes testified to how vastly unfair all of this was.

And though he'd never been one for PDAs, he got a tart out of the box and held it to her lips, letting her nibble away at it. Honest to God, he could just about feel the echo of it on his skin, right on his shoulder, then tingles on his neck, as if she were using her lips and teeth on him instead. An old line from a movie popped into his head: *What sorcery is this?*

He watched her eat like it was his reason to live, and when she licked the last crumbs from her lips, he stifled a groan. It was past time for him to go, but he didn't want to leave her until the cat situation was resolved. Making a snap decision, he texted Maya.

I need half an hour more. You and Stan can handle things?

Right away, she sent back, It's fine. But are you okay?

A reasonable question, since he rarely took long lunches. He preferred heading up the next day's prep work since Stan wasn't a certified baker and might make mistakes that could impact the quality of their products. Fine, just an unexpected errand. Tell Stan to wait for me on prep. I'll be there ASAP.

After tucking his phone into his pocket, he took the cat, ignoring Goliath's protests and her shock. "What? You're allergic. I'm not letting this jerk mess with you." Goliath hissed and tried to scratch him, so Titus repositioned him and kept him angled away from Danica. "How did you become the feline Pied Piper anyway?"

Her gaze flickered away, and her smile had a strange cast. "I have no idea. This isn't the first time, though. Goliath is the latest in a long line of obsessed cats."

"That's so weird."

"Tell me about it. I have a theory that cats chase people who are allergic to them."

Since Titus was a dog person and had no alternate ideas, it seemed like a reasonable supposition. "I wonder how Doris would feel about you."

"Who's Doris?"

"My dog." Eagerly, he dug out his phone and brought up a picture, sent it to her on chat. Easier than showing his screen with the cat actively fighting him.

I'll be covered in scratches at this rate.

"She's so cute! Huge too. Is she friendly?"

He considered that. "A little standoffish with strangers, but once she decides that you're trustworthy, she's an absolute snuggle hound. You wouldn't believe how much she hogs the bed."

"This is moving *so* fast," she said in a mock-somber tone. "First you want me to meet your dog, and now you're talking about beds."

Titus grinned. "Sorry, I won't spring Doris on you until at least our third date."

"You seem really sure that we'll get there," she said.

"There's no doubt on my end."

Whatever she would've said, he didn't get to hear it, as a round robin of a woman with hair like a mature dandelion came power walking toward them in a puce tracksuit, arms swinging like she was fighting invisible gnomes. "That must be Hazel," he whispered.

Danica only nodded, rising with an expression that went defensive the closer the old lady got. Titus didn't like seeing her that way at *all*, and he stepped in front, preemptively thrusting the ginger cat at the older woman. "Here you go, safe and sound. Have you considered a better monitoring system at home? It seems like you let him out a lot."

Hazel blinked, evidently unprepared for someone to attack her preventive measures. "He's an escape artist! I have no idea how he's getting out of the house."

"Try getting a collar with a camera in it," Danica suggested. "Maybe there's an exit that only Goliath knows about it, and when you check the footage, you'll be able to lock that route down."

Hazel cradled the cat like a baby. She clearly wanted to yell at Danica like this was *her* fault somehow, but Titus could see that his presence was acting as a deterrent.

"How am I supposed to know how to do all that?"

Right, Danica had said that Hazel couldn't even text. "Maybe a relative could help you?" he suggested.

Hazel beamed at Titus like he was a genius. "Oh! My grandson knows all about the internet. Do you think he'd be able to work a cat camera collar?"

"I'm sure. If the local pet store doesn't carry them, your grandson can probably help order one online, and then he can set everything up for you."

Clearly taken with this idea, Hazel nodded enthusiastically. "I'll take Goliath home and call David right now. Thank you!"

She hurried off without another word, and Danica stared after her, apparently speechless. Titus couldn't stop laughing.

"Really? David and Goliath?"

Smiling, Danica said, "The legends suggest her grandson is the one who can defeat that cat once and for all. Thanks for running interference."

"Hey, I was terrible at the throwing and catching parts of football but damn good at blocking. I'll be your defensive line anytime." *Ugh, no. Why did I say that?*

"Careful, I might take you up on that. Friday at what time, by the way?"

"Seven," he said at once. "And for the record, this was our first date. Friday will be the second. That's why I'm so sure we'll get to the third."

"Date or base?"

"I'm flexible."

Danica offered a smile so heated that his breath caught. "So am I."

CHAPTER 6

FRIDAY ROLLED AROUND MUCH FASTER than Danica expected.

Between work and texting with Titus, she found herself standing in her underwear in front of the full-length mirror on the back of her bedroom door. She turned sideways, trying to decide if this bra-and-panty set was good enough for a date. Not that she intended to *show* Titus, but knowing she was set up properly did wonders for her confidence. She'd bought this spicy red set a few months back, and she'd been saving it for a special occasion.

Tonight definitely qualifies.

Satisfied, she opened her closet and studied her options. The natural dress to pair with the sexy undies was this black cherry surprise—a '50s-inspired sundress, black cotton printed with red cherries. It was sexy, vibrant, and fun with a sweetheart neckline that framed her cleavage beautifully. *But is it too much for dinner and bowling?* Danica decided she didn't care.

Quickly she donned the dress and added a strand of black pearls. Nothing but her favorite red Fluevog sandals would do for this outfit. Once she surveyed the overall impression, she nodded and went to work on her makeup. Often Danica preferred going natural with a touch of lip balm and tinted sunscreen, but tonight she executed a sexy nighttime look, complete with subtle smoky eyes and bee-stung lips.

By the time she finished with her hair, it was nearly time for Titus to pick her up. She took a deep breath, tucked a pair of invisible socks into her handbag, and hurried downstairs to wait. Clem had plans tonight with Kerry and Priya, and Danica hadn't mentioned her date. Given that her cousin had warned her about Gram's proximity, Clem probably wasn't on board with Danica's plan to cut loose and have fun.

There's no reason why this has to be a big deal. I'm overthinking.

At 6:55, a rap sounded on the front door.

Despite her best intentions, her heart raced as she went to answer it. Titus stood on her front porch with a bouquet of mixed flowers, a bright blend of daisies, asters, sunflowers, and carnations. It was so adorably old school that her heart quivered. She hadn't planned on inviting him in, but she couldn't dump such a thoughtful gift on the side table where they stashed their mail and keys. Belatedly, she realized he was staring at her, like full-on gaping.

"Are you all right?" she asked instead of a more conventional greeting.

"I...think so?"

"You don't sound sure."

"It's because I never realized beauty could be a blunt object before."

"Are you saying that you've been assaulted by my attractiveness?"

"A little? In a good way," he added quickly, with a smile so bright that she considered fishing sunglasses out of her purse.

"Did you want to come in while I put these in water, or will you be pressing charges?" She tried to mask the smile, but it pulled at the edges of her mouth and got clean away from her until she felt it tugging at the corners of her eyes.

"I'll let it go this time, ma'am, but I need you to stop dazzling others with such a complete lack of regard for their safety. How many people must have driven into poles because of you?"

"It's a lot," she said somberly, placing a hand over her heart in mock remorse.

His gaze followed her motion and glanced over the curve of her breast. Well, that was why she'd worn this dress in the first place, but damn if she didn't love the color glazing his cheekbones. Danica fought a frisson of pure desire. For some reason, she wanted to touch Titus more than anyone she'd ever met. Her other hand drifted toward him like they were literally magnetic, but at the last minute she plucked the bouquet from his grasp.

"I have no doubt."

For a few seconds, she had no idea what they were even talking about. Right, the joke about her hotness putting drivers at risk. Smiling, she hurried to the kitchen and prepared a vase with water, adding sugar and vinegar to keep the blooms fresh longer. When she came back, she found Titus still standing in the foyer, studying the candid photos she and Clem had collected over the years.

"This must be your cousin," he guessed.

"Correct. That's Clementine, Clem to her friends."

"Waterhouse as well?"

Danica nodded. "Our mothers didn't change their names when they got married. It's a...unique family quirk. Waterhouse women were feminists long before there was even a word for it." That was the closest she could come to explaining their witch heritage, but he seemed to take it in stride.

"That's fascinating. Would you keep your maiden name as well?"

"If I ever got married? Definitely." She flashed him a teasing grin. "But you're pushing ahead again. At the park, you were all about your bed and meeting your dog. Now you're asking about my wedding plans."

Titus went rigid, eyeing her with tangible fear. "I'm sorry, I didn't mean—"

"Relax, I'm teasing you. One moment..." Danica went into the front room, visible from the foyer, and set the flowers on the coffee table, adjusting the magazines so the arrangement looked as if it had always been there. "How does that look?"

"Beautiful," he said, but he wasn't looking at the bouquet or her impromptu efforts at interior design.

Butterflies fluttered in her stomach. Though she was trying to control her reaction to him, there was no doubt that *he* was gorgeous. Beard perfectly trimmed, hair tousled in gentle curls, long lashes, thick brows, and a jaw so chiseled that statues would be envious. That didn't even account for his broad shoulders, his defined arms, and the soft-brown eyes currently gazing at her with so much warmth that her toes curled.

Her magic sparked a little, and she felt it in her veins, like when she tried to cast after downing too much champagne. Not a mistake she made anymore, but she'd been young and reckless once. With effort, she sealed the fluttering current of her magic and walked toward him. She could tell that he'd dressed carefully for their date, ironed his pants and shirt. Really, she was more interested in dragging him upstairs and stripping him *out* of those clothes than in finishing this date properly, but it was too soon for that. Titus didn't seem like the sort of man who was looking for a hookup, and she couldn't have anything serious with him. *Ugh, why is he so delicious?*

"You're staring," he said huskily.

"So I am. Should I apologize?"

"It depends on why."

"Shall I be tactful, or do you prefer the truth?"

He flinched, as if he secretly suspected there must be some terrible reason. "The truth is always best, even if it's disagreeable."

She took a step closer. "I was thinking that your clothes would look better on my floor. We'd better go to dinner if you want to get out of here with your virtue intact."

Titus sucked in a sharp breath and put a hand on the wall, bracing himself. "That's...not what I expected you to say. At all."

"It's up to you."

"We should...proceed with the date. I don't want to rush things between us."

Dammit. Well, she didn't think that would work anyway. Nothing ventured, nothing gained. Danica checked her bag and then gestured for him to lead the way. Outside, his Nissan Leaf was parked in front of her house, such a cute and unassuming ride, perfect for Titus. He opened the door and closed it for her afterward, and somehow it was even more adorable seeing a tall guy fold himself into a compact electric car.

"Where are we headed?"

"It's a surprise, a little place I discovered recently. They're newly opened, and I love the food. I hope you will too."

Titus drove like he did everything—with quiet confidence—and Danica settled in to enjoy the ride. He didn't protest when she fiddled with the radio, settling on a station out of Chicago. Ten minutes later, they pulled into a strip mall. None of the places looked too interesting, but he parked in front of Burma Kitchen. She tended to be experimental with her meals, and she'd never tried Burmese food.

"I didn't even know this was here!"

"You seem excited."

"Absolutely. I can't wait to try everything." For once, she didn't mean to be suggestive, but Titus stilled, his gaze fixed on her mouth.

He swallowed once, twice, and leaned slightly her way. He touched her cheek, tracing a fingertip lightly downward, drifting toward her mouth with a restless compulsion.

Then he caught himself. Pulled back.

I really want to kiss him. I refuse to go home until I find out whether his lips feel as good as I imagine.

Dear God.

With effort, Titus gave himself a silent pep talk as he slid out of the Leaf and jogged around to get her door. She already had her hand on the handle, not making it easy for him to be a gentleman. It wasn't that he thought she couldn't open her own door, but he wanted Danica to know that she was special, worth putting in extra effort.

Anxiously, he watched her face as they went into the restaurant together. The decor was simple, nothing extravagant, but they'd need to go into the city for a superposh dining experience. Burma Kitchen was half full, the tables simple wood and metal. The walls were painted ecru and bamboo green, with judicious use of fabrics and screens to attempt to add privacy and elegance.

Kham Keow, the owner of Burma Kitchen, greeted Titus with a friendly wave. "Good to see you. And your lovely guest. Sit anywhere you like."

Since the place was on the small side, he chose a table for two near the back, not so close that they could hear noise from the kitchen or bathroom. "How's this?"

Danica took her seat, smiling. "Perfect."

A server in black proffered menus as Titus spread his napkin across his lap. *Need to make a good impression and take my mind off how much I wish I'd gone upstairs with her back at her house.* Sternly he told himself to settle down. *You've waited this long. You can wait a little longer to take things to the next level.* With Danica, it already mattered more than it ever had—that he do this properly and not screw it up.

"Anything look good?"

"Everything," she said with a teasing light in her eyes as she looked him up and down. "But what do you recommend?"

Somehow, he swallowed the sexy rejoinder that sprang to

mind. "The roti is great. I usually get a veggie dish, some curry, oh, let's try the tea leaf salad?"

"Since this is my first time, I'll put myself in your hands." Danica closed her menu and gazed across the table like she was considering Titus as her main course.

Yes, please.

He ordered the samosa platter, tea leaf salad, spicy lotus roots, fried rice, and chicken coconut curry. "You don't mind sharing, I hope?"

"With you? Not at all."

"Do you like iced milk tea?" he asked, pretending his heart wasn't racing like he'd just completed a sprint.

"I do."

Turning to the server, he added, "Two milk teas, please. I'm driving, but you could have a cocktail if you prefer."

Danica shook her head. "If you're not drinking, I'd rather not. In some countries, they have a designated driver service. You ring in and someone comes to take you home."

"I suspect they must have better public transportation," he said thoughtfully. "It would work in larger cities, but out here…"

"Not so much." St. Claire had no public transportation, unless one counted the Greyhound stop at the gas station twenty minutes away. "That's what ride-sharing apps are for, though you pay for two rides instead of one. Sometimes I do that when I go out drinking with Clem and other friends."

Titus imagined a tipsy Danica, all giddy and getting in a random stranger's car; he didn't care for that scenario. It could be dangerous even if she went home with her cousin… "You can call me," he said quickly. "If you ever need a ride, that is. It doesn't matter what time. I'll come get you."

"Wow, seriously? You'll be my on-call chauffeur?"

I'll be anything you wish.

With effort, he managed to bite back the words. Luckily, the samosas arrived, and they were delicious, as always. The food came in well-timed waves, so the next hour was full of incredible flavors and casual conversation. Titus watched Danica respond to each bite, enjoying her blissful smiles and half-closed eyes. Before, he'd never realized how sensual it was to watch someone enjoy their food, but by the time they'd finished, he was slightly aroused, dazed with resisting the pull between them.

"How was it?" he asked.

"Exquisite. I'll be back. I'm bringing Clem...*and* the rest of my book club. I don't know if Margie has ever had a curry. I'm positive Ethel hasn't."

"That's fantastic. Word of mouth is critical for a restaurant."

Pleased by her response, he paid for their meal while she went to the bathroom. When Danica returned, her lipstick was freshly applied, such a gorgeous shade of red that he curled his hand into a fist against his knee to resist the urge to pull her to him and smear it thoroughly. She touched him on the shoulder, just a light pressure to call his attention, and a pleasurable shock went through him, almost electric in its intensity. It traveled throughout his body in a sensuous wave, and his cock stirred.

No, don't do that. This is not the time.

"Oh! Did you feel that?" Oddly, Danica seemed uncharacteristically anxious, her eyes wide and worried.

Titus wished he could kiss the concern away. *I will never make it through this night.*

"Probably a strong static charge. Ready for part two?"

"We're bowling next, right? I should warn you that I'm the gutterball champion. Or at least, I was in junior high."

"I can teach you," he offered.

"That would be great."

Waving at Kham Keow, he escorted Danica to the car and opened her door. She angled a look up at him through her lashes. While they were eating, the sun had gone down. Now the sky was all dark velvet. Had anyone ever looked prettier in the moonlight? Before he could talk himself out of it, he told himself to go for it.

She lifted her chin for a reason.

When he lowered his head, slowly enough that she could block the kiss if she wanted to, Danica came up on tiptoe and curled her fingers into his shirt. Her hands grazed his chest as his lips met hers. It had been long enough since he'd kissed anyone that he was slightly afraid he might've forgotten how. Then he lost all coherent thought entirely. She was all heat and softness, her mouth so delicate and tender on his, slowly warming to a lush fullness as she parted her lips and touched her tongue to his.

The erection he had been fighting in the restaurant came on strong, and he pressed her against the side of the car, kissing her ravenously. Titus tangled a hand in her wavy hair as she wrapped herself around him. This kiss was everything, alpha and omega, and it erased the memory of everyone he'd ever touched before her. His whole body throbbed with longing, like he had been waiting for this woman, this moment, his entire life.

There was no way for him to get enough. Not of her. Breathless, he broke the kiss and dragged his mouth over her jaw, down her throat, and left little nips that made her shiver, digging her fingers into his back. He imagined she would hold on to him that way when he— *Oh God*. Suddenly he realized that they were dry humping each other in a parking lot while making desperate noises.

Practically panting, he rested his forehead against hers. "Okay, that escalated a *lot* faster than I intended."

He expected her to laugh or to pull away. Instead, she touched his face with the softest of caresses, tracing every feature like she couldn't believe he was real. Her fingertip trailed down the bridge of his nose, over his lower lip, and the pleasure of it sent an uncontrollable shiver through him. Titus moved away from her then, trying his best to contain his riotous impulses—the ones telling him to find some privacy and *have* her.

In time, Danica settled in the car, and he paced around it until he felt sure he could join her without embarrassing himself. She buckled her seat belt as he started the engine.

"I admit, I've never gotten that worked up from kissing before," she whispered.

That must be in response to what he'd said five minutes ago. And hell, it was impossible not to feel smug about her confession, even as he ached for her.

"Me either."

She tried a smile, but longing lingered in her eyes, in the way her gaze glided over him, teasing him with echoes of her touch. "We have chemistry, huh?"

"*So* much," he said.

"Enough to light a small town."

"We should offer ourselves to the mayor as an alternative power source."

Danica laughed. "How are we supposed to go bowling after this? If you give me lessons, you'll put your hands all over me, and I...never mind. I retract my objection."

Titus basked in the pleasurable wave rolling through him. Desire and warmth and tenderness and...no, not that word. Too soon for that one. Affection, then. Wanting had never been so easy before, so easy and *right*.

If only it would last this time.

CHAPTER 7

THOUGH DANICA HAD LIVED IN St. Claire for years, she had never been inside Star Lanes, the local bowling alley.

It was all done up in retro style, like a '50s diner, but they served beer, not just fries and milkshakes. Since there wasn't much nightlife in town, half the local populace was here, eating or drinking, yelling across the place at people they recognized. It was impossible not to worry about Gram getting wind of this, but her crowd preferred gardening and bingo to bowling and beer. *Should be fine, right?* Titus received his fair share of greetings, and an older man broke off from his friend group to intercept them.

Titus shuffled his feet, rubbing the back of his neck like he was nervous or embarrassed. *Why is that so cute?* "Hey, Stan. I didn't know you bowled."

"I'm a man of mystery."

The self-proclaimed man of mystery extended a hand. "I'm Stan. Nice to meet you. I work with Titus at the bakery."

"You must be his assistant." Danica shook his hand and made small talk, enjoying Titus's adorable awkwardness.

Someone called loudly, "Stan, you're up! You planning to take your turn or what?"

"I'm coming, geez."

"That's it, I'll never hear the end of this," Titus said mournfully as his assistant sped back to his bowling team.

At least she suspected they must be since they all wore matching shirts with logos for the local oil-changing business on the back along with the name "Lickety Splitz." True to the claim, Stan threw a seven-ten split and picked up the spare. Danica watched him exchange high fives from everyone on the team; then she turned back to her date.

Date, oh goddess, what am I even doing right now? The memory of the kiss washed over her, leaving her whole body flushed and glowing. Somehow she got herself together enough to respond to his joke.

"I hope I'm worth the teasing."

"No question. Let's get our shoes. Sorry about that in advance," he added, leading the way to the counter, where a bored teen was looking at her phone.

"The idea of renting shoes is tremendously gross. You know that, right?"

"Trust me, I'm aware."

After putting on the invisible socks she'd packed and the ugliest footwear known to man, she followed Titus to their assigned lane. Danica had never imagined that bowling could be dorky, entertaining, *and* sexually frustrating, but with Titus, it achieved the trifecta. As promised, she was terrible, but she improved under his tutelage, which involved a lot of his arms around her, showing her exactly the right way to hold the ball. Admittedly, she paid way more attention to the heat of his body pressed against her back than the positioning. Consequently, she shorted out the electronic scoreboard with magical fluctuations. The power flickered when it sparked, and she willed her abilities to settle down.

Calm, you're calm. With effort, she steadied her racing heart and tried to quell other urges. In time, the lights came back on, but their scoreboard wouldn't work, no matter what buttons Titus hit. *I can fix it, but not with him standing here.*

"Maybe you should ask for a paper one?" she suggested.

"Good idea."

As soon as he walked off, she closed her eyes, focusing on the electronics she'd fried. Fortunately, this was her wheelhouse. The circuit was completely blown, but she used her magic to restore it, repairing all the damage she'd caused. Being a technomancer was convenient at times like this; it allowed her to mitigate unintentional harm before anyone got suspicious.

Damn. Why do mundanes screw with our powers like this?

By the time Titus got back, the scoreboard was online and functioning properly. Danica sat at the table with her hands folded like she'd had nothing to do with that. He eyed the scoreboard and sighed, setting down the paper copies.

"Just my luck," he muttered. "Shall we get started?"

"You can go first."

Since he'd given instruction at the start, she admired his form as he bowled. It was pure pleasure to drink him in, the arch of his arm, the way his body bent and dipped when he released. *And I'm thinking of filthy stuff again.* Truly, their sexual chemistry was off the charts; in English there wasn't even a word for the intensity, though German likely had a polysyllabic choice that fit the bill. On a whim, she searched and came up with "leidenschaft"— uncommonly strong passion or fervor.

Yep, I knew it.

"What are you doing?" Suddenly, Titus stood at her shoulder, peering at her phone in curiosity.

"Looking up a word in German that encompasses how much I want you."

He stared for a few seconds like he didn't know how to respond. "You just...said that. Right here. In the middle of Star Lanes."

She bit her lip. "Yeah, maybe I shouldn't have."

"The candor is fine. Fantastic even. The timing..." His look smoldered, lingering on Danica's mouth, and she felt it like a kiss.

"They do say you shouldn't ask if you're not ready for the answer," she teased.

After Darryl's indifference, it felt so good to bask in Titus's desire. His eyes practically ate her up as she slid out of the score-keeping seat and sashayed toward the ball return unit. He'd chosen a purple eight-pound ball for her, and she had to admit it was easy to handle. She tried to emulate his fancy stance, but she didn't quite nail it. He was still watching her with a heated, hungry stare when she only knocked down two pins, despite trying twice.

"Have you always wanted to be a baker?" she asked as he took his next shot.

He shook his head. "No, but my mom loved to bake, and I guess...it makes me feel close to her, even though she's gone."

That made her want to hug him...so she did. There was no reason not to. Danica wrapped her arms around him and gave him a squeeze. The move seemed to surprise him, but he didn't pull away as she said, "I get that. I've always been closer to my grandmother. Oddly, she's more into tech than my mom." There were witch reasons for that, but Titus didn't need to know as much.

"That's interesting. Did your grandmother teach you how to fix things?" He returned the embrace, delaying his turn for long moments.

"Everything she knew," Danica confirmed.

"You must have taken supplementary courses to keep up with current technology?"

She nodded, not wanting to pursue that avenue of discussion. "Do you think you'll stay in St. Claire?"

"I can't imagine myself ever leaving. This might sound strange, but my mom's buried here. It would feel like abandonment if I moved, if I couldn't stop by and leave flowers now and then. Is that...weird?" He seemed worried about her response, a little anxious about sharing that much so soon.

"Not at all. I haven't lost anyone I was close to like that, but I suspect I'd feel the same way."

"Plus, I have friends here. And while running a bakery wasn't my lifelong dream, I do love it. It's awesome seeing how happy people are, eating something delicious that I made."

"I can vouch for your skill," she said.

It took Titus ages to look away and finish his turn. He won their match by a huge margin while she barely got eighty, and she couldn't have cared less. As they returned their shoes, she wondered if he would kiss her again when he dropped her off. *Can I risk letting him?*

Crap, Clem might be home. It would be supremely humiliating if her cousin turned on the porch light like a disapproving parent. Even worse if Clem came out to stare at them with arms folded. Honestly Danica didn't know what bothered Clem more— the idea of Danica fooling around with a mundane or if she sensed the depth of Danica's attraction and suspected Danica might be tempted to break their pact.

Whatever, I'll worry about that later. The rest of the coven thinks I deserve some fun.

When they left the bowling alley, Titus touched his hand to her lower back, a faintly proprietary gesture. While the implications worried her, she also delighted in the fact that he felt possessive, even if she shouldn't want that. *I'm in so much trouble.*

"Did you have fun?" he asked as he opened her door.

"It was wonderful."

He flashed a boyish smile. "I'm glad you thought so too. I've had some terrible dates, but this one was—"

"Perfect?" she suggested.

If only it hadn't been.

That would make it easier to cut him off, if their chemistry turned out to be mostly in her imagination. Sometimes, she admired someone's physical attributes, and then five minutes of conversation cured that dazzlement. But no, Titus was sweet and passionate and delicious, exactly the sort of man who could—

No, *not* steal her heart. She couldn't allow that.

"Yes. That. I don't use that word lightly either." His eyes glittered in the neon lights from the flashing bowling pin.

Danica didn't say much as he drove her home. The station she'd selected before was playing a melancholy song. Most people connected their phones to their vehicles, but either Titus didn't mind relinquishing musical control to the radio, or he was more interested in her company than in the tunes.

In short order, Titus pulled up outside her house. The lights were on, a sure sign that Clem was home. Danica turned to him with a faint smile. "Thanks for a lovely evening."

"The pleasure was mine." He started a slow lean.

She should move back. She didn't.

But instead of trying to rekindle the flames from before, he kissed her delicately on one cheek and then the other, a soft brush of lips to her chin, and finally her forehead. *Oh goddess, the brow kiss—my kryptonite.* It was a tenderness grenade, reducing the defenses around her heart to rubble.

Titus offered a crooked smile. "I don't want to get carried away and give your neighbors something to talk about. Hope that's okay."

"More than," she whispered. "Good night."

"I'll text you," he said.

Danica rubbed her aching chest as she got out of the car and hurried toward the house. It wouldn't be easy to forget him.

Even if that was for the best.

———

Titus basked in the afterglow while watching Doris frolic in the backyard.

The dog acted like he had been gone for ten years instead of a few hours, but it was impossible to mind that sort of devotion. He ran after her and threw her soggy tennis ball until she got tired of chasing it. Doris dashed over and flopped on top of his feet, a classic plea for belly rubs if he'd ever seen one. Obligingly he knelt and scratched her belly until she was a wiggling puddle.

"Did you propose yet?" Maya teased, propping herself against the doorframe.

"You'll never let that go, will you?"

"Not likely. Fun date?"

He wouldn't fearlessly use the word "perfect" in front of his sister or the teasing would never end. "Yeah, we went to Burma Kitchen and Star Lanes after."

"I'm glad. Things have been rough..." She hesitated, and he could tell she was thinking about their mom, how Dad had moved on with Susan, and maybe the new baby as well. She might be thinking about Titus's many exes too. "For a while now. You deserve to be happy."

"It was one date," he protested.

"Still, I'm glad that things seem to be working out for one of us."

Titus wished he could find the right words to comfort her. But likely Maya wouldn't believe him if he said that they didn't do anything wrong. That it was Dad's weakness—the man couldn't stand to be alone even for a little while, and he lacked the fortitude to process grief on his own, so he immediately filled that void with someone else. Or hell, maybe the old man just had the emotional depth of a puddle. Two months after Mom passed, he'd said, "Life is for the living," just before he'd started dating Susan.

Those reflections blighted Titus's good mood. The best way for him to be happy was to pretend his dad was gone too.

And how fucking sad is that?

"Yeah, yeah. I should get to sleep. Doris, bedtime!"

The dog sprang up and raced Titus to his room, where she sprawled and took up way more than her share of space as he brushed his teeth. Once he settled under the covers with Doris draped over the other pillow, he plugged in his phone and checked. Minor disappointment when he saw that Danica hadn't texted him, but maybe she was waiting for him to do it first. *I said I would.*

Before he could think better of it, he fired up the messenger app. Thanks again for tonight. Sweet dreams. After way too much reflection, he added a heart emoji before hitting send. Maya was right about one thing: relationships had always been a struggle for him, and the idea of failing scared the shit out of him.

In the morning, there was no reply to his message—unsurprising, as his day started so early. He rushed through his morning routine and hurried to the bakery. To his surprise, Stan didn't say a word about their meeting the night before. Since the man wasn't a morning person, it seemed like he couldn't muster the energy to joke around either.

Working in the kitchen always took Titus's mind off everything else, so the hours flew in a flurry of delicious aromas. There was undeniably a manual labor component to running a bakery, but when he beheld the finished products, all lined up on trays to be sold, happiness sparkled through him. He loved inventing new recipes, developing products to surprise and delight his customers. Currently, he was working on a healthy version of a gingersnap, as his grandmother's recipe called for almost a cup of lard and way too much sugar and molasses.

"Do people even *want* gingersnaps these days? Let alone healthy ones," Maya asked when he popped out of the kitchen to relieve her for break.

Mrs. Carminian happened to be browsing the pastry case, and she glanced up with sudden interest. "*I* do. My husband loves them, but he's diabetic, and he needs to watch his sugar and his carbs. If you pair old-school taste with improved nutrition, I'd buy two dozen a week, and I'm not the only one. My Sunday school group was just talking about the gingersnaps and snickerdoodles we used to get at the weekly church potluck." She sighed. "People don't bake like they used to."

"That's better for me," Titus pointed out with a warm smile.

He was naturally friendly and courteous to older folks, but it paid major dividends with women like Mrs. Carminian. She beamed at him as she bought out his entire stock of low-carb, sugar-free treats. Silently Maya bagged up the pastries as Mrs. Carminian chattered to Titus.

"Still working as a volunteer firefighter? Maybe I'll have some trouble with my barbecue this weekend." The old lady winked at him.

He flattered her by flirting back politely. "I'll be there with bells on."

"Bring your big hose instead!"

Oh Lord. It never failed to astonish him what elderly women would say.

From somewhere to the side, Maya choked on a laugh,

and when Mrs. Carminian left, his sister smirked. "You're so smooth with the grandma set. If only that carried over to the younger ones."

"Eat your lunch," he snapped.

As usual, his sister's break proved to be ridiculously busy, and he got out fifteen minutes late. He'd been in a hurry this morning, so he hadn't packed anything. He could get a sandwich to go from the café down the road, but really, he was more tired than hungry. *Maybe I'll just go sit in the park for an hour.* Early mornings had trained him to nap anywhere, including a bench in the sun.

Since Danica hadn't responded to his text, he fought irrational fear that he'd never hear from her again. *Maybe I should break something. Then I'd have a reason to call her to the bakery.* But she was sitting on his bench when he got there—with lunch already set up.

She smiled at him, apparently unaware of his racing thoughts. "You're late. Lucky I'm feeling patient. I didn't start without you."

"That's… You…" Honest to God, Titus had no idea what to say.

He recalled that they'd discussed meeting here for lunch and she'd offered to make various healthy concoctions, but they hadn't made concrete plans for today, right? Yet here she was with two lunches and two bottles of juice and so pretty that he had to tuck his hands in his pockets to keep from hugging her. Each time, she warmed him like a summer day, leaving him hot and breathless. Actually, it *was* a summer day, so it could be that too.

"Cat got your tongue?" she teased. "If so, I can look for Goliath. In fact, I'm a little startled that he's not here already."

"Maybe David's got him on lockdown. What's on the menu today?" He seated himself like everything was totally normal.

Beautiful women always make me lunch and wait for me without prompting.

"Tuna and avocado, apple wedges, and a honeydew green tea smoothie."

"Well, that's...intriguing," he said.

"Admit it, that wasn't the first word that came to mind. Here." Danica passed over his portion of the food, and he realized he didn't have dessert to contribute this time.

Titus *hated* feeling unprepared. "If you'd given me a heads-up, I wouldn't have shown up empty-handed."

"You don't like surprises?"

He considered that. "I just...don't like getting more than I give. I can't stand being in someone's debt."

"It's a sandwich, not an auto loan." Her warm voice carried a definite thread of music, a laugh she was holding in.

With a sigh, he conceded the point and took a bite. "A super delicious one, though."

"You can make it up to me later."

"Promise?"

Her eyes locked on his then slid to his mouth. "Definitely."

Suddenly his head swam with thoughts not remotely appropriate for a public park at 1:24 in the afternoon. No, these were private midnight fantasies, ideas so dirty that he rarely framed such thoughts, let alone put someone in a starring role so fast.

With effort, he attempted a conversation that didn't involve suggesting that she get naked. "Are you interested in some freelance work?"

"That's the whole premise of our shop," she said.

"Unrelated to fix-it work. I could use a taste tester for some recipes I'm working on. It's not a paid position, I'm afraid. Maya usually does it, but she's tired of sweets."

"Not something I ever imagined was possible."

"It is if you live with a baker."

A slow smile that made him want to kiss her. "I'll take that under advisement. So you'd be compensating me in other ways?"

He swallowed hard. "I'm willing to...negotiate."

CHAPTER 8

INSIDE THE HOUSE, DANICA BANGED her head lightly against the front door.

Agreeing to be Titus's taste tester had been a terrible idea because now she had a reason to see him again and again, even without dating. All kinds of impulsive stuff happened around him, like her brain had a permanent short circuit. Just as well he'd asked her to sample desserts and not to get married because she might've blurted a reflexive "yes" and unleashed the dogs of war. Well, Pomeranians belonging to her octogenarian grandmother anyway.

I should stop seeing him. Her magic already felt like bottled lightning, zinging around in uncontrollable bursts. Yet when she thought of him heading to their bench—*oh Aradia, we have a spot already*—and not finding her there, her heart ached. Already she cared too much how he felt, if he was sad or tired, if it brightened his day to eat lunch with her.

"Did you have a good time last night?" Clem asked.

Crap. I didn't want to hash this out today. She needed time to get her head in order. Slowly, she turned, pretending that she wasn't a hundred conflicted knots.

"Yeah, it was fun. Did you know there's a Burmese restaurant in town?"

Clem tilted her head, visibly surprised. "Really, where?"

"In the strip mall, next to the dry cleaner. The food is excellent." Eagerly, Danica extolled the virtues of the dishes she'd sampled and added, "We should eat there for one of our meetings and do coven business at someone's place after. I'm dying to see what Ethel thinks of chicken coconut curry."

"I haven't had samosas since—wait, I see what you're doing! Don't change the subject." Crossing her arms, Clem attempted to look stern.

In response, Danica tried an innocent expression. "What do you mean? You asked about my night, and I'm telling you what I ate."

"Are you seeing him again?"

Danica shrugged. "I don't know. Probably. We kissed, and it was..." She pretended to wipe sweat from her brow. "You don't find chemistry like that every day, so I'm having a hard time pulling myself away, you know? I feel like it would be an irresponsible use of sexual tension if we don't orgasm together at least once."

Her cousin's eyes widened. "That good? Just...be careful, I guess. And remember our deal. Things only stay calm as long as we're neutral like Switzerland."

It sucked that any choice she made regarding her personal life could be considered taking sides. Gram would video call Danica's mom if she got serious with someone from a vetted witch family and be all "in your face" about it. Her mom would probably not react so triumphantly if she hooked up with a mundane, but it would certainly fuel the conflict. She sighed and waved a hand in her cousin's general direction.

"Trust me, I'm aware," she said finally. "Can we table this for now?"

"Of course. You get that I'm worried, right? I don't want you to get hurt again. Even if you don't admit it, even if you weren't all in on that relationship, I know Darryl messed you up. I still want to punch him over how he strung you along and—"

"Aw, Clem," Danica cut in. She hugged her cousin and breathed in the familiar, comforting scent of her favorite lotion, sweet melon and pineapple. "I'm honestly fine, I promise. What I need is a rebound fling, and this one fits the bill. If I catch feelings, you'll be the first to know."

Clem hugged her tight and then eased back to ask, "You sure you don't want to hex Darryl? I've got multiple ideas, and Kerry would help! Oozing sores or crusty—"

"Eh, no. He'd know it was a magical rash when it didn't respond to medical treatments, and I'd be first on his list of suspects. He's the type who would report us to the council, and we don't need the paperwork."

"I hate taking the high road," Clem muttered.

"You're not asking *me* to cause trouble for your ex."

"That's different. I only dated Spencer for four months. You wasted years on Darryl."

Danica had to admit that Clem had a point, but she still wasn't down for vengeance. "Anyway, what did you do with Kerry and Priya? You hung out at their place?"

Clem nodded. "They're all settled in, and they redecorated to incorporate both their styles. Aggressive elegance is what I'd call it. And to answer you, we had wine and cheese while bingeing four episodes of that new Netflix original."

"Which one?"

They talked a bit more about the plot of the show, then Danica showered and headed to her room. It was almost midnight, but she couldn't settle, even after she got in bed. Clem's fears echoed in her head—*I don't want you to get hurt again.* Danica didn't want that either, but in the privacy of her room, she could admit that she was way more attracted to Titus than she ever had been to Darryl.

Time to put on the brakes.

While she wasn't in too deep yet, she needed to take stock and consider whether her original plan was possible. It might not be feasible to have a fling with Titus with her whole being clamoring for more. She finally fell asleep at close to two in the morning and woke up late, cranky and fighting a headache. She had the vague sense that she'd been dreaming, but she couldn't recall any details.

Must've woken up in the middle of REM sleep.

Sometimes she wished she was a vivimancer instead, capable of magicking away her own aches and pains. But it was tough to make a living in that field, and most witches held mundane jobs to pay the bills, though a few worked as "holistic health practitioners." The council didn't like it, but there were enough mundane frauds in the field that most people couldn't sift through them to find those with real power.

With a mumbled curse, she swallowed a couple of ibuprofen, and before she could think better of it, she drafted a message to

Titus. We're slammed at the shop this week, so I won't have time to do lunch. We'll catch up when things settle down.

Before she even made herself a sandwich, she got a reply. Okay, thanks for letting me know. Don't work too hard, and hit me up if you need a break. I could use an impartial review of the healthy gingersnap recipe I'm developing.

Reading that, Danica closed her eyes and wished for strength. *The man wants to feed me cookies. Cookies...and maybe the best sex of my life. How am I supposed to resist?*

She fixed a stern look on herself in the mirror as she pulled her hair into a high ponytail. "Be strong. You can do this."

On her way to work, she got a call from her mother. "I'll be in town tomorrow. If you have time, would you like to get together?"

That was the difference between Gram and Danica's mom. Gram never took no for an answer while Minerva would be hurt if she didn't *make* time despite the short notice, but Mom wouldn't say anything. Danica could certainly hang out for a while, especially since she was avoiding Titus.

"Sounds good. Do you want to come for dinner? Will Dad be with you?"

"He's working, but he sends his love. Invite your grandmother too. She'll feel left out otherwise." That was Minerva, trying her best to keep the peace.

"Okay, I'll talk to her. Are you visiting because of Gram?"

Her mother sighed. "Yes, she said she has some concerns about you. I wish she'd spend more time living her own life and less time trying to manage yours."

Danica agreed, but it felt...disloyal to say it aloud. "Yeah, well. Let me know if you manage to grow a wishing tree. Oh wait, that'll never happen."

Since her mother lacked magic, she grew a garden the mundane way, and it was beautiful, but still, it was a lot of work. Danica realized belatedly that it sounded like a passive aggressive dig about her mom's life choices, and she had no idea what to say to smooth the awkward moment over. The silence lingered a little too long.

"What time should I be there?" Minerva finally asked.

"Six thirty would be good. I'll tell Clem not to make plans. It'll be a full-on Waterhouse reunion." Probably, it would also be unspeakably awkward.

"See you soon, Little Star."

"Yep. Bye, Mom."

The cuteness of that childhood nickname simultaneously made her smile and roll her eyes. Danica meant "morning star," and her mom called her "Little Star" to this day. She texted the invite to her grandmother, not wanting to deal with another family chat today.

The next night, she and Clem braced for Gram-and-Mom-ageddon. Lucky for Clem, her own mother lived in Florida as well, closer to Gram in case she needed help during snowbird season. Tonight, the pressure would be on Danica to mediate and keep old grievances from spoiling dinner. They'd picked up a roast chicken from the deli, and Clem had made a salad while Danica slow cooked a pot of baked beans last night. Neither one of them loved cooking, but they'd hear about the lack of effort if they served only takeout.

Gram arrived first in a swirl of lavender. It was mystifying how she exuded glamour at her age, but she did. Her hair was always done, sleek and silver, and her clothes were elegant. She always chose the right accessories, pearls today, along with a crisp cotton sheath. Beaming, she hugged both her granddaughters in turn and then turned her gaze to the house with an assessing air.

"Beautiful. Love the flowers." She cut a look at Danica that made her nervous.

Does she know? Clem would say, "Yes, definitely, she always does," but it seemed out of character for Gram not to mention Titus right away. Danica addressed only the surface statement. "They're lovely, but they won't last. I'll have to throw them out soon."

"As long as you know, my dear."

Well, that was pointed.

Minerva rapped on the door, waiting to be granted access before she came in. Danica hugged her mom first thing and stood back to see how she'd changed since her last visit. She'd lost a little weight, slimming from plump to average. Her face showed lines only at the corners of her eyes, and her hair was auburn, redder than Danica's. Her mom had none of the freckles—those came from her dad—and she wore an adorable tie-dye romper over a yellow T-shirt, paired with chunky sneakers and hand-strung beads. As always, she had a warm smile and soft-hazel eyes.

"You look great," Danica said.

Gram made a scoffing noise. "She looks absurd. When will you act your age, Minerva? You could be so pretty if you—"

"Dinner!" Clem called.

Danica flashed her cousin a look, grateful for the interruption. Gram had precise ideas about how Waterhouse witches ought to behave and living up to her expectations could be...challenging. Minerva didn't respond to the half-completed criticism, but Danica stayed her with a hand on her arm as Gram headed for the dining room.

"You look adorable," she whispered.

Her mom smiled. "It's *hot*. I enjoy being comfortable. And your dad thinks I'm cute no matter what I wear."

I wish I had that. I wish I was brave enough.

The dinner was every bit as tense as she'd feared. Gram ate a few bites of the chicken and then said, "Danica, dear, you can't pine over Darryl forever. Let me—"

"Mom," Minerva cut in. "Please let her live as she sees fit. Any choice she makes, as long as she follows her heart, will be the right one."

"Oh please! That's the fastest way for her to—"

"Mother." Normally, Mom's tone was soft, but it held a thread of steel now.

"Fine, let's talk about something else. Are you still heading up that garden club? You won a prize for your work, didn't you?" To Danica, Gram's praise sounded...forced, as if she couldn't find anything to admire about gardening like a mundane.

It hurt to see her own mother dismissed this way, but since Minerva didn't defend herself, Danica didn't make waves. Instead, Minerva ate some beans, then calmly replied, "Yes, I'm still the point person. Hobbies are important, far better to invest your energy in something you enjoy."

Maybe Danica was imagining this, but that sounded almost like chastisement. She traded looks with Clem, who raised her brows as if she thought so too. This could get ugly before dessert. Quickly she asked, "Who wants cookies?"

"I'd better not," Gram said. "It's so unbecoming when women let themselves go."

Yikes. Mom wasn't as slim as Gram, but so what? Danica opened her mouth to counter, but before she spoke up, Clem did. "Go where? Body-shaming is wrong, Gram. How would you feel if someone said you're annoying and out of touch because you're old?"

"I can't control the aging process," Gram snapped, obviously stung.

Danica tried to mediate, as she always did. "Hey, she said *if*. Hypothetical. No need to get upset. Just remember that judgmental comments are hurtful. Coffee?"

"I'd love some." Mom rose and touched her shoulder. "I'll help you make it."

The night didn't improve from there, but they did manage to prevent the elders from fighting. Gram left first after multiple cheek kisses, and Mom refused an offer to spend the night with a soft smile. "Your father's waiting for me. He says he can't sleep without me."

"Give him my love," Danica said.

"Mine too," Clem added.

In the morning, Danica felt like shit.

It seemed like *way* longer than a few days since she'd seen Titus. Now she was reliving that kiss, ending up so flushed that even a cold shower wouldn't work. Not that she could take one at Fix-It Witches. To make matters worse, her abilities were fritzing when she tried to repair gadgets at the shop.

Her phone buzzed on and off all day. After the awkward meal last night, Gram was sending Bindr profiles again, along with messages making it clear that she wanted their bloodline carried on and that she'd never be satisfied until Danica chose a proper witch family. Sighing, she turned off her phone. *I don't need this.*

Time crawled by.

Around three in the afternoon on day seven of Danica's self-imposed exile from the land of delicious men and sweet pastries, Clem pointed at the door. "Go see him. I've never heard of sexual frustration causing this, but there's a first time for everything."

"Are you sure? I only worked half a day—"

"You made that microwave radioactive!"

"Oops?" She made a cartoonish expression of regret, all puppy eyes and hunched shoulders, and Clem never could resist.

Her cousin laughed, shaking her head. "You're a mess. It won't kill me to close the shop. I don't have any plans tonight anyhow."

"Thanks!" Quickly she hugged Clem and gathered her bag before the other woman could change her mind.

Not that Danica thought she *should* be working with her power going haywire. It couldn't be what Gram had warned about already, right? It made no sense logically that desiring a mundane and going on one date could completely disrupt her magic. Lack of concentration, frustration, anxiety—all those emotions must be scrambling her focus.

It will be better once I see him.

For Titus, it had been a long, lonely week.

Saturday looked to be no better, though there were plenty of customers judging from the noise out front. He was supposed to play poker tonight with Trevor, Dante, Miguel, and Calvin, but he had no taste for it. Impossible not to fear that his curse was kicking in. After two lunches and a single nighttime date too—that was unusual. Apart from his junior prom date hooking up with someone else, he usually managed to hang out for a while before everything went sideways.

Maya popped her head into the kitchen, interrupting his grim reflections. "You have a visitor."

"Who is it?"

"The reason for your moping."

With a spike of desperate hope, he washed his hands and pulled off his apron, coming into the front of the shop to find Danica sipping a latte at one of the bistro tables. She also had an assortment of cookies arrayed before her, and she was perusing her choices like it was a life-or-death decision. *Maybe I was worried for no reason?* It wasn't like she'd stopped responding to his texts, and it was possible the shop really had been busy. His past might be making him irrationally skittish about normal relationship ebbs. A regular guy probably wouldn't get worked up because the woman he liked was wrapped up in work for a few days, right?

Be cool. It's not a big deal.

"Hey, you." A few customers watched openly as he joined Danica at her table. Gossip was as good as currency in a small town, and their interaction would be discussed and dissected in multiple chat groups.

"Cookie?" She offered him one of his own macaroons.

Titus shook his head with a smile. "Did things settle down at work?"

Something flickered in her pretty brown eyes, and she shook her head with a sigh. "My cousin is irritated with me because I couldn't focus. She finally shooed me out."

"And you came immediately in search of me?" Titus wondered if he dared to hope that *he* was the reason she couldn't concentrate, if she'd missed him even a fraction as much as he had her.

It was too soon to feel this way, of course. Such swift attachment was more than a little needy, so he tried to minimize the feeling. With limited success.

"I hope that's all right. This is your busiest time." Danica gestured with her half-eaten cookie at the line of people. "Do you need to help Maya fill orders?"

Titus sighed. "I probably should. Give me fifteen minutes?"

"No problem."

He teamed up with his sister. With her dealing with the customers and running the register, he shifted to packing up the baked goods, and soon they had the backlog caught up. There was little left in the case when he returned to where Danica sat, gazing out the window with her chin propped on her hand.

"Is everything all right?" he asked.

Titus had no specific cause to think she was troubled, but she lacked her usual brightness. It could be the result of an exhausting week at work. He tended to overthink these issues, creating major problems from minor inconveniences. It was all he could do not to immediately offer to cancel his plans with the guys.

Don't be like this. You're playing poker. Keep some perspective, for God's sake.

She glanced from the sidewalk outside to his face and regarded him steadily for a few seconds. "I'm dealing with some complicated family stuff."

"So am I," he said. "Want to talk about it?"

"You first." Her words sounded almost like a dare, as if she were testing whether he'd open up to her.

This wasn't the ideal setting, but he didn't mind talking. Not to her.

Still, he lowered his voice because this wasn't something he wanted customers repeating, and if Maya overheard, she might be hurt all over again. "We talked about this briefly before, but... my mom passed away, just after I opened the bakery. Within six months, my father remarried, a much younger woman that he met on a dating app. He moved to Arizona to be with her, and he's basically tapped out of our lives..." Titus tipped his head at his sister. "And now, we just found that they're expecting. It's..."

"A lot?" she supplied.

After a moment, she put down her cookie and reached across the wrought-iron table to put her hand on his. Relieved that she seemed to understand, he nodded and turned his palm up, wrapping his fingers around hers.

"There should be a manual, you know? I'm so conflicted because I know I'm being a bad son because I'm not happy for him. I should be glad that he's not miserable, but honestly, I fucking *hate* how fast he moved on. I resent his new family, and Susan is...well, she's fine. I guess." That admission was grudging.

He didn't want to like her because she'd stolen his damned dad. *There, I admitted it.*

"Were there...problems? Between him and your mom?"

It was a reasonable question, one he'd secretly agonized over. "If there were, I never knew about them. They seemed happy together. Then she got sick, and we all thought—we *hoped*—that she'd pull through."

"I'm so sorry," Danica said softly.

She didn't pull her hand away, offering silent comfort as a few more customers trickled in. Nothing Maya couldn't handle on her own.

"Thanks. You're a good listener."

"I didn't do anything."

"You cared enough to ask."

And he did feel better for airing the bad feelings. Danica didn't seem to judge him for his reactions, and it was absurd how much he liked holding her hand. She gazed at their linked fingers, polishing off her cookie as they sat together.

Finally, she said, "My family problems are a bit different. Basically, my grandmother is very...old-fashioned. My mother married someone Gram disapproved of, and I've been caught in the middle of their feud since the day I was born. I had dinner with both of them last night, and..." She jerked a thumb across her throat.

Titus took that to mean that death might have seemed like a merciful escape. "That's tough. Older people often carry deep biases, and there's nothing we can say to change their minds. But even if she's terribly wrong about your father, she's family, and you love her."

Danica stared at him, eyes wide, as if she couldn't believe what she was hearing. "Most people tell me to cut her off. But she was so good to me when I was little. We were so close. Clem and I spent our summers with her here, and she taught us so much. She waited until I was older before she started...sharing her opinions about my dad."

To Titus, that sounded manipulative. He could understand why other friends had tried to get Danica away from her grandmother. No matter how the old woman felt about her son-in-law, she shouldn't shit talk him to his child. Most likely, she was a hateful racist who made sure her bond with Danica was strong before revealing her bad side. But he sensed he'd lose the ground he'd gained by pointing that out.

"It must be painful and tiresome. Getting it from both sides."

"It is. My dad doesn't know," she confided quietly. "Gram's never said anything in front of him, and I'm grateful for that. But both my mom and I hear about it."

Privately he thought that was nothing to be thankful for. Her grandmother sounded like a horrible, controlling witch.

"I'm so sorry," he said, echoing her earlier words.

Her cinnamon-brown eyes locked with his, a connection so strong and deliciously fraught with unspoken yearning that he shivered, leaning forward unconsciously. Danica stroked the back of his hand, and the spark of pleasure blossomed into a current, a tingle that went up his arm into his shoulder and down his brain stem. His whole body felt alight, burning with the need to touch her.

Then she whispered, "Would it be weird if I asked for a hug?"

"Not at all. I'd have offered if you hadn't." He let go of her hand and stood, rounding the table to draw her into his arms with more assurance than he usually felt.

But at this moment, he had no doubt. This was what he was supposed to do, console this woman like it was his reason for living.

And when she settled against his chest, resting her head on his heart, Titus wondered how he could ever let her go.

CHAPTER 9

THIS WAS THE BEST DANICA had felt all week.

Leaning on Titus and listening to the comforting thump of his heartbeat. His body was so big and warm, strength she could rely on. This... It was more than sex. More than chemistry, though they certainly had that in abundance. It was so easy to talk to him, no matter how deep or difficult the subject, and the warmth of him might honestly cure any ailment. *That* was how good he felt.

Oh no. I've caught feelings.

Her first impulse was to shove him away and bolt, but that would make her seem demented, so she waited a few seconds, then extricated herself carefully. *I was the one who asked for a hug.* She ought to have known that sharing personal confidences was a bad idea. But he'd surprised her with his kindness regarding her family problems.

I promised I'd tell Clem if this escalated.

Titus was talking, but she hadn't heard all of it. She focused as he was saying, "...busy tonight, but if you're free, I'd love to have you over tomorrow. I'll make something delicious, and you can meet Doris. Maya will be there, so it will be more like a family meal than a date. I hope that's okay."

Her heart turned over. He was inviting her home to *cook* for her. And it scared the shit out of her how much she wanted that. To share Sunday supper with him, joke with his sister, and roughhouse with his dog, like there could truly be a place for her in his life. In his home. With every beat of her heart, she imagined how lovely it could be.

If she wasn't a witch. If she wasn't torn between two worlds and obligations to Gram and promises to Clem, who had torpedoed a functional relationship. For her. *I shouldn't have come today. I was fooling myself that this could ever be a simple fling with neither of us getting our emotions involved.*

She forced a smile. "That sounds fantastic, but I've got plans with my cousin and some friends."

"Members of your book club?"

"I'm surprised you remember." It wasn't a formal coven meeting, but Kerry and Priya were coming over to hang out. She and Clem were closest to them, though everyone in the coven counted as friends.

"Everything you say makes an indelible impression."

Why did he have to be so...so wonderful? Not perfect but flawed in ways that made him even more endearing.

Why aren't you from a witch family? If she followed in her mother's footsteps, in time, she'd lose her magic entirely, and she would never be able to share everything with him. To Danica, living a lie sounded painful, a constant burden on the soul. She wondered how her mother had borne it all these years, if that explained the way Gram talked about her as if she was terribly fragile, already broken.

"You're sweet," she said softly. "But I should get going. You need to get back to work, and I have some errands to run."

That was a blatant lie, an excuse to get away, but he didn't know that. And she felt horrible for deceiving him—on multiple levels. When Titus smiled, she immediately wanted to kiss him. *I'm in so much trouble.* It took all her self-control to offer a cheerful wave to him and Maya, who was watching with unabashed interest.

"I'll talk to you soon," Titus called as she hurried out of the bakery.

I really shouldn't.

Danica couldn't go back to the shop in this state. Before she talked to Clem, she needed to clear her head. In a daze, she wandered until she found herself at the memorial bench where she'd eaten lunch with Titus. Her magic snapped wildly in her veins, threatening to overflow, and she sat there willing herself calm until a plaintive meow drew her attention. Goliath gazed up at her with adoring eyes, then sauntered around her ankles, purring audibly as he rubbed against her.

"You stalker! I thought David defeated you."

The cat responded with a haughty swish of his tail. On closer inspection, she noticed that he wasn't wearing the camera collar; apparently nothing stopped him from getting out of the house. She was in no mood to deal with Hazel, but she couldn't leave this needy ginger unattended either.

"Fine, let's go. I'm not carrying you and I'm not waiting for

Hazel to pick you up either. You walked this far to find me. You can do it again." As she set out, Goliath chased after her, as she'd known he would. This cat would follow her to compete in the Iditarod, so getting him to walk home with her was no challenge. "You know this can't happen, right?"

Goliath mewed. For such a large cat, he had an absurdly squeaky voice.

"Okay, I get that. But Hazel would be so sad if you abandoned her. You're the only one she has to talk to."

Another mew.

"Well, it's not my fault either!"

Danica attracted a few looks conversing with Goliath as they made their way back, but she was used to being considered "quirky." Most people viewed her eccentricities as cute, but the truth was, she did get impressions from animals, especially those that desperately wanted to bond with her. It was an extension of her magic, though she didn't otherwise have a knack with living creatures. Priya, on the other hand, could literally talk to squirrels; it came with vivimancer territory. She could also mutate living things, which resulted in some truly exotic houseplants.

By the time Danica got to Hazel's house, she was calmer. She knelt on the porch and rubbed Goliath's head. He practically fell over in ecstasy, as she rarely did this. If she didn't wash her hands straightaway, she'd be sneezing with red and swollen eyes for a full day.

"Thanks for being a good friend," she said.

Then she rang the bell to return the cat to his crotchety caretaker. For once, Hazel didn't scold Danica, only gathered

Goliath in her arms like a baby. "I'm calling David. He's the only one who can figure this out."

"Good luck," Danica said, heading home.

To test her magical control, she unlocked the front door with a flick of her fingers, then went upstairs and took a full shower, rinsing off any cat residue. Too bad she was allergic; she did like cats and having one as a familiar would be amusingly on brand. To keep busy and stop obsessing, she fixed a quick meal of spaghetti pomodoro and salad, and she was setting the table when her cousin came in.

Clem sniffed the air appreciatively as she kicked off her shoes. "You cooked? What's the occasion?"

"I was hoping you'd yell at me less if you were full of delicious carbs."

"Why, what did you do?"

"Let's eat first, then talk."

"You know I'm not the patient type," Clem said.

But she did come to the table, and they ate quietly while Danica figured out what to say. As she made them both coffee for after dinner, she decided it was best to spit it out. She carried two steaming cups to the table, hoping Clem wouldn't be too mad.

"Okay, there's no easy way around this. The minute I saw Titus today, I realized I'm already falling for him. You were right. I need to put a stop to it, but I don't think I can go cold turkey." Battling deep inner alarm, she reached across the table and took comfort when Clem clasped her hand. "What should I do?"

"You're lucky I'm a nice person, or I'd be saying 'I told you so' right now." Her cousin squeezed her hand once and then got up to pace, wearing what Danica termed her "problem-solving" expression.

Over the years, Clem had applied herself to all sorts of conundrums, from sneaking out after curfew to getting revenge and, really, any problem Danica might have. If she asked her cousin for help, Clem never backed away from the challenge.

I can always count on her.

Overcome with a wave of love, Danica bounded out of her chair and hugged Clem. "We'll figure it out, right? I can't stay away from him on my own, and I don't want to lose my magic. It's so sad, seeing how my mom lives."

Softly, Clem embraced her and patted her back. "Don't worry. We'll figure it out." Then her cousin snapped her fingers. "Where's the spellbook Gram gave you? She said the magic would activate when you need it most, right?"

With a wild thrill, Danica realized her cousin was right. "You think there's a new spell waiting? Should I use it if there is?"

Clem nodded solemnly. "This is serious. We can run it by the others first if you want, but I think it's time to bring out the big guns."

The next day, Titus went to Fix-It Witches with a batch of gingersnaps.

He was forty bucks poorer from losing at poker, but he was also glad that he hadn't offered to cancel his plans to hang out with Danica. Taking it slow might be tough, but he sensed he'd scare her off otherwise. Clearly she had some personal stuff going on, drama between her mom and grandmother, and she might not have the mental energy to dive into a relationship headfirst right now.

But if he proved he was patient and willing to wait, he'd gain a friend at least, and he could always use more of those. Danica was worth having in his life, no matter what form their connection took. Nervously, he smoothed his hair, probably doing more harm than good, and then he stepped through the front door. The shop was open on Sunday, albeit for limited hours, just from one to five. As for him, he closed the bakery—not because he was especially religious, but both he and Maya deserved a day off.

I don't even know if she's working today.

But Danica emerged from the back with a professional smile that flickered when she recognized him. Something flashed in her eyes, too fast for him to figure out what. He held up the container, pulling the top off the tin to reveal the cookies.

"You offered to taste test, remember?"

"Sugar Daddy's isn't open today," she said, like that mattered.

"I develop recipes in my spare time. During work hours, I focus on products that sell well. Sometimes I pull pastries that aren't moving like I expected." Truth was, he'd wanted to see her, and this offered a plausible excuse. Titus set the container down on the front counter. "Give them a try?"

He set down a latte, made just the way she liked it; he'd even checked with Maya, who had been fixing Danica's drinks for much longer. Carefully, like she thought a snake might pop out, she pulled the cup toward her. After taking a cautious sip, she regarded him with wide eyes.

"This is exactly how I order my lattes."

For a few seconds, he wrestled with how to respond. He could display confidence and say something like "I'm just that good," but...that wasn't his style. And part of him wanted her to know that he'd cared enough to ask about her preferences. In the end, the truth won out, even if it made him look dorky and try-hard.

"My sister clued me in," he admitted.

Her smile dazzled him. "That's so sweet."

Danica selected a cookie and bit into it, tilting her head as she chewed. "These are delicious! They're soft inside but crispy at the edges, and they give the same feeling as old-school gingersnaps. You said they're healthy?"

"More so anyway. I used raw honey, coconut oil, and almond flour, among other things. Don't even ask—I won't give away my secret recipe."

Not that he'd make *her* pay for them. She could come into the bakery and he'd happily fill a box with whatever she wanted.

"Definitely add these as a test item," she said, stuffing the rest of the gingersnap in her mouth.

"Yeah?" Titus became aware that he was staring at her lips. She had a crumb at the corner, and it shouldn't have been cute. Only it was. He restrained himself from reaching out and said, "You have a little something there."

"Here?" Seeming self-conscious, she brushed at her mouth with the back of her hand, but she still didn't get it.

Knowing this was the cheesiest move ever, he dusted the cookie bit away from the edge of her lips, and oh God, they parted on a soft sound at his lightest touch. Her eyes darkened and she leaned forward infinitesimally, as if she might crawl over the counter to kiss him. Titus, shifted forward, leaning on his elbows just to get a bit closer. He hadn't come here for this, but he might not have the willpower to resist if she made the first move.

Slowly, Danica lifted a hand and touched the corner of his mouth; then she traced the line of his jaw. Just a single fingertip, skimming along his features, a fluttering caress to his cheekbone, his eyebrow, and the curve of his ear. Desire roared through him, a flash fire completely disproportionate to the level of contact.

Her breath hitched like she felt it too.

His heartbeat thundered in his ears, and if there were any other noises, he couldn't hear them. Danica eased a little closer, so he could breathe in her delicate scent. Flowers and...fruit? A hint of lemon. She smelled amazing, and it took real effort not to reach for her. Maybe it would be okay since she'd touched him first, but he feared frightening her off.

"I really want to kiss you," she whispered.

He swallowed hard. "You have my permission."

She reached across the counter and stroked his lower lip, the sexiest invitation he'd ever received, and then her mouth grazed his. Raw lust careened through him. God, he wasn't even *prone* to this. He'd wanted people before, but nothing so intense that it shorted out his brain. But he got hard just looking at Danica, and kissing her?

It wasn't nearly enough.

Dilemma—he wanted to feel her body against him, but if he moved to get closer, he'd have to break this delicious kiss. Before he could resolve the issue, a sizzle and pop exploded around them.

To his dazed senses, the cascade of sparks felt like an extension of his intense arousal. Belatedly, he realized that every damn light bulb in the shop had spontaneously exploded. Danica scrambled away, her eyes big and fearful.

"Damn. You should get an electrician in to look at your wiring. There must be a short somewhere. It could start a fire."

Her laugh sounded strained. "I'll do that. You should go. There's so much glass dust, and I don't want you to get hurt."

"I can help—"

"Thanks for the cookies," she cut in.

Danica walked to the door pointedly and opened it, waiting for him to leave with a tense air. After Titus stepped out, she flipped the sign to closed and locked it behind him. While he didn't blame her for being freaked, it did seem like she'd hurried him out, like he was to blame for her shop's wiring issues. Come to think of it, the juicer had shorted when he was there too. It would be just his luck if his curse was getting worse, spreading from relationships to appliances.

That would explain why my oven broke.

Dispirited, he walked a block to where he'd parked his Leaf and drove home. At least Doris would be happy to see him. Maya was there when he got back—she'd spent the previous evening with a friend so he could host poker night. He had put the house back in order first thing, so his sister was in a good mood as she chopped vegetables for a salad.

"You're back early. It didn't go well?"

"The shop needs repair work." For some reason, he opted not to share all the details. Maya might be willing to dissect the encounter, but he preferred not to scrutinize it too closely. "I think she's got some family issues as well."

His sister sighed, setting the knife on the cutting board. "Don't we all. Have you talked to Dad recently?"

"Not since…" He hesitated.

"You can say it. Not since he told us about the baby?"

"Yeah."

"Well, I spoke to him a few days ago. He's asking us to visit again, before Susan gets 'too pregnant to be social,' whatever that means."

"Do you want to?" Titus asked.

For his own part, he'd rather clean the gutters and dredge the septic tank than fly to Arizona to "bond" with his father's new family, but he shouldn't infect Maya with his bias if she didn't share it. Patiently he waited for his sister to gather her thoughts. She traced circles on the cutting board, her eyes sad and shadowed. Finally he stopped her when she began moving bell pepper seeds into abstract patterns.

"No. And I feel bad about it. But Susan makes me feel like an intruder, and her kids…"

"Lucy isn't so bad. Jared is—"

"A perv," Maya finished.

A chill settled over him. "Did something happen? I saw him hitting on you, but if he touched you, I'll beat his ass."

She shook her head. "He just says gross, inappropriate things."

"That's still way over the line. We won't go. Dad has his own life now, and we're not part of it. But I'll always be here for you, Mini."

When Maya hugged him, Titus almost forgot the weirdness at the shop and his highly illogical fear that Danica was about to bolt.

CHAPTER 10

AS DANICA TIDIED UP THE shop, she worked to center herself.

What should I do?

She hadn't expected Titus to drop by and get her all excited. The situation was dire, no doubt about it. Somehow, she controlled herself as she cleaned, fixed the wiring she'd overloaded, and replaced all the bulbs. By the time she finished, she was calm, more able to think clearly about the problem. Clem was right on both counts. If possible, it was time to use the special spellbook, and this afternoon offered the perfect opportunity since Kerry and Priya were coming over. Having two skilled witches on deck could only help when she deployed the book of spells Gram had created as a gift. The old woman had poured most of her magic into it to prepare Danica for the future, as she feared for the stability of Danica's powers, given that she had a mundane father. Clem had no such disadvantage since her father came from respectable witch lineage.

With her resolve firm, Danica biked home from the shop and was sipping chamomile tea in the kitchen when Kerry sounded her signature "Shave and a Haircut" knock. Clem went to answer, and she heard her cousin laying out the situation succinctly as she ushered the other two inside. Priya came straight in and gave Danica a hug from behind. Danica leaned her head back against the other woman's shoulder and closed her eyes, taking comfort in the softness and the gentle brush of Priya's hand against her hair.

This... This is what I'm giving up if I choose a life like Mom's.

Minerva had chosen romantic, mundane love over the bonds of sisterhood. She seemed to have become a standard PTA mom, participating in bake sales and food drives, doing what any average wife would do. And her magic had dwindled.

Mom must have found herself in my situation, irresistibly drawn to Dad.

And she'd made the decision to let it happen. To lose part of herself as the price of gaining a life with Laurence Yaeger. She'd honored tradition only far enough to keep her maiden name, as Waterhouse witches had done for centuries, but otherwise, she lived as a mundane, and she'd irreparably damaged her relationship with Gram. Possibly, Danica had been unduly influenced by her grandmother over the years, but it was impossible not to see her mom as a bit...weak. Like at dinner the other night, she never argued with Gram. She bent over backward to keep the peace, and she didn't even defend herself.

The idea of walking away from Margie and Ethel, Vanessa and Leanne, Kerry and Priya, made her heart ache. Danica loved these women every bit as much as she could love a life partner. In their way, they all mattered as much, and she had to stop this obsession before it took over her life. *I'm not willing to sacrifice my relationship with them. Not ever.*

Not even for love.

Maybe it was too soon even to be thinking of the L word, but her magic seemed to think that Titus Winnaker was her Waterloo, judging by the way it was fritzing. Danica exhaled in a shuddering breath as Priya kissed the top of her head and gave her a last squeeze. Kerry was less physically demonstrative than her partner, but she patted Danica's arm as she settled on the other side.

"I hear you're in crisis mode," Kerry said.

Clem took the chair closest to Danica, setting the book in the center of the table. "I'm glad you're both here. I've never seen her like this."

Part of her feared opening the book. It was a gorgeous artifact, power glimmering from the dark-leather cover. Every other time when she'd checked, the pages had been blank. Supposedly, the first spells wouldn't appear until she truly needed them. Today was likely that day. In her heart, she suspected she was facing the first major challenge of her life, and the course she charted going forward would decide...everything.

Whether she lived as a witch or mundane.

"What are you waiting for?" Priya asked. "We're here. You know we'll back you up."

Taking a deep breath, Danica flipped the grimoire cover open, and it settled on the first page on its own. Magical energy crackled around her, a corona of light visible even to the naked eye. Across the table Kerry's hair lifted, fanning out around her head. Priya took a seat on her other side, and the four joined hands. Without even speaking, they fell into a strong partner-ship, and the edges of their power slid together like interlocking puzzle pieces. Two vivimancers, two technomancers, a closed circuit.

The spellbook buzzed, a low rumble streaming from it. And on the formerly pristine page, shapes and sigils appeared: instructions on how to cast "The Right Path." She had never seen anything quite like this spell; it would be a powerful working.

"It's there," she whispered.

Kerry leaned closer. "That's odd. I don't see anything."

Baffled, Danica glanced at her cousin for confirmation. "Do you?"

Clem shook her head. "You're the only one who can use this."

Damn. She'd known that Gram was a powerful witch before the investiture of this grimoire, but this was some next-level shit. It took incredible skill to craft customized spells, intended only for one practitioner. Her heart ached over how much time her grand-mother must have devoted to this. And guilt percolated through her over the way she tended to blow the old woman off, ignoring her messages for days at a time because she didn't want to go on Bindr dates.

I'll spend more time with her while she's here for the summer.

"Uh-oh," Priya said. "I know that look. We've got a four-alarm remorse conflagration. Someone call the fire department!"

"Very funny," Danica muttered.

While she tried to center herself—because casting when she was emotional was almost as bad as doing it when she was drunk or hungover—Clem bustled around setting up the various implements for a working. Knife, candles, bowl of water. Her cousin paused to ask, "Do you need anything else? Special ingredients?"

Danica skimmed the spell again, then shook her head. "No, this seems to be mostly ritual gestures and verbal intonation, though I'll need the candles and the knife to shape a few sigils."

She read the words again. *A spell to guide you onto the Right Path and eliminate detours.* Titus certainly qualified as the latter, but...this wouldn't hurt him, would it? While witches didn't take a vow against harm, she never practiced malicious magic. Neither did Gram, so far as she knew, but her grandmother could also be a bit callous about the fate of mundanes. *Look at how they've treated us,* the old woman would say. *Do you know how many witches they've drowned, hung, and burned? To say nothing of innocent mundane women who were only guilty of being a bit odd.* If Gram started on the witch hunters, the rant could go on for days.

"Are you ready?" Priya asked.

While Danica was ruminating, Clem completed the prep work, down to the salt circle that should theoretically protect everyone. Inside, there were four white candles lit, one in front of each witch. Danica nodded and took up the knife. Here, a mundane would expect some blood to be spilled, but instead, she cut only the air, shaping the sigils according to the symbols listed in the spell—alchemical representations of fire, water, earth, and air. In her mind's eye, she saw the lingering shapes, burned into the ether. Triangle for fire, inverted triangle for water. Triangle bisected by a line for air, inverted triangle bisected at the bottom for earth. Energy gathered within her, a comforting hum when she'd feared that she might be losing her power.

No, it's still here. It's not too late. I can fix this.

She focused her will and spoke the words. "By the powers of east and west..." Danica pointed her knife in each direction, offering respect to the witches who occupied each cardinal point. "North and south..." At the last, she angled the blade in her own direction, as she was anchoring one of the loci. "Aradia, I invoke your blessings. Please protect and guide me to the proper path."

Danica's magic flared, a wild and uncontrollable spike that knocked the candles in all directions; one slammed into the window, and the curtains caught fire.

Of all the damn luck, Titus got a call on what was supposed to be his day off.

But he'd become a volunteer firefighter to give back to the community, so he grabbed his gear and suited up. St. Claire didn't have a large paid fire department, so smaller issues were often delegated to volunteers like him. So far, he'd never fought an actual fire. Usually, he dealt with minor medical situations like dog bites or bee stings and lockouts. Sometimes he literally rescued cats from trees or cleared debris from the highway after a crash. But the address dispatch had given him seemed oddly familiar...

When he turned down the tree-lined street, he realized he was headed for Danica's house. He slammed his foot down on the gas pedal, suddenly scared to death, but the Leaf responded slowly. For the first time since he was a kid, he wished for a fast car, one that could rocket him down the block to make sure she was okay.

If it weren't so dangerous, he'd already be texting or calling her. *Why didn't I connect to the car before setting out?* As it was, he had to be patient and he barely kept his shit together long enough to grab everything out of his car. He'd done extensive training in his first year of service, and now he was even trained as an EMT. He feared what he might find when he ran up the walk to her porch. Smelling smoke, he pounded on the front door with both hands.

"Fire department! We got a call. Is everything all right? If there's no response in thirty seconds, I'm coming in."

To be precise, he tapped the stopwatch on his phone, and at twenty-nine seconds, a young woman threw open the door. With deep-brown eyes, short brunette hair, and elfin features, she looked a bit different from the photos he'd seen when he picked Danica up for their date. Clementine resembled her cousin, but to his mind, Danica was prettier. The smoky smell was stronger, but nothing seemed to be actively on fire.

"Who reported us?" she gasped.

Two more ladies popped into the foyer. One was tall and elegant with fair skin; the other had silky black hair and bronze skin, and she wore a beautifully embroidered sari in coral and yellow. Both of them stared like he'd threatened to chop the door down with an ax. Which, *maybe*, he sort of had, and he was carrying a bunch of firefighting gear, so possibly their reactions were appropriate.

Titus set his pack down and took a step back. "I'm not sure, but it's usually one of the neighbors if you didn't call in a request for help."

"Who's at the—*Titus*." Danica gaped at him like she'd seen a ghost, and she clutched the doorframe for support. "What are you doing here?"

Judging by everyone's reactions, the fire must've been minor. It seemed like he'd been overzealous in his response. "Sorry if I alarmed you. Time is of the essence in these situations, however. It's best to be sure nobody's actively in harm's way."

The other three women were silently swapping looks. He could tell they were talking about him with their eyes, and they seemed to be extrapolating *something* from Danica's reaction, but hell if he knew what. While it was a bit frustrating not to understand what was going on, relief also bobbed to the surface like a fishing lure. Danica had told him the truth about her plans today. She'd said she would be hanging out with her cousin and a couple of friends; here they were, proving that his fears were unfounded.

She wasn't lying to me. I can trust her.

A huge weight slid from his shoulders. He'd been blown off so often and through so many creative means that he had trust issues. Hell, Titus knew that was the case, and still, his imagination ran wild, predicting all kinds of ways that a new relationship could go off the rails. Sometimes he even feared he was sabotaging himself somehow, and he wanted more than anything to stop, to make this woman stick around.

Eventually, Danica's friends and her cousin concluded their silent conference, then the pale woman moved toward him and stuck her hand out. "Well, everything's fine now, though we did have a bit of a scare earlier. I'm Kerry, by the way."

"Nice to meet you."

He exchanged handshakes and greetings with Priya and Clementine while Danica seemed to steady her nerves. Finally she said, "I had no idea you were a volunteer firefighter. Do you work at animal shelters and nursing homes too? Maybe fight crime on the side?" Her voice held a note that he couldn't identify, both teasing and not, rich with reluctant admiration.

More like, I'm too good to be true?

That put a smile on his face, one that felt like it must be stretching his cheeks. When she looked at him that way, it felt like they were the only ones in the world. "Are you asking if I'm secretly Superman?"

"It's hard not to wonder," she said.

The rising heat within him, it was ridiculous. Inappropriate even. He shouldn't think about kissing her with her friends in the room. But he couldn't pull his eyes away from Danica, from her flushed face and overbright eyes. *What's even happening right now?* If he didn't know better, he'd swear he was under a spell.

"Holy shit," Priya whispered. "I'm not even involved, and I'm a little turned on by all this ambient sexual tension."

Someone laughed and shushed her. Titus tried to recall what they were even talking about. "No crime fighting, but we have activities at the fire station for the elderly. We run a coffee klatch most mornings from eight to ten, and the firefighters on duty chat with the old folks who come in."

"How does that work? Do you subsidize the expense?" Kerry asked.

Titus glanced at her, vaguely surprised that other people still existed in the world, let alone were standing in the room. "No, members of the coffee klatch donate for the supplies, and it doesn't cost anything to use the meeting room at the station."

"Probably much cheaper than a fancy caramel macchiato," Priya noted.

"And they like seeing the same people daily, hanging out with the firefighters. From what I hear, it's tough when you don't have anywhere to go in the morning and nothing particular that you have to do," he said.

Kerry was nodding. "My grandfather had a rough time after retirement. We work hard our whole lives, only to earn the right to be lonely and feel useless."

He smiled, eyes still on Danica. "As for stray animals, I'm always pulling cats out of trees. Does that count?"

She couldn't seem to stop staring at him either. "Absolutely."

Titus shuffled his feet. He shouldn't flirt with Danica or chat about fire station activities before resolving the outstanding report. "May I assess the damage? Since I responded to the call, I need to document what happened. If you file an insurance claim, I may be asked for corroborating information since I'm the responder on record."

"Everything is fine," Clem said, "and we don't intend to file a claim, but by all means, follow me."

Leaving his bag by the front door, he trailed her to the kitchen, where the smoky scent lingered. Charred remains of synthetic curtains lay in wet, dark tatters in the sink. Judging from the broken glass and recently snuffed candles, he guessed there must have been a mishap with the mood lighting. Feeling like a bit of a tool, he gave his standard safety speech with regard to open flames.

"We'll be careful," Clementine replied with an edge to her voice.

Danica hurried to her cousin's side and put a hand on her arm, shaking her head silently. Though Titus wasn't sure about the undertones, he guessed that Danica's cousin wasn't a fan of being scolded after the fact. She probably already knew what she'd done wrong, and he hadn't intended to make her mad, but there was certain verbiage he had to use in these situations. *Not trying to be a dick. I should probably go.*

"It can happen to anyone," he said easily. "I went over to an apartment building recently where a college girl set her own TV on fire because she didn't realize that candles on a lower shelf could burn that hot."

Priya laughed. "Sounds like something I would do."

"You would not. Stop acting like you're not an absolute genius," Kerry scolded.

"I'm also a bit of a ditz when I'm distracted."

"Since I've done what I came to do, I should go," he said.

Danica finally appeared to get herself together, apparently more shaken by the small fire than she'd let on at first. "I'll walk you out."

CHAPTER 11

"SORRY WE PULLED YOU AWAY from family time," Danica said.

At this moment, she didn't know how she was supposed to feel. From the flickering curtains at Hazel Jeffords's house, she guessed the old lady had called the fire department when she saw a little smoke. Gram's special incantation could *not* have meant to summon Titus, yet that was exactly what Danica had done. What a colossal misfire. Her magic really couldn't be trusted these days, and she had no damn idea what to do about it.

"I don't mind at all," he said. "At least I got to see your face and meet some of your friends. That's time well spent."

"You wanted to meet them?"

Oh goddess, I shouldn't be happy about that. It makes everything more difficult.

"Of course, though I hope for better circumstances next time."

Next time? No. She managed a smile and stretched up on tiptoe to kiss his cheek, wishing she could erase the ache in her chest when she faced certainty that this would be the last time they touched like this. While their paths might cross—it was a small town, after all—she couldn't get closer to him. Not with her magic already going haywire.

Danica waved. "Say hi to Maya for me."

"Will do!" Titus was already jogging back down the walk, lugging his bag easily, but he glanced back with a brilliant smile. It seemed to make him happy that she cared enough to greet his sister.

Family's important to him. And he's got that shitty situation with his dad's new wife. I wonder if—no. Focus. You cannot get more involved than you already are.

When she went back inside, Clem, Priya, and Kerry were sitting in the front room with cups of tea. There was one waiting for her as well. She braced herself as she sat down, waiting for shots to be fired. Her cousin must have ten thousand words to share, none of them good. But the others sat quietly, sipping and waiting for her to speak.

"That's him," she finally said. "As I'm sure you already know."

Kerry smirked at her. "Your fling is the CinnaMan! I can't believe you kept this from us, you heartless—"

"Don't tease too much," Priya cut in. She touched her girlfriend lightly on the arm. "Not everyone is as lucky as we are."

Their eyes met, held, and that melting look just before they kissed warmed Danica's heart even as she despaired of ever having it for herself. Kerry and Priya were perfect together, and both families supported their relationship. When they were ready, they planned to use a witch-only sperm bank, and they'd each have one child with the same donor—imprinted with each other's energy through vivimancy—to continue their bloodlines. No conflict, no sides to be taken. Just happiness, full partnership, and beautiful, magical babies in their future.

Danica let out a wistful sigh. "The spell didn't work."

Clem sat beside her and wrapped an arm around her shoulders. "I know you're worried, but it'll be okay. Every problem has a solution. We just haven't found it yet."

Privately she admitted that it *hurt* to hear Titus described that way. *He's such a good person. He deserves someone who can treasure him.* And hell, that hurt too.

"Definite 'too much' teasing," Kerry said then. "But come on, nobody's going to say it? The *obvious* joke about him arriving to put out Danica's fire."

Danica pointed at the door. "I need you to leave. Now." But her stern expression was spoiled because she couldn't contain the reluctant chortle. "It's just so absurdly apropos, isn't it? I swear, my magic has a sense of humor or the universe is screwing with me."

"Could it be both?" Priya wondered.

She shrugged, leaning her head against Clem's briefly. "Maybe. I don't know about the rest of you, but even *I'm* tired of my issues. Why don't we hang out as we originally planned, eat some delicious food, and binge that show?"

"Putting off your problems won't solve them," Clem muttered.

True, but neither will obsessing.

And Danica didn't want to become someone who had no dimensions outside her romantic struggles. She wanted a rich, full life with multiple connections, and if she stopped hanging out with her coven sisters over this, she might as well marry Titus and become a mundane. Then she could do…whatever magic-less women did for fun.

They all snuggled in and watched a few episodes, and afterward, she fixed Kerry's phone to prove that she had enough control to return to work tomorrow afternoon. Before she left, Priya tended to their languishing houseplants. Before, they were withered and wan; after, they shot up lush and green, changing the energy of the space entirely.

"You know, you can do this without magic," Kerry pointed out. "Millions of mundanes raise houseplants with no help at all."

Danica swapped a look with her cousin and grinned. "We've heard those rumors but remain unconvinced. They must have a little vivimancy in their blood."

When Priya hugged her, she whispered, "Message me if this gets to be too much. Clem can be a bit…intense about your family stuff, so if you need to chill, just let us know. The door's always open at our place."

"Coming, love?" Kerry was already waiting by the front door, twirling the key fob on her index finger.

"On my way!" Priya offered a final pat and hurried to join Kerry, where they said farewell to Clem and headed out together, fingers softly interlocked like it pained them to be apart even to walk to the car.

"What was that all about?" Clem asked. "Are you plotting with Priya?"

She shook her head. Goddess, nothing escaped her cousin's hawkish eyes. "She was just offering support, that's all."

And an escape hatch. But she'd never say that in front of Clem. It would hurt her feelings to hear that she came off as over-the-top. Danica understood why. Just sometimes, it was a lot, balancing her promise to Clem against her grandmother's wishes and then, of course, her mother's quiet disappointment that she wasn't forging her own path. *Who would've thought a free spirit could be so let down because I care what other people think?*

It also didn't escape her that she was trying to cut ties with one person who didn't expect anything from her to please those who did.

Clem smiled, thankfully seeming not to notice the undertones. "Priya's such a sweetheart. Kerry is so lucky."

"I'm aware," she said softly.

Danica was the only one who knew that Clem had had her eye on Priya first, but she hadn't been sure if it was a good idea to date within the coven. While she'd pondered, Kerry had swept into town, joined as a full member after having chatted with everyone online for a while, and fell for Priya like a ton of bricks. Kerry had no doubts, no hesitation whatsoever, and within a month, they were an item.

Clem wasn't generally an impulsive person; she analyzed the angles before making a move. While that was great for the business, Danica had never known Clem to give her heart without weighing all the pros and cons thoroughly. Consequently, she couldn't say her cousin had *ever* been completely, messily in love. Just…occasionally attracted, which made it much easier for her to keep their pact. That was also why it meant more that Clem had dumped Spencer like a package of bad cheese, choosing to support Danica without a flicker of hesitation.

"Hey," Clem said. "Don't look so sad. I'm happy for them, seriously. It's not like I was completely gone for her or anything. I was just…weighing my options."

Like you always do, Danica almost said.

But that observation would start a fight, and when she and Clem went at it, it was wicked and vicious, just like real sisters. *I don't have the energy, and I don't want to argue with her.* She didn't want to open the door to hearing about her own faults either.

"Understood."

With a sigh, she powered on her phone at long last. Ten texts from Gram awaited along with five voicemails. She had told her grandmother repeatedly that she didn't listen to them, but that didn't stop Gram from leaving them. And she acted like the beep was a pause button and would just pick up where she left off when she ran out of time. Consequently, the voice messages always sounded like an interrupted monologue. If Danica didn't answer soon, she'd find Gram on the porch again. She *wanted* to spend time with Gram while she was in St. Claire. She just didn't want to talk about this.

"What did she send you?"

"Profiles, of course. Oh hell." Danica stared for a full minute, and then dissolved into giggles at the posed photo of a "sex wizard" sporting a black goatee and matching cape. Clem crowded close to see. "Do you suppose Ivar Magicstaff is his legal name?"

"Everything okay?" Maya called as Titus came in.

He'd stowed his gear bag in the trunk, ready for the next call.

Which hopefully wouldn't be today. Ducking out once on family time wouldn't piss his sister off, but if it happened again, he'd hear about it. Particularly about his habit of overcommitting. He wanted to give back to the community, but Maya thought he did it to the exclusion of having his own life.

And maybe that was a *little* true.

"Just a minor kitchen fire. I'll do the paperwork later. Where are we on meal prep?"

"I just put the roast in the oven." She put her hands on her hips. "It's like you plan these 'emergencies' to get me to make food."

Titus rubbed his hand across the top of her head, grinning when she smacked his arm. "Don't even lie, you love our Sundays at home."

"I do," she said quietly.

In her sad eyes, he glimpsed the memory of happier times. When it wasn't just the two of them joking around, but Mom and Dad too, giving each other shit and rambling about stuff that happened when they were kids. Nothing dramatic or spectacular, but moments that were gone forever now, lost to time and change. To talk to Mom, they had to visit the cemetery, and Dad had stopped listening entirely after she died.

"You'll love this even more. I've got a buttermilk pie in the freezer. Want me to get it out?" Probably he should offer Maya a hug instead of sweets, but she worked hard enough to enjoy both.

"Is it Memaw's recipe?"

"Obviously," he said.

Memaw had taught Titus's mother everything she knew about

baking, and he'd learned from both of them. Their maternal grand-mother had been gone for twenty years, but he still had a box full of her old recipes written in cramped penmanship on stained index cards. One of these days, he planned to update all of them, see if he could retain the flavor while improving the nutrition and health benefits, just as he had the gingersnaps.

Maya nudged him. "What are you waiting for? I was promised pie!"

A few hours later, they were settled at the table, eating pot roast, potatoes, and green beans. Titus hadn't mentioned this because he knew she'd tease him, but he couldn't hold it in any longer. "You'll never guess whose kitchen was on fire."

"Mrs. Carminian? She mentioned lighting up her barbecue." His sister waggled her brows. "I hope she was waiting for you in her sexiest housedress."

"How are you so right all the time? Her husband had a camcorder and said he was bi-curious but also open to being cuckolded."

Maya's mouth fell open, a bite of potatoes arrested on the way in. "*Really?*"

"No, not really." He cracked up at her expression and submit-ted when she rounded the table to force a mid-level noogie on him.

"You're not funny." She pointed her fork at him, resuming her seat when she finally felt she'd evened the score.

"I'm hilarious. Admit it, I had you going. You were about to start texting everyone that the Carminians are secret swingers."

Her face pinked. "Shut up, I was not."

"Anyway, back to my original point. I was sent over to check on Danica's place. Apparently she was having some friends over, got a little wild with the candles. Set the kitchen curtains on fire."

"Aw, so you got to see your dream girl...and confirm she's not cheating on you already. That's nice." Maya leaned over and patted his arm in a mock supportive gesture.

It's embarrassing how well she knows me.

Titus deliberately cut a bite of beef. "We're not exclusive. It's too soon for us to have had that talk."

Not too soon for me to think about it, mind you, or to want her for myself. But he was trying his best to keep his expectations reasonable, stick to a rational timetable and not scare the crap out of this woman.

"Bro. I know you. You were already wondering if she's blowing you off when she said she couldn't come over today." Maya paused, assessing his expression. "Am I wrong?"

"No," he mumbled.

"Therefore, you were secretly relieved to find her at home, doing what she said she would be."

"That...is also true."

"You want some advice?"

"Yes, please."

"Try to stop being scared and just let this unfold as it's meant to. Danica doesn't know your history. This is probably her normal getting-to-know-you pace. If you obsess over how it will go wrong...look, if it goes sideways, it'll be because of your behavior. And not some random curse."

They'd argued about this before. Maya did think he must be doing something, as each failure made him more skittish and desperate, more prone to clinging like a squid. And apparently, most people weren't into that. Frankly, it might be alarming if they were.

"Thanks. I'll try to be cool."

"Respond to her texts. I'm not advocating some bullshit push-pull nonsense. Make sure she knows you're happy to hear from her and spend time with her, but definitely don't tell her that you're already dreaming about marriage and babies."

Despite himself, Titus grinned. "You sure? Maybe I ought to be ring shopping by now. After all, we've had dinner. Gone bowling. Eaten lunch twice. What else is there?"

"You're such a dork," she said fondly.

"Since you're related to me, that makes you dork-adjacent."

She threw her napkin at him as he went to the kitchen to slice the buttermilk pie. They watched some TV, and later, he took Doris for a run, played with her in the backyard afterward. When he came in, Maya was heavily texting someone, so into it that she didn't even seem to notice that he was in the room. Lately she'd been like that, and sometimes she went to her room to voice chat. He heard the murmur of conversation if not the actual words. So far she hadn't told him what it was about. Doubtless she would when she was ready.

Hopefully she wasn't planning to visit Dad in Arizona when she'd made it clear she didn't want to. *If he's pressuring her...*

Titus got mad just thinking about it, but he couldn't call his old man to ask.

Instead, he texted Trevor, who acted like he was twenty-two instead of thirty-two most of the time. Maybe this wouldn't do any good, but it would be better than stewing. The guy was always around, unlike everyone else, and Trevor knew the situation with his dad, so he only had to tell him about the baby and how it was impacting Maya.

He ended with, Do you think my dad's giving her a hard time about the visit?

I'll give her a hard time. Your sister's hot. 🍆

Fucking Trevor. Titus glared at his phone for a full minute before sending Stay away from Maya. Seriously. I will literally kill you.

I think you mean figuratively, Trevor sent back. Kidding! Sisters are off-limits. I just like the eggplant emoji. Anyway, I guess it's possible, but if she wanted to talk to you about it, she would. Just keep being a good dude.

That was...surprisingly not a terrible suggestion, coming from someone who earned his money by cutting other people's grass using his dad's lawnmower. Trevor thought being responsible was a contagious disease, and if he wasn't stoned, he considered the day a complete loss. His parents had basically given up on the idea that he'd ever move out or get married, so they focused all their attention on his older brother.

Thanks, Titus answered.

You should come over. We can play and smoke, just like old times.

Titus had to laugh. In Trevor's head, those had been the glory days, but he had no desire to go hang out in Trevor's basement when he had a whole house. Besides, like always, he had to get up early. Maybe one day, when the bakery was paid for, he could afford to hire another baker and relax a bit. Until then, the profits went toward paying the loan, and he had to work like an Australian cattle dog.

A little voice whispered that the long hours would be worth it if his efforts went toward building a life with someone special.

Someone like Danica.

CHAPTER 12

DANICA FULL-ON DODGED HER PROBLEMS for the rest of the day.

After she finished giggling with Clem over the eligibles Gram had forwarded, she refused to hear another word about Titus, her family, or haywire magic. Thankfully, her cousin took the hint, and they binged a bunch of goofy romantic movies, ones that always ended happily, no matter how messy it seemed in the middle. This was exactly the way Danica liked her fiction too. Sometimes she branched out to other genres, but those books often left her with a deep sense of trepidation, reading without the assurance that characters she cared about could survive until the end.

Hell, if I wanted to feel shitty, I'd watch the news.

A knock sounded at the door, and she found her grandmother waiting, wearing an impatient look. She hadn't seen the older woman since that disastrous dinner, and judging by her frown, Gram wasn't here for a pleasant chat. She raised both brows as she took Danica in and stepped inside without waiting for an invitation.

"I see that you're alive after all," she said with a sniff. "You didn't even look at the Bindr profiles I sent. Honestly, Danica, you're not even *trying* to get over Darryl."

She stifled a sigh. *Not remotely ready for this.* "Want a cup of coffee?"

"It's too late for that." Those words sounded unaccountably ominous. "I'll get heartburn and I won't get to sleep if I have coffee at this hour."

Right, she's talking about caffeinated beverages. That wasn't a warning.

"Chamomile tea then?"

"Sounds good."

Tension boiled in the silence, louder than the burble of the kettle. "Here you go. Do you want something to nibble along with it?"

Danica knew damn well Gram hadn't come for tea or snacks.

The older woman fixed a gimlet stare on her. "Do you want to explain why you're leaving me unread? I try to be understanding, sweetheart, but nobody's that busy. We used to be so close, and the fact that we're not anymore... It hurts." She glanced around the house, as if remembering how it used to be. "We had such *fun* here when you were small. You probably don't remember your grandfather, but he loved you so much. He'd fall asleep with the two of you on his chest, and when you woke up from your nap, I'd entertain you with little illusions. You said it was better than television, and I didn't mind even though those spells exhausted me for days. It was worth it to see you smile. I'd do anything for you and Clementine." She reached across the table and took Danica's hands as a wave of guilt deluged her. "You understand that, right?"

"Yes, Gram."

Clem was home, but she didn't come down. Maybe she thought Danica needed this tête-à-tête with Gram to wake up from her delusions about Titus. She ended up agreeing to narrow the Bindr profiles down. "I'll pick the two best ones," she finally muttered. "But I'm not promising anything."

"That's all I ask." Gram rose and kissed her cheek. "Just keep an open mind. You'll see, sweetheart. Your life will be so much better if you heed my advice."

That night, Danica didn't sleep well, and she skipped lunch the next day, opting for a glum bowl of ramen at home instead of meeting Titus like she desperately wanted. But the strength of that desire meant she shouldn't. Things had already gotten away from her, and they'd only kissed. *Look at what happened at the shop! I'll blow a substation if we go all the way.*

Danica showed up to work on time, and Clem sighed over her expression. "Oh damn. You're even wearing your 'Don't mess with me' T-shirt. Are you sure that sends the right message to our customers?"

"I'll work in the back," she muttered.

"That...is a terrible idea. Radioactive microwave, remember? Look, I'm sorry you're struggling, but this is our livelihood. Get your shit together!" Clem slapped the display counter for emphasis, frowning fiercely.

Sometimes tough love was the only cure for an emotional ailment. Reality check: her cousin was right. If she ruined their business with personal stuff, she'd never forgive herself. Danica did her best to compartmentalize all the conflict and confusion while doing some breathing exercises she'd found online. While she couldn't claim she was okay with everything, at least the lightning in her veins settled a little.

"I really don't understand," she said softly.

"What?"

"Why do Waterhouse witches lose their power if they marry mundanes? I mentioned it to Margie and Vanessa, and they've never heard of anything like that. I mean, obviously there's some weakening of magical strength in the descendants, but neither one of them has heard about a curse that kicks in that way."

Clem leaned on the glass countertop, looking troubled. "I heard Gram talking to one of her cronies once, and it seems like it's unique to our line. It has to do with what happened to Agnes Waterhouse so long ago, and I suspect it's meant to protect us."

"From persecution? If we don't mingle with mundanes, we can't be singled out?" It was tough to know what had been on anyone's mind four hundred years ago.

"I guess so. It *has* kept us safe. And is it really so wrong? Those who choose a mundane love over sisterhood should pay the price."

Danica stared at her cousin. "You sound exactly like Gram."

"She's not wrong. Both our mothers eventually gave up everything for their mundane lovers, and look at them now. Witches descended from a goddess, born with incredible blessings, and they threw it all away."

Wow, she's really mad.

They tended not to discuss Minerva and Allegra because Danica chose to cut her mom and aunt some slack since she knew all too well how hard it was to please Gram. But she hadn't realized that Clem was still so angry about Allegra marrying her mundane boyfriend. Danica didn't know all the details surrounding the divorce, but Clem's dad, Auntie Allegra's first husband, had been an absolute asshole.

Families are so complicated.

She tried for a conciliatory tone. "That's why we made the pact."

"Exactly. In a few years, when we want kids, we can use the same donor service as Kerry and Priya. And we can raise our kids together without all the drama our parents put us through. We have each other. We have the coven. You'll see. Everything will be so much better this way," Clem said firmly.

Will it?

Her cousin seemed to think they'd both be fine with a series of discreet affairs, but how could anyone control that? She wasn't a sex robot, programmed to take only pleasure and incapable of experiencing emotional attachment. Come to think of it, she studied Clem silently for a few seconds, worried about her mental state. Maybe the family shit had done more damage than she'd realized if her cousin believed this was the only way to attain peace and contentment.

"Let's check the spellbook again," Danica said at last.

"Tonight?"

She nodded. "Just you and me this time. Maybe it's a more personal spell than I realized, but I have to sever the connection this time. It...hurts."

I shouldn't miss him this much already. It's too fast, too soon.

Clem's expression softened, her anger slipping away like a leaf boat hitting the rapids in a rushing river. "This sucks, but we'll get through it. You know I'm here for you, right? No matter what."

Nodding, Danica hugged her cousin. She *did* know that. Even if they disagreed sometimes about family crap or fought like wet cats, they always had each other's backs. Always. Calmer now, Danica went into the back and managed to work without wreaking any havoc. By the end of the day, her wild magic had been drained to a manageable level, and she hoped that boded well for their second attempt at the spellbook. Clem had gone home earlier to set up, and after Danica locked up the shop, she biked home in a pensive, melancholy mood. This felt like the bitter end of something beautiful, like getting a mouthful of dregs at the bottom of a sweet cup of tea.

She found the ritual set up for the second time at the kitchen table with Clem waiting at her usual anchor point. Mechanically, Danica washed up and got herself in the proper headspace, focusing on a gentle stream of magic as she opened the grimoire. *I'm in complete control. No more misfires.*

The same spell she'd found the day before was still there, but faded and blurred as if it hadn't been executed right. *Imagine that.* This time, she kept a strong mental grip on the proceedings and spoke the incantation, slowly throttling back on her power. *Let me go. Forget me. We aren't meant to be. I'm so sorry.* The candles flickered, and she *felt* the energy spiral outward in a soft shockwave, power sent to do her bidding as the book must have intended the first time.

"Did you feel that?" she asked.

Clem nodded, easing forward. "It's still blank to me. What about you?"

When Danica checked, she nearly burst into tears because this time, the spell was gone. *I did it right. Titus will probably forget about me.* At least, that was the form she'd wished for when she released the spell. She didn't want to hurt him, just for him to gradually lose interest, like someone getting over a crush. Her magic would ease the sting, and eventually, it would seem completely normal to him, just one of those things.

Despite her best efforts, the tears overflowed. Whether she'd wanted to admit it or not, this was a breakup. *And I never even got to bang him.* That unfair fact was salt in the wound. Clem rounded the table and put an arm around Danica's shoulders, stroking her hair.

She sniffed. "You have to pick up the pastries from now on. I can't. I just...can't."

"You got it." Clem wiped up her tears with a napkin then said, "Ice cream? We have mint chocolate chip in the freezer."

"Hell yes. Get the tiny spoon. I want to feel like a giant."

When Clem laughed, it made her feel marginally better. This was what she'd chosen. Her cousin understood her quirks from a lifetime of making silly jokes together, and she had shared context like that with her coven sisters too. Maybe it wasn't right that she had to choose, but nobody ever said life was fair.

There were so many kinds of love, and as she'd heard for her entire life, a Waterhouse witch had to take great care in matters of the heart.

Tuesday morning seemed to arrive even faster than usual.

Which was weird because Titus was spinning a theory that time had stopped for a while on Monday. That would explain why he hadn't heard from Danica at all. Though he was trying not to be an obsessive weirdo, following Maya's excellent advice, he still checked his phone compulsively. People who were dating sent each other occasional texts, right?

Why am I so bad at this?

The lunch rush gave him no time to think, and he was thankful to be busy as he covered Maya's break. He'd left his phone in the kitchen, better that way. And he had been filling orders nonstop for half an hour, chatting up old ladies, when he finally took a breath and stretched his neck and shoulders. Really, he only enjoyed the baking part of this job. It was a good thing Maya liked managing the front end or he'd be in trouble.

Suddenly, the front door banged open, and a massive guy in a black leather jacket stormed in. He looked...dangerous, Titus thought, and rather out of place in St. Claire. Not that he was prone to judging people by what they wore, but everything about this dude raised his hackles. The man slammed a motorcycle helmet on the counter.

"Where is she?" English accent, not posh, Brummie, more like, or somewhere rough.

"Who?" Titus squared his shoulders. If *this* was Maya's boyfriend and he was asking for Titus's sister like that? Oh *hell* no. Every muscle in his body tensed, prepping for a fight.

"The fucking witch, you cunt. Followed her trail straight here, and I'm *never* wrong about these things. Where is she?" The asshole reached across the counter and grabbed the front of Titus's uniform, trying to yank him in for some intimidation.

But Titus didn't let that happen. He dug in with dough-kneading strength and broke the other man's grip. "Don't touch me. And get out. Now."

"Right, I shouldn't have called you a cunt. I apologize. I've been riding for eighteen hours. This is a shop, yeah? Maybe she's one of your customers..." Leather Jacket paced away from the counter, moving around the front of the café like a hound following a smell.

He didn't seem to be looking for Maya in particular. Just...a random witch? Titus sighed. *It's going to be one of those days, isn't it?* Running a business meant anybody could wander in the door, and sometimes his clientele ran to tinfoil-hat types. There was a prepper named Dale who lived on a farm outside town, only came in twice a year for supplies, all furtive and unwashed. He spent his life waiting for the apocalypse in the root cellar, but every March he bought confetti cupcakes for his birthday, a ritual even a doomsdayer couldn't quit. People were weird.

"Apology accepted." Maybe this didn't have to escalate. The guy didn't seem to be tweaking, but Titus couldn't get a look at his eyes behind the dark sunglasses. "If you're not shopping for baked goods or buying a drink, you still need to leave, though."

"Then I'll have a black coffee." LJ dug into his pocket and produced some grimy, wrinkled bills, just enough to cover his order. "Now then, I'm a paying customer. You want to keep me happy, right? Just answer the question."

Titus ground his back teeth as he filed a to-go cup. He wasn't about to give this dingus a ceramic mug.

"The question of...which of my customers is a witch? I'm saying this with your best interests at heart, sir. Please get help."

"That supposed to be funny? I don't expect gratitude for this thankless bullshit, but I'm dead tired of people insinuating that I'm daft when I know damn well what I'm about. There's more going on in this sleepy little town than you possibly imagine, Cletus."

He closed his eyes and counted to ten. *This bastard did* not *just call me Cletus.* Before he could respond, Maya came back from her lunch break. She greeted the jackwagon cheerfully, but without even a flicker of recognition, thank God.

"That must be your bike outside. It's awesome! I've only seen pictures of vintage Ducati like that. Must've cost a mint."

"Hell if I know. I inherited it from my old man. Looks like you work here too, eh? Maybe you'll be more reasonable. I just have a few questions for you, sweetheart, and I've bought my coffee right and proper. Can we have a little chat?"

If the jerk hadn't been so gruff and angry five seconds ago, Titus wouldn't have been so surprised at his sudden shift. Now he was trying to charm Maya, and just...none of it was normal. This dude had to be mental and suffering from rapid mood swings. Titus came around the counter and put himself between the two.

"We're not helping you with your witch hunt," he said deliberately.

Maya flashed him an "oh crap, one of those" look, and he inclined his head slightly. She pressed her lips together briefly, sighed, then added, "Have a nice day!"

It was practically illegal around here not to end a conversation on a friendly note. He smiled at his sister and stepped around the asshole to open the door. With a frustrated roar, the guy chucked his coffee—big surprise—dashing it against the floor, and then he lunged. Titus's first instinct launched him at Maya to shield her, but the bastard gave the cash register a furious shove, flipping it upward. He stormed out as it slammed on the floor; it didn't break into pieces, but it didn't turn on when Titus righted it.

Maya stood in stunned silence, gaping at the widening pool of coffee on the floor. "What the *hell*?" she finally managed to say.

Titus shook his head, already going for the mop. Stan poked his head out of the kitchen. "Do I need to call the sheriff?"

"Maybe?" Probably it would be smart to get this on the books in case that whack job came back raving about witches again.

"The fun never ends," Maya muttered.

"You're telling me."

His sister seemed shaken, and Titus wasn't a lot better off. He did call the sheriff and filled out a report, showed footage of the strange encounter and the subsequent property damage. Sheriff Mulvihill frowned and shook his head when he finished up.

"I have no idea what to make of this. But I'll keep an eye out. If I spot this perp, I'll haul him in and teach him some manners."

They ended up closing early, with baked goods left, which almost never happened. He bagged them up to donate to the St. Claire Food Bank. Hopefully his loss would be somebody else's gain. Titus liked to imagine kids being surprised with unexpected treats.

"You're stopping by the food pantry?" Maya guessed.

He nodded. "When life gives you lemons and all that."

"Don't you ever get tired of looking on the bright side? You're always telling me things are fine, even if they aren't. That they'll get better, even if they're terrible. What will it take to make you admit that our lives suck and things may always be crappy? That's just how it is for us because even our own fucking dad wanted a do-over."

Maya dashed out, leaving him with a powerful ache in his chest. *Goddammit. I didn't even see that coming, and I should have. I knew she was hurting.*

The only bright spot in this shitty situation? Now he had an excuse to call Danica. The bakery couldn't operate without a working cash register. Really, he just wanted to hear her voice, though. *Bad, so bad.* The black hole inside him might swallow up the last of his optimism if he didn't talk to her. Without hesitation, he rang up the shop, knowing Danica would be working, not her cousin.

"Fix-It Witches, how can I help you?" Her voice was bright and professional, like a ray of sunshine shot directly into his bloodstream.

Some of the tension and stress scaled back. Desire filled in the cracks, leaving him aching for her from head to toe.

"I have an urgent need for service," Titus said.

CHAPTER 13

THAT DOESN'T MAKE ANY SENSE.

Danica clutched the phone until the handset dug into her palm. Titus shouldn't be calling, not after the spell yesterday. His interest in her ought to be fading, but the desire making his voice so husky and low came across the phone line so clearly that her toes curled. As her heart quickened in response, she attempted to scale back, but there was no leashing the excitement quivering through her.

Is he magic-resistant or something? There were rare cases of mundanes who shook off spell effects, but she'd never met anyone like that before.

Trying for a modicum of professionalism, she said, "What can I do for you?"

"Take a look at the cash register? We had an…altercation with a weirdo, and he knocked it off the counter. Now it won't turn on." It seemed like Titus was trying to collect himself too.

While his initial request had come out sounding like pure sex, his account became more matter-of-fact. It sounded like he did need repair service; this wasn't a ruse to seduce her. *Dammit.*

Impossible not to feel slightly disappointed about that, however ill-advised those feelings were.

"I'll lock up early and bring my toolbox. It will be hard for you to open in the morning without it, right?"

"It will make Maya's life tough," he said softly.

"I'm sure I can do my thing and get it going again. No worries. I'll be right there. And…" She hesitated, wondering if she ought to get this personal when she was trying to cut the connection between them. In the end, tenderness won out over caution. "I'm sorry you're having such a shitty day."

"It's looking up. I'll see you soon."

Danica rushed through the usual closing procedures, set the magical alarm, and locked up. Before leaving, she did remember to grab her gear, a toolkit she and Clem had purchased as a prop. She set it in her bike basket and rode the six blocks to Sugar Daddy's, which was already closed. But Titus was there, watching out the window for her, and he let her in before locking the door behind them.

That motion sent a little shiver of anticipation through her. *Nothing's going to happen,* she reminded herself. *That's just to keep customers out.*

As Titus had said, it was obvious that the cash register had taken a knock. This thing wasn't quite an antique, but it wasn't a fancy POS unit like you'd see in a larger establishment. It was a model with programmable keys and an electronic totaling system, along with a simple cash drawer. These had been popular in the early 2000s, still serviceable with good upkeep.

"Is there any hope, doc?" He regarded her with a glum expression.

Danica wanted to hug him. Like, a lot. To cover that impulse, she said, "Definitely. I hate to be predictable, but do you have the owner's manual?"

Titus shook his head. "Bought it used. Let me write down the model number. I can probably download it from the company website."

Danica opened her toolbox as he headed for the back. With any luck, she'd have time to repair the register before he came back. And if he wondered about how fast she'd allegedly cracked it open and put it back together, at least he'd have a working till when the bakery opened. When she was sure there were no witnesses, she closed her eyes and cast magical senses toward the breakage inside. Two vital parts, one cracked entirely and the other disconnected from its dock. She poured her abilities into mending the damage and even more energy into guiding the displaced section back into the proper slot. Physical manipulation took a lot out of her, and she was trembling when she opened her eyes.

Carefully she plugged the cash register back in and beamed when it powered on. *There, not bad for five minutes.* Part of her did feel guilty charging so much for spell work that could be completed so quickly, but they wouldn't earn a living if she only charged for the actual time involved. Plus, it factored in recovery time needed for her to be able to do magic again.

I should let him know I'm done, though.

Cautiously she pushed through the galley door into the pristine kitchen. A muffled curse from the office suggested he wasn't having much luck finding the owner's manual. Danica rapped lightly on the open door, and then stepped in.

"Hey, I..." She trailed off as she took in his defeated posture. Titus stood with his back to her, the browser on his desktop open to a search page, but he had both arms on the wall, braced with his head down, and his breath was coming fast. "What's wrong?"

"Everything," he muttered.

I shouldn't get involved.

But there was no stopping her mouth. "You can talk to me. I'm here for you."

"My sister is heartbroken about the new baby, and there's nothing I can do to make her feel better. And then today, in the bakery... That asshole could have hurt her. It just feels like everything is fucked up, and it's probably my fault. Because—"

"Nope," she cut in. "You're a great brother. Even I can tell that. And you're an amazing person. I get that when you're having a terrible day, everything feels worse than it is. But here's some good news: The register is fixed. And Maya will be okay."

Ignoring the inner voice ordering her to retreat, she crossed to him and rubbed his back, soothing circles that created little sparks. Their sexual chemistry was so fierce that it still crackled even when she was offering comfort. He spun too quickly for her to step back and pulled her into his arms, his hold hot and desperate. The moment Titus touched her, she forgot all the reasons why this was a bad idea.

He cradled her close, pressing his face into her neck. It felt like he was breathing her scent in like she was emotional ether that could stop the pain. "You make everything better. Just you. Only you."

"Titus..." She had no idea how her face must look as he pulled back to gaze at her. But she felt like begging.

I've never felt this way before.

There was no tentativeness in his kiss. His mouth took hers like he had been waiting to kiss her his entire life. He went deep, devouring in tender strokes of his tongue. She bit gently on his lower lip, tugging with her teeth, and he moaned, the hottest sound ever. It swept over her like a sexual tsunami, making her quiver from head to toe. Already, she was getting wet, just from kissing and feeling his body against hers. His big hands roved down her back, teasing lower with each maddening sweep, until she rose on tiptoes to get some pressure between her legs. It also nudged her ass into his hands.

"God, yes," he groaned, closing his palms on her and dragging her body against him.

So hard.

His cock throbbed between them, contained by his pants, but they were soft cotton and she could feel more of him in his uniform than the night they'd kissed in the parking lot. She ran her hands over his chest, toying with the buttons on his white jacket. He wasn't wearing the apron—less for her to strip off. Teasingly, she moved and he pushed in response, never breaking the kiss. Instead, he kneaded her ass cheeks with incredibly strong hands, working her against him until she gasped against his mouth.

I want him so bad. Right here. Right now.

Everyone else was gone for the day. There would be no interruptions.

Am I really doing this? Witches couldn't get pregnant unless they willed it and released a little magical energy. It was a bit more complicated than a mundane conception, and thanks to two vivimancer coven sisters, she was inoculated against mundane diseases. There was nothing stopping her from taking exactly what she wanted for once.

"You're a goddess," he whispered.

He shifted the angle, rubbing against her just right, and she saw stars as he kissed downward, nuzzling her jaw, her throat, while he caressed upward, hands skimming her hips, her waist. When he touched her breasts over her T-shirt, she made a sound she hadn't even known was possible, somewhere between a growl and a moan.

"I need you. Now."

Titus stared, dazed and uncomprehending as Danica pushed him backward.

He fell into his padded office chair, and she pulled at the elastic band of his trousers. Before he could do more than groan, she had his cock in her hands, stroking him until he couldn't think, let alone speak. She bent and pressed a kiss to the slick tip, utterly without hesitation or shame.

"Fuck," he whispered.

"That's the plan. Do you mind if I'm on top?"

"Please?" In his muddled mind, he didn't know if he was asking or agreeing, but it seemed to be enough.

She stripped out of her bottoms in record time and settled on his lap. Just as well she was taking charge because he had no idea what he was doing. Part of him believed if they could get past this point without disasters or interruptions, maybe his curse would be broken too. He kept quiet, opting not to tell her that this was his first time.

"I'm sorry," she murmured. "I can't wait. This probably isn't how you imagined it, but I've got to have you."

Hell. Titus had certainly never pictured hot, greedy sex in his office chair, but after this, he'd probably never work in here again without a hard-on. "No, this...is good," he gasped, as she sank straight down on him.

No condom. I don't—I should...

Bare skin. Hot. So hot. Slick.

There were reasons he should object to this. It wasn't safe for her—well, it *was*, but she didn't know that. *If she gets pregnant—*

Danica raised her hips. Pressed back down. Lightning pooled in his pelvis, stealing his ability to breathe for a few seconds. Nothing in life had prepared him for how good this felt. Romance novels had hinted at it, but Jesus Christ.

If she gets pregnant, I'll marry her.

The thought alone almost made him come. His cock jerked as she rode him, and he tried to get himself under control. It would be embarrassing if he went off in two minutes. *I have to make it good for her too. Think about her needs, not how good her pussy feels.*

"Top off," he managed to say.

It was all backward to peel her shirt over her head and fumble to unfasten her bra while she moved on his dick, but everything was always topsy-turvy between them. The first time he saw her, a blender spewed piña colada all over her. Remembering that put filthy ideas in his head, stuff he normally wouldn't even watch in porn.

He touched her breasts, watching her eyes go lambent. She picked up the pace, dropping down on him hard. Slowly, he learned how to answer, shifting, pushing up, and watching her head fall back when he grazed the right spot inside her. Once he found it, he hit it again and again, until her breath was coming in ragged gulps. Focusing on her made it easier not to get lost in the burning pleasure, but the feelings tugged at him relentlessly until he couldn't hold back.

Titus kissed her deeply. "I'm getting close."

"Me too. Just…a little more."

"This?" He grazed her clit with his fingertips and couldn't resist caressing between their bodies, feeling how wet she was, how wet *he* was. His hand grazed his own cock, caressed her slick labia. He wished he had a better view of where they were joined. Touching just there felt incredible, and that was a mistake because now there was no stopping the pressure building in his balls, at the base of his spine.

Suddenly, her head fell back, and she clenched on him. "It's happening."

His cock throbbed. "Do it. All over me. Let me feel you."

Soft, desperate pants against his neck as she came, grinding down on his cock. His orgasm rocked his whole body, deep tension releasing in hot spurts. He pulled her down on him, hard, rolling his hips to draw out the incredible sensation of coming inside the woman he loved. No first time could have been better than this.

Dizzily, he tracked that thought back. The woman he…? *Yeah. Fuck.*

I love her so much.

It was too soon, and he knew it was, but he was so damn gone for Danica. As his breath and heartbeat slowed, he cuddled her against his chest and stroked her back, not wanting her to feel like this was a fast and dirty fuck that she should immediately regret. *God, I hope she doesn't have sex remorse after this.*

"Wow," she whispered. "That was...wow."

Not bad for my first time.

Maybe one day, he might even tell her. Possibly five years after they got married. He could imagine the conversation, snuggled up together in bed. She would be awed and disbelieving, maybe even praise his self-control. *I had no idea; you didn't fumble like a nervous virgin.* She'd made it easy by taking the lead, showing him exactly what she wanted and not giving him space to doubt.

"You're so beautiful."

"I'm a sweaty mess."

"Agree to disagree. Remember, I participated in bringing out that...glow, and if you want my opinion, the results are gorgeous."

"You did not just say that." But she laughed and pressed a kiss to his cheek, right above the start of his beard.

Titus hated to bring this up, but it would be irresponsible not to. "So that was glorious and all, but—"

"You're concerned about safety," she guessed.

"Aren't you?"

"I have a clean bill of health, and I'm on birth control. But if you want me to get tested, I'm happy to do that. You don't need more stress in your life."

"Likewise," he said.

He could have clarified right then. *It's impossible to get STDs when nobody else has ever touched your junk.* Wait, that wasn't entirely true, but he'd never had a blood transfusion or done drugs either.

"Then let's do the work to give each other peace of mind."

"Should we have done that beforehand? Before we…" He couldn't decide what to call this interlude. He'd hugged her because it was impossible not to.

I didn't expect…this.

"Some people do. They show each other the paperwork before getting intimate. I know enough about you to trust that you don't do this casually, though. And I hope you feel the same about me." She paused, massaging the back of his neck lightly.

Titus tilted his head back, unable to believe she was still sitting on him while his cock softened inside her. If she stayed long enough, he'd want to go again.

"I really don't do hookups," he agreed.

"If you did, the town grapevine would be on fire with people gossiping about it." Her eyes held a soft, affectionate light. "Lucky for you, I don't flaunt my conquests, since this constitutes mad bragging rights." She wriggled a little on top of him.

Titus held her to him, unable to control the possessive urge. "You think so?"

"I know so. As for me, I've only slept with my ex in the last three years, and we both got tested before starting that relationship."

His stomach clenched. The idea of someone else touching her made him want to growl. And the fact that her ex had had her for two years, then married someone else? The jackass must be out of his mind.

"Great. Let's never talk about that fuckface again."

"Fine by me." Danica kissed his nose, an affectionate gesture that melted his heart into clarified butter. "Much as I hate to move from the best seat in the house, I need to wash up. Okay for me to use the bathroom first?"

My dick. Is the best seat in the house.

He couldn't stop grinning. His face might literally split, Joker-style. *It's terrifying to be this happy.*

"Go for it."

Titus groaned when she slid off him. He wasn't prepared for how sensitive his skin was nor for the soft stroke of her hand across his head as she moved away. His whole body was an erogenous zone. If Danica touched his elbow, he'd probably pop an erection.

For a few moments, he simply sprawled in the office chair, trying to process. *The curse is broken. She's the one.* None of the usual bullshit that plagued and terrified him applied where Danica was concerned. The woman was gorgeous, gifted, and fearless, taking what she wanted with both hands.

It's a miracle that she wants me.

CHAPTER 14

DANICA SPLASHED WATER ON HER face.

She had cleaned up, just as she'd said, but she was also battling a colossal wave of panic and regret. After making up her mind to stop seeing Titus, after casting *two* spells to that effect, she'd just banged his brains out in his office. *This is so out of control.* It would be some comfort if the sex had at least been mediocre, but no, it rocked her world every bit as much as she'd imagined.

Dammit. What now?

Pulling herself together, she dried her face and donned a smile before heading to look for Titus. She found him still sprawled in the office chair, as if he were boneless. He'd straightened his clothes, even if his hair was still messy. The brightness of the smile he directed at her made her feel like shit. *He thinks this is the start of something, not an impulsive mistake.* Danica didn't have the heart to address the issue. Not today, not right after such fantastic sex. Asking her to have that convo right now was both cruel and unusual.

"I wish I didn't have to invoice you, but don't get it twisted. It's purely for fixing the register. Not for—"

"Other services?" Titus supplied smoothly.

"Exactly."

He rose, taking her hands in a gesture so adorable that her heart quivered. "I hope you don't provide this level of attention to all your clients."

"I think you know that I don't."

"Then I'm special," he pronounced with an absurd air of satisfaction.

If only you knew.

"Definitely." Her mouth just loved answering before her brain caught up. "I have to run. Book club is—"

A soft kiss interrupted her, and she got lost in it for several dreamy seconds. *I could live off kissing this man.* Danica fell out of the daze when he traced a finger down her cheek.

"Have fun tonight. I'll text you before bed."

That sounded very...official, but from the glimmer in his eyes, it also offered all kinds of promise. Probably she should discourage him, but instead, she said, "Sounds good."

"You know, I'm starting to think that weirdo did me a favor," he said, smiling.

"How so?"

Is he talking about the dude who wrecked the register?

"He barged in here ranting about witches, and when I suggested he seek help, he...reacted badly. Big guy, tough-looking. British accent. If I had to guess, I'd say he has a drug problem and maybe a mental illness."

Oh shit.

For several long seconds, she couldn't even breathe. Titus

kept talking, apparently not noticing her preternatural stillness. "Anyway, that turned out to be a blessing in disguise. You fixed what he broke, and then we...you know. A bad day turned out great, thanks to you."

I fixed what he broke...magically. And magic leaves a trail for those who know how to follow it.

If the stranger wasn't deranged, this destruction could've been a trap. *One I walked right into.* She needed to purge the trail, but Titus would walk her out like a gentleman. She had no excuse to linger alone in the front of his shop, and she couldn't do magic in front of him. Normally the energy would disperse on its own, and it couldn't be detected long range, exactly why her ancestors had settled in a small Midwestern town, away from where you'd expect witches to congregate. Witch hunters had been off their trail for decades. Until now.

I have to warn the others.

She shivered a little. "Likewise. Talk to you later."

Regardless of whether that was even a suitable response, Danica hurried out front and collected her gear, darting to the door before he could unlock it. Titus rushed after her, seeming confused by her sudden urgency, but she didn't pause to soothe him. If her bad feeling turned out to be true, the coven could be in deep shit.

Kerry and Priya were hosting tonight, and Danica raced home to catch a ride with Clem. Her cousin could tell she was agitated, but she didn't explain. Better to tell the story just once. The other two women welcomed them after a short drive, and she said the right words about their newly redecorated home while pacing as everyone else arrived. Margie came next, followed by Vanessa and Ethel; then Leanne arrived last.

Ethel took one look at Danica and grinned. "You got laid. And it was *powerful*."

At the old witch's words, Leanne took a closer look. "Damn. So she did."

"It's been ages for me," Margie said with a sigh. "I demand vicarious satisfaction."

Danica made a shooing gesture while her cousin glared at her. "I'll take questions about my sex life later. Something big might be looming." Quickly, she summarized what had happened at the bakery, glossing over the personal details.

Kerry cursed quietly. "You've made two service calls there recently. If this guy's the real deal, he could have followed your energy trail."

Danica let out an unsteady breath. "Exactly what I'm thinking. I haven't bothered using a dispersal ritual in ages. I got comfortable. And careless."

"He hasn't got us yet," Ethel said with a pragmatic air. "My mother told me about one who came sniffing around in the '30s. They didn't find us then either. Try to calm down."

Priya came over and rubbed Danica's shoulder. "It's not your fault. I suspect that none of us have been as careful with our magic as we could've been."

Vanessa nodded. "It could have been any one of us that pinged on his radar."

Sighing, Danica shook her head. "But I'm the one who's spiking like crazy. My output is off the charts lately."

"At least you admit there's a problem." Clem's tight tone made it clear there would be a reckoning for this, but her cousin had the grace not to call her out in front of everyone.

I'll hear about having sex with Titus later.

Ignoring that, Danica turned to Ethel. "You said there was a hunter here in the '30s. Did your mother tell you how they got rid of him?" She didn't mean it literally, of course.

If witches went around murdering hunters on their trail, it would only confirm the suspicions and result in even more hunters tromping around. The solution had to be clean and clever. Hopefully the elder witch knew what to do.

"First, we protect this place so he can't sense our workings," the old woman said. "And then we do a joint casting to confirm if he's the real deal."

"Divination is your forte," Vanessa said.

Ethel nodded. "That's why I'll be taking the lead. Priya, can you lock the apartment? You've lived here for years, and your imprint is stronger than Kerry's."

"Understood. I'm on it." Priya went room to room, strengthening her wards, until not even a glimmer of energy should bleed through to the outside.

Danica could feel the protections building, a soft glow that radiated security. Usually, they'd be laughing and chatting, noshing on the various food and drinks that Kerry and Priya had set out. Clem had bought cinnamon rolls as she promised, relieving Danica of that responsibility, but nothing else was turning out like they'd planned.

Once Leanne confirmed that the seal was solid, Kerry and

Priya got the implements Ethel requested, white candles and purified water in a copper bowl along with various ceremonial herbs. The old witch took the lead, intoning softly as she scattered the carnation and mugwort, finishing with sea salt for purity. Without prompting, they joined hands around the table, allowing Ethel to pull from their energies as she peered into the glimmering water.

At first, it was cloudy as she whispered, "Tell us, spirits, true or false, false or true. Him we seek and him we find. Let none hinder this quest of mind. Hunter, the water reveals the truth of you."

The liquid roiled inside the bowl, gentle bubbles that slowly clarified into the image of a large man, reclining in a vinyl chair. A leather jacket was slung over the back, and he was drinking a beer in a cheap motel room. As Titus had said, he was big, but more, he emanated intensity and determination. At his feet lay a battered leather satchel full of goddess knew what, maybe tools for killing witches. He wore battered boots and torn jeans. From head to toe, he radiated danger, and if that wasn't enough, he was ruggedly appealing too. Strong jaw, dusted with dark stubble, a shock of hair so black it gleamed, and his eyes were an eerie silver gray. And though it was impossible, he *stirred* as they gazed on him, glancing around as if he felt the invisible weight of their attention.

Carefully, Ethel drew back, pulling out of the bond so deftly that Danica barely felt the disconnection. She rubbed her hands together nervously. "Well?"

The old witch stared into the now-quiescent tureen. "We're in it now, my darlings. He's the real deal."

Her coven sisters sat quiet for a bit, each likely wrestling with their own fears. Then Clem squared her shoulders with the air of a maiden agreeing to be chained to some rocks as bait for a sea monster. "No worries. I'll handle him."

Titus went home in a hell of a good mood.

He greeted Doris with an enthusiastic belly rub. As he played on the floor with the dog, Maya came to greet him. It was rare for his sister to beat him home, but it was kind of nice not coming back to an empty house. After the way she'd bolted before, he feared she'd still be upset, but she looked better now.

Spatula in one hand, she pointed it at him like it was a microphone. "Inquiring minds want to know. Did your magical lady friend make our problems disappear? Will business proceed as usual tomorrow?"

"Yes and yes."

"Damn. She really can fix anything. I wish I had that superpower."

"She told me she learned everything she knows from her grandmother, but I doubt an older person would know how to repair all the latest gadgets. I—"

"And I'm done with this conversation. If you're curious, you should spend more time asking about her life and less time..." Maya made kissing faces and pressed her folded fingers together in an especially obnoxious impression of hand puppets making out.

Give me a break. I literally just had sex for the first time. Also, I did ask where she went to school, but she never answered me.

"Your advice is noted," he said, giving Doris a final belly pat.

After changing out of his uniform, he played outside with the dog until it got dark. Maya had pasta primavera on the table when he came in and was lazily grating parmesan cheese while she watched something on her tablet. They'd talked about getting a small TV mounted in the kitchen, but he'd absorbed some of his mother's old-fashioned ideas about electronics where they cooked. Plus, the heat wouldn't be good for the circuits, and the TV might fritz. Then he'd have a reason to lure Danica to his house. Incredibly, a spark of arousal fluttered through him as he imagined her in his bed, riding him like she had in his office. Unbidden, other images rolled through his mind.

God, I'm dirty. No getting a kitchen TV if that's why I'd be buying it.

Shaking his head, he forked up a bite of pasta. "Thanks. This is great."

Having sexual fantasies while eating dinner with his sister was *not* something he'd ever imagined doing. Maybe it was because he'd gone without for so long, but until meeting Danica, he'd always shrugged over his lack of a sex life. He occasionally masturbated to take the edge off, but he'd always seen it as... exercise, almost. But now, he wanted to learn all the ways he could make her feel good.

"No problem. It was my turn to cook." She studied him. "You're awfully quiet. Shall I guess what's on your mind?"

Before Maya could start teasing him, the house phone rang, usually a telemarketer at this hour. They had talked about disconnecting the landline, but Titus couldn't bring himself to cancel it since the number had been in his mother's name before she died. He had transferred the account, but this number had sentimental value to him, silly as that might sound.

"I'll get it." He headed over to answer the wall phone, not even a cordless unit either. This thing was an antique, butter yellow and still functional. "Hello?"

His dad's voice came across cheerfully, and the rotini he'd eaten immediately clumped in his stomach. "Titus! So glad I got through. I think there's something wrong with your cell phone. It keeps sending me straight to voicemail."

Yeah, that's not an accident. I don't want to talk to you.

"What's up? We're in the middle of dinner."

"Oh damn, right. I always forget that we're not in the same time zone. Well, I'll be quick. Check your email. I sent your itinerary. You and Maya have to come see us. Susan wants you both at the baby shower."

What the hell?

"I hope those tickets are refundable," he said, trying not to snap. "I can't just close the bakery on a whim. We have set hours and—"

"This isn't open for discussion. Put a sign on the door, and act like my son for a few days. It won't kill you to show your mother some support."

Fuck. He did not just say that. Breathe. Count to ten.

Titus's tone was icy when he responded. "She's your wife, not my mother. And we never agreed to this trip. I'll talk to you later." Titus cut the call and left the phone off the hook, trying to seem calm as he sat down at the table.

Maya was sitting with a blank expression, staring at her bowl. "He really expects us to drop everything just because Susan asked. Close the business, maybe lose customers. What the hell is wrong with him? He called her our..." She couldn't even say it, and as if that was the last straw, she burst into tears. "I hate him. I hate him so much. And I hate it even more that he tries to make us feel like the bad ones, like we're ungrateful and selfish for not supporting everything he does, no matter how shitty it makes us feel."

Titus got up and hugged her, patting her back awkwardly. "I know, Mini. And I wish I knew what to do about it, but the conversations I've tried to have with him about this... They didn't go well."

"That's because he just wants what he wants. He's the selfish one! If he'd given us any time at all to adjust or paused to consider our feelings, the situation would be better. As it is, I constantly wonder if he was cheating online with Susan while Mom was dying."

Shit. She said it.

The same suspicion had chased around Titus's head more than once. People didn't just move on from death and get remarried that fast, did they? Not unless the seed had already been germinating for a while.

"I haven't asked," he said softly. "Because I'm afraid of the answer."

She made a scoffing noise. "Like he'd even tell us the truth. I'm sure he'd blame us for asking instead of owning up to it."

"That sounds about right." Gently he patted her shoulder and went back to his food, although neither his mood nor his appetite was the same.

Finally, after ten minutes of pretending, they got up to clear the table. Titus loaded the dishwasher while Maya put things away and wiped down the counter and table.

When they were done, she said, "I think…I'm going out for a bit. Sometimes this house…" She shook her head. "Do you mind if I take Doris for a run? If you're in bed when I get back, I'll keep her in my room."

"Go ahead, I know she'd love that. Wear the reflector strips!" he called after her, as she got Doris's leash and the dog practically fell over wagging her tail.

It was a double-edged sword, living here. All their happy memories as a family were tied to this place, but this was where everything fell apart too. Usually he got comfort from being here, but tonight, it was all melancholy. With a sigh, he went up to his room and wished he didn't want to call Danica so much. Texting was more casual, but maybe they were in a place where that didn't matter?

Throwing himself on his bed like a teenager, he stared at his phone. And he did try to resist for a while, opening a book that failed to distract him, even though he had been enjoying this romance before Danica blew his life to smithereens. In a good way.

Just past nine, he gave up. Dialed her number. *I'll only let it ring three times. If she doesn't answer—*

She picked up on the second beep. "Hey, you."

That greeting sent pleasurable shivers through him. Most likely it was her husky tone more than the words. But somehow, she made those two words sound so intimate, like there was nobody else she'd rather hear from.

"Am I bothering you? I know you have book club tonight, and I'm not sure how long it runs. I can—"

"It's fine. Meeting's over." He heard sounds like she might be settling in. "What's up?"

Should I say this? Why not? It was the truth, and he wasn't the kind of person who could play games or pretend not to need people.

"To be honest, after you left, the day took a crappy turn again, and I wanted to hear your voice."

CHAPTER 15

"OH YEAH?" DANICA'S RESPONSE INVITED Titus to elaborate. Probably she shouldn't be so pleased to hear from him.

Not after she'd just impulsively ravished him after two different spells failed to quell her unquenchable thirst. But as Leanne had put it just before the coven meeting ended, "Look, you've got it bad for this guy. Maybe the universe is telling you to indulge, get him out of your system. These intense sexual obsessions usually burn fast and hot."

Her eyes had widened. "You're saying I should satiate myself? Stop resisting."

Leanne waggled her brows. "Honey, I've seen the CinnaMan. The only thing I don't understand is why you were trying to resist in the first place."

Everyone but Clem seemed to agree with this statement, and the meeting broke up after they'd confirmed that they did indeed have a genuine witch hunter on their hands.

On the way to the car, Ethel had worn a serious expression as she took Clem's hands in hers. "Be careful. He's grim and determined."

Her cousin had nodded. "I'll be careful. Did you get a sense of where he is?"

"Oh, he's holed up at the motel off Route 30, but he'll probably return to the bakery if he gets a whiff of Danica's magic." The old witch turned a somber gaze on both cousins. "Be watchful, both of you. I wasn't around when my mother dealt with the hunter back in the day, but from her stories, it wasn't pretty."

Clem didn't waver in her resolve. "Understood. I'll call if I need help."

The rest of the witches had given hugs all around, then Kerry and Priya had gone inside while the others headed home. Her cousin had barely said ten words to Danica after they got back, and she'd dashed off to her room as soon as possible, presumably to make plans to ensnare the witch hunter. Danica had no doubt there was a big quarrel brewing, which was why she was hiding in her bedroom when Titus called.

Belatedly, she realized she was only half-attending to his response. Fortunately she tuned in soon enough to get the gist. It seemed like his dad had bought plane tickets for Titus and his sister without confirming that the visit was possible on their end, and now he was demanding that they shut down the bakery to attend a baby shower. *Damn. That's messed up. I'm not the only one with family issues.*

When he finally paused, she said, "If you want my take—and I'm guessing you do since you shared that with me—the whole situation is unfair. He forced this on you, and he's using guilt as a wedge, like you're a bad son if you don't do exactly what he wants. You're an adult, and you can buy your own plane tickets. When it's convenient for *you*, not him."

"Wow," Titus said.

"Did I overstep?"

"No. But that's precisely how I feel. Sometimes you wonder if it's in your head because you're too close to a situation to be impartial."

Danica shook her head then realized he couldn't see her. "Your dad is being selfish. I don't presume to know about his relationship with your mom, but him expecting you to act like she never existed? That's bullshit. I'm not saying he shouldn't live his life, but he can't demand that you stop grieving and treat his current wife like she's always been your mother, you know? He needs to back off and give you time. Instead, he hurts you every time you talk because he wants to retcon your family history."

"Exactly. And Susan is only ten years older than me. Even if I accept their relationship, I'm *never* seeing her as a maternal figure."

"I get it," she said, snuggling deeper into bed and pulling up the covers. She'd already brushed her teeth and put on pajamas, planning to read a little before falling asleep. "From what you've told me about your dad, he's not the type to admit fault. So he'll transfer the blame to you and leave you questioning whether he's right."

"Thanks."

"For what?"

"Listening. Cheering me up. Even if you hadn't said all the right things and reassured me, hearing your voice still would've helped. It's like I got a two-fer."

"Now you're just being excessively sweet."

"Nah, it's the truth. Talking to you is the best."

Hell, his voice in her ear, deep and low, did something to her too. Her core heated, still soft and sensitive after sex despite the hours in between and the shower she'd taken. Somehow, any contact with him at all left her slick and needy. If she accepted Leanne's cure for what ailed her, she should embrace her instincts where he was concerned, gorge on the Titus experience until her need subsided and she could walk away. Trying to stop this rising tide had drawn a witch hunter down on them, for the goddess's sake, so maybe this was the right move.

"It's...good for me too," she said huskily.

There was a short silence, as if he was processing her tone. Then he whispered, "Am I imagining it or are you—"

"Turned on by your voice? Yes."

Danica had never tried phone sex, but they might be headed in that direction. Quietly she got up and locked her bedroom door, just in case, and then slid back under the covers, listening to the quickening of his unsteady breathing. To her ears, it seemed like her admission had gotten him hot too.

"I'm not sure how I'm meant to respond."

"What do your instincts tell you?"

The audible gulp of him swallowing carried across the line. "It would be impolite to leave you wanting if there's something I can do about it."

She smiled. "There is. Are you interested in a video chat?"

"Oh God. Yes. Give me two minutes."

Titus disconnected, and she dimmed the lights, propping all her pillows against the headboard. Then she plugged in earbuds so there was no chance of her cousin hearing any sexy sounds he made. When he called back on video, he was set up similarly in his bedroom, shirtless and so gorgeous that he made her mouth water. Danica wanted so much more than a quick, hard fuck; she wished she could lick him everywhere.

"I'm keeping the camera on my face," she said softly. "I hope you'll do the same. I want to hear you and see your expression, during." Hopefully that would be enough to get the point across, as she wasn't experienced at this.

"Okay. But...I've never done this. I'm not sure how this is supposed to go."

A wave of gentle warmth suffused her. "It's my first time too. We can just do what feels good. And say what seems right."

"Got it. Then...I'm starting. I'm thinking about how you felt this afternoon."

Danica listened to his movements and his ragged breathing for a few seconds, gaze locked on his face. His cheeks were already flushed, his eyes heavy-lidded, and he bit his lip, adorably sexy. Even without him dirty talking, she had to put her hand in her panties, already wet and aching.

"Does it feel good?" she whispered.

"Fuck, yes. I'm imagining your hand on me."

"Me too."

For a few seconds, there was only the wet glide of their fingers on their bodies, quiet gasps and the occasional grunt from Titus. Danica knew she had to be quiet, but that somehow made it hotter. She couldn't get enough of the minute shifts on his face as he worked his cock, licking his lips, little frowns as he chased his pleasure, and it was so delicious watching him get closer. His excitement fueled hers, and she rubbed frantically, tension coiling deep inside her.

"God, Danica..." His head fell back against the pillows, and the image trembled on screen, like it was getting tough for him to keep the phone steady.

"I'm getting close."

"Do it for me."

By their gasps and moans, they came within thirty seconds of each other, both panting in the aftermath. Her entire body relaxed, boneless as slow pulses quivered through her. She smiled at the dazed look on his face.

"Mmm. Thank you. I feel like passing out. Sweet dreams."

In the morning, Titus still couldn't believe the way his life had changed.

Sex was great and all, but to him, it was a miracle to have someone to call late at night who would listen to his crap and make him feel better. Obviously, the mutual masturbation helped too. Endorphins were powerful as hell.

He hummed through his morning routine and danced with Doris quietly in the kitchen, singing a silly song as he set up her timed food dish. Then he headed to the bakery ahead of schedule, and he had a lot of the work done when Stan showed up half an hour later. The assistant wasn't late; Titus was just brimming with energy.

The older man grunted at him as he tied on his apron and fell into his role without a word. Normally, Titus appreciated Stan's laconic early-morning manner, but today, it would've been nice to have someone to share his good mood with. He wasn't misguided enough to message Danica at this hour. Normal people didn't keep the schedule he did, as even regular businesspeople started later in the day.

Hours flew, and the bakery opened. Soon, Titus had to give Maya a hand. If things kept going as they were, they would need to hire an assistant to help on the front end. That was a good problem to have. He wished he could afford to hire someone full-time, but it wasn't in the cards yet. Fortunately, retirees often needed part-time work, and they had a wealth of experience to offer.

"Wonder if Mrs. Carminian is looking for a job," he muttered.

No, that wouldn't work. She'd flirt with him all day and never get anything accomplished. Smiling, he shooed Maya off to take her break and weathered the usual lunchtime rush. Titus was tired by the time the constant flow of customers abated. He leaned against the counter with a crick in his back. He could use a massage, but there was only one place in town for that, and he knew both masseuses, one of whom had been his biology lab partner. It was weird to pay to get naked in front of someone he used to dissect frogs with. Some services were easier to purchase from a stranger.

Maybe he should still be bummed about the conversation with his dad the night before, but he couldn't work up the energy to care. Though the situation wouldn't resolve itself, he didn't need to obsess over it. Maya had been quiet and subdued all day. Clearly she was holding onto the issue in a big way, worrying it the way Doris did a rawhide bone.

At last, he grabbed his packed lunch and stopped by the clinic to get the test he'd promised done. Then he headed to his usual bench. A flutter of disappointment flowed through him when he found only a couple of birds pecking at crumbs on the ground nearby. As he approached, they flew off and waited in the branches of a nearby elm tree to lurk in case he dropped some choice tidbits. While he ate, his phone buzzed twice with messages from his old man. Aggravated, Titus nearly turned the damn thing off and only didn't in case Maya or Danica needed to get in touch with him.

He glared at the screen instead. "Leave me the *fuck* alone."

"Whoa, that's harsh. I know I'm late, but I thought I built up some goodwill yesterday." Danica's teasing tone cut into his grumpy haze.

Full of happy incredulity, he bounded to his feet and dragged her into an impulsive hug. "I thought you weren't coming."

"Got held up at the shop. There was a hair-straightening emergency, if you can imagine that. Don't tell anyone, but I fixed it for free since the girl was crying, and she—oh, never mind. You're not interested in all the ways my day got weird."

"I am, though. Fascinated, even." Titus sat down, inviting Danica to join him with a gesture. As she did so, she passed him another concoction. "What's this?"

The juice was green, ever so green. He regarded it with trepidation.

"Cucumber, kale, pineapple, lemon, and ginger."

Oh God.

"Did I offend you in some way?"

Danica laughed. "Just wait until I make my beet cocktail for you."

"Is there any way I can talk you out of this?"

To make her happy, he downed half the bottle in one swallow. Surprisingly, it wasn't the worst thing he had ever tasted, but it had a weird mouthfeel. He didn't know if he'd ever be pleased with drinking vegetables. Fruits were one thing, but when people started juicing beets and celery, it was a slippery slope.

"Any plans for tonight?" she asked.

Is she asking me out? Or about to?

God, he hated saying this. "I'm stopping by the station after work, part of the volunteer firefighter gig. And there are some related responsibilities. Why?"

"Oh, I'm not trying to spring something on you last minute. I was just curious."

Part of him was disappointed to learn she was only asking from idle interest. "What about you?"

"I'm pretty sure I'm fighting with my cousin."

Titus blinked. "Like in a cage match or...?"

Her smile was like sunrise over the ocean, sudden and so brightly beautiful that it took his breath away. "You're so cute. No, but we've put off some...personal conflict, and if I know her half as well as I think I do, we'll have it out soon."

"Nothing serious, I hope?"

"She disapproves of some of my life choices."

He wished she would trust him with her problems, especially after the way he'd unloaded on her last night. "That's cryptic."

Instead of explaining, she finished her sandwich and took a sip of her juice. "What can I say? I'm a woman of mystery." Sighing, she shook her head. "It's a long story, but it has to do with our family stuff. I talked about Mom and Gram, right?"

"Oh, right." Comforted, he sorted through what she'd told him. "I guess your cousin is ready to take sides and maybe is pressuring you to do the same?"

She tilted her head, seeming pensive. "That's not...entirely wrong. Clem definitely agrees with Gram on some points, and she's got her own issues with our mothers."

"They're sisters, right? Who both kept their maiden names after getting married? But that was the limit to their feminism, and your grandmother doesn't like their partners."

"Damn, your memory is amazing. Yeah, that's the situation overall. Though minor correction, she was good with Auntie Allegra's first husband, but he turned out to be a cheating hell beast, and my aunt is happier with her subsequent pick."

"But I'm guessing he doesn't have the right...pedigree to please your grandma?"

"Got it in one. You're really good at this."

"Does your cousin disapprove of me for some reason?" It was a shot in the dark, but given her family dynamic, the supposition made sense.

He didn't expect her to freeze and gaze at him with enormous eyes, as if he'd developed mind-reading powers. "How did you know? Did she say something to you?"

Oh shit. Her cousin hates me?

"No, I extrapolated from context."

Danica groaned and buried her face in her hands. "Why do you have to be both absurdly hot and wickedly smart?"

That compliment wrapped around a complaint puffed him up to an incredible degree. He tried to rein in his ego with limited success, rubbing her back gently in the meantime. "She doesn't know me yet. I'm sure she's protective of you because you're like sisters, and she doesn't want you to get hurt again. After what happened with your ex, I can understand her caution. I'm confident I can win her over. What's her favorite dessert?"

"You are too good to be true," she mumbled.

"Nah, that would be you."

Titus half-closed his eyes in pleasure when she shifted closer and snuggled into his arms like she belonged there, all warm and soft, smelling of lemons and flowers. Her voice was so soft that he didn't catch her response.

He stroked her back gently. "What was that?"

"Never mind. It's pointless wishing for things that you can't change."

Racking his brain, he tried to understand the bias against him. Maybe her cousin thought any relationship Danica had would be doomed due to rebound? "Why can't we? There must be some reason that your cousin is already dead set against me. Is it because—"

Before he could finish the question, she kissed him.

CHAPTER 16

DANICA HATED DOING THIS TO shut Titus up, but on the plus side, she was still kissing him, and that was *always* awesome.

He cupped the back of her head and deepened the kiss. His beard scraped her cheeks while his mouth plundered hers deliciously, and when she pulled back, she was breathless. Titus stroked a finger down her cheek, traced the line of her lips, and pressed against the small indent in her chin. It was like he was memorizing her features, and damn. She couldn't say that anyone had ever looked at her like that before, as if the sun rose and set in her eyes. Her heart went wild.

"Maya has plans tonight," he said softly. "And it won't take me that long at the station. Do you want to come over for a while? If the quarrel with your cousin can wait."

His brown eyes practically simmered at her, and she immediately forgot all the reasons why this was a bad idea. "What time?"

"Seven."

"I'll be there," she said.

There would be questions when she got home, but currently,

she didn't care. Quickly Danica packed up her lunch and hugged him impulsively. She wasn't prepared for the sheer power of it, the way he wrapped himself around her and laid his cheek against the top of her head. Titus hugged like his life depended on it. She felt the goofy smile forming when he finally let go.

"I might make it through the day now," he said. "Thanks for the top-up."

"Uh, no problem."

"I'll text you my address. See you tonight!" He waved as she walked off.

He's so sweet and open. What if I hurt him?

Guilt surged as she hurried back to the shop. She'd stopped by the clinic first thing so she could keep her promise to Titus, and the afternoon kept her too busy to worry about personal problems, as a small series of emergencies kept her hopping. Clem left soon after she returned, looking every bit as cranky as she'd feared. Goddess only knew what her cousin would say if she knew Danica was headed over to Titus's place tonight. She tried to tell herself it was a booty call, not a date, but even she didn't believe it entirely. He just wasn't that guy.

If Leanne was right, a few more hookups and it should be easier to let him go, right? She just had to keep her magic locked down, no wild spikes in unprotected locations. It was safe to do normal repair work in the shop; they had it shielded until not even a trickle should escape, and she thought the witch hunter would find the name a bit obvious, which was exactly the point, letting them hide in plain sight. Service calls were another matter.

How are we supposed to earn a living with that asshole sniff-ing around?

"Oh!" Sudden inspiration struck, and she called Ethel, as the older witch didn't like texting. Too bad.

"What's up, hon?" That was Ethel, cutting right to the chase. If only more people were like that on the phone.

"I'm worried about doing repair work on location under the circumstances. Do you have any shielding charms?"

"Not ready-made, but I could whip up a couple for you and Clem. Not for free, you understand. I'm on a fixed income."

"I'm not asking for a handout," she said, smiling.

"Then I'll get right on it and have them done by tomorrow. Bring cash for pickup because I don't take checks, and I don't accept Venmo, unless it's an online transaction."

Danica stifled a chuckle. "I'm surprised you know what that is."

"Don't underestimate me. Do you know how much I earn for a picture of my feet?"

The laugh Danica had been suppressing spilled over. "I wish I thought you were joking."

"Not even slightly. I earn most of my gambling money that way." Ethel was partial to blending in with other seniors and taking casino trips, usually local ones, but she'd gone to Vegas a few times as well.

Sighing, Danica said, "I can't believe we have to do this. Who knew witch hunters were even still a thing?"

"They've been dwindling in the last forty years, but a few family lines still take it seriously. Can't accept that it's terrible and unnecessary. Ironic because they use their own sort of magic in tracking us down and suppressing us!"

"Magic is okay only in *their* hands," Danica muttered.

"Don't I know it. Be careful, honey. I have a bad feeling about this."

She chatted with Ethel a bit more before returning to work. All afternoon, she watched the door, afraid of the witch hunter storming in like he had at the bakery. She considered warning Gram, but the woman's spy network put the Bratva to shame, so she probably already knew. Finally, Danica finished her shift, set the magical alarm, and locked up. The late-afternoon weather was swelteringly hot, even for summer. *This is the kind of thing they used to blame witches for, back in the day.* Still, it was lovely to bike home, and she waved at people walking their dogs or taking their kids to the park on the way.

As luck would have it, Clem wasn't home, an unexpected bonus, but she had the car. Not a big deal. Danica took a quick shower and changed her clothes, choosing a cute cotton sundress patterned in blue. She put her hair up in a messy bun that she imagined Titus would have fun unraveling and did light makeup because it wasn't fun scrubbing the smears away after the sort of sex she was hoping they'd have.

As she ran down the stairs, she ordered a ride through an app, and soon one of her neighbors showed up. *This is the downside of a small town. At least it's not Hazel Jeffords.* She hadn't seen Goliath lately either. Danica got in the front seat of the Toyota Corolla, smiling at Mr. Carruthers, who had owned the hardware store until his retirement. His son ran the place now, and apparently the elder Carruthers kept himself busy driving folks around.

"Hot date, Miss Waterhouse?" The old man's eyes twinkled at her.

"I hope so."

They made small talk until he dropped her off at Titus's place. Fortunately he didn't seem to know who lived there, and she didn't enlighten him. The old man drove off as Danica took in the homestead. It was a beautiful place, mellow and welcoming. She could see how much he loved the house from how well kept it was. That couldn't be easy working the hours he did.

Before she even got to the front door, Titus threw it open, and a huge black-and-white dog peered around his leg. "This must be Doris."

"Oh no, it's starting."

"What is?"

"People only pay attention to Doris once they meet her. I become invisible."

She shot him a heated look. "That's highly unlikely."

The big dog was clearly taking her measure, so Danica gave Doris plenty of space as she came in. He'd said Doris was cautious about strangers, and Danica could sense the wariness rolling off her through the passive stream of her magic. Something bad had happened to this poor pup, though Danica didn't have the ability to determine what. Priya or Kerry would be able to *ask*, such a cool power.

"Would you like something to eat? Or drink?" he asked, gesturing toward the kitchen.

I can't believe I'm saying this.

"We both know why you invited me over, and I'd rather have sex on an empty stomach." With a sultry smile, Danica pulled her dress off, tossing it aside in what she hoped was a bold, confident move.

He can't resist. I'm even wearing my good underwear.

Titus wore an expression that she absolutely couldn't interpret, something like a Vitamix blend of lust and panic. He rushed her, but before he got there, Maya popped out of the kitchen wearing a friendly smile that froze as her gaze slid up and down. Danica knew exactly how she looked, hip cocked, wearing a matching bra and panty set—pink satin and lace..

"Uh. Nice to see...so much of you. I like your lingerie. And I agree with you about the empty stomach, it's..." She paused, communicating silently with her brother. "Never mind. I'll be in the kitchen while you get dressed."

Oh goddess, why? Take me now.

Titus had never been so embarrassed...or so turned on.

He hadn't imagined that Danica would strip in his front room before he had a chance to tell her that Maya was home. Maybe he ought to have sent a message, but who could've guessed that Danica would come out so strong? A hot flush covered her entire upper body as she hastily got dressed, and he wanted nothing more than to carry her upstairs. But he'd never been in this position before.

It seemed discourteous to do that when Maya was home. Not that she was an impressionable kid; they were both adults. Possibly he was overthinking it, but they should have a conversation about how to handle things respectfully as housemates first. He'd be okay with her bringing a partner home too, just with a discussion beforehand setting ground rules, like no sex or nudity in public areas.

God, this is awkward.

He became aware that the silence had gone on too long and stepped toward Danica, pulling her into a comforting hug. "I'm so sorry. This is my fault. I should've told you, but I haven't been home that long, and I had no idea her plans had changed."

Her voice came out muffled with her face tucked against his chest. "No, it's on me for being...impulsive."

"Your impulses are sexy as hell, and I'm lucky to benefit from them."

"I should probably go. There's no way I can hang around here after flashing your sister. The problem is, I don't have the car. I thought I'd be here a while and that you could take me home later if you were so inclined."

"I don't really want you to leave, but I need to talk to Maya. Why don't you wait in my room? I'll be there soon."

"You think we can just..." Eyes wide, she seemed hesitant even to say it.

"Why not? We'll need to be quiet, but that might be kind of hot. You're allowed to say no, of course. Say the word and I'll drive you home instead."

He waited in silence, trying not to pressure her. Obviously he wanted to have sex—it was like she'd lit a fire under his libido and now he couldn't get enough—but not if she felt too upset. Nothing mattered more to him than her feelings.

Finally, she said, "You know what? I'd laugh if this happened to someone else. Might as well own it. Go ahead, talk to your sister. Which room is yours?"

"Up the stairs, down the hall, second on the left. It's the room with an en suite bath."

"Got it. I'll be waiting."

Maya hit him as soon as he walked through the doorway to the kitchen. "You've been holding out on me. Things are progressing much faster than I imagined, Captain Awkward."

"Please, I will never be mentally ready to discuss this with you. But we *do* need to have this conversation. Do you mind if Danica stays over?"

"Not at all. You won't go big brother on anyone I bring home?"

"I'll do my best to be polite and welcoming." Quickly he outlined his suggestions for not making it weird.

Maya agreed. "Reasonable. No sex in public spaces, no roaming around naked. If you keep it in your room, I'm fine. And to make it less *eek* right now, I'll take Doris out for a long run. But damn, bro, give me a heads-up next time."

"You assume she'll see me again after I let this happen," he said mournfully.

"Titus, the woman chose *you* over hot food. Stop being a downer."

"Sorry. I'm disturbingly bad at…" He waved a hand toward the stairs. "All of this. With her, though, it doesn't matter. I won't walk away unless she gives up on me first."

"That's quitter talk. Oh, and Titus?" Maya's tone turned teasing.

"What?" he asked warily.

"Well done. She's fire hot."

Oh God. I wish my sister didn't know that about...my girlfriend? In all honesty, he didn't even know if he could use that word yet. Maybe they were supposed to eventually have a conversation about it after dating for a while and decide if they were exclusive. With every fiber of his being, he wanted that already, but Danica might not. He didn't know how she saw him, if she considered him a rebound fling as her cousin seemed to suspect.

Hell, I'm getting too much in my own head when I have a seriously sexy woman waiting in my bedroom.

He scrubbed at his beard with a flustered hand. "Please don't ever say that again. Don't even think it."

"Deal. Doris, let's go, girl! Daddy has a job to do."

I might never hear the end of this.

Fortunately, the dog didn't care what else was up when Maya waved the leash. Titus made his escape, bolting upstairs like embarrassment could tackle him from behind. Danica was still fully dressed when he opened the door, not that he expected otherwise after the debacle earlier. She'd perched on his bed and was reading one of his books. Bending to read the cover, he saw she'd chosen one of his favorite romances.

"I love that one."

She glanced up with a tremulous smile, and he noticed the tear streaks on her cheeks. *Crap, she's been crying? I'm such an asshole.* Quickly, he settled beside her and wrapped his arms around her. His heart tried to ricochet out of his sternum when she cuddled against his chest, taking comfort instead of shoving him away. That was what he feared most: Danica getting tired of his ineptitude and bailing, like everyone always did.

"Please don't feel bad. If anything, this is my fault, and Maya's totally fine. She was laughing about it when she took Doris out for a jog."

"She probably made herself scarce to spare me further shame. Your sister is a sweetheart, and I'm—"

"Amazing," he cut in.

"I'm the only one who could end up like that, trying to be sexy."

His throat went dry, remembering just how hot and powerful she'd looked. "Trust me, if Maya hadn't been here, we'd have already done it once, and I'd be resting up for round two. You seduced the hell out of me. The timing was just off." He hesitated, wondering if this would make her feel better or worse. "It's not just you. The first time someone other than me tried to touch my junk, I almost got arrested."

She stared up at him for a few incredulous seconds. "Okay, I have to hear this story. Tell me everything."

If baring past humiliation could cheer her up, Titus would fall on that grenade. "I was a senior in high school, and I'd just realized..." Hmm, best to get it out now. Hopefully she wouldn't have a problem with it. "That I'm bi. There was a boy I'd been hanging out with, although I didn't realize I *like* liked him at the time. We took some beers to the reservoir, made out a lot, and just as he stuck his hand down my pants, there was a knock on the windows we fogged up. You can imagine the rest."

Truthfully, it had been worse than he was letting on due to

the rumors that went around in a small town. Danica stroked his cheek. "Did they call your parents?"

"My mom, thankfully. She lectured me about the beer, but she didn't say a word about anything else."

"I bet it was tough for a while. Small towns have a lot to say about that sort of thing."

Surprised, he studied her face, but he saw only warmth and kindness, regret for what he might have suffered. "It blew over. We weren't the only kids groping each other, and the QB got arrested for doping."

"Sportsball is always big drama." Softly she leaned in and kissed him on the corner of his mouth, nuzzling into his beard to find it. "Thank you. That can't be an easy memory to share, and you did it to make me feel better. I...don't deserve you."

"Why would you say that?"

For a moment, her expression was haunted, holding more secrets than he could grasp, and then her gaze heated, glittering as her look raked him from head to toe. "It would be a waste not to seize the opportunity we've been given. Don't you agree?"

Sheer longing cascaded through him. "Carpe diem," he whispered.

CHAPTER 17

DANICA CHASED THE KISS, EVEN before Titus leaned.

She saw the decision in his eyes and moved to meet him. Their lips met and clung; his were impossibly lush. Before him, she'd never made out with anyone who had a beard, and she was starting to like the opposing stimuli of soft mouth and the abrasion on her cheeks. Their tongues tasted and teased, and then he pulled his mouth away to kiss down her throat, mark her on the curve of her shoulder.

Yes, right there.

He grazed with his teeth, just strong enough, and her nipples puckered. Without hesitation, she pulled his big palm to her breast. The other, he wrapped around her hips, dragging her entire body against him. It was a clumsy move, not a practiced one, somehow sexier for all that because it felt like he wanted every part of her so much that he couldn't choose. He tried to pull away a few times and kept falling back into the kiss.

Finally, he hauled himself back and stumbled to the door, locking it for peace of mind, she assumed. And then he was back, pressing her down on the bed with greedy hands that stroked every inch of her. Danica couldn't get her breath as her excitement rose. Titus slid his hands under her dress, massaging her thighs as they kissed, but he seemed determined to tease.

"Should I get naked?" she gasped against his mouth.

"Do you want to?"

"Yes, please."

He released her long enough for them to scramble out of their clothes, and when they came together again, it was all glorious skin on skin. She shivered at how good he felt, how *right*—but she shouldn't think that way. *Just live in the moment. This is what you have with him; make the most of it.* Danica pulled him on top of her, running her hands down the firm plane of his back.

Titus groaned, and she felt the throb of his cock where it rubbed against her. "I don't know how long I can hold out."

Deliberately she shifted, working her pussy against him in slow, indulgent strokes. "Is there some reason we have to delay?"

"I wanted to kiss you all over."

If he did that, if he took his time and cherished her, how would she ever let him go? Freaking out a little over the idea, she wrapped her thighs around his hips. "Next time. I really want you, and I can't wait."

"Jesus, Danica."

A heavy flush colored his cheeks, and his eyes went lambent as he tilted her hips with one hand and stroked her pussy with the other. Then Titus licked his lips, and she couldn't have looked away from him if her life depended on it. With slow, inexorable demand, he pushed inside her, thumbing her labia apart, utterly absorbed in watching her take him. Danica couldn't stop gazing up at his face, drinking in every minute shift of his expression. The way he gasped a little when he seated fully, how he bit his lip when he began to move. And goddess, it felt good. Those sinful, smooth strokes, working her deep inside, even as he continued to caress her. Soft touches along her sides, kisses pressed into her neck as he gathered her close.

She moaned when he lifted her hips, cupping her bottom and kneading as he thrust deep and slow, rolling her against him. Danica responded helplessly, arching and tightening on him with the start of a powerful orgasm. Titus stole her breath with a ravenous kiss.

"That's it. Come for me, love. You're so beautiful like this. I can feel everything."

The endearment should have shut her whole nervous system down, but instead, her whole body went rigid as she came, fingers digging into his back. Sparks flashed in her head, and the lights flickered. *No, no, no. Not now.* As her orgasm ebbed, she got her magic under control, and she held Titus as he shuddered, filling her with heat.

"I should have told you before," he said breathlessly. "My test results, I have them. I'll show you when I can move again."

She laughed, running a gentle hand through his hair. "I believe you. And…me too. I went in this morning, and they emailed me this afternoon. We'll swap phones in a bit."

I should already be running.

Leanne had been catastrophically incorrect. No amount of sex would ever get Titus out of her system. He wasn't a bad case of viral gastroenteritis. Closing her eyes in despair, she buried her face in his shoulder and breathed him in, possibly for the last time. No matter how much it hurt, she had to stop this soon. Or it might destroy her family.

To rub salt in the wound, Titus was a professional-caliber cuddler. He spooned her and nuzzled her hair, her cheek, the nape of her neck while caressing and soothing like he could never get enough of her skin. The man smelled amazing, somehow like cinnamon, sugar, and sex; she wanted to weep over the forbidden sweetness of it.

"I wish you could stay," he whispered eventually, "but I have to leave ridiculously early tomorrow, and I suspect you don't want me dropping you off at 3 a.m."

That much was true. Moving slow underneath an avalanche of regret, Danica got dressed. As promised, they showed each other the emails proving that their impulsive trysts wouldn't have unpleasant consequences, and then Titus pulled on a worn gray T-shirt and torn jeans. Casual and just fucked, the man was smoking hot.

Dammit.

"Ready," she said.

Though she wasn't, not really. Not by a long shot. The mood was quiet as he escorted her to his Nissan Leaf and opened the door, a proper gentleman until the end. Even if they'd just banged like bunnies, and it had been more of a booty call than a proper date. For a while, they drove in silence until Titus finally broke it.

"Are you okay?"

She aimed a sideways glance at him, drinking in his profile. "Why?"

"You're not saying much. I'm afraid you're afflicted with hookup remorse."

His word choice stung a bit. *Is that what this was for him?* If so, maybe she didn't need to feel bad about getting off and getting out.

With effort, she tried to shake the bleak mood. "No, I'm good. How could I regret sex as awesome as that?"

"Really?"

Danica raised a brow. "Are you seriously fishing for compliments after the fact? It was pretty evident that you rocked my world."

Titus cleared his throat, and when he spoke, he still sounded strangled. "I did? Wow. Okay, that's...excellent feedback."

He seemed strangely startled by the revelation. Had prior partners not praised him? Just thinking about him with someone else pissed her off, and she crossed her arms, irritated with herself for being jealous when she had no right to be with him in the first place. By the time they pulled up outside her place, she was calm, at least.

Only the house was lit up like Clem was throwing a hell of a party, and she recognized all the cars parked in the drive and on the street. It wasn't time for their regular coven meeting, but everyone was gathered nonetheless. *Looks like a magical intervention.* Or she hoped it was that and not an emergency related to the witch hunter.

Her heart racing, she turned to Titus. "Thanks for dropping me off."

"It looks like you have friends over."

"I guess so. Clem must've felt like being social. I'd invite you in, but..." Hell, she couldn't even come up with a good excuse.

Judging by the way his face fell, he agreed. "No, I get it. You probably aren't ready for me to hang out with your friends." His tone, though, goddess, his tone ached with sadness.

This is a terrible idea, especially when I'm breaking it off. I shouldn't. But she couldn't let him drive off thinking she saw him as a fuck boy. Not when he was everything she wanted and couldn't have.

"It's not that," she said. The reason to explain her hesitance arrived in a burst of brilliance. "I'm afraid they've been drinking. They might try to get you to strip." Leanne, definitely, Vanessa, probably. Ethel, maybe. Priya and Kerry would leave him alone. Margie was a sweetheart even under the influence, and Clem had a mean streak. "Just keep your clothes on, okay?"

Now he looked amused and mildly alarmed, much better than the hurt from before. "Thanks for the heads-up. I'll run if they get handsy."

Titus rolled his shoulders as he came around to open Danica's car door.

He hadn't realized he was tense until it seemed like she was icing him out. But really, he was always watching her, waiting for some sign that she was like everyone else—that she already had a foot out the door. There had to be something about him, something that drove people away. Nobody apart from his sister and his dog seemed to think he was worth sticking around for, and it didn't matter how much he did at the station or how much he gave back to the community. Good deeds kept him busy, but they didn't earn him love.

Honestly, it was funny that she was worried about her friends perving on him during girls' night. He could handle some of that, as long as Danica came with the mild drunken harassment. He didn't seriously think she'd let anyone grope him, but still. Her concern was endearing.

She climbed out of the car and beckoned. "Let's go. I'm sure there's food. As I recall, I didn't even let you eat dinner."

Titus chuckled as his stomach rumbled on cue. "I'm not sorry about the delay, but I *am* starving now."

Inside, there was music playing, a pop singer with a catchy hook, and he heard a lot of women talking. Danica called out, "I'm home. Titus is with me!"

He didn't think the announcement was *that* momentous, but the music cut off, and a slew of women crowded into the front room. Though he hadn't put much thought into what Danica's friends would be like, this group was more diverse than he would've expected. Clem stood near the back, arms folded, and, yeah, her stare was confrontational, bordering on hostile. He remembered Kerry and Priya from the fire call, and the rest of the women seemed familiar, like maybe he'd seen them around town.

"Nice to meet you," he said, shifting a little under the intense scrutiny.

Danica shot a look at her cousin that he couldn't interpret, then she said, "Let me make the introductions. This is Ethel." She indicated a curvaceous woman in her late sixties or early seventies with silver pixie-style hair. She wore a flowing rayon dress, lots of beads, and bright-pink lipstick.

"Charmed," Ethel said, extending a hand.

He shook it instead of kissing it, but from the old woman's expression, maybe that was the wrong call. He turned as Danica pointed out everyone else. Margie was in her forties with medium-brown hair and tired eyes. Vanessa was dark-skinned with pretty braids and delicate bracelets marching up one arm. He nodded to Kerry and Priya, whom he'd met before, while Leanne undressed him with her eyes. Now he saw why Danica had been worried. Leanne had red hair, a spray tan, and she looked like she wanted to eat him on a cracker. Danica put a plate in his hand, and he ate absently, listening to multiple conversations—work, child support, books, and vacation plans. He wished his poker nights were this entertaining.

Danica went into the kitchen with Ethel and seemed to be buying some sachet bags. That was sweet, likely serving to augment her friend's fixed income. Or maybe she just really liked making her clothes smell delightful. *He* certainly appreciated it.

"Nice to meet everyone," he said eventually. "Since I don't want to intrude further, I'll let you get back to ladies' night."

Leanne winked at him, swirling some wine in his general direction. "Why not stick around? Every night is ladies' night."

Oh damn.

"You're not encouraging him to drink and drive?" Danica cut in sternly.

The redhead smirked. "Not at all. He can drink as much as he wants and then sleep it off in your bed. Problem solved."

"Tempting as that sounds, I have to be up at an ungodly hour. I wouldn't subject Danica to that this early in our relationship." But one day? Maybe he'd have to worry about how to sneak out of their shared bed without waking her.

I'd love to have that problem.

"Understood," Margie answered, offering him a genuinely kind smile. "It was such a pleasure to meet you."

A chorus of "Take care" and "Bye, CinnaMan" followed as Danica walked him to the door. "Whew. That wasn't as bad as it could've been," she said.

Smiling, he bent and kissed her cheek. "They seem like a fun group. I love that you don't discriminate by age either."

To his surprise, Danica responded quite seriously. "Never. We all learn *so* much from Ethel. She's a treasure."

"I'll see you soon."

It was hard to make himself go, but he was doing so much better this time around. Not letting himself become obsessive or needy or clingy. If he kept it up, there was a good chance that this could work out. *The curse is all in my head. There's no earthly reason I can't have a normal relationship, date like everyone else.*

Proving the universe could be merciful, Maya didn't tease him when he got home. She was in front of the TV with a bowl of popcorn, and she waved as he went past and up the stairs. He needed a shower in the worst way. Afterward, he played with Doris in the backyard, and just before ten, he went to bed early, as he always did.

The morning breezed by as usual, and Maya took her lunch break at noon, like normal. As she stepped out of the bakery, a pretty young Black woman greeted her with a kiss on the mouth, and they walked off holding hands. Finally he had confirmation that Maya was seeing someone; she was squirrelly about sharing private details these days, and he had his suspicions as to why. Titus hoped Maya would introduce her girlfriend soon.

Just then the bell tinkled as someone came into the shop. *The rush must be starting already.* He pinned on a smile that faded as soon as he recognized the asshole who'd wrecked the place before. Only this time, he seemed…different, somehow.

"I came to apologize," the man said politely. "And to recompense you for the property damage. Will five hundred dollars suffice?"

Titus stared. This jerk had a thick wad in his wallet when he didn't look like he had two nickels to scrape together. What the hell? He must be involved in shady shit to carry that much cash. *I want him gone.* Really, everything about this dude rubbed him the wrong way, but he couldn't call the sheriff on someone trying to make amends.

Shaking his head, he pushed three of the bills back across the counter. "Two hundred covers the cost of the repairs, but I'd rather have an apology."

"I'm truly sorry. That day, I was exhausted and, frankly, not right in the head. I ought to have gone to bed instead of… Well, you know what I did."

"Yeah, well, everyone has an off day now and then." None of his had ever made him run into a store yelling about witches, though.

"Fantastic! You're the forgiving sort. If you're really over it and we're good, maybe you'd be willing to have a beer later?"

Is he asking me out? Or is this an "olive branch" sort of beer?

Titus hesitated. Either way, he wasn't super into it, but in the end, Midwestern politeness won out. *Maybe I'll call Trevor in case this dude thinks he can roofie me and steal a kidney and half my liver.* "Sounds fine. Mind if I bring a friend?"

"The more the merrier. I'll be drinking at O'Reilly's tonight." The big guy's easy acceptance reassured him.

Maybe it truly was just a shit day when he snapped. *It doesn't seem like he has an agenda.* More like he was offering a free beer in addition to the cash as an afterthought.

Titus made a sudden decision, extending his hand in a friendly gesture. "I'm Titus Winnaker. I don't think it was my fault that we got off on the wrong foot, but I'm willing to start over if you are."

"Gavin Rhys." A firm handshake, given by a man who'd done plenty of manual labor. "And I admit it was all my doing. Glad you aren't holding it against me, as I might be staying in St. Claire for a while."

"Oh yeah?"

Before Gavin could answer, the bell chimed again, announcing Mrs. Carminian. She sashayed in wearing a fuchsia velour track-suit. "Good day, boys!" She took a long look at Gavin and then fanned herself. "This bakery is the hottest place in town, I swear."

"I'll check the air conditioning. What can I get for you?" Titus asked.

"That's my cue," the other man said. "Later, mate."

Mrs. Carminian pretended to swoon as he left. "That accent! Tell me he's single. My granddaughter is visiting and—"

"Your order?" he prompted.

"Right, I'll find out somewhere else. You're the worst at gossip."

Maybe that was true, but he was the *best* at overthinking, and he couldn't shake reluctant curiosity about what would keep a guy like Gavin Rhys in St. Claire.

CHAPTER 18

"HI, MOM!" MINERVA'S CALL TOOK Danica's mind off Clem's uncertain temper at least.

"Hey, Little Star. Everything good in your world?"

"Not entirely. There's a witch hunter in town." Before her mom could panic, Danica added, "Clem's handling it. We're okay, don't worry."

"Do you want me to come?" Mom asked.

"No, we've got this." Without magic, her mom would be safe, but that also meant she couldn't offer much help. There was no need for her to make the trip again so soon.

"If you're sure. Have you talked to your grandmother?"

Danica shook her head, momentarily forgetting that it wasn't a video call. "No, but I'm sure Gladys told her. The woman knows everything that happens in St. Claire."

"True enough. Gladys says the trees whisper secrets."

She blinked. "Is that possible?"

"Who knows? Every witch has a different relationship with her major affinity."

Just then a customer came in. "I have to go, Mom. Talk to you later."

She took a toaster oven in back and fixed it while the woman waited. Clem had already left for the day.

All day at work, Danica had flinched at every fulminating look, but Clem held it in. Danica didn't look forward to what awaited her at home, and sure enough, when she walked in the front door, she found her cousin highly irate. Pacing, Clem wore a stormy expression, and she compressed her mouth like she didn't trust herself to speak. For like five minutes, Danica watched this display until she couldn't take it anymore.

"I was hoping you'd calm down if I let you be, but you're like a double boiler right now. Just spit it out. Whatever it is, we'll figure it out."

"Gram *knows*."

Instant ice formed in her veins. "Oh shit. What happened?"

"She ambushed me outside the shop, asking about Titus, and when I tried to obfuscate, she said, 'Never mind, I'll take care of it.' Trust me, you do not want Gram paying attention to him. There's no telling what she might do."

"Fuck."

Now she understood why Clem was so upset. When Gram interfered, it was never fun, less so for Titus. While the woman had invested her power in the spellbook that was currently malfunctioning, she had lots of connections, and many witches owed her favors. Her cousin wheeled on her.

"Exactly! I told you to end it. I told you! But now we've got a witch hunter in town, a problem *I* have to deal with, Gram's on a tear, and you're introducing your mundane boyfriend to the coven? What's wrong with you lately?"

When her faults were listed like that, Danica felt like shit. She felt her lips tremble, and goddess, she didn't want to cry because Clem would accuse her of doing it to get sympathy, but everything was so screwed up. And her cousin was right.

It's my fault.

"I'm sorry," she whispered.

Seeing how sad Danica was seemed to mitigate Clem's anger somewhat. Her cousin rounded the couch and sat beside her. She set a gentle hand on Danica's shoulder. "The time for self-indulgence has passed. You know that, right? It's time for damage control, and that means putting some distance between you and Titus immediately."

Danica hiccupped, trying to staunch the flood of tears. "I know. S-sorry. It's so dumb, being this upset over someone I haven't been seeing that long, but Clem, he's...*perfect.*"

With a muffled curse, her cousin offered a hug and let Danica cry it out. Clem mumbled something that Danica didn't quite catch; it somehow sounded like "Tell me about it." But when she asked for clarification, Clem shook her head.

"Never mind. We can talk about my problems another time."

"Did you meet the witch hunter, by the way?"

For a moment, Clem looked startled, almost guilty, and her gaze cut away, over Danica's left shoulder. "Uh, yeah. I definitely did."

"He doesn't suspect, right?"

"Please, who am I? Of course not. I made it look like the usual bar pickup."

"How did you track him down?" Anxiously, she imagined

the witch hunter finding them because Clem had searched for him magically.

"It was easy. I stopped by the fire station during coffee klatch and followed the senior gossip. Apparently he likes to drink at O'Reilly's."

She had to admit that was clever. O'Reilly's was a dive on the way out of town, a white building with a deck and plenty of free parking. The owner, Tim O'Reilly, called it a pub, but it was a regular bar, decorated by someone who had never been to Ireland or a pub. The beer was decent, the music was terrible, but the pool tables were pretty fun.

Biting her lip, she studied her cousin's closed expression. "I'm worried about you. How far will you go to distract him?"

"Does it make sense for you to focus on me right now? You've got Gram in town, wild magic, a mundane boyfriend to let down easy, and—"

"Okay, stop listing my problems, please. I get the point. And I'll listen to you from now on, I promise."

"About time," Clem muttered. "I just hope it's not too late."

"Why isn't the spellbook working?" That was on her mind a lot, and deep down, she feared it was because she was already losing her powers, the Waterhouse curse kicking in.

"Who knows?" Her cousin gave her a one-armed hug.

"What's the hunter like anyway?"

"His name's Gavin Rhys. He's big, angry, got a great ass and strangely compelling eyes. Very into mouthy brunettes." Clem winked as she stood up. "And I need to get ready because I'm meeting him later."

"Be careful," Danica said.

Her cousin waved a dismissive hand, jogging up the stairs presumably to turn herself into a walking wet dream. Normally, Danica would be up there, sitting on the bed, offering wardrobe suggestions, but this wasn't a normal date, and she couldn't treat the risk Clem was taking lightly. Imagine how furious Rhys would be if he figured out Clem had played him. Witch hunters were stern and allegedly incorruptible. He might well snatch her cousin and disappear her into the labyrinth of hunter justice.

"Maybe I should go with you?" she called.

"Hell no," Clem yelled back. "He's looking for you in particular, dumbass. There's a chance you'll ping his radar, no matter how well you're shielded. I'd rather not risk it."

"Fine."

Eventually, her cousin came down in a sleek red dress that didn't look like much until she turned; nearly her entire back was exposed, with little beaded ropes that swayed gracefully against her spine holding the garment together. She wore no jewelry, but her makeup was on point with focus on eyes and lips. She'd chosen retro-sexy shoes, red-and-white lace-up Mary Jane pumps with thin heels. All told, Clem looked like a witch who meant to slay.

"Wow," she said.

Her cousin twirled. "Right? Honestly, he'll be lucky to remember his own name when I'm done with him."

Danica bit her tongue, restraining more cautionary words. Since she was the reason they were in this mess in the first place, it hardly made sense for her to rein in Clem. Soon after her cousin left, her phone buzzed with a two-word message from Gram. Call me. Ice surged in her bloodstream again, but delaying the confrontation would only make matters worse. Maybe she could calm her grandmother if she responded promptly.

Taking a deep breath, she put the call through, giving thanks that she no longer found her grandmother's face peering out of her cereal bowl. The old witch answered on the second ring. "We need to talk."

That never goes anywhere good.

Still, she tried to feign innocence. "About what?"

"Your current dalliance," Gram said sharply.

Wow, what a word.

"It's not cool to spy on me." Danica came out strong, knowing this was a lost cause.

"People tell me things when I'm visiting. I can't help that." Surprisingly, her grandmother's voice softened. "I know how it is to be young and impetuous, my dear, but I can't permit you to ruin your life as your mother did. Please understand…if I seem harsh, it's because I don't want to see you throw away your power and our family's heritage over a momentary infatuation. I want you to experience how beautiful it is to live a full life, partnered with a witch who can bolster your magic and touch your very soul. I only interfere for your own good."

She sighed. "I know. I'm sorry."

"I've lived longer than you, Danica, seen so much that you can't even imagine. Maybe mundanes seem harmless. But remember, they murdered over fifty thousand of us openly during the trials, and it's been twice that since the hunters went underground. The executions are private now, only after they torture us and try to get us to admit we're in league with the dark one and give up our sisters and brothers. We can't forget. We can't *ever* forget that they loathe and fear us, and if your Titus knew the truth, he'd turn from you in an instant. With him, you can never live as your true self. Is that what you want?"

The words hammered like nails into Danica's flesh, and she hated how conflicted she felt, even now. She let out a shuddering breath. "I know. And I'll take care of it."

Her grandmother's tone firmed to a quiet promise. "See that you do, dear. Or *I* will."

After work, Titus called Trevor, mostly because he was his best friend, but also because he wouldn't have other plans. Dante had shared custody of his little girl, Miguel was married, and Calvin worked a lot. "Feel like drinking tonight?"

"You buying?"

"Yes, you asshole. I'll pick up the tab."

"Then absolutely! Can you drive too? The lawn maintenance industry is in a downturn, and I'm a little short on gas money."

Titus tried not to laugh. He would bet that Trevor had spent his cash on weed instead and had smoked away the last of his customers, mostly elderly neighbors who could easily find someone else to cut their grass. There was no reason to point out the flaws in his entrepreneurial strategy, however.

"No problem. I'll be there in an hour or so."

That gave him time to shower, change clothes, and spend some time with Doris. Maya wasn't home; she usually went somewhere after making the bank deposit, and now he guessed she was with her girlfriend. Titus chose his dog as the first order of business and threw the tennis ball in the backyard for a good half an hour; then he roughhoused with her and rubbed her belly.

"Be good, okay? I'll set your dinner on a timer."

It probably made him ridiculous that he worried about his dog feeling lonely as she ate, but he went out so rarely that he shouldn't feel guilty tonight. He'd spent more than half his allotted time on Doris, so he rushed his shower and got dressed in a hurry. Nothing special since he was just getting a beer with Trevor and that weird guy.

Trev was waiting out front in ratty jeans, a Bob Marley shirt, and a beanie. *Who even still wears those?* Obviously, the answer was Trevor. At least Trev had gotten rid of the dreadlocks. White guys should never, ever wear them; a fact he'd spent like six months trying to explain. Now his old friend had a 'do that reminded him of Brad Pitt in that old movie where he played an absolute stoner. Damn if he could remember the name.

True Romance, that was it. That was the only Tarantino film he could stomach. *Watched that one because Mom liked it.*

He waved as Trevor ambled down the walk and got in the Leaf. "Bro, this car—"

"Don't start. I'm not the one trapped at home for lack of gas money."

"Okay, fair. So where are we headed?"

"O'Reilly's. There's a guy who wants to buy me a beer." Quickly he laid out what went down the other day, and by the end, Trev was shaking his head.

"Sounds like he was tripping balls, man. Maybe he got ahold of some bad shit."

"Maybe."

"That why you invited me out, in case he flips again? Maybe I should remind you that I'm a lover, not a fighter."

Titus laughed. "Okay, asshole, but surely you can film me getting my ass kicked and maybe dial 911?"

His friend aimed an easy smile at him. "That I can do."

Since it was early when they arrived, the bar was half empty, and they ordered burgers and onions rings for dinner. Most of the food was crap here—even the pizzas came frozen—but their fried meat tasted decent. Part of him was relieved when he thought Rhys might have flaked, but then the other man strode in, larger than life. He waved and headed straight for their booth.

"Here we go," said Trevor.

"Hey," Titus said to Rhys and then made quick introductions.

"What're we drinking?" Rhys asked. "I've got the next round."

"Bud is cheap and plentiful." His friend raised his mug.

Honestly, Titus had never much cared for the stuff, and from the way Rhys twisted his mouth, he agreed. "I'll see what they've got in bottles."

Shortly Rhys returned to the table with Sam Adams Boston Lager. "Hell if this isn't the best they could do. Cheers, lads."

With a shrug, Titus took the free beer. He knocked back a swallow, relaxing a fraction. This dude didn't seem to be after anything in particular. Maybe he could take the goodwill offer at face value.

"Thanks," Titus said.

"What's there to do for fun in this town?"

"You're looking at it," Trev said. "Oh, there's bowling, I guess. Or a dollar movie? If you're feeling reckless, you could visit one of our eight churches."

Rhys laughed. "Seriously? Eight?"

"You're not from around here, but we're Bible-Belt adjacent," Titus said.

"Right, I'll pass on the religion, but..." He trailed off, and Titus followed his gaze to the front door, where Danica's cousin Clem stood, dressed to kill in a red dress. "If I'm lucky, maybe I'll see God before I go."

Trevor had been finishing his burger with single-minded attention, and he swiveled in the booth to see what was drawing both their eyes. "Damn. I didn't know there was anybody *that* hot in the whole town."

Irrationally, Titus felt like bragging about Danica, but it would probably be a dick move to do that when they were admiring her cousin. With effort, he kept his mouth shut. "I guess you're taking off?" he said to Rhys.

"Correct. I've a prior engagement, and I wouldn't want to disappoint someone so eager for my company. Bought the beer like I promised. No hard feelings?"

"We're good," Titus said.

He and Trevor shot the shit while nursing their beers, finishing their burgers and onion rings. After that, they played a few rounds of pool, lingering a couple of hours to make sure those beers metabolized. Liquor wasn't his preferred vice, Trev's either, so they headed out without ordering more, and Titus felt fine, good to drive.

"That was surprisingly chill," Trev said as he slid into the Leaf.

"Yeah, we should hang out more often."

"I'm glad you didn't get your ass kicked."

Titus laughed. "Same."

After dropping his friend off, he drove home thoughtfully, wondering if Danica knew about her cousin's new love interest. It wasn't his place to meddle, though, even if the guy had seemed slightly unstable at first. *Maybe I should mention it.* He didn't know if Clem had noticed him since she'd been on Rhys like red paint on a barn, but if she had, Danica might wonder why he didn't mention seeing her cousin tonight.

Damn, I'm overthinking again.

As soon as he pulled into the driveway, he fired off a quick text. Saw Clem at O'Reilly's. With the guy who broke the register. Miss you.

Maybe the last line was too much? Ah well, no point in regrets now. He'd already hit send. Doris greeted him at the door as if he'd been gone for days, and he crouched to rub her from head to toe, getting so much love that he could wallow in it.

"You're back?" Maya called.

Something about her voice alarmed him. Giving the dog a pat, he stood and strode into the living room, where his sister was sitting mostly in the dark, hugging a pillow to her chest like she did when she was upset. It was a defensive habit, one she'd learned as a little kid. The TV wasn't even on, not a good sign.

"What happened?" he asked. "Did Dad call again?"

Since he wasn't supposed to know that Maya had a girlfriend, he couldn't ask if they'd had a fight. It was more probable that the old man was causing trouble, guilting her and making unreasonable demands. Gently he put a hand on her shoulder.

Maya shook her head. "It's just...I've been thinking about what he said."

"You can't let him get to you. That's just how he is. It sucks, but—"

"No, some of what he says is right," she cut in unexpectedly.

That was the last thing he expected to hear. Titus sat back, angling his body into the corner of the couch to face her. "What?"

Doris nudged against his leg, evidently sensing his distress. Absently he put out a hand and rubbed her head when she settled close protectively. He was glad she didn't leap up onto his lap like she sometimes did. But honestly, Doris did a better job of reading the room than many people did, and she could probably sense his tension.

"We're mad at Dad, and we're not giving Susan a chance. If we blow her off while she's pregnant, she may not let us have a relationship with baby Aubrey. And Titus, that kid's part of our family." Maya squared her shoulders. "I think...we have to close the shop for a few and go to Arizona for the baby shower."

CHAPTER 19

"SHIT," DANICA SAID, STARING AT her cousin with wide eyes.

A chill crawled slowly over her skin, sinking in with the deepest foreboding. She rubbed her palms over her forearms, trying to will the feeling away. But it was no use. The dread was real and profound as she analyzed the implications of what Clem had said about seeing Gavin Rhys with Titus at O'Reilly's the night before.

"I think—"

"The hunter is trying a new tactic?" she guessed.

Clem nodded. "It's the only thing that makes sense. First he wrecks Titus's shop, and then he's buying him a beer? He must have figured that the aggro approach didn't work, so he's decided to make nice and observe him up close, see who he spends time with. It's a smart way to track us down."

Danica shivered. Before, the idea of a hunter had been bothersome in the abstract, but now it added another layer of fear to an already-tense situation. *I have enough to worry about with Gram getting involved.* Part of her brain was already imagining what it would be like, being dragged off by a hunter. Since they couldn't do public trials anymore, their justice would be swift and terrible, conducted in private, with her body never to be found.

"I'm so sorry. This is all my fault."

It wouldn't have surprised her if Clem had said *I told you so* yet again, but her cousin hugged her instead. "Hey, I'm the one who said we should use the grimoire. That first spell went wildly wrong, so I'm at fault too. And really, it doesn't matter who did what anymore. We should focus on mitigation."

She's being nice.

While that was technically true, any spells that misfired on their home ground couldn't have drawn the attention of a witch hunter because of the protective wards in place. Still, Danica let that go because Clem was trying to absolve her. And it would be ungrateful and pedantic to insist on taking all the blame when her cousin was being magnanimous. She smiled slightly.

"Okay, fair point. I'm worried about you, though. How do you know—"

"Don't worry about me. I've got this. I'm keeping Rhys distracted. You concentrate on keeping your magic under control and handle Gram if you can."

She winced. "Easier said than done. I'll avoid Titus until I can figure out what to say."

And how to say it.

Since they'd never officially gotten together, it couldn't be a straightforward breakup. If she knew Titus, however, he wouldn't be content until he understood why she didn't want to see him anymore. And that would be damned hard to explain since she did want to see him—quite desperately, in fact. Making matters worse, she sucked at lying, and he always seemed to read her effortlessly.

I wonder if the "it's not you, it's me" speech would work.

Just then, her phone buzzed. Sorry to drop this on you out of the blue. Talked to Maya & she thinks we should go to the baby shower. Long story short, we're on the red-eye tonight cos my dad's cheap. The bakery will be closed for a few days. (Hope we don't lose all our customers.) Miss me a little?

Clem had been scanning her face as she read. "What now? More bad news?"

"More like…the universe cut me a break." Rather than explain, she shifted her phone so her cousin could read the message.

"That gives us some breathing room," Clem said with an approving smile. "And it's easier for me to distract the hunter if he's not trying to run surveillance on Titus."

With a groan, Danica let her head fall back against the sofa. "I don't love that you're doing this. How are you so *calm*? One wrong move and—"

"You know I'm all about precision and planning. He's dancing to my tune every step of the way. Trust me, I'm enjoying this." From her grim smile, that might even be true. "And speaking of which, I'm supposed to meet him tonight. Don't wait up."

Before Danica could object, Clem made a beeline out the door. This worried her on multiple levels. If anyone got caught, it could lead to others in the coven being snatched as well. With effort, she pushed down the panic and replied to Titus with a series of emojis. She couldn't leave him on read; that would be cruel and unusual. But she had no words either, hence—heart, octopus, airplane, cactus.

Probably she should meet Gram and try to sweeten her up. Their last call had ended on a sour note with what she took as a threat. *I can't let anything bad happen to Titus.* But she couldn't make herself reach out because her grandmother would ask if she had resolved the situation, and in truth, she hadn't. She'd never been able to lie to Gram either.

In the end, she took a long bath and went to bed early. The next morning, she woke up to Goliath crying on her front porch. Danica leaned her head against the inside of the front door as Clem laughed at her. She didn't know what time her cousin had gotten in, and she didn't ask either.

"That cat really loves you. Maybe you should see a doctor, get some pills for the allergic reaction, and just adopt him. Hazel won't live forever."

"Clementine Waterhouse!"

Her cousin made an innocent face. "What? Is it too early for me to say true things?"

"It would serve you right if I took him in and taught him to pee in your shoes."

Muttering darkly, she went out onto the porch and called Hazel. The fool ginger jumped up on the porch swing, making it sway, and promptly fell over, waving all four paws in invitation. His belly was white and fluffy, and unlike most cats, this wasn't an adorable trap. Goliath would hug her hand, but he didn't bite. Sometimes she gave in to temptation and rubbed his tummy until he practically purred himself into pudding.

"Why do you love me so much, huh? Why?"

Goliath regarded her with devoted, unblinking eyes as if to

say, *You already know.* She sighed, noticing that he'd somehow gotten his camera collar off. Ten minutes later, the old woman finally showed to reclaim her cat, making all the usual complaints. She propped one arm on her hip, the other cradling Goliath over her shoulder.

"I don't believe for one minute that you aren't doing something to cause this," Hazel snapped. "There's no other explanation. This just isn't…normal."

Shit, that's the last thing I want her saying around town with a hunter sniffing about.

"Maybe it's not me. I've read that cats get attached to places. They start feeling territorial, so maybe Goliath thinks the whole zone around your house is his to patrol?"

Did that sound plausible?

Hazel stared at Goliath for a few seconds, and then she squashed his furry face between her palms, baby talking on full auto. "Huh. Is that true, wookums? Does the whole neighborhood belong to you? Is that what you think, my little king?"

"Did you ever figure out how he's getting out?"

"Goliath only wore that expensive piece of junk for an hour. Then he squirmed out of it and hid it somewhere. David looked at the footage, but it's just Goliath prancing around the house. That was a complete waste of time and money." Hazel scowled and flounced away, as if that was Danica's fault too somehow.

Goliath gave an anguished look over Hazel's shoulder, but Danica didn't intervene. Instead, she dashed inside feeling like she'd dodged a bullet. She didn't have to work until later, and Clem had left at some point while she was dealing with Goliath and Hazel. Exercise might clear her head, so she decided to go for a leisurely bike ride before her shift.

The weather was perfect for it, not too hot yet, only the problem with pedaling on automatic was that her course took her right to the bakery. Which was thankfully closed while Titus and Maya were in Arizona. A sign on the front door read CLOSED THIS WEEKEND FOR PERSONAL REASONS. They weren't open on Sunday anyway, so they'd only lose today and Saturday. *And why am I thinking about this? It's not my business.*

Movement registered in her peripheral vision, and she caught someone hurrying away down the alley. Chasing them would be suspicious; just as well she didn't need to. Because she could *feel* the energy rippling over the shop, a powerful hex designed to drive away customers. She hadn't *seen* the witch, but this had Gram written all over it. Though she was in town, it wasn't her style to do such things personally, even if she'd still had sufficient power. No, she preferred calling in favors.

Glancing around to make sure nobody was paying attention, Danica quickly purged the spell. Then she worked a cleansing to strip away any signs of the working from her person. This was risky as fuck, but she couldn't leave that hex in place to dig into Titus's business and erode his customer base for no good reason. Hexes were like burrs; the deeper they sunk in, the more difficult it was to root them out.

Danica spun and nearly slammed into the witch hunter, Gavin Rhys. *No, I'm not supposed to know his name. Dammit, I hope I didn't screw up again.* Her heart pounded like a drum in the middle of a Wagner symphony.

She forced a friendly smile, tipping her head back to meet his intent, silver-gray gaze. "Sorry, I didn't see you there. Looks like the bakery is closed."

The curve of his lips didn't reach his eyes. "So it is. But I found what I'm looking for, and it wasn't cinnamon rolls."

"This is hell on earth," Titus whispered to Maya.

His sister nodded, her smile so plastic that it might have been melted into her face. "The weather certainly supports that theory."

No joke, the temperature spiked over a hundred early on with the heat index even higher, and stepping outside felt like immersing themselves in a dry-heat sauna. It was weird to live like that, running from air con to air con. If he couldn't go outside to play with Doris... Titus winced, thinking of how sad his dog had been when he'd left. At least Trevor had agreed to hang out at their place, give the dog her food, and play with her in the backyard.

They had been saying all the right things all day. They'd arrived at five in the morning, local time, and were functioning on precious little sleep. The damned house was overflowing with people they didn't know, and Susan had been so busy opening presents and beaming at anyone who spoke to her that she didn't even seem to realize they were there.

To make matters worse, Dad was casual about the whole thing. He'd even said, "Oh, I'm so glad you decided to come after all," like he hadn't issued an ultimatum.

Like it was our choice.

Titus crammed a corn dog bite into his mouth and chewed

angrily. They had played some dumb games and pretended to enjoy them. *How much longer will this damn thing run?* He wanted to escape for ten minutes to call Danica, but not if it meant leaving Maya alone. Jared was still giving Maya the eye every chance he got.

How does Dad not see this?

"Ugh," he said, only moving his mouth a little.

His lips might well be frozen in this fake smile as he fielded random congratulations and people speculating whether it was a boy or a girl. Susan was telling anyone who would listen that they wouldn't force anything on the baby. Little Aubrey would wear green and yellow until they were old enough to express a preference. His dad made a face over this pronouncement, but he had the sense not to contradict. Titus thought Susan had a point, and he was less mad at her, overall, than at his old man.

"We just have to get through tomorrow night," Maya whispered then.

Their return flight was another red-eye, getting them back just in time for him to begin work. If this weekend was shit, Monday would be even worse. He wouldn't have done this for anyone but Maya. His sister thought this was the right move, so here he was, pissed at the world and missing Danica.

Dad and Susan lived in Gilbert, and their house was typical Arizona style, all white and beige, inside and out. It was modern, lots of windows, with arches instead of doorways. The outside was desert landscaped with palm trees, cacti, rocks, and wood chips, more environmentally responsible than trying to grow a lawn. Titus hated everything about this place, not least the open floor plan and how there was no privacy. Dad and Susan wouldn't let them stay at a hotel, but instead, he and Maya were sleeping on air mattresses, crashing with Jared and Lucy in their respective rooms.

The good part about that was, at least he could keep an eye on that asshole at night. Jared was headed to college at the end of August, vacating his room before the baby was due. That would give them six months to redecorate. Jared might not have a place to sleep next summer, not that Titus gave a damn. When he checked his plate, he realized he'd rage-chewed through all his food, tasting none of it.

Lucy was a quiet girl with brown hair bobbed short, freckles, and glasses that gave her a Velma Dinkley vibe. She joined Titus and Maya in leaning on the island, hiding out in the kitchen, though that was a misnomer. *Open fucking floor plans.* This house had no doors, apart from bedrooms and bathrooms. *Nothing like our house. It's like Dad wants to burn out those memories, replace them entirely.*

"Are you guys excited?" Lucy ventured softly.

He tried to come up with a diplomatic response. "It's a lot to take in."

As ever, Maya went the extra mile. "Yeah, especially for you. I mean, you've always been the youngest, and now suddenly you'll be an older sister. Are you okay with that?"

The girl hunched her shoulders. "Does it matter? I'm basically invisible anyway."

Shit. Suddenly, Titus felt like the world's biggest asshole. If it was bad on his end, seeing his dad rewrite history, at least he was independent. *I have a home waiting for me. Lucy has no choice but to put up with their crap.* From what he knew, Susan had been a single mom for years, and her ex was out of the picture. Plus, he had no clue if Lucy even got along with Jared—and he was leaving at the end of the summer anyway—so it must be like she'd lost her mom and she had nobody in her corner. Some people claimed being a teenager was awesome, but he knew better. It meant being old enough to realize how fucked up certain things were while having no power to impact them. All the anxiety of adulthood and none of the control, worst of both worlds.

Knowing he might regret the answer, he asked anyway. "Is it that bad?"

"It's worse. Half the time, they don't even know I'm here. I stayed out two nights last week, and they didn't even notice. My online friends are all like, *Damn, this rocks, you can do whatever you want,* but..."

"No, that sucks." Maya put an arm around Lucy and suggested with her eyebrows that Titus make a move, though he had no idea what she expected him to do.

Hesitantly, he patted Lucy on the shoulder. "How much school do you have left?"

"Two years. Jared got an athletic scholarship, swimming. Otherwise I don't know how he would've gone to college. His grades are shit." Lucy pulled off her glasses and rubbed her eyes, but she didn't pull away from Maya. "I don't even know why I'm telling you this. I'm aware that you don't like any of us."

Titus swapped a look with Maya, edged with a wince. *Great, we hurt a kid who's already in a crappy place.* Then he said, "I don't know you or your mom that well."

To his surprise, Lucy laughed. "You didn't mention my asshole brother."

Maya smirked. "No. No, he did not."

Maybe he'd regret this, but it was the right thing to do. Even without conferring with Maya, Titus knew she'd agree. "Look, if things become untenable here, for whatever reason, call us. My dad is right on one point. We're family now. I'll get you a plane ticket and pick you up in Chicago. We can get you in school in St. Claire, and you can help at the bakery for pocket money. Or if you'd rather, you can finish high school online or get your GED."

"The point is, you have options," Maya added. "Trust me, I know fully how you feel. Like you don't matter and you're being replaced."

Lucy bit her lip. "Oh my God, seriously? You might hate having me around."

He shook his head. "I don't think so. There would be rules, though. And consequences if you don't follow them."

His stepsister grinned. "Are you offering to parent me, Titus?"

"To sibling you, anyway."

Maya hip checked Lucy as she let go. "Just wait, he'll give you a terrible nickname. That's when you'll know there's no escape from his brotherly clutches."

"Oh yeah? What's yours?"

"Tell her, Mini." Titus pretended to cower from the dirty look Maya shot him.

"Okay, that's adorable," Lucy said.

They were all laughing when Susan and Dad wandered up. Neither of them appeared to notice that they all froze or that their arrival instantly killed the mood. Instead, Susan beamed at everyone, as if she couldn't be happier. Titus didn't know if she was naturally this dense or if pregnancy had made her unusually self-absorbed.

"I'm thrilled to see you getting along so well!" She turned to Dad with an adoring smile. "See, I told you this visit was a good idea. I'm so glad I suggested it."

Suggested? Ha! No, don't make a scene. Only one day left. You can do this.

CHAPTER 20

UP CLOSE, THE WITCH HUNTER radiated intensity.

Black hair, dark stubble, strong jaw, and a nose with a bump in the ridge, as if it'd been broken multiple times. In person, his light-gray eyes were even more eerie, fringed by inky lashes. Dark ink crawled up his neck, and his hands were scarred, like he made a habit of hitting people. Or walls. Possibly both.

Probably both.

She gulped in a soft breath, but Rhys went on as if he couldn't sense Danica's panic. "You must be Clementine's cousin. She couldn't raise you on mobile, and I offered to keep an eye out. She said I couldn't miss you on the mint-green bicycle, and she was dead right."

"Oh, my phone's on silent. You know Clem, I take it?" It took all of her self-control not to tremble, and she didn't let her voice shake either.

How the hell is Clem doing this? She must have nerves of steel. Danica wanted nothing more than to escape and call Gram, demand an explanation for what she'd narrowly prevented, though she already had an inkling what the old witch would say. She fell into step with the hunter, waiting for him to respond as she pushed her bike toward the shop.

"She's been kind enough to show me the sights."

Danica laughed. "In St. Claire? I hope she took you to Star Lanes. You shouldn't miss their frozen pizza or bowling to the oldies night."

"I do enjoy a fine frozen pizza." His eyes warmed a little, the smile nearly reaching them, but Danica could tell that he was still watchful.

Maybe that's just his nature. If he was positive I'm the one he's looking for, he wouldn't be talking, that's for sure.

She grinned. "Well, they do bake it first. Did something happen at the shop?"

"That's my fault. I wanted to take her to lunch, but she said you hadn't arrived to relieve her yet, so she tried to ring you—"

"And I didn't answer."

"Which brings you up to speed," he finished.

"Understood. Then we should kick it up a notch. If I keep her waiting too long, she'll be hangry, and nobody wants that."

"You got that right."

"I'd offer you a ride on my bike, but I don't think you'd fit on the handlebars, and I'm pretty sure your legs would drag if I let you ride pillion."

A bark of startled laughter escaped him. "You might also find it difficult to pedal with my weight on the back."

"That...is true."

"Are you calling me a husky lad?"

Danica laughed. "Hey, you brought up weight, not me."

And it was indisputable that Gavin Rhys was a big man, over six feet tall. She was bad at guessing weight, and it didn't matter, except that he was basically a wall, all chest and shoulders and legs. *I wonder if Clem is really okay with distracting him?* Right now, she didn't even dislike Gavin Rhys; she only wished he hadn't bought into such bullshit ideology that painted witches as brides of the dark lord. More likely, he'd been born to a witch-hunting family, and it was tough as hell to shake beliefs indoctrinated at birth.

They made amicable small talk on the way to the shop, and outside, Rhys peered up at the sign Danica had insisted on. "That's a cute name."

"I thought so. We brainstormed forever trying to come up with a memorable brand."

"It's certainly not a name I'd forget." A certain darkness flickered in his expression; then he masked it with an adroitness that made her nervous.

"Come in, then. Or would you rather I send Clem out?"

"I'll wait. She seemed amenable to grabbing a bite at the café around the corner."

"Trust me, you'd know if she wasn't." With that, she went inside and found Clem wiping down the appliances they had for sale out front. "He's waiting for you," she said, not trusting herself to offer more.

Her cousin only nodded and slung her silver-mirrored tote over one shoulder. "I'll be home late. Don't wait up."

Danica grabbed her phone and called Gram. Finally. It only made things worse when her grandmother let the call roll to voicemail.

She never does this. It must be serious. Her own anger edged with fear, she called four more times but only left the one message.

Around five, the old witch finally called back, her voice overly sweet. "Something you need, dear? I was helping Gladys in the garden." That was the name of the friend who'd rented a room to Gram for the summer.

That was probably a lie. Unlike Mom, Gram had less of a green thumb than Clem or Danica, and they were slowly killing all their houseplants with the best of intentions. She didn't call her grandmother out because she couldn't afford to aggravate her further.

"Do you have time to get coffee later?"

"What time?"

"After the shop closes. We can meet at Java House." The café around the corner had simple meals, good coffee, and it was close.

"See you then," Gram said.

This meeting might not be friendly despite Danica's best intentions. She fretted about what would drive Gram to this level of anger until closing time. After rushing through the nightly security procedures, she hurried to Java House, where Gram had already gotten a table. Today, the older woman wore a light-gray pantsuit with a blush tank top, elegant as always, from her curled hair to her painted toenails.

"How's Gladys doing?" Danica asked once she'd placed an order for a vanilla latte.

"She has rheumatoid arthritis. Vivimancers have helped some, but it's not curable even with magic. That's why I was in the garden with her despite my lack of proficiency."

Maybe it wasn't a lie after all. Gram would do anything for

people she cared about. Danica had no idea how to bridge this subject without sounding hateful and accusatory, but without Gram's interference, other witches had no reason to hex Titus.

They made small talk for a while until Gram finally said, "Something on your mind, dear? I suspect you didn't ask me out for a simple chat, though I wish you had."

Guilt flickered through her at the obvious hurt in her grandmother's voice. She tried to soften the allegation. "I dispelled a hex today."

"Yes, Ruby told me that things didn't go as planned."

Wow. I guess…I didn't expect her to admit it right away. Hurt warred with anger within her, and the fire won out. "I can't believe you tried to ruin Titus's business! He hasn't done anything wrong. He's a good person, and you need to leave him alone." *There, that ought to be forceful enough.*

A long silence followed. Gram stared, eyes wide. Likely she couldn't believe Danica had spoken to her like that because she was always the soft, conciliatory one, while Clem offered more open defiance.

Finally her grandmother said in a soft, icy tone, "Well, that depends on you, dear. I found out that there's a witch hunter in town, likely because of you. How long did you plan to hide the fact that your magic is malfunctioning?"

Oh shit. Danica had expected Gram to hear about the hunter, but her grandma had already learned Danica's secret too? *Nobody in the coven would've told her. How does she know?* If Danica wasn't sweating bullets, she would be seriously impressed with her grandmother's information network.

Still, she tried to bluff. "What are you talking about?"

"Really, Danica. I can't believe you kept something so important from me. I spoke to your mother, and you told *her*, even though she's two hours away and in no danger whatsoever. I can't believe this is what we've come to. And we used to be so close." Actual tears shimmered in Gram's eyes.

She bit her lip. "You've never needed me to warn you about anything. I mean, you're basically omniscient."

Gram took a moment to sip her drink and compose herself. She wasn't the sort of woman to cry in public. "Me having access to information and you caring enough to tell me are two separate issues. Or do you plan to argue about that as well?"

Is this why she flew off the handle and hexed Titus? She blames him for the distance growing between us? Maybe for my magical problems too. That wasn't remotely fair.

"I don't want to fight with you," Danica said quietly.

"Then don't. It's quite simple. You'll stop seeing him. And I'll have no reason to harm the man. He's just a mundane, after all. No one of any importance."

I don't want to do this. Not because she's blackmailing me.

"Are you seriously threatening to hurt Titus if I don't break up with him?" That wasn't the right word since they'd never even had the "we're exclusive" talk, but it hardly mattered at this point. Rage frothed in her brain like a Keurig gone rogue.

Gram set her coffee cup down with an audible clink, though her voice stayed quiet. "It's not a threat, Danica. You know perfectly well what I'm capable of. I will do whatever I think necessary to safeguard you and protect your future, to preserve the power you seem entirely too willing to throw away." Gram's tone turned dark and bitter, practically seething with vitriol.

She closed her eyes, hating this with every fiber of her being. But hadn't she known it would come to this eventually? It didn't matter what she wanted. It never had. And more importantly, she absolutely couldn't permit Gram to go after Titus, to injure him or destroy what he'd built to prove a point.

I have to protect him.

She bit her lip. "Okay, yes. I'll...I *will* end it. I was planning to anyway. Just...give me some time to do it gently so I don't hurt him unnecessarily."

"I can offer a grace period," Gram said. "But I'll need something in return. A show of good faith, if you will."

Ugh, what now?

Stifling a sigh, Danica said, "I'm listening."

"Those Bindr profiles? All those witches are local and willing to meet immediately. Choose one. You'll get together for coffee right here if you like. If this doesn't occur within the week, I can't guarantee what might happen to that mundane."

Fuck. She'd laughed at these bachelors with Clem, assholes who quoted Baudelaire and pretended they spoke fluent French. Despondently, she recalled their pictures and attributes, like she should think of them as potential sperm donors. She'd never come closer to hating Gram than at this moment.

Swallowing her outrage, Danica clenched a fist beneath the table. "Deal. I'll agree to coffee, but anything else is up to my discretion and on my timetable."

"That's fine, dear. Just keep an open mind. Any of them would give me lovely grandchildren with a bloodline that any witch would be proud of."

She didn't trust herself to speak, barely keeping her tears in check.

As Gram marched out of Java House, Danica imagined how Titus would feel when she left with no satisfactory explanation, and she cried like she would never, ever stop.

For days after Titus got back to St. Claire, he tried to fight his growing unease.

Danica hadn't exactly ghosted him, but she was...elusive. She replied to his texts after some delay, but there was distance in her answers that hadn't been present before. That was a weird thing to intuit from texts, but she wasn't joking or using emojis. Her answers came across as...brusque, and he didn't know what to make of it.

Stop thinking about it. Don't be obsessive.

Tonight, he was hosting the poker game, and Trevor had just arrived to help him make the multiple pizzas that his buddies would devour. The others thought he was extra for making them instead of ordering, but no pizza joint in town could compete with Titus's recipe. His crust was delicious, and he splurged on the freshest toppings.

"Do you think she's mad?" he asked Trev as he dumped the yeast into the warm-water-and-sugar mixture.

"Who, bro?"

"The woman I'm seeing." *Was seeing? Who the hell knows.*

"Oh, remind me about the details."

Sighing, Titus ran through the situation, ending with, "Things have been different since I got back. I haven't seen her at all."

"Huh. Maybe she is? You did leave town with only a text. I haven't had a girlfriend in five years, but I think they *do* get pissed about stuff like that. Before Sarah left that last time, she told me we needed to 'work on our partnership' and that she wanted to be 'consulted on important decisions.'"

Titus had no idea why Trev was using air quotes when Sarah had literally said those things. Maybe he didn't know how air quotes were meant to be deployed? But overall, it was a sad day when Trevor made sense and gave surprisingly decent relationship advice.

"Think I should apologize?"

"Do it in person, dude. With flowers. Or chocolate. Maybe both? If that doesn't solve it, I'm out of ideas."

"Flowers are a good idea." The more he thought about it, the more he liked it. "Maybe I made her feel like she's not important to me?"

"Hell if I know. Probably, though. I mean, would you be upset if she did it to you?"

Titus thought about that. "Probably. Texts are convenient, but they're...easy. I might feel like she didn't care enough about my feelings to call or stop by."

"There you go." Trevor peered into the copper mixing bowl. "How long do we let that sit? Those are some serious bubbles."

"It's probably time to get the dough started."

He didn't want to be that guy, so he spent the rest of their cooking time talking about stuff pertinent to Trevor's interests, ergo video games and weed. By the time Dante, Miguel, and Calvin arrived, the house smelled fantastic, and Titus had a wide range of homemade pizzas ready to be devoured. Several hands of poker later, he felt much more cheerful. It was good to drink beer and shoot the shit, no expectations, no pressure.

Maya came home around midnight, the usual cue for the game to break up. His friends headed out as he picked up the mess. She hesitated in the kitchen doorway.

"Something up?" he asked.

Maya leaned against the kitchen counter. "Has Lucy messaged you?"

"Actually, she has. We're talking more now."

"Same. I like her. And..." She hesitated. "I feel bad for her."

Titus sighed. "Me too. I can only imagine how it is, living with Dad and Susan and being treated like wallpaper."

"I wish she'd move here," Maya admitted. "They'll probably use her for free babysitting without caring how that makes her feel."

"It's really like they don't care what collateral damage they inflict in starting their new lives as long as they can write over the old ones."

"Pretty much. Well, we made the offer. The rest is up to Lucy."

He nodded. "She might not want to leave her friends. Maybe it's better for her to tough it out for two years."

Just then, his cell rang. *Lucy,* he mouthed at Maya, before he answered. "Hey, we were just talking about you. What's up?"

A soft sniff reached him then a shuddering breath. "Really? You were?"

"You sound like you're crying. What's wrong?" His voice got louder without him meaning to, and Maya grabbed his arm, frantically shaking her head. With effort, Titus modulated his voice. "I'm here. Talk to me."

"I had a huge fight with my mom. She was being all moody, yelling at me, and I snapped. I...said some things. They were all true, I swear! You saw how she was at the baby shower. But then your dad started screaming at me for being disrespectful. He said—"

"Let me guess. 'If you live under my roof, you keep a civil tongue in your head and do as I say'?"

Lucy's breathing steadied. "Verbatim. I guess he's consistent at least."

"Where are you? Are you safe?"

"I'm at a friend's now. But...if you were serious, I want to talk to my mom about living with you guys for a while, maybe until I graduate. They're driving me crazy, and...I like you and Maya. I won't be any trouble. I'll follow the rules. And I won't fight with either of you or make a mess—"

"Hey," he cut in quietly. "It would be your home too, so you can make a mess. We'll add you to the chore roster and rotate the work. Do you like dogs?"

"I've always wanted one."

"Then you'll love Doris. Stay at your friend's tonight, then when everyone is calm, go home and we'll do a video call tomorrow night. Maya and I will do our best to make this happen if that's what you want."

"I really do. It sucks so bad here, you have no idea."

His sister leaned in. "It'll be okay, I promise. Even when it seems like the end of the world, it passes. I'll give you a big hug when you get here, and Titus will bake cookies."

"Oh my God." It sounded like Lucy was crying again. "You're the best, I swear." Someone spoke in the background, and then she added, "My friend made popcorn. I'm gonna go decompress. Tonight...was a lot. Talk to you soon."

He stared at his phone for a minute after they hung up. "It feels like she's—"

"Really our sister?" Maya finished.

Titus nodded emphatically. "Don't think I'll ever get there with Jared, maybe not Susan either, but Lucy's family."

He went to bed feeling okay overall, though sleep eluded him after he settled in with Doris. His brain kept making plans on how he'd make amends with Danica, then it moved on to convincing Susan to let Lucy go. She'd probably get hysterical, and he wasn't looking forward to a fight, but maybe she'd eventually understand that it was for the best. Was the woman capable of acting solely for Lucy's benefit?

Guess we'll find out.

By the time his alarm went off, he hadn't gotten much sleep at all. He took a long shower and took care of the usual morning chores, like setting Doris's timed food bowl and programming the coffeemaker for Maya, who got up later. *Wonder what it'll be like when Lucy's here.* Suddenly, it occurred to him that he'd done it again, made a major life decision without consulting Danica. If they were dating seriously, she'd want a discussion before he essentially became a guardian to his teenage stepsister.

If he didn't live with Maya, this whole situation could be majorly misconstrued.

Fuck. I have some explaining to do. Maybe Maya was right and he did self-sabotage because he couldn't come up with any other rational explanation for how badly he was fucking this up. *And it started so well too.*

His nerves got worse as the day progressed. Titus was a mess when he took his lunch break and dithered for fifteen minutes over what flowers to buy. Finally, he grabbed a random bouquet and headed for the repair shop. *I don't need food. I just need to see her.*

And then he did. Sitting in Java House with another man, one wearing a tailored suit, an expensive watch, and a fancy haircut. As he watched, the guy reached across the table and took Danica's hand, stroking like he had every right. And she *let* him.

Clutching the apology flowers, Titus wanted to die.

CHAPTER 21

RICHARD LEITCH, PRONOUNCED "LEECH," LIVED up to his name.

This jerk was everything Danica had feared, and he couldn't keep his hands to himself. So far, he'd stroked her hands, her shoulder, and brushed her hair away from her face. He took the fact that she'd messaged him on Bindr to mean that she was DTF, right out of the gate, when she was only doing this to cool Gram's wrath while she figured out how to let Titus down gently. Admittedly, Leitch was easy on the eyes, tall and fit with a symmetrical face, coiffed blond hair, and *really* soft hands.

To the point that his hands felt gross, smooth, and overly sleek, as if he'd magicked away his own fingerprints to prevent being caught doing crime. Her smile tightened as he touched her yet again, telling some endless anecdote about how awesome and successful he was. He ran a brokerage firm, calling himself a "financial wizard" with no tangible sense of irony. Richard seemed convinced that he had her eating out of his smooth palms, but Danica was searching for spies. Gram might have someone watching them, but if not, there would absolutely be magical surveillance.

Maybe I should visit Mom, ask her for advice. Clearly Danica's mom had handled Gram when she'd married Dad, so any suggestions would be welcome. That felt like taking sides, though, and she'd tried *so* hard not to do that.

Wow, he's still *talking. Really doesn't need any input at all.*

Richard laughed at his own joke, inviting Danica to do the same with another stroke to the back of her hand. *Just give this fifteen more minutes, then you can say you need to get back to work.* But before that happened, a shadow fell across the table. Danica glanced up reflexively, and her heart dropped into her shoes. Maybe literally—she tilted her head to check for red splatter. Then her gaze slid back to Titus.

Yeah, still here.

This...is bad.

From his stricken, frozen look, he was *not* okay with her having a coffee date. She tried to tell herself that his reaction was over-the-top. *We dated a few times, hooked up now and then. I never promised to be his girlfriend.* Only she knew that was semantics, and she was in the wrong. But if Gram's spies reported back, as she knew they would, she had to handle this the right way, or he'd get hurt. Possibly his business or maybe even—

Surely Gram wouldn't harm him physically?

But honestly, after that last conversation, she wasn't 100 percent sure. Gram gave no damns about mundanes, and Danica understood that to her bones. The stakes had never been higher.

She forced a cool smile, staying in her seat. "Titus. How have you been?"

That wasn't how people greeted someone they cared about,

and he appeared to absorb that, his attention roving between her and Richard. Who stood and offered a feeble handshake. "Richard Leitch. You must be one of Danica's friends. Today you've caught us at an awkward time, our first date." He shot her a look that he doubtless believed was charming and irresistible. "Hopefully not our last."

"Hmm." A noncommittal response as she assessed the flowers in Titus's hand.

Are those for me?

Possibly, he might be seeing someone else too. If so, it would be hurtful but likely for the best. That way, he could write her off as a narrow escape and go be happy with someone else. She clenched a fist against her thigh under the table. *Ugh, why am I so upset?*

But Richard was studying the bouquet too, and he stepped back with a knowing look. "On the way to meet someone special? Don't let us keep you."

Titus waited. And she *knew*, she knew what he was waiting for. His eyes didn't hold a shred of deceit. He was waiting for her to admit that the flowers were for her—that he'd been headed for her shop when he saw them through the glass. There was no one else; that was her guilt prompting a momentary doubt when he wasn't that type of man. For about thirty seconds, he waited and *hoped*—and Danica witnessed the precise moment when the brightness and expectation died. Not natural causes, more of a murder.

Pain flickered in his dark eyes, and then they shuttered. "I've… intruded," he said at last. "Sorry. It won't happen again."

And then he wheeled, striding for the door like the building was on fire. If it was, they might dispatch him to deal with it. Outside, he pushed the flowers into the hands of a baffled middle-aged woman, and then he rushed away, out of Danica's line of sight, leaving her with Richard Leitch, who was still here. Utterly unable to read the room. He genuinely seemed to have no idea how little Danica wanted to be with him, how much she wished she could chase Titus down and try to explain.

I guess there's no need to think about what to say.

There was an argument in their future, and she owed it to Titus to let him express whatever he needed to in order to get closure. She'd take whatever he dished out because when he stopped yelling at her, they'd be done. And her heart ached over that, more than it should, surely, because they hadn't been together long.

An inner voice that sounded irritatingly like her mother whispered, *When it's right, it's right. When you know, you know.*

"That was random," Richard said, returning to his seat like he couldn't wait to resume their scintillating conversation. "Anyway, I was telling you about my rare pottery collection, I think?" He droned on, utterly unconcerned with her lack of engagement.

Their "date" stretched for nearly another hour before Danica unplugged it from life support with the desperate excuse that Clem was covering for her at Fix-It Witches. Richard seemed momentarily surprised that she had free will and could choose to wrap things up, but he recovered swiftly and grabbed her to press a wet kiss to her cheek.

"This has been fantastic. I had my doubts initially, but then I saw your pedigree, worth driving an hour to meet you. It's *crucial* to mingle with the right people, if you know what I mean." His casual elitism rendered her breathless, not in the good way.

He's just like Gram.

"Right," she said, her tone dead as a tree that had been hit by lightning.

Richard didn't hear that or see her flat expression. "I'll call soon. Look forward to it."

She was a womb to him, a potential boost to his bloodline. He leaned in to kiss her cheek again, but she dodged. *I would rather scoop my own eyes out with a spoon.*

They left together and went their separate ways, Richard to his flashy red convertible that made zero sense in the Midwest, since he couldn't drive it with the top down year-round like people did in balmier climates, and Danica toward the shop. Only she diverted course at the last minute. With tears trembling in her throat and grief fresh like salt on her tongue, she couldn't bear to see Clem. Not yet. Instead, she veered toward the courthouse—the memorial bench beneath the elms.

And Titus was there. Of course he was.

She'd sensed it through a knowing deeper than magic, though she didn't want to use the word when it was too late. He sat forward, studying the ground between his knees with hunched shoulders. *I put that sorrow there.* She could practically see it, pressing between his shoulder blades. *We never had a chance. Not really. I'm not brave enough. And he... He deserves better.*

Sudden heat stung beneath her eyelids. Somehow Danica blinked away the tears. If he saw them, he'd know something was wrong. She had to be cold now, icier than she'd ever been in her life.

For his sake.

———————————

Titus had no idea how long he'd been grieving.

He sat there, deep in mourning for a relationship that maybe he'd imagined. It was possible that Danica had never been the person he thought she was, the one he wanted her to be. Maybe it had always been a bit of fun for her, a rebound to make her feel wanted after her ex screwed her over. And that sucked profoundly for him, but it didn't make her a bad person. Those pitiful hopes just made him...desperate, lonely in a way he'd never even tried to articulate. Because he'd given himself over to good deeds and community service, like he could *earn* love from someone if he put enough good back into the universe.

His head snapped up as every nerve prickled to life. When he turned, she was there. Still as midnight and just as beautiful. But no smile, no life in her pretty eyes. Whatever this had been, it was certainly over. He saw that now. Possibly he'd known before, judging from his unease over her terse replies to his texts. Yes, he was dense and hadn't gotten the message, and she was too kind to ghost him. Unlike a few others.

"We should talk," she said.

"I'm listening." Childish, perhaps, but he wouldn't make it easy for her.

"Actually, I thought that you might have something to say."

"About what? The fact that you've fallen in love with Leech at first sight and you're eloping to Peru to raise alpacas together?" He couldn't keep the angry bite out of his tone. The sad bit was that wouldn't even be the weirdest reason someone had dumped him.

A startled laugh escaped her. "What? No."

His phone vibrated, not the first time. Maya must be wondering where the hell he was, as he rarely took long lunches and he always texted when he got held up. Titus couldn't bring himself to answer. What would he even say?

"But you're seeing him. Just like you were seeing me." Past tense, no reason to pretend he didn't understand that they'd had an expiration date in her eyes and she was done with him, chucking him like a carton of bad yogurt.

"It was just a blind date," she said dismissively.

That made things worse, not better. If she'd accepted a setup from mutual friends or started using a dating site, she couldn't be remotely as into him as he was her. *God, I'm glad I never told her she was my first.* Now, it was just an embarrassing secret to keep, and nobody ever needed to know he'd had sex for the first time at thirty-two in an office chair.

"Ah." He had no idea how he was supposed to react because she wasn't giving the usual speech. *It's not you, it's me. I'm not ready to commit* or maybe *we're just not a good fit.*

Instead, she radiated chilly calm like a field of snow nobody had walked through. But he remembered too well how she looked on top of him, her head thrown back while they both lost their minds. If he was different, she might not be giving up right now on something he'd thought was special. He hated that he had no words for this. Was it even a breakup if they hadn't been official?

"You're allowed to be mad," she said.

And that made him angrier, like he needed permission. Titus gritted his teeth and wished he didn't still care what she thought of him—that he could just cut loose and call her names. He opened his mouth, but the shitty words wouldn't come.

Finally he managed to say, "I guess we're done hanging out?" *Is that the right word?*

"I'll miss you," he added then immediately wished he hadn't.

Because she looked away, over the top of his head to watch the squirrel scrambling up a branch nearby. "Yeah, we had fun, huh? Sorry I didn't get a chance to tell you face-to-face that it—"

"Just wasn't working out?" he supplied smoothly.

Yeah, that's an old standard.

"I'm not ready for a relationship right now."

Sure, that's the other excuse. And it made zero sense when he thought of her with that asshole Leech. Before, he never asked for a play-by-play or autopsied a failed relationship—fear and awkwardness prevented it—but this time he would, out of curiosity and despair. Because he'd thought they were good together—that she was different. Maybe even the one.

"Did I do something wrong? Is it because I left—"

"It's nothing you did," she said firmly, so much that he almost believed her. "We're just not right for each other. That's all."

All? It was everything. And Titus was starting to think that he was *born* for solitude, isolation etched into his bones. Archeologists would be mystified and amazed to find "Forever alone" stamped on his femur, thousands of years hence. On some level, he knew he was being ridiculously dramatic, but he was so damn angry over this current, inexplicable failure that it felt like his skin couldn't even contain it. Yet he couldn't lash out at her, and that left him to swallow it or to flail in the fury until he drowned.

But nobody could go forever without breathing. The lack of oxygen made him testy. He snapped. And the words poured out like poison. "You should have told me. If we were done, you should've said so. Not sent me vague texts and let me find out when you were on a date with some random asshole."

Danica squared her shoulders and nodded. "That's entirely fair."

It made it worse somehow that she was taking it. "God, I think I had a near miss. If that's what you're looking for, no wonder you're not into me. Your taste utterly sucks. Is that what Darryl is like too?"

She nodded. "Cut from the same cloth."

"Then what the hell were you thinking with me, huh? Did you lose a bet?" Hell, he couldn't even be mean to her without cutting himself on the backswing.

Her eyes softened, flickered, and she took a step before her hands clenched into fists. "Okay, I think I've been more than fair. Let's stop now."

"Screw you, I'm just getting started. I have all kinds of shit to say."

"No. You don't. And you have no right either. Frankly, we weren't even a thing. I was being courteous to give you closure, and now we're done. If you have a problem with that, get drunk with your friends and shit talk me to them like everyone else." She whirled and walked away.

Like an absolute dipshit, he watched her go, every step of the way. He ate up the slope of her shoulders, the curve of her ass, the way her arms swung because she was presumably pissed. Which was better than nothing, better than the icy pond she'd brought for him to skate on, and fuck, he was no good at winter sports, always off-balance and windmilling, exactly how he felt right now.

His phone rang. For Maya to resort to voice calls, she must be worried. He picked up on the third ring and willed himself to sound fine. "What's up, Mini?"

"Where the hell are you? Your break was over forty minutes ago. Are you okay? I've sent you like twenty texts."

"I had some stuff to take care of. Is something wrong at the shop?"

"The cash register is acting weird. I managed to restart it and it's working for now, but you might want to get Danica to look at it again."

Fuck that.

"We'll buy a new one if need be. That was used when we got it, and it's served well. After a certain point, some things can't be fixed once they've been badly broken."

Thankfully she didn't seem to hear the grim undertones in his voice. "True enough. Are you ready to have the big family video conference tonight?"

Shit. Right. Not even remotely.

But maybe focusing on Lucy's problems would numb the pain of his own. "We promised, so yeah. I'll do my best to sell the idea."

"Awesome. And just so you know…" Her tone turned teasing. "You're an amazing brother, and Lucy agrees. Don't get conceited."

Titus almost laughed—no chance of that, none at all.

CHAPTER 22

"HOW LONG HAS SHE BEEN drunk?" Leanne asked.

Danica peered up from the kitchen table blearily, but it didn't interfere with her next shot. If she could just stay numb long enough, maybe she'd stop hating herself for hurting Titus and stop loathing Gram from threatening him like a villain from a children's story. She didn't hear Clem's answer, but it was about two days, give or take. Her cousin was holding down the fort at the shop and yelling at her during downtime, but she was also in the middle of something with that damn witch hunter.

Which meant Danica had plenty of time to drink.

Until Clem called the rest of the coven, and now they were working up to an intervention. Danica grabbed the bottle of whatever this was—vodka maybe—and stumbled into the living room because she'd just recalled that she was mad at Leanne. Danica aimed her drink at the redhead, sloshing some on the area rug.

"This is your fault!"

Leanne arched a well-groomed brow. "How do you figure?

I'm not saying you're wrong, mind you, but I'd like more information before I take the blame."

"You said I should go for it, get him out of my system. Instead, he's all over my system! I miss him, and I'm mad at Gram, and my magic is…" Misery overwhelmed her, and she dropped into a squat, protecting the last of her drink with her life.

"It was pretty over the top, what your grandmother did." That whisper came from Margie, who acted like it might literally kill her to speak a bad word about someone.

Ethel chortled. "Over the top? Listen, Old Ms. Waterhouse is as mean as a honey badger where her family's concerned. I'm not saying I agree with her actions, but she thinks she's defending her brood."

"I'm not a brood," Danica snapped.

"Nobody said you are." Priya smoothed Danica's hair.

At least she thought it was Priya. The room was spinning more than a little. Soon, people were helping her to bed. She recognized the feeling—she was about to pass out—and her coven sisters would probably pour out any liquor left in the house. That would mean she'd have to function like a sober, proper adult when she woke up. Because she didn't want to, she closed her eyes and acted like she was already out as the others tucked her in.

Then they had a conversation, apparently believing she was unconscious.

"What do we do?" Vanessa asked. "I've never seen her like this."

Clem sighed. "It's unfair. I can't even *yell* at her, and I'm so mad. It's like she forgot our pact the minute she met this guy, and she hears nothing I say these days."

Guilt seeped in, staining the deeper corners of Danica's soul that were already ragged and sore. She kept her eyes closed, knowing she owed her cousin an apology. *I let everyone down. How do I make this right?* Muzzily she wondered if faking her own death was out of the question.

"Maybe the spellbook?" Priya suggested. "Not right now, obviously. She's in no shape to cast. But when she sobers up again, there might be something that could help."

"Maybe. But the thing didn't seem to be working as intended. Last time we used it, the witch hunter showed up, and I'm leery of trying it again, but if Danica wants to…" Clem didn't sound too enthused.

Truth be told, neither was Danica. Their quiet voices lulled her, and she drifted, or, hell, maybe she passed out at long last. Either way, her bladder was screaming when she woke fourteen hours later, a fitting accompaniment to the hammers banging in her head.

Perfect. It started with a hangover. It ends with one too.

After peeing, she took a long, long shower and downed a liter of water with some pain pills. *That's enough self-indulgence. I owe Clem so big. She's been dealing with the hunter and keeping the shop open and…* Danica sighed, drying her hair more briskly than necessary. The towel abrasion made her head throb worse. *And I deserve it.*

Her phone, which she hadn't looked at in days, was on fire with messages from Richard and Gram. He was pressing for a second date while Gram offered congratulations—her sources indicated that everything had gone well—and suggested they get together for lunch, just to have fun like they used to. The old witch acted like everything was good in her book while Danica nursed a deep and seething rage tempered only by this shitty hangover.

I miss Titus so much.

Honestly, it was ridiculous the way the ache sat on her chest like a night hag devoted to devouring dreams. The pressure didn't abate, even after days of drinking. She wanted to run over to the bakery and apologize on her knees, for everything, and promise to make it up to him. But even if she did, it didn't solve the problem with Gram. He wouldn't be safe.

She wondered if her grandmother had made threats against her father before her mom got married. And if so, how did she handle the situation? But Mom would absolutely freak if she found out what Gram was doing. No exaggeration, this could split the family down the center, leaving a crater too deep and wide ever to be patched.

It's better this way.

Danica wished she could convince herself of that fully, but until that time, she'd keep looping it in her head. Until her heart accepted it.

But...she couldn't let this go either. Right now, Gram was gardening with Gladys or doing sudoku, imagining that she'd won, a complete rout. Danica was dating some jerk, just as she'd demanded. A pureblooded witch. And she'd prevented a potential mixed marriage. The sheer hatefulness of it all made Danica clench her fists.

Before she lost her nerve, she rang her grandmother. "Yes, dear?"

"I met Richard Leitch, just as you demanded. He's an asshole. I won't be seeing him again. More to the point, I'm not meeting any of your matches. Never again. Not for coffee, not a movie, not a walk in the park. If you ever try anything like this again, I'll tell Mom exactly what you're up to."

A long silence followed, and then Gram forced a laugh. "So dramatic. You act as if I did something truly dreadful rather than just looking out for your best interests."

"Bullshit. Someone who cares about my best interests would care about my happiness, not just about my power. I'm not saying I intend to sacrifice the latter, but the way you've been acting, it's clear where your priorities lie. I have to prove I'm worthy of the Waterhouse name because of my mixed heritage, and I'm fucking done, do you hear me? I deserve better, and I'll have it, or you won't be part of my life anymore."

"Danica! You can't—"

"I can. I did. You're my grandmother, and I appreciate everything you've done for me. Your time and your love and the priceless gift of the grimoire and the house, but…if you didn't give me those things freely, if there are strings attached, then take them all back. Because I'm my own person, *not* your puppet, and I deserve to be happy."

"That's all I want," Gram said softly. "All I've ever wanted."

"Only if that happiness fits your specifications. It's controlling, and I'm done, do you hear me? No more pressure, no more threats— against me or *anyone*! Going forward, I will date whoever I want. I'll live as I see fit, and we'll see if you get to be a part of that."

Her heart was racing so fast, it felt like arrhythmia. Never in her life had she imagined speaking to Gram like that. It went against every instinct, like she'd been quietly ensorcelled with the need to please the old witch. Probably it wasn't an actual spell, just the fading effects of hero worship. As a little girl, she'd wanted to be just like her grandmother, tough and fierce and full of mysterious strength.

Danica didn't give Gram a chance to defend herself. Instead, she hung up and stumbled to the bathroom to barf up some weird-colored bile. Unsurprising, as she'd been on a liquid diet for several days. She clung to the commode and waited, but the nausea passed. Then she felt a gentle hand on her head, brushing back her hair.

"You sure told her," Clem said, sounding a little proud.

"Uh. I guess you heard that?"

"Every word. It's about damn time too." Between the two cousins, Clem had always been the more openly defiant one. She'd fought Gram *and* her own mother without quarter.

"I had to. I'm done trying to live inside the lines she's drawn for me."

"Understood, but it was hilarious when you threatened her with Auntie Minerva."

Danica laughed a little at that. It was rather like threatening to set a toy poodle on a Rottweiler. "I know, right?"

"Will you be okay?"

She tilted her head, silent sarcasm about her position of worship before the porcelain goddess. "Not soon, but…eventually. Best thing about rock bottom is that I can only go up from here."

As promised, Titus persuaded Dad and Susan that it was best for Lucy to have a change of scene.

Because Dad was an asshole, Maya thought if they framed it as less stressful for Susan so she could focus on her pregnancy, it would work like a charm. And it did.

Basically, as soon as the old man realized it would mean less in-house conflict, he was all for it. Susan took more convincing, but by the end of the video call, she'd finally agreed that it might be more peaceful. She asked a lot of questions, though, raising issues that Maya and Titus had already considered. Unsurprisingly, neither Dad nor Susan conferred much with Lucy, so it was a good thing she wanted this life change, or it would be just another decision made without her input.

Two days later, he and Maya called Lucy to chat privately. The tablet screen flashed, and then Lucy appeared, lounging on her bed. Her room was mint green with twinkle lights hung up, movie posters on the walls. It occurred to him that they should probably redecorate the guest room, Maya's old one, before she moved in.

Part of him was grateful that Lucy needed sanctuary. Without this extra responsibility, he might fall into a mental black hole and not crawl out for quite a while. He wanted to drink over losing Danica, but with the bakery and two younger sisters relying on him, he had to be strong. No chance to act otherwise, and that was a good thing. If he let himself go, he'd end up like Trevor after Sarah, just all gaming and weed, until maybe he'd forget there was supposed to be more to life.

"Still good to go?" Titus asked, hoping Lucy didn't feel quite as abandoned anymore.

"I'm excited. I'm nervous, but it's cool too. I've gone to school with the same kids my whole life. Once you get...ranked, it's hard to change how people think of you. In St. Claire, I get a do-over, and I'm looking forward to helping at the bakery too. Am I working in front or back?"

Right, I offered her a part-time job.

"The front. Maya could use the help, and it's safer. We've never had a student working for us, so I need to look into it before I let you do any baking." There was no issue with Stan helping in the kitchen, but he wasn't a teen, not by a long shot.

"Um. I don't know if I'll like it, but I enjoy making cookies and stuff. And maybe I'm presuming too much, but if I enjoy it and I work hard, maybe I could go to school. Like you did, Titus? And learn to be a baker?"

He blinked. Sure, he'd thought about bringing on another baker at some point when the business was stable and loans were paid off, but he'd never in a hundred years imagined that Lucy might be interested. Her face fell as he held silent.

She rushed on, "No pressure. I mean, I know it's a family business, and I'm not counting on that or anything, so—"

"It *is* a family business," Titus cut in. "If you want in, you're in. Just know that you're allowed to change your mind, no hard feelings. Nobody expects you to have everything figured out."

Maya squeezed his shoulder, outside the range of the camera. She mouthed, *Good save.* He flicked his hand at her without letting his expression shift from the warm smile he was offering

Lucy in reassurance. The kid really was a love sponge, so desperate to please that it pissed him off. *How do Dad and Susan not see this?*

Lucy sniffled. "Thanks. I can't tell you how much this means to me."

"We're here for you," Maya said.

Even if they aren't.

Everyone heard the unspoken words, but Titus went on to business. "Okay, so we need to get you moved because school starts at the end of August and there's a lot to do. Maya and I will fly out to pick you up late Saturday. We'll stay through Monday. That way we only have to close one day. Does next week work?"

"You're coming to get me?" Lucy asked.

Maya said, "Of course. You're packing up your whole life. We're not asking you to get in an Uber and find a way here on your own."

From what he'd gleaned, Susan had worked too much as a single mom to travel much with her kids, so Lucy had only been on a plane a couple of times in her entire life. She tried not to show it, but she was overjoyed that they were taking off work to collect her. That was how you proved to people they mattered— with actions.

After chatting a bit more and making concrete plans, Titus hung up to book their tickets. Round trip for him and Maya, one way for Lucy. He got them seats together on the way back, a decent price too, as airlines were still desperate for travelers. As soon as he got the confirmation email, he sent the details to Lucy so she'd know the arrangements were set, that he and

Maya weren't grown-ups who talked a good game but would ultimately let her down.

"You okay?" Maya asked as he stood and stretched, rolling his neck.

Nah, I feel like somebody stepped on my actual heart.

He was embarrassed to be that dramatic out loud. Saved it for the inner monologue. Shrugging, he knelt to pet Doris. "Just tired, I guess. Why?"

"I don't know. You've been acting weird. Even quieter than usual. Are you having second thoughts about Lucy?"

"Oh, hell no. We can't be worse for her than Dad and Susan."

Maya laughed. "I'm not ready for parenting, but...my thoughts exactly."

"It'll be more like mentoring. She just needs to feel like we care and we're looking out for her."

"Have you thought about painting my old room? Right now it's kind of a junk repository, and it's *so* lavender."

"Full of unicorns too." He couldn't help the snide tone, didn't even try.

"So help me, I will end you."

"I'll invite Trevor over on Sunday. If we all pitch in, I think we can redecorate pretty quick."

Maya nodded. "Painting won't take that long. I just hate all the fiddly prework, the tarps and the taping of windowsills and doorframes."

"Trev and I can handle that. Can you order some stuff? Lamps and furry pillows and soft afghans? Whatever you would've wanted in your room at her age."

His sister did a little dance. "I hope she likes it when we're done."

"The fact that we're trying will probably mean a lot." Titus didn't intend that in a bad way; it was just obvious that Lucy needed attention. "And if we get some details wrong, we can change things according to her tastes. It's more important that she feels at home."

"I know I'm gonna sound like an asshole but...we are seriously awesome people," Maya said, acting like she might even pat herself on the back.

Titus laughed. The sound hit him strange, like he hadn't thought he could ever feel...well, happy was the wrong word. But even humor had been sliding by him, as if his sadness was too thick for it to penetrate. A wall of scar tissue too tough to permit *anything* to pass, let alone light or joy.

And you're doing it again. Dial it down. This isn't the end of the world. You've been here before. It's not the first time or even the worst.

Maybe it would be the last, however, because he didn't see how he could muster the optimism ever to try again. Even when it felt perfect, wholly right, it wasn't.

Some people were bachelor uncles from birth. Titus could live for his extended family, maybe have nieces and nephews one day, be good to a series of dogs and give back to the community. He could be a volunteer firefighter for years; maybe he'd join the Rotary Club too. And when he died, a bunch of strangers would be sad at losing such a useful—

Fuck this. Fuck it all the way down.

CHAPTER 23

"WHAT DO *YOU* THINK I should do to move on?" Danica asked Goliath.

I'm asking a cat for advice.

It was a low point, admittedly. Sure, Danica was doing better than she had been, but improvements were relative. She might not be drinking until she barfed, but the world was grimly monochrome, like the moment she hurt Titus, all the color leached out of her world. Clem had been unbelievably generous and given her a day off despite how much she'd slacked recently.

Maybe I should've gone to work. I have too much time to think.

The ginger cat circled her ankles and mewed, whiskered face uplifted in perpetual hope. Today was his day, however; she was in the mood to torture herself. Stooping, she scooped the cat into her arms and settled in the porch swing with him purring like mad and rubbing all over her. Soon, the watery eyes and sneezing would start. Maybe she'd even break out in a rash. She petted the damn cat like he'd always dreamed she would, rubbing his head, between his ears, stroking down his spine, and scratching his butt. Goliath purred until he fell over, then he waved all four paws, twisting wildly on his back.

Danica let him.

By the time Clem got home, Danica's eyes were nearly swollen shut, and she had some nice welts going. Goliath was in heaven, though.

"What the hell are you doing?" her cousin demanded, pulling the purring ginger furball out of her arms.

"Punishing myself and making this cat's day?"

"Cut it out! It will take you days to recover from this. I'm taking the cat home, and then you're going with me to the clinic to get a shot."

"Just call Kerry or Priya. They can take care of it." That was the benefit of being attuned to vivimancy.

Clem leaned in, lowering her voice. "This doesn't require magic. Modern medicine will do the job, and you know damn well it's safer, especially now. Gavin was asking me about our last name, and I think I played it off. But he mentioned the shop too. One is a coincidence, two is suspicious, and three—"

"Is a pattern," Danica finished. "Fine, I'll put compresses on my eyes and be ready to go when you get back."

"I've had about enough of this self-imposed penance. The only reason I'm not yelling more is... Well, you'll see when you look in the mirror."

Goliath cried and stretched out a white-tipped paw as Clem carried him off, reaching for Danica like they were Romeo and Juliet, separated by feuding Venetian families. With a crooked smile, crooked because her face was swollen, she soaked a cloth in cold water and winced when she saw how scary she looked. If someone claimed she was the first wave of a terrifying outbreak, anyone would believe it.

The cold pack helped a little. An allergy shot would help more. She was waiting as promised when Clem returned. Her cousin grabbed the keys and drove to the clinic without saying a word. Things weren't exactly…right between them, but Danica didn't have the energy for the kind of fight it would take to clear the air. Mostly she appreciated how present Clem always was, no matter what mess Danica had made.

"Sisters for life," she said aloud. More than once, they'd chanted it drunkenly, affirmed it when they'd sobered up.

Clem glanced over, and her set jaw softened a little as she did the call back. "Sisters for life."

She let out a long breath. "Thanks for always being there, even when I act like a dumbass."

"I admit, you've been a challenge lately," Clem muttered.

"Hey…"

"Yeah?"

"You called the hunter 'Gavin' before."

Her cousin slid her an unreadable look. "What? That's his name."

"It's not so much what you said as how you said it."

"I do not want to talk about this," Clem snapped. "Not even slightly."

Quickly Danica held up her hands before her cousin could go off. "Okay. Just know that I'm here, a prime maker of bad decisions, if you ever want someone to listen without judgment. I live in a glass house, no stones here."

Clem's look eased into a reluctant smile as she pulled into the clinic parking lot. It was a small brick building in the strip mall parking lot, detached and offering twenty-four-hour urgent care. Inside, the place was full of crying toddlers and worried-looking women, a few elderly people, and a teenage boy cradling his wrist. It took about an hour for a doctor to see Danica, only a few minutes to get an allergy shot and a harried lecture about being more careful.

Clem was silent until they were nearly home, and then she said, very softly, "I like him," as if she was confessing to a crime.

Danica replied just as quietly. "I suspected. What are you going to do?"

"Hell if I know. Aren't you going to tell me what a terrible idea this is?"

"I'm the queen of those, if you hadn't noticed. Yeah, I'm worried about you, but I can't tell you what to do."

Clem sighed. "Started with me running a game, feeling so clever because I was putting one over on him. Making the almighty, dangerous hunter forget why he even came to St. Claire in the first place. But now... Fuck it, never mind. I'll figure it out. I haven't forgotten our pact. This is a blip, that's all."

That seemed to be all Clem intended to say on the subject, and as she parked, Danica changed the subject. "I've been thinking, and I want to use the spellbook one last time. Before, I was all messed up emotionally. I think that's why the spells kept going wrong. But I've reached equilibrium, and I want..." She took a deep breath. "I want to help Titus. If I can nudge him toward getting over me faster, so he doesn't feel as hurt and he forgets faster, that would be better. It's all I can do to make amends, you know?"

To her surprise, Clem nodded. "I get it. Let's do that. If there's a spell in there that looks like it'd help the CinnaMan, I'll back you up."

She couldn't resist the urge, hugging her cousin from behind as they headed into the house. "You're the absolute best. I'll get the grimoire."

Clem set her hands atop Danica's and pressed gently. "I'll set up in the kitchen. Try not to start any fires."

"It was one time," she muttered, stifling a smile.

For some reason, the spellbook felt heavier in her hands this time. The tome represented all her grandmother's hopes and dreams, the weight of all her expectations. With each step, she wished she could drop this thing down a well. *No, tamp down the anger or the spell will go wrong again. I need to fill myself with positive energy and selfless intentions. This is for Titus. I genuinely want him to be happy.* Danica imagined the joyous life he'd build—with someone else—and it felt like her chest might crack open.

Danica stood and breathed until her mood leveled out. Then she went on to the kitchen, where Clem sat with lit candles, all the accoutrements in place. It was impossible to know what they'd need exactly until she perused the spell. Taking a breath, she pulled out her chair and sat. Opened the grimoire with hopeful eyes and—

Yes. It's perfect.

"Anything?" Clem asked.

"Yes. There's an incantation written. Beautifully simple—a spell for Letting Go." Why did it hurt so much? Goddess knew, she might do herself a permanent injury casting this, but if it helped him...

"That sounds promising."

Danica closed her eyes for a long moment, and when she opened them next, she was braced and ready. "Let's begin."

―――――――――

Sunday should have been Titus's one day off, but it was better to stay busy.

That way, he could pretend he wasn't hurting, brush off Maya's mild concern. Earlier in the week, he'd thrown himself into activities at the fire station, run with Doris until he couldn't think. Even then, the anguished throb of his maimed heart startled him now and then. He breathed through the worst of it and told himself it would get better.

It always does.

And this wasn't a new experience. In fact, it would've been more surprising if things had gone any other way. Like always, he had no clue when or why everything had gone wrong. He let out a shaky breath and restrained the urge to punch the wall he was prepping for paint. Instead, he washed it down with controlled, meticulous motions.

The furniture was out in the hall, stacked up so they could barely pass. Trevor was taping borders that shouldn't be painted with a precision that belied his usual carelessness. His friend hadn't always been so devoid of dreams, more evidence of how thoroughly love could wreck a man. Maya squatted, pouring a little of the paint they'd chosen into a tray.

Her gaze was anxious when she lifted her eyes to meet his. "Think she'll like it?"

The color was a gentle shade at the intersection of green and blue. At the store, the worker said it was called "Waterfall," and he suspected Lucy would be thrilled over their effort, if nothing else. Maya rambled on about how it was a cool and calming hue, and Titus swallowed his impatience. *It's not her fault.*

Lately, he was angry about everything, and he worked not to take it out on people who didn't deserve it. Hopefully, he'd pass from the furious stage of grief soon; that way he'd make it to acceptance faster. But he had to pass through bargaining en route, and, God, he hoped he could keep from drunk dialing Danica, begging her to explain what he'd done wrong and making desperate pleas for her to allow him to fix it.

"She'll love it," he said firmly.

The new bits and pieces Maya had ordered from some online outlet were downstairs, still in cardboard boxes and plastic packing. He didn't have any clear idea how it would all look when they were done, but hopefully his sister had a master plan. He grabbed his roller and sighed. Since they were covering lavender walls, they had to do a layer of primer first, let it dry before they could proceed with the main event.

"You should have gotten a sprayer," Trevor said.

Maya scowled at him. "That wastes so much paint. And

it gets everywhere. Rollers are slower, but it's less of a mess overall."

His friend lifted his roll of masking tape in a mock salute. "Yes, ma'am." He turned to Titus as he finished up the window-sill. "You're paying me for this, right? Not just in pizza and beer."

"Of course. Twenty bucks an hour plus pizza and beer."

That was cheap as hell compared to a professional painter, but Trevor didn't qualify for top rates either. He didn't seem to mind, as this was a hundred bucks, guaranteed, and probably more. It wasn't like Trev had anything better to do.

Once Titus got into the groove, it was fun redoing Maya's old room.

They watched a couple of movies while waiting for the primer to dry and with three of them working, it only took a couple of hours to get the actual paint on the walls. Around the ceiling and edges first with brushes then the rollers. Titus could hear his mother's voice telling him the proper way to do this. How would she feel about Lucy moving into their family home? Since she had been a genuinely kind person, she'd probably be okay with it.

Before leaving the room, they opened the windows, and Titus threw together a few pizzas from dough he'd frozen after he'd made the big batch on poker night. They kicked back, joking around during a buddy comedy that Trevor picked. Doris knocked over a can of beer and roughhoused with everyone and then sprawled on top of Titus, finally dragging a real smile out of him.

I have good people in my life. I'll be okay.

He should get to sleep, but Maya wanted to finish the room, so against his better judgment, he enlisted Trev to help him move the furniture back in, and then she added all the little touches—a cushioned footstool and fuzzy white pillows, an area rug in all the colors of the sea, glittery mirrored boxes to set on the dresser. It was all stuff he'd never have thought of, but when everything came together, the room looked beautiful. Maya had ordered new linens too, patterned in white and teal. Altogether, the space was bright and feminine, a little glam, and a lot cool.

"Looks great," Titus said sincerely.

Maya yawned and arched her back. "Finally. Remind me never to do this all in one day again."

He understood her hurry, though, because they were leaving as soon as the shop closed next Saturday, flying back to Arizona. And maybe it would've been okay to wait, involving Lucy in the process, but this felt like more of a gift. *Here, we cared enough to take the time to do this for you. Enjoy the room, it's yours, no effort required.*

"Give me my money," Trevor demanded, holding out a hand. "I've been here for like ten hours."

He'd been drinking beer and watching movies for a good portion of that time, but Titus gave him two hundred bucks anyway. "Can you crash on the sofa for a bit? I need to get a little sleep before I open in the morning."

"No prob. You've taken me home at 4:00 a.m. before."

Usually Trev stumbled out to the car, snored all the way there, and then passed out again as soon as he got inside the basement at his parents' place. He'd sleep until noon, at least, then play video games all day. It must be nice having permanently given up both stress and ambition.

The next morning, it went as he predicted, and Titus centered himself making the delicious pastries the citizens of St. Claire adored. When the cinnamon rolls came out of the oven, he thought of Danica, and Titus almost doubled over. *Fuck. That's new.* It was like an internal rebellion within his body, as if his cells were trying to tell him this breakup was wrong—that he was supposed to be with her.

Fuck, I know that. What do you want me to do about it?

Stan shot him a concerned look as he clutched his side. "You good? That's not appendicitis, is it?"

"Nah. I need to work out more. Think maybe I pulled something lifting that last tray."

"Try getting old. You should hear how my knees pop in the morning."

Titus laughed because he was meant to. Stan was always more talkative in the afternoon, disproving the stereotype that all old people were early birds, up at 5:00 a.m. and cheerful about it, eating senior dinner specials at 4:00 and snoozing by 8:00 p.m. Hell, Titus lived more like an elderly soul than Stan did.

The rest of the week buzzed by. Soon, Titus was wrapping up in the kitchen on Saturday afternoon, making sure everything was set for a longer-than-usual shutdown. "Don't leave any valuables," he called to Maya. "I hate that we're closing, but—"

"I'm not a kid," she shouted back.

Mrs. Carminian had been headed out when he popped out from the back. "Oh, hey. Sorry about the yelling."

The old woman wore a troubled look, but she let herself be herded, and Maya locked the door behind her. "Hey, apparently they moved our flight up forty minutes."

Shit. That meant they had to hustle. He hadn't printed the FAMILY REASONS sign yet, so the usual CLOSED one would have to do. St. Claire might be mildly inconvenienced when they didn't open on schedule Monday, but he'd give away some samples on Tuesday, apologize profusely. It should be fine.

Titus thought quickly. "Grab the deposit bag. I'll drive you to the bank and swing by for Trev. We'll head home, get our bags, then go directly to the airport. Half an hour tops?"

Maya nodded and put her hand over his like they were starting a team scrimmage. "And break!"

CHAPTER 24

DANICA WAITED A WEEK BEFORE she yielded to the temptation to check on Titus.

The spell hadn't felt like it worked exactly *right,* just a maddening tingle. But neither did it go catastrophically wrong. He didn't call her or wander past the shop, which was a good sign, except that it made her feel terrible.

Maybe he's already seeing someone else.

If so, that would be a good thing. Totally.

But Saturday afternoon, she figured she'd swing by the bakery. Just…a little light stalking of an ex. *God, I dated Darryl for two years, and I wasn't like this.* She'd put the blocking charm Ethel had made in her purse, just in case. With a witch hunter around, searching for her magical signature, she couldn't be too careful.

To her surprise, the shop was already shut, lights off and locked up tight. Sometimes they did wrap up early when all the baked goods were sold. No point in staying open for sporadic coffee sales when Sugar Daddy's wasn't the only coffee shop in town. As she stared through the front glass at the darkened storefront, Mrs.

Carminian trotted by, walking her two adorable Yorkies, Fiddle and DeeDee.

"It's sad, isn't it?" the old woman said.

Danica turned, raising a brow in question. "What is?"

"I overheard them talking earlier. It seems like they're closing the doors."

Ice speared through her, right into her heart. "No way."

"The business seemed to be doing well, but he and Maya were talking about shutting down today. Titus was telling her not to leave anything of value behind, and I heard from Mr. Stevewell that they left town in a hurry, driving hell for leather for the highway."

"They're coming back, right?"

Mrs. Carminian shrugged, not seeming too concerned. "How would I know? Guess we'll find out sooner or later. I asked Walter to keep me in the loop, but he's being cagey. If he puts a For Sale sign on this property, then I guess they aren't."

Walter Reynolds was a real estate agent; Danica had worked with him in setting up Fix-It Witches. Her mind racing, she waved as Mrs. Carminian finally yielded to the impatient tugging of tiny pooches and continued on her way. She could drive out to Titus's place to check for herself, but that was clearly over the line. *Maybe something's wrong?*

It bothered her that she had no clue what was going on with him. But why should she? She'd burned that bridge and been more of a bitch than she needed to be.

What if the spell messed up his life? Shit, what if Gram...

"Okay, that's it," she muttered. "I just need to check, that's all."

After dropping an emergency emoji in the coven group chat,

Danica sprinted home, nearly a mile, and she wheezed for three solid minutes on the porch, skirting Goliath, who showed up hoping for a second snuggle session. She'd already tried to scry when a few of the others arrived, but her hands were shaking too much for the spell to work.

"Titus is gone," she babbled.

It took about ten minutes and lots of interruptions to get the whole story out, then Ethel took over. "Let me look, sweetheart. Scrying's my game."

While Danica paced and chewed at her cuticles, the older witch settled in front of a copper basin. Vanessa hugged her while Margie made chamomile tea. Kerry still hadn't arrived; neither had Priya or Leanne. Their day jobs were demanding. Clem must be dealing with the witch hunter, or she'd have at least responded in chat.

"Anything, Ethel? Anything? Did my grandmother—"

"I don't think so. There doesn't seem to be any *malicious* magic attached, though I can't be sure about the unintentional effects of the spell you cast last weekend."

That was a kind way of saying that her working might have backfired. Again.

"It's possible that the magic decided he'll be happier if he leaves town for good? Gives up the life he's built here for a fresh start." Dammit, that didn't sound like a decision Titus would make in his right mind. He loved St. Claire, and he was proud of the bakery.

Maybe I accidentally severed all the roots he's put down here, made him feel like there's no reason to stay? Oh crap. It was called a spell for Letting Go.

As Margie brought over a steaming cup of tea, Vanessa rubbed Danica's back. Danica took a breath to center herself and said, "Okay. Hmm. Just...tell me where he is. Do you know? Can you *find* him?"

"Piece of cake," Ethel answered.

The old witch fixed her gaze on the water, whispering to it and sprinkling fresh herbs. First the cloudy liquid bubbled, and when it cleared, there was a house clearly depicted. From the style and landscaping, it must be out west somewhere.

"Does he know anybody in Arizona or New Mexico?" Vanessa asked.

"Arizona," Danica said at once. "His dad lives there. I can't remember where exactly."

"I've got this." Another tweak of the spell, and then Ethel delivered the address. "That's in Gilbert. You think your spell made him decide to move to Arizona?"

"I can't let him go. He belongs here. This is his home and..." Suddenly the truth hit her like a ton of bricks.

The reason why things felt right with Titus, why it was beautiful and effortless—he was the missing piece of her jigsaw puzzle. He made her laugh, no matter the situation. She couldn't imagine that ever changing. She would never get tired of his smile, his warm eyes, or his silly sense of humor. Eventually, she wanted to wake up with him every morning and always find his arms open when she had a crappy day.

"He's my home too. We belong together. I want to build a life with him, whatever it costs. I *know* it's fast, but I don't care anymore. Not about the Waterhouse curse or what Gram says.

My mom says all I need to do is follow my heart and she'll be proud of me. So...I have to get him back." She grabbed Margie's arm, nearly spilling the tea the other witch was about to drink. "I have to."

"Okay," Margie said in a soothing tone.

The attempt to calm her only agitated her more. "You don't understand. I can't let him sell the bakery and move to Arizona! His father is terrible!"

The front door banged open, and Leanne rushed in, breathless. "I lied to the mayor. What's the emergency?"

Tapping a high-heeled foot, Leanne twirled her car keys, waiting for an answer. Danica locked onto that immediately. "You're driving me to the airport."

The redhead didn't even blink, proving once again that she was ride or die, no questions asked. "Let's go. Fill me in on the way."

"Hold up, you need a few things. Give me three minutes." Margie raced upstairs and returned with a packed bag. Vanessa grabbed Danica's purse, a good thought since she couldn't fly without ID. "Update us when you know something."

"Don't do anything I wouldn't do," Ethel called.

Waving, Danica dashed out the front door, knowing her cousin would be mad as hell over being cut out of this decision. *I'll take the punishment when I get back. Better to ask forgiveness than permission.* Leanne's car was sleek and fast, a little yellow Mazda Miata that she'd bought after her second divorce settlement.

"Do you even have a plane ticket?" Leanne asked as she backed out of the driveway.

"I'm on it." Quickly she grabbed the last seat on a flight leaving in three hours. *This is insane. I can't believe I'm doing this.* "Next flight to Phoenix. If we make good time, I'll have no trouble."

Leanne slammed her foot onto the gas pedal, accelerating past a minivan on the way out of town. "Please. 'Good time' is my middle name. Midway or O'Hare?"

"Midway, the seven fifty-five on Southwest." Coincidentally, it was also the fastest flight, and since she was gaining time, it would be weirdly early when she arrived.

Probably still too late to show up at his dad's house, but she didn't dare wait. Besides, it would *not* be better to show up bright and early on Sunday morning. Either way, this would be awkward and embarrassing, best to put her groveling face on and get it over with. Anything to keep him from making a terrible, life-altering mistake with her misshapen spell buzzing about his head like a swarm of misguided bees.

She took a deep breath and summarized the situation for Leanne, who listened without judgment. If anyone knew about following her heart, it would be her. Not always with fantastic results, but so what? Better to have loved and lost and so forth.

"We've got the usual traffic, so we're looking at fifty-five minutes according to the GPS. I'll shave it if I can. Might be tight."

Danica shrugged, unconcerned with trivial issues any longer. "I've sprinted through airports before. At least Midway is usually less crowded."

"Hopefully the line at security won't be bad."

"Doesn't matter if it is." Now that she'd made the mental leap, nothing would get in her way.

Leanne shot her a warm smile, maneuvering lane to lane like a boss. "Attagirl. Come back with your man or on him."

For some reason, that quintessentially Leanne tweak to the Spartan code made Danica laugh until she couldn't breathe.

Thanks to the shuffle forward, inefficient security procedures, and a gate change, Titus and Maya barely made their flight.

Even after they belted in, it took him an hour to calm down, and in three more, they were on the ground in Phoenix. The travel industry still wasn't what it was, as people still weren't moving much, but people who'd gotten the vaccine early were starting to resume long-delayed vacation plans. Titus preferred to stay out of crowds, but that was more a personal preference than a necessity.

The sun was setting when the driver dropped them off at Dad's house. He and Susan had opted not to do an airport pickup, surprising no one. Jared was gone, some last-minute road trip with his high school friends before they all went their separate ways. *At least I get my own room while I'm here.*

That was better than the last visit, when he'd crashed on an air mattress and listened to his stepbrother complain about him audibly in some group chat. Dad and Susan did greet them at the door, but Lucy beat them by offering huge hugs. The kid could hardly keep still, stumbling over herself to ask a hundred questions about the house and St. Claire and even Doris, who was at home with Trevor.

Titus showed off a few pictures of the dog, house, and yard, though he didn't mention the quickie update of Lucy's room. Some of the edge had finally come off his anger. He might never love Susan, but he did have to accept that Dad had moved on. Faster than Titus thought was kind, but it wasn't his life.

Susan had made chili in the slow cooker, a weird choice, but he supposed living in hell's own furnace, where the seasons were hot and really hot, one couldn't let the weather dictate the menu, or it would be salad and cold cuts, all day, every day. The food was good, and Susan insisted on topping it with all kinds of stuff, including shredded cheese, scallions, sour cream, and Fritos. He swapped a look with Maya and Lucy, who indicated that he should just eat it that way and be quiet.

He took a bite. Yeah, not his first choice; the Fritos were too much. Since Susan was watching him so expectantly, he gave a big smile. "Wow."

"See? I told you this is the best." Susan devoured half a bowl and then dashed to the bathroom with his dad chasing her.

"Okay, now dump it and make it however you want," Lucy said quickly. "Do it fast. Otherwise, if she finds out you think her condiment style needs improvement, she'll cry and say it's because you hate her."

Maya made a face as everyone sprang into action and activated the garbage disposal like it was the bat signal that would summon a food crusader to save them. They were all seated eating their dinner calmly when Dad and Susan came back, looking a bit green. The old man was nagging her, by the sounds of it.

"Babe, the doctor told you to lay off spicy food. You can't keep it down."

"But it's all I want right now," she wailed.

Oh Jesus.

He shot an alarmed look at Maya. Part of him had thought that maybe Lucy was exaggerating, but it was clear that Susan was 60 percent hormones, 35 percent tears, and 5 percent fetus. Since he'd been four when his mom had been pregnant with Maya, he couldn't remember if she'd acted this way or not. Honestly, it was funny watching his old man try to step up and be comforting when his go-to mode was to yell at people for fucking up.

Try that on your pregnant wife. I dare you.

Thankfully, this wasn't a long trip. Tomorrow, they'd participate in whatever surprise Susan had planned and suffer through a communal meal. She wanted to bond as a family since she was ambivalent, at best, about Lucy leaving. Susan had already asked a thousand awkward questions about Titus's social life, like he'd make Lucy listen to him knocking boots all night long. Ironic, really.

"Should we watch a movie in the den?" Susan asked.

Dammit, he just wanted to withdraw to Jared's room and crash—it had been a long day—but he forced a smile. "Sure. Nothing too scary, Maya will have nightmares."

His sister nudged him. "Whatever, you're the one who cried when I sang the *A Nightmare on Elm Street* theme song outside your bedroom door. One, two—"

"That's enough," Dad said, just like when they were kids.

Susan decided they were having a Will Ferrell marathon and started with *Eurovision Song Contest: The Story of Fire Saga*. That sounded bananas, and he wasn't too into it until a bearded guy named Olaf came on and started yelling about a song named "Jaja

Ding Dong." Titus laughed until he almost fell over, and he saw that everyone was relaxed, cracking up, and it was...okay. Good, even. He'd thought that visits would always suck, but maybe... they didn't have to.

He had a sister on either side, poking him, rocking forward at the funniest bits while Dad was rubbing Susan's feet in the loveseat. Even that didn't bother him any longer, sort of like being furious that someone forgot to shut the barn door after the horse got out. The only thing left to do was catch the horse, really. Hmm, the baby wasn't a horse, so maybe that wasn't the best analogy.

Everything about the movie hit just right: wholesome, hilarious, and surprisingly heartwarming. When he first sat down, he intended to watch one movie begrudgingly and bolt as soon as possible, but when Susan suggested a break before the next one, he didn't move. *Two, two is a good number. Shows goodwill more than perfunctory participation.*

During the intermission, Susan made popcorn on the stove using spicy sesame oil. Titus had never tasted anything like it. Really good, peppery without being dusted with powder that got all over his fingers, and the heat built as he ate. Before, he'd felt guilty enjoying anything his stepmother did, like it made him a bad person and a disloyal son.

"This is delicious," he said softly.

"Yeah? That's quite a compliment coming from you! I got the idea from a food blog I check regularly. If you're interested, I can send you a couple of links."

"Sure, I'd like that."

The next Will Ferrell wasn't quite as good as the first, but he enjoyed it nonetheless. It was late now; surely it had been long enough for him to go to bed without Dad thinking he was being difficult or uncooperative. But before he could voice that intention, the doorbell rang.

Lucy bounded up. "I'll get it." She trotted off, and he heard her talking to someone, but he couldn't make out the words, just the rise and fall of their voices.

"Do you think it's about the coyotes?" Dad asked.

Susan shrugged, picking up the dishes, and Maya plucked the glasses and bowls from her and took them to the kitchen, more than she would've done for Susan a month ago. Their stepmother followed, and he could hear them chatting, not monosyllables like Maya used to offer. Like it or not, things were changing. When a pan clattered, Dad hurried into the kitchen, presumably to help.

He never did that with Mom.

Or maybe he had when Titus was small. He just couldn't remember. The past his parents had shared was gone, known only to his old man. And maybe that was why he'd moved on so fast. Because otherwise, he'd drown, trapped in the amber of those old memories, inherited by him alone.

"It's for you," Lucy called.

Titus blinked as she stepped into sight. "Are you sure? I don't know anyone here."

"Positive. This woman's really apologetic but insistent. I invited her in, but she said she'd rather talk outside." Lucy gestured toward the foyer. "She's out front."

There must be some mistake.

He was fucking exhausted, head teeming with questions, and

as he stepped out into the night air, the warmth surprised him after the chilly air-conditioning. There *was* a woman waiting for him, and his heart trembled in his chest as she turned, when he recognized her.

She's beautiful in the moonlight. No, none of that. Remember how things ended.

"Danica," he said flatly. "What the hell are you doing here?"

CHAPTER 25

YEAH, HE'S NOT HAPPY TO see me.

And why would he be?

Danica took a breath, mustering her resolve, and then she started talking. "Don't sell the bakery. Don't move to Arizona. I don't know how far you've come in the planning, but St. Claire needs you. *I* need you. It's all my fault, and I'm so sorry. I didn't even like that asshole. I met him to appease my grandmother, but I don't care about that either anymore. I don't want to live my life to please her, and more importantly, I want to live it with you. I want to see where this goes if you'll give me another chance. You're the one. I knew it ridiculously early on, but you were supposed to be a rebound, and everyone knows rebounds don't work out, and—oh my God, please say something."

Titus blinked at her in the glow from the streetlights. The night sounds were different here, birdsong she couldn't identify, but the call felt lonely. He unfolded his arms—that was something, right? It was a lessening of defensiveness.

"What are you even talking about? Why would I sell the bakery?"

"Mrs. Carminian said you're closing up shop and that Mr. Stevewell saw you and Maya leaving town. The way she talked, it was like you weren't coming back."

To her shock, Titus started laughing. "That old woman thrives on drama. She put two and two together and got forty-seven. We're only here for a couple of days, Danica. I would've been back Monday night. My stepsister will be staying with us because living with pregnant newlyweds is stressful for everyone and she needs a change of scene."

She covered her hands with her face. "Oh my God."

"How did you even find me?"

Crap. That's another question I can't answer easily.

"Public records. I dug up your dad's name and found him as the property owner here. You'd mentioned that he'd moved to Arizona." Hopefully, that was all possible because otherwise, she had no explanation for how Ethel had acquired the address. It wasn't like she could say it was magic.

"You did deep data mining and then flew four hours to beg me to forgive you? To plead with me not to leave town for good." His smile widened.

Yeah, he's enjoying this.

"Possibly I didn't think it through. It's...a little over the top."

"A *little*?" But from his expression, he'd shifted from angry to amused. His body language was softer.

"Okay, a lot. But you don't understand how serious Mrs. Carminian made it sound. I might have panicked. She was talking about Walter Reynolds and real estate listings and—"

Titus took a step toward her, grasping her upper arms. "I'm

not interested in any of that. Explain this shit with your grand-mother and how I can trust you not to let her get in your head again. I can forgive one mistake, but I won't let you break my heart."

"Are you saying I have that power?" she whispered.

"You damn near ruined me, woman. I was already planning my lonely life as a bachelor uncle. I almost joined the Rotary Club! I was two steps from checking out the solitary drinkers at the VFW."

She probably shouldn't laugh, but she couldn't help it. "I'm so sorry. If I'd known, I would have come sooner."

"Would you?"

Daringly, she stepped closer, and as she'd hoped, his grip on her biceps loosened, allowing her to settle against him. He still smelled faintly of sugar and cinnamon, remnants of his workday. Danica closed her eyes and breathed him in before remembering he'd asked for particular assurances.

"Look, my grandmother has certain expectations about my potential life partner. I think I already mentioned that my mother followed her heart and the family's been at war ever since with me square in the middle."

"Yeah, I know that much. And I guess the goal must be for you to marry money, judging by the car that jerk drove."

She jumped on that assumption because it was the only thing that made sense. "I'm sorry. Gram only uses one metric for measur-ing worth. I shouldn't have met Leech, even to placate her. I'm so sorry for hurting you. If you give me a second chance, I won't let anyone come between us ever again. I want to be your permanent taste tester. I want random puns during the day and to talk to you late at night just before you fall asleep. I want—"

"You talk a good game," he said softly. "But can you stay the course?"

"More words won't convince you. Only actions can. Are you willing to let me make it up to you?"

Titus smiled slightly and lowered his head to kiss the tip of her nose. "Your actions are already on the job. Hell, you panicked, stalked my family on the internet, and got on a plane because you were afraid of losing me for good. That's more than anyone has ever done to keep me around." From his tone, it seemed like he'd been abandoned a lot, something she found incredibly hard to fathom.

"Their loss is my gain," she said fiercely.

"You were right about one thing before. We weren't exclusive, so I didn't have the right to feel as hurt and betrayed as I did. But if we're doing this, I'm all in, no living like we already have one foot out the door. You're my girlfriend, I introduce you as such, with all the rights and privileges attached."

Danica laughed quietly. "What would those be?"

"I get to do this." He kissed her cheek. "And this." Another kiss, edging closer to her lips. "And this, if I feel like it…"

She lost patience with the teasing and kissed him and, oh, that kiss. It was the heat of a desert night and the calls of lonesome birds that finally received a reply from potential mates, the twinkle of stars in a sky so black that it was like ice melting after a long winter. His mouth was silk and heat, and his beard rasped against her skin in a way that made her open her mouth on a moan.

"All in favor, motion carried," she managed to say as he leaned his brow against hers.

"I'll make your family like me. Right now, I'm nothing to brag about, still paying off loans, but the bakery is turning a profit. In a few years, the outlook will be brighter. There's no money owed on the house, though I have to buy Maya out if I want to—"

"Hey." She cut him off with a finger pressed to his mouth. "I don't give a damn what you earn or owe. You asked how I can guarantee I won't let Gram scramble my brain again. Well, I already told her off. I made it clear that she'll have to fight my mom *and* me if she tries to interfere again. For years, I refused to take sides in the family feud, but you're worth throwing down for."

"You fought with your grandmother? Over me."

"I mean, not physically. It was a phone call." Technically, it hadn't been about Titus either, more about Danica having the right to choose her own path.

And I pick him.

Titus gave her the softest look, and she felt the warmth from head to toe. "I didn't think you actually punched her."

"Does this mean you forgive me? And we're together."

"It does. *I* never wanted us to be over in the first place," he pointed out.

"I'm sorry," she said again.

"You don't need to knee grovel or anything. I just... I can't believe you came back. Once they leave me, nobody ever comes back."

He'd hinted at a messy and tragic relationship history before, and he'd seemed weirdly convinced she was moving to Peru to raise alpacas the day they'd fought over her date with Richard

Leitch, but she wasn't in the mood to hear about his past. Danica snuggled deeper into his arms and let out a happy sigh when he rested his bearded chin against the top of her head.

She rubbed his back, taking pleasure in the flex of his muscles. "I should probably book a hotel room."

"Oh no you don't. If I have to stay here, so do you. You can meet Dad, Susan, and Lucy. It'll be nice to introduce my girlfriend to the family. I've never done that before."

"Never?"

"Well, Maya's met a few, but nobody ever makes it past a couple of months."

"I'll be the first," she declared.

"No time like the present." He took her hand and tugged her toward the house.

———————

Titus was acting a lot calmer than he felt.

This was rom-com-quality big-gesture territory. Part of him couldn't believe Danica had freaked out so much over the idea of him leaving town for good. God bless Mrs. Carminian and her bad assumptions. Between the meddlesome old lady and his neighbor Mr. Stevewell, they seemed to have fanned Danica's nerves into a full freak-out.

She's really here.

He squeezed her hand just to be sure, and she returned the pressure. As they approached the front door, it swung open, revealing Lucy, who glanced between their linked fingers with poorly concealed curiosity. "Friend of yours?"

"My girlfriend decided to surprise me," he said.

It was the simplest explanation, but his stepsister didn't look like she bought it entirely. "That's...cool. I guess."

Danica seemed to read hesitance from Lucy as well. "The truth is we had a fight before he left. Titus didn't answer when I called and texted—"

"I was on a plane," he cut in. "Forgot to switch airplane mode off when we landed."

"Anyway, I decided to apologize in person. It was my fault, and I wanted to meet his family anyway. I'm sorry for intruding." She extended her free hand. "You must be his stepsister. I'm Danica Waterhouse."

Lucy seemed to like the adult introduction. She shook hands, then said, "I'm Lucy Pike. For now. They're talking about changing that."

"You don't sound enthused," Danica noted.

"I've been Lucy Pike my whole life. Lucy Winnaker sounds like someone else."

Titus had mentioned that Lucy was moving to St. Claire, and he hoped Danica wouldn't be mad that he hadn't talked it over with her first. If she was, it was her own fault, frankly, but from her warm expression, it seemed like she genuinely cared about what Lucy was saying. That wasn't the expression of someone who would come across pissy later.

"Hopefully they won't push it," she said with what seemed like real sympathy.

Dealing with her cantankerous grandmother had likely taught her a lot about friction within families, so she probably did empathize with Lucy. Smiling, he wrapped an arm around her shoulders, moving past Lucy into the house. It seemed like everyone was done in the kitchen because Susan, Dad, and Maya all stepped into sight as soon as they did. Fucking open floor plan.

"Surprise," he said with what had to be a goofy grin. "My girlfriend's here. Dad, Susan, this is Danica."

Polite greetings followed, though he could tell that Dad and Susan were shocked that Danica was here so late without even a heads-up. Nothing he could do about that, so he glossed over it and emphasized how happy he was that she could meet them and that she'd wanted to help Lucy get settled so the girl would feel more at home after the move.

Susan softened immediately. "That's so sweet. I've been worried about sending her so far away. I'm glad to know she'll have lots of adults she can rely on."

Lucy collapsed on the couch and buried her face in a pillow. "Oh my God, Mom."

"It's our pleasure," Danica said smoothly. "I've lived in St. Claire for years, and before that, I came every summer to stay with my grandmother. It's a really great town."

"That's true," Dad said, almost against his will. His tone was quiet and sad, as if he was letting himself remember the old days.

"And I'm so sorry I showed up out of the blue. I was raised better than this. If it's inconvenient or uncomfortable, I can get a hotel room." Danica glanced earnestly between Dad and Susan, and it amused him to see how fast the old man melted.

"Oh, that's not necessary," Dad said.

"She can bunk with Titus," Susan put in. "We're not old-fashioned."

From the old man's look, he might've protested, had Susan not spoken up. He hated thinking about the age gap between them, and if he objected, it made him look uptight, something he avoided like the plague around his younger wife. Titus tried not to reveal how funny he thought it all was as the family said good night and gave hugs.

Maya lingered long enough to whisper, "Thought you broke up?"

"Just a speed bump."

"I like this one, bro. She's not afraid to go big."

Danica must have overheard that because she laughed. "Go big or go home, right?"

"That's what I'm talking about. Try to keep it down, you two. Remember there are minors in the house." With a cheeky grin, Maya headed off to Lucy's room.

Titus led the way to Jared's room. It was a typical teen boy lair, posters of bikini girls sprawled over shiny cars and sports team memorabilia scattered throughout. There was also gear unique to Jared, related to swimming, goggles, eye drops, and a whole drawer full of Speedos. Not that he planned to show those to Danica.

"This must be the stepbrother's turf. I'm afraid I don't remember his name."

"Jared. He's road-tripping and will be off to college after. I suspect they'll turn his room into a nursery. Or maybe Lucy's."

Danica made a face. "She's not thrilled about getting a younger sibling and being used for free childcare?"

"I wouldn't be either," Titus said.

"My parents are together, so it's not a problem I've dealt with. But I admire you for helping Lucy. I meant it when I said I'll do whatever I can to make her feel at home after the move. I wasn't just kissing up."

"That so?" he teased.

She stretched up on tiptoe, bracing her palms on his chest, and her touch seared through his shirt. Immediately, he wanted more, more than he could have in a lifetime. Even then, when she was old and gray, a mischievous old woman like Mrs. Carminian, it still wouldn't be enough. With every beat of his heart, he knew— he *knew*—that he would die, still hungry for her.

"Are you a witch?" he asked.

She froze. "Excuse me?"

"Because it really feels like you've cast a love spell on me."

Her laughter had a strange, strained note, but then she kissed him. "Mmm. Your sister's right. I want the makeup sex, but we need to wait. It would be weird to do it here. Can you behave if we sleep together?"

"What's the other option?"

"I could crash on the couch."

"Forget it, I can keep it in my pants. And I want to hold you." "Want" was the wrong word. "Need" was the right one, twisted up like barbwire, as if it would wound him physically to let her go.

It has to work this time. Has to.

She kissed him again. Again. Her mouth was magical, sweet and salty at the same time. "When we get home, it is *on*. Don't make plans for three days."

"What about work and food?"

"I'll take it under advisement. Do you want to shower first or should I?"

"You can. It's next door on the left."

It was best for them both to wash up tonight, avoid the rush in the morning. Maya preferred morning showers. If Lucy did too, there might be a jam-up, delaying whatever Susan had planned. Fortunately, his stepmother drove a minivan, so they would all fit, no special accommodation needed to add Danica to the party.

Danica grabbed her bag and ducked out with a quick kiss. When she came back, she smelled soapy clean, her hair falling in wet tangles. She flipped it over one shoulder with an adorably sheepish look.

"I forgot to pack a brush."

"Want to use my comb?" Before she could answer, he got it out of his backpack and started slowly working out the knots from her damp hair.

"That's even better," she said, tipping her head back.

"I'm so glad you didn't hesitate. Nobody's ever made me feel like I was worth chasing before. It's..." He let out a slow breath, wishing he could find the right words.

"Just wait," Danica whispered, casting him a simmering look. "I've barely begun to make it up to you. Look forward to it."

Titus groaned, his gaze locked on hers. "You know it'll be Monday night before I can enjoy what those eyes are promising, right?"

She smiled, all joyous temptation as she traced a teasing fingertip down the center of his chest. "Oh, trust me. I know."

CHAPTER 26

I'M SLEEPING WITH TITUS. IN someone else's bed.

It was a standard full-size, which meant it wasn't quite long enough for him. Wrapped around Danica like he was, Titus didn't seem to mind. He kept stroking her in innocuous places as if he couldn't quite believe she was here.

Frankly, neither could she. But she wasn't sorry about the grand gesture, even if she'd come across as impulsive in a big way.

"No idea what we're doing tomorrow?" she whispered.

"None. Susan keeps calling it a 'super fun surprise,' so I really don't know what to expect. I hope it's not an outdoorsy activity. None of us are used to the heat."

"Since she's pregnant, she'll probably go easy on the physical strain," Danica said.

"That makes sense. Hey…"

"Yeah?"

"Thanks for freaking out over me. I'm apparently quite into this." Titus laughed softly when she poked him.

"I'm never living this down, am I?"

"Sweet dreams," he said instead of offering false reassurance.

There were still problems to be dealt with, and she doubted she'd heard the last of Gram, but she intended to look on this as a vacation from all those issues. It had been a long enough day that Danica drifted off at once, secure in his arms. In the morning, Titus was already gone when she woke up, understandable since he was on a much earlier schedule normally. From the kitchen, she smelled something delicious—

Oh my God, he made cinnamon rolls.

Her stomach let out a horrendous noise, but before she could follow the delectable aroma of cinnamon and sugar, Titus rapped on the closed door and then let himself in without waiting for a reply. Since he was holding a plate with a giant gooey cinnamon roll and a cup of coffee, made exactly as she liked it, Danica fell in love with him all over again.

"You're incredible," she said in a ridiculously airy tone. "How are you this perfect?"

If eyes could beam out hearts, hers must be doing that right now. Titus grinned, perching on the edge of the bed. "Now you're just flattering me."

"Have you *seen* your pastries?"

Deliberately, he cut a piece of tender, steaming cinnamon roll, and the frosting trickled down over the soft inner roll. Danica moaned as he fed her the first bite. She considered insisting that she could feed herself, but it was more fun this way, eating from the fork he was holding. He passed her the coffee mug so she could sip when she needed to cut the glorious sticky-sweetness. She licked her lips, and his eyes heated, gaining a sheen that made them look almost like polished bronze. In the end, he fed her every bite, and it was almost like foreplay, even though he never touched her.

"Okay, so if I don't leave the room now, I won't let you get out of bed," Titus said huskily. "And that—"

"Would be bad?" It wasn't supposed to be a question, though it came out as one.

"Not bad per se, but you've made a fairly good impression on my family so far. I'd hate for them to decide that you're a sex maniac."

Danica grinned. "Even if I am one, it'd be best to leave that under wraps."

"I'll keep your secret." He leaned in for the best ever *good morning* kiss, and she felt confident that any morning breath was well concealed by the sugar and cinnamon.

"Then let me get dressed and brush my teeth. I'll be ready shortly."

Since Danica didn't know what they had planned for today and she'd already slept in, she hustled in getting ready. Grateful to Margie for packing a few decent outfits, she put on a cute summer dress in primary colors and added a filmy scarf to keep the sun off her shoulders. Her hair was a little wild from being left to dry on the pillow, so she dampened it and put it up, the best she could do without starting over. She brushed her teeth thoroughly, added tinted sunscreen and lip balm, then she hurried to the front room where everyone else was already waiting.

"I'm sorry. I hope we're not running late."

Susan shook her head. "Not at all. I hope everyone has fun

today. This is one of my favorite places. It's actually where Greg and I had our first date."

Greg. Did I know Titus's dad was named Greg?

"Greg and Susan" had such a sitcom ring to it. Danica made some noncommittal response as everyone piled into the gray minivan. Titus headed all the way to the back, so she followed him, leaving Maya and Lucy in the center, with Greg and Susan up front. She laughed softly as the powered doors swooshed closed.

"What?" Titus whispered.

"I feel like I'm being driven on a junior high field trip."

He grinned. "Don't tell anyone that we're holding hands."

His long fingers curled around hers, pulling her hand onto his thigh. With a happy sigh, Danica leaned into him. Now that she wasn't constantly living in a state of panic, it felt good to enjoy being with him. Endlessly right, if she was honest with herself. *Maybe my mom nailed it when she said that I just needed to let love in. I really need to talk to her.*

Danica didn't pay much attention to the conversation in the car, partly because she couldn't hear all of it with the elders blasting ABBA. That was probably more Greg than Susan, though his wife didn't seem to mind, and, hell, Danica had enjoyed the film version of *Mamma Mia!* as a teen. She was familiar with most of the songs and could sing along to "Waterloo." Soon, everyone was, even Lucy, though she would've been a toddler at the time.

The impromptu sing-along kept any tension from cropping up until Greg pulled into a huge parking lot, an entertainment center in the middle of the desert. Honestly, the complex was impressive, the sandy hue standing out against the red of the mesa rocks. As they drew closer, she saw that it was an aquarium, the perfect indoor activity.

"This is fantastic," she whispered.

"It won't be as good as Shedd," Titus predicted, "but at least we're not hiking in this heat." He waited for everyone else to climb out, then he gestured for Danica to precede him.

She crab-walked out of the back and came out of the minivan butt first. Maya steadied Danica as she got her footing in the parking lot. Though it wasn't even noon, she could already feel tightness in her lungs. Late afternoon would be miserable.

"So? What does everyone think?" Susan pressed her hands together, and Danica wondered if she realized it was an unconscious gesture that revealed how much she cared about receiving a favorable review.

"It's awesome," Lucy said.

"Really? I'm so happy." Mom and daughter hugged, and it was obvious to Danica that things had been messy between them for a while. "I wanted us to have fun together for once, without fighting. Especially since you're l-leaving."

"It's not like you'll never see me again," Lucy said.

Danica felt like maybe she shouldn't be listening in on this private moment, but if she rushed toward the entrance, that would send the wrong message too. Titus quietly put a hand on her shoulder, telling her wordlessly not to worry about it.

Maybe he's saying that I'm family now too? Or close enough.

"But you want to go. That wouldn't be true if you were happy."

Lucy sighed. "I don't want to do this in a parking lot, but…

here's the thing. I need some space. To *let* you be happy. If I stay, I'll feel jealous of the new baby, and we'll get on each other's nerves. This way, the distance will give us the time to...adapt. Does that make sense? You deserve a fresh start, Mom, but so do I."

To Danica, that sounded surprisingly mature. It didn't seem like Lucy would give Titus and Maya a hard time.

Susan sniffed and wiped her eyes. Then her husband stepped in, wrapping an arm around her shoulders. "We've been over this, babe. It makes perfect sense. Now let's stick to the plan and have a good time. I made reservations like you wanted for a nice lunch later. Now give me a smile, crying will upset baby Aubrey." He rubbed her belly once.

Frankly, none of that made Danica like Greg better, but Susan cheered up at once. "You're right. Family fun awaits!"

Surprisingly, it was an awesome day.

As predicted, the aquarium wasn't as nice as Shedd, but Titus enjoyed the visit. There were penguins and butterflies and a cool feature in the ladies' room, where they could look at sharks while washing their hands. That he didn't experience personally, but Maya, Lucy, and Danica told him all about it.

"I've never been anywhere that the bathroom was a recommended stop," Danica said, laughing.

Titus didn't kid himself. Sharing the experience with her made all the difference. She held his hand while they walked through the exhibits, soaking in the tranquility of the exotic marine life swimming or floating in their tanks. They paused often so Susan didn't get overtired, and it was…nice. No drama, just the sense of what things could be like in time. He liked sitting on the bench with Danica, holding her hand.

That's kind of our thing.

They ate lunch at Olive and Ivy. Hummus, of course, bruschetta, various flatbreads, and salad to share. Until today, he would've bet that his dad had no freaking clue what couscous was. But here the man was, saying, "You're right, the couscous is fantastic."

The food was great, but his dad was a steakhouse guy, and he wouldn't have chosen Mediterranean without a nudge. Sometimes it was hard for Titus to see the old man changing, as he'd refused to do for Titus's mom. As if she sensed Titus's ambivalence, Danica lifted a piece of white truffle and prosciutto flatbread to his mouth. He nibbled the food from her hand, and her kindness eased some of the sting. *Bear with it. He loved Mom too. Believe that.*

By the time they got home, it was late afternoon, time to help Lucy with the packing if she needed it. Susan had to work in the morning, so she'd be saying goodbye then. Dad was retired, though he did some day-trading. And wonder of wonders, he'd volunteered to drive them to the airport. Titus didn't like thinking of people as lucky charms, but really, everything about his life got better when Danica was around. The family had been on their best behavior the entire time, likely not wanting her to think badly of them.

He made Susan happy by asking to watch *Eurovision* again. It seemed to please her that he'd enjoyed it enough to want to share it with Danica, who laughed her ass off in all the same spots. It was just as fun the second time too.

Around eight, Titus poked his head into Lucy's room. "Need any help?"

"We've got it," his stepsister answered.

Both Maya and Danica were lending a hand, helping Lucy decide what clothes would translate best to the Midwest. "We definitely need to get you a winter coat," Maya said, frowning at the collection of thin jackets they'd assembled.

"Will it snow?" Lucy asked.

Danica smiled. "It usually does. I bet you're hoping for a white Christmas."

Lucy's eyes brightened as she considered the possibility. "That would be amazing. I've been reading up, and apparently Christmas lights are a big deal in your area."

"Oh definitely," Maya said. "We'll take a drive. East Peoria, Alton, Aurora, Lisle, Effingham, all awesome and worth seeing. If you don't mind time in the car, I'll make hot cocoa, and we could make a night of it."

"Oh my God, I'm so excited. I probably seem really basic, but I'm all in for this heartland heartfelt stuff."

"You're awesome," Danica said firmly. "And there's nothing wrong with being enthusiastic. Acting bored as a shortcut to coolness is so 2008."

"Studied ennui dates back to the nineties," Maya pointed out. "What do you think grunge was all about?"

Lucy grinned as she zipped up her second suitcase. "You're both pretty. And I think I'm set. I just need to pack my carry-on, toiletries, and electronics in the morning. Thanks for your help, both of you. It was good having local guides for clothing questions."

"I'm entirely superfluous," Titus said.

Maya offered, "You get to carry the heavy suitcases. We'll even let you drag them around the airport tomorrow, all the way to baggage check."

He pressed a palm to his heart, pretending to be overwhelmed by her generosity. "Wow, really?" Catching Danica's eye, he flexed. "Lucky for you, I'm ready."

His sister laughed and made a shooing motion. "The power of the flour bag workout in action. Let us get ready for bed. We have a big day tomorrow."

"Uh, it's not even nine," Lucy said.

"Fine, I want to call my girlfriend. I'll be in the backyard for a bit." That was the first time Maya had spoken of the woman Titus had seen with her outside the bakery, but he didn't tease her. Not when it seemed to be brand-new.

"Understood," Lucy said.

Danica followed Maya out and stepped into Titus's arms without being coaxed there with pastries. That felt...miraculous, if he was being honest with himself. On some level, this still didn't feel real—that she'd gotten the wrong idea from Mrs. Carminian and dropped everything to get him back. This probably wouldn't endear him to her cousin, however, as she must be stuck minding the shop while Danica was off being romantic and impulsive.

"What does Clem like to eat?" He'd asked this once before and not gotten an answer.

"Why?"

"Because I'm going to stuff her full of baked goods until she likes me."

Danica laughed so loud that she put her palm over her mouth to muffle it. When she calmed enough to speak, she moved her fingers aside, eyes glittering with amusement. "Okay, that's calculating and fantastic. As plans go, I give it fair odds. Let's see... She loves snickerdoodles and white chocolate macadamia nut cookies. Cherry pie is her favorite, though any fruit but peach is safe. Cake, she adores red velvet for some reason." She made a face. "*I'm* not a fan, but she freaking loves beautiful little red velvet cupcakes with all the fancy touches."

Titus got his phone out, taking notes as fast as he could. "This intel is exactly what I needed. Don't worry—I'll succeed in this mission."

"I believe in you," she said softly.

As he leaned down to kiss her, his dad called, "Titus? Where are you? If you're not busy, I'd like a word."

Yeah, that's code for "get in here."

Quickly, he dusted a kiss against Danica's forehead instead. "I'll be right back. This probably won't take long."

As it turned out, his dad wanted a heart-to-heart, and it took a while, nearly two hours. Titus listened to Dad's worries about being too old to be a good father to baby Aubrey and whether a geezer like him could keep a woman Susan's age happy. Thankfully, Titus didn't need to say much and the old man ended by thanking him for his willingness to help with Lucy.

"We had a fight... Jared's furious about the baby. That's why he's gone. I don't even know if there *is* a road trip. He may have made himself scarce before college starts, and it's eating Susan up that she might hurt her older kids by giving them a younger sibling."

It never even occurs to him that Maya and I might mind too. And the way he puts it—like this is a gift we've been given, one we don't appreciate.

Briefly, Titus considered bringing up his feelings, but all the other times he'd tried, it had always ended in a fight. Honesty didn't solve everything. Sometimes it just made everyone involved feel shitty.

"Yeah, it's tough," he said.

"Anyway, I wanted to thank you. If you need money for Lucy's expenses..."

Is he seriously offering child support right now?

"Forget it, Dad. Maya and I can look after our little sister."

The old man froze briefly and then swiped his hand across his eyes. "Damn. I didn't expect to get so girlie so fast. Maybe I have couvade syndrome, you ever heard of that?"

"Can't say that I have."

"It's where an expectant father gets symptoms from his pregnant wife. Look it up—it's an actual thing. Point is, it means a lot to Susan and me—and Lucy too, I'm sure—that you've warmed up to her. She's a lonely kid." Dad sighed. "Never invites anyone to the house, seems like most of her friends are on the internet. Susan's been worried for a while."

"We'll do what we can to help her make friends in St. Claire," Titus promised.

"By the way, I like your girlfriend. Seems like a sweet person. I wasn't sure when she showed up so late without calling, but I like that she loves you enough to travel halfway across the country to apologize. You don't find devotion like that every day."

Titus swallowed hard. "No, you really don't."

CHAPTER 27

KNOWING IT WAS RISKY, DANICA still performed the spell.

She didn't have all the accoutrements, but for a gifted witch, such issues were a challenge, not a deal breaker. True magical soundproofing was impossible, but she could send a suggestion that others should forget what they heard. Because who was she fooling? There was no way she'd last another night with Titus, curled up in platonic cuddles. The night before had been snuggly and gorgeous and also sheer torture because she'd wanted to strip off his clothes and lick him all over. Titus was seriously deluded if he didn't understand how hot he was.

There was no way she'd ping on Gavin Rhys's radar all the way in Arizona, though there was a small possibility that another hunter might notice something since the house wasn't warded. That said, they were leaving tomorrow, so there likely wouldn't be time for anyone to get here. Anyway, what were the odds? She'd lived for thirty years without attracting undue attention, going about her witchy business.

At any rate, anything that went down in this bedroom tonight wouldn't get talked about; she'd made sure of that. When Titus returned from chatting with his dad, she had the lights off and was under the covers, completely naked, although he wouldn't discover that until he joined her. He came in quietly, tiptoeing, like he suspected she might already be asleep. The day hadn't been *that* exhausting.

Danica peeked at Titus as he stripped down to boxer briefs and put on a worn white T-shirt. As he slid beneath the covers, she rolled to face him, and he put an arm around her, freezing when he touched bare skin.

His voice sounded hoarse. "You're...not wearing anything."

She smiled in the dark. "You should be a detective, cracking cases left and right."

"I don't want to discourage you from being comfortable, but this could prove...difficult," he said hoarsely.

"Are you sure? Because I feel like sex with you is the easiest choice in the world."

Titus sucked in a shaky breath. "I thought we agreed to wait until we got home."

"Yeah, but I changed my mind. Waiting is terrible. Instant gratification is the wave of the future. And I can be quiet, I swear. Nobody will suspect a thing."

Thanks to my diversion spell, everyone will pay attention to something—anything—else.

"Danica..."

She kissed his neck, and a shiver worked through him. "If you don't want to, I'll put on my pajamas. I'm not trying to pressure you or make you feel uncomfortable."

"That's not the issue here. I feel...guilty. And a little..."

"What?" she breathed.

"Bad. As in wicked."

"Let your conscience be your guide. Never let it be said that I pulled you from the path of righteousness."

He stroked a big hand down her arm, seeming unable to stop touching her. "We strip the sheets in the morning and throw them in the washing machine before anyone gets a look at them."

"It's adorable that you're worried about—"

Titus peeled his underwear and T-shirt off in record time. Then he kissed her, possibly to prevent additional teasing, but his soft, lush mouth framed by the scratch of his beard distracted her. His tongue stroked hers, deep and luscious. He pulled her on top of him, and she fell deeper into him, loving the flex of his muscles and the rigid cock burning against her belly as they kissed. She spread her thighs, opening so he could feel how wet she already was.

"Wow. Oh damn. Wow."

He flipped her. "Last time I wanted to kiss you all over and you said 'next time.'"

"Mmm. Excellent, have at me."

Maybe she should have tempered that invitation because Titus took her at her word. His mouth and hands were everywhere, licking, nipping, nuzzling, stroking until she could barely breathe, let alone think. Danica twisted and panted, not letting herself moan to keep up the pretense of being quiet. When he put his face between her legs, she practically launched off the bed and framed his head with her thighs. She sank her fingers into his hair and worked against him, losing her mind over the sheer, sharp pleasure of his talented tongue, his teasing mouth.

"Fuck. Oh fuck," she gasped. "I don't usually come like this..."

Titus paused, replacing his tongue with a teasing fingertip on her clit, and left her hanging at the precipice. "But...?"

"I'm close."

Maddeningly, he kissed away from her pussy then, licking and nibbling down her thighs and back up, like he meant to drive her wild. She bit down on her lower lip, hot and cold shivers rolling through her. Danica had never been turned on to the point that it felt like an out-of-body experience.

"I have to punish you a little," he whispered. "For what you put me through."

"Shit. I thought you forgave me too fast."

"I do forgive you, but I'm planning to imprint on you so you can't get off without thinking about me. My lips, my fingers, my cock."

She swallowed hard as he traced a teasing caress inches away from her slick labia. "Oh yes."

"Tell me that you belong to me, Danica."

"I do. I'm yours."

"No more running, no more excuses. We can date for as long as you want, but this is permanent. We're good together."

"So good," she whispered.

"I bet you need to come. Should I let you?"

In answer, she lifted her hips, and he stroked her clit as he went in with his mouth. Two more licks, and the orgasm rocked through her. Her thighs tensed as he settled between them, thrusting his throbbing cock inside her as she came, and he groaned as she clenched around him. He kept a light pressure on her clit until she pulled his hand away, shaking and breathless. Somehow she managed to wrap her legs around his hips as he fucked her through the aftershocks. Honestly, she thought she was done, but a few minutes in, her body stirred again, pulled into arousal by his demanding strokes.

"That's it. You'll go again for me."

He kissed her neck, the top of her breasts, while working into and out of her body in measured strokes. His control troubled her; she liked it better when he was helpless and unhinged. Danica bit him on the chest.

"You jerked off today."

Titus hitched, mid-glide. "How can you tell?"

"Because otherwise you'd be as desperate to come as I was."

"You're right, love. I did it right here in bed with you this morning, quiet as a mouse while I yanked my cock. Woke up hard as a rock, and I couldn't walk down the hall like that. It wouldn't subside with you right next to me either."

She arched up to meet him, digging her heels into his ass. "Fuck. When you put it like that, a secret wank offered the only sensible solution. Was it good?"

"So fucking good. I listened to you breathe, and I came so hard, all over my hand."

"Did it make you feel filthy?"

"Yes. And I loved it." Titus groaned, pushing into her deep and hard. "I can't stop. You feel too good. I'm coming."

When his climax filled her with heat, she came too, a soft little flutter that wrung the last of her energy. Danica went boneless beneath him, stroking his spine in languid motions while their heart rates settled. She brushed his hair back and cuddled him until he got self-conscious about his weight and rolled to his side, snuggling her against him.

"I feel like I should say something profound, but my head is so fuzzy," he whispered.

"You're saying I blew your mind."

"No question."

Titus made a genuinely happy sound, and she could tell he was about to drift off. Gently, she ran her fingers through his hair and caressed every part of him that she could reach, marveling at how beautiful they were together. He had been right to worry about the sheets, as there would be major damage in the morning. She shifted out of the wet spot and waited for the fear to set in. Only... it didn't.

Nothing had changed. She just loved him enough to accept the prospect of losing her magic. Because life without him was a bleak, lusterless existence anyway. No spell could replace him; there was no better partner waiting for her anywhere in the world.

If she had to choose, it would be Titus, every time.

———————————

It was just as well that Titus and Danica already had mind-blowing makeup sex.

In the morning, everything was chaotic, and he needed the

endorphins to tide him over. They managed to wash the sheets on the DL and said goodbye to Susan amid sniffles on both sides. Traveling home was harried, as Danica had forgotten to book a return ticket. They managed to upgrade Maya to business, and that freed a seat for Danica in coach. Titus got the aisle, Lucy preferred window, and Danica snuggled against Titus's side, content at being in the middle.

This is incredible.

Normally Titus hated flying, but with Danica next to him, the hours breezed by. After collecting Lucy's stuff, he paused at the ATM and then led the way to the parking garage and did some fancy Tetris-style packing to fit all their stuff in the car. In St. Claire, he needed to focus on getting Lucy settled, and that would take a few days. Luckily, Danica understood that, and she didn't press when he dropped her off at home with a quick kiss.

Maya and Lucy had been dozing in the back seat. As he returned to the Leaf, Lucy asked, "Are we there yet?"

"She's been saving that since we landed." Maya pointed toward the other side of town. "About fifteen minutes more. We live out in the country, no close neighbors."

"Oh wow, that's different. We always lived in apartments until Mom married Greg." Lucy sat forward, checking out everything as they drove back through town and onto the county road that led home. "St. Claire really is cute. Is that your bakery?"

Titus answered without looking. "That's it. You can come to work with Maya when you feel ready, once you've settled in."

"Not with you?"

He laughed. "I leave at four in the morning."

Lucy bit her lip with an expression of abject horror. "Seriously? Maybe I don't want to be a baker after all."

As he pulled into the driveway, he wondered what she'd think of the house. Judging by her bright smile, she liked it fine. Doris burst out of the front door, wagging her tail so hard that she almost fell over. Trev ambled out afterward, mellow as always.

"Right on schedule. Where's my money?"

Titus laughed because he'd predicted this. Since Trev didn't have an actual job, he never helped friends out of the kindness of his heart. And that was fine. Lately, Titus had needed his services more than ever.

"Here you go. Stopped at the airport ATM just for you."

Trev put the money in his worn-out Avengers wallet without counting it. "Pleasure doing business with you." He turned to Lucy, extending a hand. "I'm Trevor. You must be the famous Lucy Pike."

Titus was a little surprised that Trev remembered Lucy's whole name, but she seemed happy about it. Hopefully not in an inappropriate crush way since Trevor was twice her age, even if he acted like a college student. *Oh crap, are these Dad feelings? Do I have to worry about every person Lucy talks to from now on?* Titus shot an anxious look at Maya, but her laughing eyes told him not to freak.

"I'm famous? Since when?"

"Since I helped—"

"Shut it, Trevor." He landed an elbow to silence his friend. They'd done such a good job of keeping the room reno a surprise. No screwups at the last minute.

Trev grabbed his stomach. "Oof, right. Shutting up."

"Let's get inside," Maya said. "Titus, get the bags. Your room is this way," she added for Lucy's benefit, who hurried after her with the carry-on like a baby duckling.

Titus made Trev haul one of the suitcases, and when they caught up, Lucy was crying a little, both hands pressed against her mouth, and she kept saying, "Oh my God," over and over. Which he hoped was a good thing.

Maya hugged the girl while shrugging one shoulder at him, like *I don't know what's up either.* "You okay?" she asked eventually.

"You spent time, effort, and money doing this for me. That means you really want me here, you know? It's not sympathy. You wanted me to feel at home, like this is my room. And it's so pretty." Her eyes sparkled as she touched all the little details that Maya had thought a sixteen-year-old girl would appreciate.

For a moment, Titus admired their handiwork too. "Glad you like it. We emptied the dresser and the closet so you can arrange your stuff however you want. And if you're missing anything, just let us know. If we can't get it locally, we'll order online."

Maya laughed. "What the hell do you think she needs? Rare, exotic sanitary pads? A mystic blood cup?"

Embarrassed, Titus rubbed the back of his neck. "Hell if I know."

"Whoa, if you're planning to talk about periods, I need hazard pay," Trev mumbled.

"Moving on," Lucy said firmly.

Titus thanked God that his stepsister wasn't as committed to messing with him as Maya. He might not survive a tag-team bout.

"Right. I'll throw together something for dinner, and afterward, we'll get you registered for school. I checked it out, and we can do it online. Susan gave me a folder with all the pertinent documentation before we left."

"Sounds good. Do you need help cooking?" From Lucy's expression, she really wanted to unpack, but it was sweet of her to offer.

"I'm fine. Make yourself at home. I'll call when it's ready." Titus heard Maya pointing out the bathroom, going over the house rules they'd agreed on, and talking about the chore list. Trev followed him downstairs and into the kitchen. "You're staying, I take it?"

"Hell yeah. You're a better cook than my mom."

"Don't you dare make the 'wife' joke."

Trevor feigned shock, donning a wounded expression. "That would be badly done, dude. Anyone can be good at cooking and/ or kitchen chores. It's not a wife thing."

"See, this is why we're friends."

Pasta was fast, so he whipped up a simple red sauce for the penne they had on hand. Caprese salad was easy as well; he put Trev to work slicing tomatoes. In half an hour, Titus had a nice meal ready. The ladies joined them as he shook some hand-grated parmesan onto each dish.

Lucy beamed. "Did Mom tell you that pasta is my favorite?"

It seemed like a bad idea to refute, so he smiled instead. "Dig in."

Trev kept the conversation from getting awkward, as he never met somebody he didn't like and was incapable of rambling to. Lucy laughed a lot at his dumb jokes, letting Titus reflect on what delicious baked good he would make to bribe Danica's cousin. Cookies? Pie? Or the super-fancy red velvet cupcakes she'd mentioned?

First, though, he worked with Lucy on her school registration. By the time he finished, he figured he ought to get to bed, as his day would start bright and early. *I can make Clem's cupcakes tomorrow at work.* Mind made up, he tidied the kitchen and headed out back to play with Doris, who was already chasing a tennis ball with Trevor.

"Are you crashing here tonight?"

"I'd rather go home if that's cool. If you're too tired to drive me, I can get a ride."

"Dude. It'll take half an hour for anyone to get out here, presuming there are even any drivers roaming around tonight."

"Then get your keys, bro. I'm tired of sleeping with your dog, and I miss my bed." Though Trev tried to be cheerful, tonight he seemed...down somehow. Like something had happened he didn't want to talk about.

"You okay?"

"Got an e-vite. Sarah's wedding. Good for her, right? She didn't let a guy like me fuck up her life permanently."

"Shit. I'm sorry, man."

"It's whatever. Like, I knew she wasn't coming back. I've known for years, so I shouldn't be bothered by this. If I was genuinely a nice guy like everyone says I am, I'd be happy for her, but mostly I'm sad for me and a little pissed."

"Anything I can do?"

"Just take me home. I'm gonna brood, Batman-style. It's not usually my go-to move, but it feels right for the occasion."

"To pull that off, you need a rooftop, not a basement."

Trevor laughed. "With the greatest respect, fuck you, my guy."

Titus wished he knew what more to do, but he did as requested and ran Trev home. His friend was quiet most of the way, staring out into the darkness in a way that made Titus think he was seeing mainly his own reflection. And maybe not liking much of what he saw.

It's not too late, he wanted to say.

But he was the last person who ought to be giving advice; he really had no clue why he and Danica were back together. He just wasn't looking a gift horse in the mouth.

"Thanks a bunch," he finally said as he parked the car.

"No prob. Things better for you, at least? Maya told me you got back together with Danica. She flew to Arizona for you, man. That's wild."

"I know."

"No obstacles left, only true love?"

"Her cousin doesn't like me. I'm planning to woo her with baked goods."

Trevor forced a smile as he got out. "Good luck storming the castle."

CHAPTER 28

DANICA EXPECTED TO FIND CLEM waiting like an angry parent, but the house was empty, even though the car they shared was parked in the drive.

Trying not to worry, she dropped a message in the coven group chat. Anyone seen Clem recently? On a scale of 1 to 10, how mad is she?

At first nobody answered. Then Kerry finally sent, Pretty pissed, but it's your life. She was talking about broken promises, so I think you owe her an apology.

It will be okay if you mean it, Priya added.

Soon, Leanne chimed in. Forget family drama. Did you get the D?

Smirking, Danica sent an eggplant emoji.

They were right about the apology, but she wouldn't do it over text. Some things went better face-to-face. It was impossible not to wonder if Clem was okay, if she'd gotten in too deep with the witch hunter, but all Danica could do was be here for her when the time came. She wouldn't even give Clem a hard time.

With a soft sigh, she wished she'd asked more about her

mom's early relationship with her dad. Or hell, it would be nice to know how long it would take for her to lose her power. Minerva Waterhouse was a soft soul, tender as a spring blossom; that was how Gram talked about her anyway, usually not in such flattering terms. The old witch made comments about how Minerva was all sentiment and sensitivity, so Danica never asked her mom difficult or awkward questions.

But…there's always more than one side to a story.

The back of her head tickled, making her wonder why she'd never questioned this before. Honestly, it felt like a veil lifting, the mere possibility that her grandmother might not be right about absolutely everything. Danica frowned, rubbing the side of her head. *Gram wouldn't have…done something to us, right? For our own good.*

She got a message from Clem. Don't worry about work tomorrow. You must be exhausted from the sudden trip. I'll cover the shop.

She didn't feel great about it, but her cousin didn't reply to any of her texts, and she didn't answer when Danica called either. Vaguely upset by this radio silence, she went to bed feeling out of sorts, like her family was falling apart. If Clem came home, she was gone again by the time Danica got up.

Suddenly, Danica wanted to see her mom more than anything. Since she left home, she hadn't spent that much time with Mom, and usually Gram was there too, and it was always awkward. She sent Mom a text:

Are you busy? I'd like to stop by later.

Never too busy for you, came the immediate reply. Looking forward to it.

She threw a few things in a backpack and grabbed the car keys. Clem must be furious, so she'd grovel when she got back and work nonstop while Titus was busy with his stepsister. Before she set out, she sent a message telling him that she'd be at her mom and dad's tonight. Then she copied the text to Clem as well.

The drive to Normal was familiar, two hours or so on I-55. Danica made good time, and she exited the highway just before dinnertime. Nostalgia overwhelmed her as she drove through town, seeing all the places where she hung out as a kid. Auntie Allegra had raised Clem here too, relying on Minerva and Laurence to help.

She pulled into the driveway. Mom and Dad's place was newer than the house she'd bought from Gram, a simple three-bedroom ranch. Only one full bath, but for a small family like theirs, it had never been a problem. The garden, though, the garden was lavish and beautiful. People regularly stopped to take pictures because of the incredible profusion of herbs and flowers. As usual, Mom was working in the yard when Danica got out of the car.

Minerva had on cutoffs, a ratty tank top, and a baseball cap; she completed the look with heavy work gloves and rubber boots. Gram would have so much to say about her daughter's style, but Danica went in for the hug, regardless of potential grime. Frankly, her mom looked fantastic, content with her life choices.

"I'm so happy you're here," Mom said. "I baked after I got your text, and there's a pitcher of fresh lemonade in the fridge. Before we settle in a for a visit, I need a shower, but would you mind doing me a favor?"

"Not at all. What do you need?"

"I'm looking for a book I marked for donation by mistake. It might be in some boxes I stashed in the guest room. Would you check? This rhododendron desperately needs help."

"What's the name of it?"

Minerva told her then added, "Ten minutes, fifteen tops, and I'm all yours."

"No problem."

Danica followed her mom inside the house, breathing in cool air and the faint scent of fresh flowers, vases of them in every room. She kicked her shoes off and headed for the guest room, where she found cardboard cartons chock-full of her mother's history. It didn't take long to unearth the gardening book her mother had requested, but on top of another box, she found what looked like old journals. Curious, she flipped one open.

March 18, 1989

I've never felt this way before. With everyone else, it's work, an endless struggle, but not Laurence. It's easy. And he's unbelievably sweet. He drove forty miles to get a tape that I've been looking for, and he played it in the car when he took me home. We kissed for ages—

Okay, maybe not. She skimmed the sexy stuff and found another entry dated a few months later.

June 20, 1989

I think we have to elope. Mom will never give her blessing, and she's threatening to hurt Laurence. She even made up the craziest story about how I'll lose my magic if I marry

him. Everyone I've talked to said it's absolute nonsense,
that they've never heard of the Waterhouse curse. Ethel
said that if it's not true, Mom is mean enough to hex me
herself. And frankly, I don't care if she does. I can't live
without Laurence. I won't. Fuck her, it's MY LIFE.

Danica blinked. "Holy. Shit."

Did that mean the Waterhouse curse started with Minerva?
That Gram actually fucking laid a curse on her own daughter?

"That's so messed up." She ran an anxious hand through her
hair, knowing she had to talk to Mom about this when she got out
of the shower.

"Did you find it?" Mom asked. She was dressed in clean khaki
shorts and a sleeveless blouse, hair still up in a towel. She seemed
to notice the notebook in Danica's hand. "My old journals... I used
to write constantly, but I don't have that much to say these days."

Is that because you lost your magic? She couldn't bring herself
to ask the question aloud, but she hugged her mom tight, realizing
that she'd gotten stingy with physical affection as she got older.
Startled, Mom put her arms around her and rubbed her back.

"Something wrong, Little Star?"

"Will Dad be home soon?"

"Around six. He's meeting with a new client this afternoon, so
we have plenty of time to chat before dinner."

Danica nodded, relieved that she had a little private time with
her mom. "Let's talk over cookies and lemonade."

They settled at the kitchen table, and Danica opened up to
her mom as she hadn't in years, outlining all the problems she'd

run into with Gram, her spontaneous romance with Titus, Gram's coercion and the forced Bindr dates, the way she'd fought with her grandmother like never before. Finally, she explained how she'd told Gram off over the phone, threatened to set Minerva on her, and eventually decided that her happiness lay with Titus. A mundane. Though Mom listened to everything without comment or judgment, her expression darkened.

"I'm sorry. It sounds like things have been crappy." Mom pushed the plate toward her.

Food couldn't solve these problems, but they did sweeten them up a little. Danica ate a cookie and took a breath, bracing for the toughest issue of all. "Now I need to know, did Gram curse you? Is that why you don't have any magic?"

Such a long silence. Then Minerva started laughing. "Oh, baby. Is that what you think? Is that what she told you? That I have no magic."

"No. Yes? I'm not sure. I'm really fucking confused right now."

"Let me straighten things out for you, Little Star. Your grandmother and I fought, just like you did, about me seeing Laurence. She didn't hex me, though she did try to con me into believing I'd lose my power."

"Same," Danica muttered. "But...does that mean you've been a witch my *entire life*?" That didn't even make sense. "Why did you turn my training over to Gram then?"

"I'm a vivimancer," Minerva said, taking her hand. "I couldn't train you myself. I learned from Aunt Gladys because Mother couldn't teach me."

"Then...the gardens..."

"Are my magic. I've always been low-key about it, and I do a fair amount of regular gardening as well. Because I wanted *you* to grow up feeling like you had a choice. Not like me. I wanted you to see that it was possible to be happy with a mundane partner. Your dad hasn't cost me anything, except a little of your grandmother's favor."

"This is batshit," Danica muttered.

"I'm so sorry. I had no idea Mother would—"

"Try to brainwash Clem and me, threaten someone I love, and generally act like a villainous overlord?"

"Yes. If I'd *known*, I would've stepped in ages ago. But the two of you were so close, and you hated it when we argued in front of you... I'm so sorry. This is all my fault."

"Wait, if the curse isn't real, why did my magic go haywire?"

I didn't hallucinate that. It happened.

Mom nibbled a cookie, eyes thoughtful. "I can't be sure, but stress and anxiety? It's not as bad as drunk-casting, but doing spellwork when you're agitated is a bad idea."

Oh goddess. Danica realized she'd suspected that in the beginning, before Gram got into her head. A thought struck her then, and Danica brightened. "But...that means you've been practicing all these years. Living with Dad? How? Teach me your ways!"

"There's a simple solution, Little Star. Tell him you're Wiccan or pagan or new age, whatever modern verbiage you prefer. Then live openly as a witch, but don't ever explain more than that."

Danica blinked. She'd known Mom had told Dad that she was pagan—but she'd had no clue why. She'd always suspected it was

Mom's way of honoring what she'd lost, turning magic into religion so she could at least celebrate their festivals. And she'd believed that gardening had replaced magic in her mom's life, but that *was* her magic. Danica's heart sang with the unexpected brightness of it.

"Wow." This revelation felt like a miracle.

Mom went on, "Meet with your 'book club,' as you always have. This circumvents the council's ruling, and you don't have to hide. I've been doing it for thirty-five years."

"Oh goddess," Danica breathed. "I think you might be a genius."

Her mom sipped her lemonade. "Protective spells are quite literal, you know. When you're a bit crafty, it's easy enough to work around the rules, and the council leaves you be."

"Everything I thought I knew was wrong. There's no Waterhouse curse, and Gram is an incredibly bigoted asshole."

"Well. Yes," her mother said softly.

And it was so funny and sad that Danica didn't know if she ought to laugh or cry. "She lied to me, my whole fucking life. Tried to make me hate people for no reason. I don't know if I can forgive her."

"I need to…*speak* with your grandmother," Mom said tightly. "Let me deal with her. I won't let her off easy. Messing with my daughter?" Her tone turned steely. "I don't think so. I wonder if Allegra knows."

"I'm not sure. Clem fights with her more, so maybe?"

"Hmm. I'll check into it. Leave everything to me. Your grandmother won't bother you again. Oh, quick question, Little Star?"

"Sure."

"Is your young man a virgin?"

Danica choked on her cookie because weirdly, her mother had been asking this for years. "What the hell, why is that *always* your first question?"

Tapping her fingers, the other woman appeared to make a decision. "Since you're sure Titus is the one and we're being up front, I have a confession to make."

Oh no.

"Don't tell me Dad isn't my—"

"Nothing like that! I told you that your grandmother was... difficult about your father as well. I went through the same thing you did, meeting people she approved of. Struggling with my desire to please her weighed against my need to live my own life."

"I'm sorry, Mom."

"That's not the point of this story. Like you, I dated a pure witch asshole, but unlike you, I was fond of him. He...hurt me. Cheated over and over before I worked up the nerve to leave. After I made the break, Auntie Allegra took me out drinking. We talked some serious shit, and..." Her mom mumbled something.

"What? It *sounded* like you said you two might've cast a drunken hex, but that can't be right."

Mom met her gaze squarely this time. "It's true. We cast a forbiddance spell. *My* daughter would never know the pain of being cheated on. Her soul mate would literally be unable to... er, seal the deal. With anyone else."

"Oh my God. Poor Titus. Do you think *that's* why the spells I was trying to cast on him went wrong? Your magic was interfering with mine."

Mom thought for a moment, finishing her cookie. "Yes, I suspect so. This is so funny!"

"It's not! Poor Titus. You almost ruined his life."

When Minerva stopped laughing, she said, "I'll do something nice for him, now that he's finally found you. Maybe cast a blessing for his business?"

What a fucking day.

"Do that. Should we make dinner for Dad?"

Her mother reached across the table to take her hand. "Definitely. He'll be so happy you're here. I am too."

It was impossible for her to stay mad when her mom was smiling that way. "I'll come home more often. And I'll bring Titus next time."

Shortly before Titus fell asleep, he got a call from Danica.

"Hey, you." He settled against the headboard, absently scratching Doris between the ears. The dog rolled over and presented her belly, ever one to capitalize on a scritching opportunity. "Miss me already?"

"Yes, definitely. But...I have a weird question for you. Are you willing to answer?"

"No to latex, yes to a little light bondage, and I'm flexible about who gets tied up."

She laughed softly. "Okay, noted. Yes or no, willing to answer?"

"Sure. I'm slightly concerned but curious enough to move forward."

"Was it your first time when we did it in your office chair?"

Holy shit. How did she know?

Titus had thought he'd done a good job not showing just how inexperienced he was, but maybe he was clumsier than he'd imagined. Sighing, he admitted, "Yeah, it was. To be honest, my romantic history is a train wreck. I have the weirdest breakups on record, like seriously. I didn't tell you that before because I thought you'd run. Nobody who knew the *Titanic* would sink ahead of time would've boarded, right?"

"Titus, you're not a behemoth boat destined to be scuttled in icy waters."

"Until I met you, I was pretty sure I'd die alone," he admitted quietly.

"That's sweet and terrifying in equal measure. But can you back up and maybe tell me about a couple of those breakups?"

"Why?"

He didn't really think she would hurt him with the information, but this whole call felt...strange. And he couldn't take another round of push-pull with her.

"I might send thank-you notes to all your exes. Because they have terrible judgment and poor impulse control, I get to spend my life with you. I mean, if that's something you'd want," she added in a studiedly casual tone.

"Oh." His heart melted. If she was just feeling grateful because he might've married someone else, then he didn't mind sharing a few of the wilder stories.

"You might think I'm unhinged, but I'm positive now that we belong together."

"Soul mates?" he asked, wondering if she'd think he was too cheesy for words.

Danica didn't even hesitate. "I'm glad I'm not the only one circling that word."

Feeling bold, he said, "See, I thought that the moment I met you, and I tried to back up off it because I didn't want to freak you out. I've never felt that way before, like I finally found the missing piece of myself."

"Wow."

"Good wow?"

"The best."

"Well, if *that* didn't scare you off, I don't mind talking about my exes. The last time I got sort of serious with someone, she left me for a biologist who studies puffins."

"That's not so bad?" Her voice rose on the end, making it a question.

"In Iceland."

"Yikes."

He dug deep for another painful story. "Before that, the girl I was dating fell for my sister. Maya didn't encourage her, but after Ashley said she'd rather be with Maya..."

"Yep, that's awkward as fuck."

He laughed, finally able to see how ridiculous it all was. If he believed in magic, he'd swear someone had hexed him a long time ago and had finally seen fit to remove the curse so he could be with Danica. "You want to hear another one?"

"I don't know, do I? In all seriousness, not if it's painful for you, CinnaMan." She didn't sound like she was too sure about that endearment.

"Is that my official pet name now?"

"Do you hate it?"

"Nah, it's growing on me. And this shit happened a while ago. I guess…I'm over it. Or I *will* be, as long as you don't come up with a completely irrational reason to leave."

"Like moving to Peru to raise alpacas? I did wonder about that. It seemed like an oddly specific thing to say during an argument."

"Hey, it wouldn't have surprised me even a little."

"Fair point. Sure, hit me with one more ridiculous breakup."

"Since I mentioned I'm bi before, you won't be surprised that I've dated a few guys. The last one dumped me to perform full-time on cruise ships. Timo is kind of a huge deal on Royal Caribbean. I used to creep his Pictogram account, and honestly, his cabaret candids are fun. Seems like he lays mad pipe with the vacation crowd."

"You did not just say that." Danica devolved into helpless laughter, and Titus enjoyed listening to her, not even minding her amusement at his awful history.

"It's Trevor-speak, contagious as hell."

"I haven't met your friends yet," she said softly. "We should change that. I want to blend our crowds. Mingle your poker night with my book club. Sound fun?"

It seemed like she was done poking into his past, and as much as he didn't mind being open with her, he breathed a silent sigh of relief. *I told her. And it didn't change anything. That's…amazing.* Danica didn't seem to have anything else to say about his former virginal status, much to his amazement. *This woman is so cool.* Finally, the relationship he'd always dreamed of was within reach.

We can date for a while before we talk about moving in

together. I'd rather jump straight to a proposal, but that might freak her out. I can be patient as long as I know she's not going anywhere.

Belatedly, he said, "Yeah, I was just considering logistics, but I'd love that if you're into it. Maybe we could play poker, drink, and talk about books."

She laughed. "That sounds amazing. Tell me more about Trevor. I guess he's your closest friend, so I need tips on making him like me."

"It won't be difficult. He likes free food and hanging out." At her urging, he told her a little more, how long they'd been friends and the way his life had imploded when his girlfriend left him. "It's been years now, and he's showing no signs of being ready to get his shit together. And I let it slide because he's a good guy and most of the time, he seems happy enough, but sometimes—"

"You get hints that maybe he's not, but he doesn't know any other way to be after so long? It's hard to pick yourself up when you hit bottom. Sometimes you need your friends to speak the hard truths, then offer a hand up. Have you ever done that for him?"

Guilt percolated through him. "I have not. Mostly I slip him odd jobs and avoid the subject. I should be a hard-ass, huh?"

"Maybe. I'll be able to judge better once I've met him."

"We'll set something up soon," Titus promised.

"Wow, this is weird. We just spent the weekend together, but I literally can't stop talking to you. I know damn well you need to get to sleep, but—"

"I feel like I could talk to you forever," he whispered.

"Oh, compliments like that will *so* get you in my pants, mister."

"Promise?"

"No revving the engine when I have to drive home alone," Danica muttered.

Titus grinned, hardly able to believe this was his freaking life. *I am the luckiest guy in the world.* "Noted. Sorry for teasing you, beautiful."

"Mmm, liking that too. Er, right, how's Lucy settling in?"

"I think she'll be fine. So far, so good. And on that note—"

"You need to sleep. Dream of me?"

"Only if I'm lucky."

CHAPTER 29

DANICA DIDN'T SEE CLEM UNTIL the next day.

She got up before dawn and drove back to St. Claire, only to find that Clem still wasn't home. *Holy shit.* She parked it on the couch to make sure she wouldn't miss her cousin. At 7:57 a.m. she heard the key in the lock. They had a lot to talk about. She straightened as Clem walked by, maybe thinking Danica was still at her mom's place.

When Clem reached the stairs, Danica spoke. "Busted!"

Her cousin started way more than she thought the moment called for, fumbling her purse so much she dropped it. But she spun in an aggro move, folding her arms to show she was in no mood. "Okay, let's go. You're in *no* position to comment on anything I do. You fucking *left the state* without talking to me about it. You disregarded our promise like it was nothing and didn't even have the courtesy to text me. And you left me minding the shop for *how* long? Cousins who are like sisters, my ass."

"You're absolutely right," she said. "I'm pleading temporary insanity. And scientifically speaking, falling in love creates a similar—"

"Oh no, you don't. If you make me laugh, I have to forgive you, and I'm not ready to do that yet."

Danica sat forward on the couch, pressing her palms together in a penitent posture. "I'm so sorry. The way I handled everything was shit. In hindsight, I'd have done so many things differently. But I have something important to tell you, and I think it might affect your commitment to the pact when you hear it."

Clem dropped into an armchair with a tired sigh. "Start talking."

Quickly she summarized what she'd learned from the journals and the subsequent talk with her mom, ending with all of Gram's egregious lies. "And that's it. There's no Waterhouse curse. I'm not losing my magic. Gram made the whole thing up."

"Holy fucking shit," her cousin breathed.

"My thoughts exactly. It was a way to control us, to keep us fearful and from going against her wishes."

Clem snarled another curse. "Aunt Min really said she'd take Gram on."

"Shit's about to get heated."

Her cousin laughed. "I mean…it's summer, so it's already—oh crap. I laughed."

"Yes! Does that mean I'm forgiven?"

"You're cooking in my place for two weeks, but yeah. There's no reason for us to worry about taking sides anymore. She's still our grandmother, but she's—"

"A hateful, manipulative old witch?"

Clem closed her eyes with a sigh. "Yeah. It's so hard to reconcile with how awesome she was when we were kids. Guess we have to remember that just because she was nice to us, it doesn't mean she didn't hurt other people."

Danica nodded, pulling the blanket up around her shoulders. "Agreed. I haven't decided if I'm cutting her off entirely yet. I probably need to talk to Mom more. That's where the problem started. Gram raised us believing that our mothers were weak—that they didn't have anything of value to teach us. Maybe she didn't say it outright, but—"

"It was insidious, this slow and careful indoctrination. Fuck!" Fists clenched, Clem leaped to her feet. "I need a shower."

Before her cousin could dodge into the bathroom, Danica opened her arms. "Hug it out? We'll always be best friends, even after we mate for life."

"Ugh, fine."

As she stepped closer, she spied several sex marks on Clem's neck and shoulder. "Something you want to tell me, Clementine Odette?"

"If you *ever* drop my middle name again, I won't be responsible for the consequences."

Danica stifled a smile. Her cousin freaking hated her middle name and the fact that Auntie Allegra hadn't realized her initials spelled COW; everyone had teased her in kindergarten, leaving pictures of cows all over her desk. Clem would never have anything monogrammed in her life—what a terrible struggle.

"You didn't answer the question."

With a groan, Clem buried her face in her hands. "I'm in so much trouble."

"What's wrong?"

"I can't stop sleeping with him!"

Her eyes widened. "The hunter him? Gavin Rhys."

"Yeah."

"Fuck," Danica said.

"That's precisely the problem. It's like I'm bewitched."

She shared her appreciation for the joke by quirking a smile, but she stayed on topic. "I guess that's one way to distract him. Not the path I would've chosen, but maybe..." Trailing off, she couldn't decide how to complete that sentence because honestly, even if the Waterhouse curse wasn't real, that just meant Clem could safely be with a mundane. None of that made hooking up with a witch hunter safer or more advisable. And this wasn't like her normally logical, organized, in-control cousin. If the affair wasn't life-or-death stakes, maybe she'd even be in favor of it.

Clem sighed. "I'll figure it out. And for the record, you're forgiven. We're good."

"Okay. Just remember that we're here if you need us. Oh! I just remembered. I promised Titus I'd get our friends together. I'll ask in group chat to see what night works for everyone."

"Leanne will bang one of his buddies," her cousin predicted, heading for the stairs.

"That...is plausible. Take today off. Tomorrow, too. I'll work from open to close for the next week if you want."

Clem turned. "You sure?"

"Definitely. You need to sleep." She didn't say it aloud, but her cousin looked like microwaved shit with circles under her eyes and her makeup smeared like Harley Quinn after a hot night. "And I owe you big-time for my drunken bender and the vanishing act."

"True. You do. Okay, I'll take a few days off. Try to get my head on right."

Danica hadn't showered at her mom's house, so she cleaned up quickly and crept out of the house like a shadow. To preserve Clem's peace, Danica didn't even go in the kitchen. Everything was different now. She didn't need to resist Titus, so she'd stop by the bakery every day if she felt like it. And today, she did.

There was a line, even this early. At least it wasn't out the door like it had been most mornings when she queued for cinnamon rolls. Maya greeted her with a reach-across-the-counter hug. "Morning, sis."

"Wow, okay. Can I get a regular vanilla light latte and a ham-and-cheese croissant?"

Lucy popped up from stocking the cups in the café area. She looked happy in the uniform, delighted to have work to do. "On it!"

As Lucy filled the order, Maya processed Danica's payment. "I hope she likes it here. She was so eager to get started."

"Everything happens for a reason?" It was such a dorky thing to say that Danica regretted it immediately, but Maya nodded.

"I really think so. You want me to call him out briefly?"

She waffled. A good-morning kiss would be awesome, but she didn't want to be needy. "Is he busy?"

To her embarrassment and the amusement of everyone waiting in line behind her, Maya shouted, "Titus! Your girlfriend's buying breakfast. Want to see her?"

"Be right out!" he called back.

It was no more than thirty seconds, long enough for her to take back her card and step aside for the next customer, and there he was, all dressed in baker's gear with the apron. He was dusted in flour, smelling utterly delicious. *God, he's so hot even in that hat.*

"Hey, you," he whispered, leaning down for a fast, steamy kiss.

"Morning. See you for lunch?"

"Wouldn't miss it."

Impossible not to be delighted with that response. "Meet me at the shop, okay? I'm giving Clem some time off. She had no choice but to cover for me while I was gone."

Both times.

"Sounds good. See you then." Another quick kiss, then he hurried off, the tips of his ears red, likely over the whispers and laughter from other customers.

Danica took her sandwich and coffee to go. If she jogged, she could make it by opening. She held her coffee with care and managed not to spill any of it, and at 8:59 she raced up to the front door. Nobody was waiting, as they sometimes were. Older people were often frustrated that all businesses didn't unlock their doors at 7 a.m.

Though she didn't usually open, she ran through the routine like clockwork. Then she ate her breakfast, savoring each bite of the flaky croissant. *This could be my new normal. I see him quickly before work. Eat lunch together.* That prospect didn't feel like dating so much as entwining their lives, like trees that grew together from separate entities to one beautifully enlaced whole.

Dreamily, Danica sipped at her coffee. Perfect, as always. But before she dove into the day's repair work, she sent the promised message on group chat.

I promised to host a mixer. My friends, his friends. Just need to know what night is good for everyone. LMK!

It took a couple of weeks for everyone's schedules to align, but after some back-and-forth, Titus hammered out the details with Danica.

He'd never done anything remotely like this. Never been in a relationship solid enough where his partner wanted to meet all his friends. In the meantime, he'd baked two batches of cookies for her cousin, and he'd bring these gorgeous red velvet cupcakes to the party later. He tweaked the decorations on top, regarding them with a critical eye. *More red sprinkles? No, they look perfect.* Sometimes he opted for red sugar dusted on top instead, but that had more of a Christmas vibe.

The best thing about his friends was that *none* of them would rib him about showing up to a get-together with dessert. He was picking Trevor up in half an hour. Maya had said she might stop by, though technically she was his sister, not his friend. Arguably, since they had grown closer since Mom passed, she could be considered both. It was more likely, however, that she'd hang out with Lucy. She'd said she was inviting her girlfriend, Keshondra, over for dinner. Hopefully, she arrived before Titus headed out. That way he could meet her without it being awkward.

As luck would have it, a silver Honda Brio pulled into the

drive as he opened the front door. The pretty Black woman he'd spotted outside the bakery hopped out. He didn't know the protocol, but he didn't want to make her nervous, so he smiled.

"Hey, I'm Titus, Maya's brother. Good to meet you."

Are we supposed to shake hands or what? A hug would be too much.

"Likewise." Thankfully, she solved the issue by offering her hand, and they shook politely.

Whew, level cleared.

"Maya's inside, go on in. I'm heading out now, but I left cupcakes in the kitchen for later. Hope you enjoy them!"

"Are you kidding? I'm obsessed with your desserts. That's how I met your sister." Keshondra's brown eyes sparkled. "I have no idea how she stays fit working with you."

"I'd say she has good genes, but that might come across as self-congratulatory since I share them."

She laughed. "Okay, I like you."

Titus waved as he set the box of treats carefully on the passenger-side floor. He'd learned the hard way—deer in the street, pastries slammed to pieces—not to leave anything delicate on the seat. Doris wagged her tail hopefully, and Maya came to make sure she didn't chase him down the road. As he backed out of the drive, she kissed Keshondra and tugged the other woman into the house.

I wonder if she was skittish about bringing her dates home because I've been professionally single for so long. Or because she felt guilty about Ashley...? Maya hadn't set out to seduce his girlfriend; that was just... Well, it didn't matter anymore. Those days were done, thank God.

He swung by Trev's house, and his friend was already waiting outside, dressed in clean pants and a decent Henley. Since he'd half expected cargo shorts and a cannabis shirt, the reality was a pleasant surprise. Trev opened the car door, smelling like Dial and deodorant, another interesting shift.

"Don't step on the cupcakes," Titus said. "I need those to bribe Danica's cousin."

"She still doesn't like you? Damn, what did you do to that woman?"

He shrugged as Trev picked up the box and carefully settled it on his lap. His friend belted in, and then they drove the seven minutes onward to Danica's place. From the cars lined up, they weren't the first to arrive. Music thrummed through the open windows, something mellow and danceable.

Danica's entire squad was already assembled. He recalled their names and matched them to the faces as he greeted everyone and introduced Trevor around. The redhead locked onto Trevor right away and maneuvered through the front room to get to him. Then she slid Trev a smile and put a hand on his forearm.

"I'm Leanne. Want to be my third husband?"

Trev blinked. "I mean...maybe? Because I could get on board if you're looking for a low-key, no-ambition type to look after the house. I cook and clean, do most general maintenance as well. Ask Titus, I've got references."

"As a handyman, not my third husband," Titus clarified.

Danica slipped up beside him, kissing his check. "Are we letting this happen?" she whispered. "Leanne may destroy him."

"Live and let live. He looks...intrigued, which is higher energy than I've seen from Trev in a while." Checking around, he found her cousin chatting up the wild-looking guy who'd wrecked his register. He recalled seeing them at the bar together. *Huh. So that's still happening.* "Just let me deliver these." He circulated until he could put the box in Clem's hands. "Here, red velvet cupcakes. Hope you like them."

According to Danica, they're your fave.

Clem clutched the bakery box like he'd given her diamonds. "Okay, you win. You've earned my seal of approval. Love my cousin and make her happy, but stop stuffing me with treats. They're going straight to my ass."

"Thanks for that," the big dude said. "I'm rather a fan."

"Of my baking or Clem's ass?" Probably Titus shouldn't have asked.

"Both." He leaned in for a kiss, one steamy enough that Titus looked away.

Damn. No accounting for taste. Clem seemed quite careful and methodical, so he'd never have matched her with an impulsive, hot-tempered biker.

The party seemed to be going well though. As Danica had predicted, Leanne was getting handsy with Trev already. A knock at the door heralded the arrival of the rest of Titus's poker buddies: Dante, Miguel, and Calvin. He waved them in and shepherded them around, making intros until the groups started to mingle on their own. Vanessa seemed to be getting along with Cal while Dante conferred with Margie about being a single parent. Miguel swapped recipes with Ethel, and everybody was drinking. Priya and Kerry were a couple, and he wondered if he should introduce

Maya and Keshondra. That might be weird? Like he was trying to set up double dates or something.

Danica settled against his side, prompting him to wrap an arm around her shoulder. "This is nice. I love everything about it."

"Two worlds enter, one world leaves?"

"I love that you compared our party to Thunderdome. My money's on Leanne." With a thoughtful air, she added, "How do you even know that quote?"

"Watching old eighties movies with my mom. We marathoned stuff she loved because she was afraid of running out of time to share it with me."

"And she loved Mad Max?"

"Among other things. She passed just after *Fury Road* came out."

There were no words that helped, even after all this time, and somehow Danica knew that. She hugged him and let him bury his face in her hair. He would never get tired of her scent. Maybe one day he'd ask why she always smelled like lemon cream.

"I love your friends," she said as he pulled back.

"Sorry, but I don't think I can talk them into including you in the poker game."

"That's cool. There will be book club events you're not invited to."

Titus smiled. "I'm good with that. I want to be part of your life one hundred percent, but I'm not interested in taking it over."

"Even if we get married? You'd still be okay with us having those nights?"

"Definitely." He loved the easy way she mentioned

commitment, none of the waffling that had made him so nervous in the beginning. "And just so you know, if things had been okay between us, I would have talked to you before inviting Lucy to move in. In the future, I won't make major life decisions without discussing them with you first."

"Wow." Danica rose on tiptoe and kissed him, cupping his bearded cheek in her hand. Her lips were magic, sheer heat and starlight, and her tongue... She stole his breath and his sanity, and he'd spend the rest of his life adoring her.

"Wow?" he repeated.

"I *really* appreciate that, and I totally understand why this happened without my input. That's all my fault anyway, so consider the topic closed. I know you're a considerate person. I have no qualms at all about putting my heart in your hands."

Titus wanted her so bad he could barely breathe.

CHAPTER 30

IF DANICA READ THE GLEAM in Titus's eyes right, he'd be amenable to this suggestion.

She put a hand on his shoulder, his cue to tip his head so she could whisper, "Everyone is getting along. You think they'd notice if I showed you my bedroom?"

"The better question is if I care," Titus said.

"Do you?"

"Not even slightly. It's a little 'college sophomore' to sneak away for sex during a party, but I want you. Bad."

She took his hand, leading him toward the steps. "You assume we're doing it. I might be showing off my impressive pog collection."

"Then I'll prepare my suitably awed expression. How's this?" He covered his mouth and widened his eyes.

"You look like you found a bug in your soup."

Luckily nobody chased them up the stairs or shouted obscene suggestions. Danica dodged into her room and locked the door behind them. As she pulled her shirt over her head, Titus said, "No pogs."

"Get those clothes off. We need to be fast or we'll never hear the end of it. And it's my turn to lick you all over."

He groaned. "I may not survive."

"You love it. On the bed. Now!"

Titus obeyed so fast that he practically left cartoon blur streaks. His cock was already hard, revealing how much he liked it when she got bossy. At base, it meant she wanted him too much to wait, too much to take it slow. Danica peeled off the rest of her clothes and crawled toward him. His gaze heated as he tracked her movements.

She started with a deep kiss, but before he could tug her on top of him properly, she pulled free and ran her lips over his shoulder, down his chest and lower, biting and licking as she went. When she tasted his nipples, he moaned and sank his fingers into her hair. He seemed to have no hesitation about receiving pleasure.

"A little more teeth," he whispered.

She bit his nipples very gently, and his cock jerked against her, slickness coating the tip. *Wonder if I could make him come from other stimulation.* He probably had no issues with ass play, but she'd save that for next time. They had a lifetime to explore.

I haven't even blown him yet. Time to change that.

Danica kissed her way south, nuzzling his chest and abs, and he seemed like he couldn't get his breath. "Are you—"

"Going to suck you? Most definitely."

With the party getting louder downstairs, she didn't want to risk someone interrupting them, so she filled her mouth with his length, no more teasing. Hardness covered by silky skin, heat and salt, gently throbbing on her tongue. She used her lips and throat fully, moving up and down with an eagerness that surprised her.

"I can't last much longer. You know why."

Because he doesn't have a lot of practice.

"Let's go together."

Rolling onto her side, she showed him the position she had in mind, with her thigh across his hip. He slid inside her, and she moaned at the hot, delicious friction. This position would help him last longer, hopefully enough for her to get off too. Since he was so damn sexy and it was also sort of hot to be fucking with a house full of people, her whole body started to tingle. She had no fear of her magic going wild anymore, and it didn't, just a constant hum to accompany the onrush of pleasure.

"You feel incredible," he whispered, gathering her close.

Yeah, that was exactly why she'd decided on side-by-side sex, that tenderness and intimacy. They weren't just fucking. This was full-on making love, and she lost herself in the sweetness of his touch, of the pure intensity of his devotion. Danica kissed Titus when the tingles blossomed into waves.

He pulled his mouth away again. "I really want to bite you. Can I?"

"Don't break the skin."

"I wouldn't. It's okay to leave a mark, though?"

She shivered. "Fuck, yes. Right here."

Tilting her head, she offered the curve of her shoulder. He started with a soft kiss, intensifying the pressure to suction, then he nipped. She clenched on him, and he pushed deep, his body vibrating. Hers might go nova when she came.

"I'm getting close."

He kissed her, sucking gently on her lower lip. "Me too."

His chest against her breasts, his belly, the slow glide of his cock, the firm pressure of his hand on her thigh, keeping her exactly where he wanted her. She felt cherished and taken and— *Oh. Yes.* She tightened and went over, holding him to her with all her strength. As he lost control, his thrusts becoming jerky and shallow, Titus took her mouth, his tongue stroking hers, drinking down her gasps and cries.

"Just so you know," she whispered, cupping his ass. "I'm probably ordering a strap-on. At some point, I'd like to do the dicking."

Titus barely even stirred, breathing heavily with his eyes closed. "I see. Do I have a say in this?"

"Obviously. It's your fine ass in question."

"Mmm, that's virgin territory too, but I'm definitely curious. I'll let you if you let me."

Danica pretended to be shocked, hiding her amusement. "Let you borrow my strap-on? I mean, sure, but why?"

"You know I'm talking about tapping this ass." He smacked it lightly, and a little shiver of sensation went through her. Since they were still joined, he felt it too. "Oh, you like that idea. Awesome, I'm in. Just...let's work up to it. I might get hurt if we go from zero to anal in eight seconds."

"You're worth waiting for," she assured him. "I've been waiting my whole life for you, after all."

"Talk like that will *so* get you in my pants," he teased, quoting her.

"What pants? The ones on my bedroom floor?"

"Please don't say they look better there. You tried that line on me once before, and I resisted it. Took every ounce of my willpower."

Danica grinned and kissed his nose, an adorable boop of a caress. "You know me so well. Can't say that I mind."

"Should we get back to the party?" he asked.

From his tone, he'd be happy rolling around in her bed some more. And she almost said yes, then she remembered they had one last hurdle to clear. *I have to follow Mom's advice and speak to him. Carefully, so carefully. So I can live as my true self without bringing the council down on us.* Really, it was a genius solution.

Danica took a breath. "Actually, I need to talk to you first. It's important."

Titus froze.

While he suspected it couldn't be as dire as Danica was making it sound, his lizard brain tried to go into panic mode. Firmly he shut it down. "Okay, I'm listening."

"First, I need to say this because it's overdue. I love you, Titus. More than anything. I want to build a future with you."

His heart quickened, and he couldn't decide if he was excited or terrified. *Is she proposing?* "I love you too. Do you have a ring hidden somewhere on your naked body? Because if so, I'm intrigued but also concerned."

She laughed and hid her face against his shoulder. "No ring. Yet. When I propose to you, I'll do a proper job. Flowers, balloons, maybe a mariachi band. It'll be cheesy as hell and over the top, and we'll both ugly cry."

"Wait, you said 'when.' I'm receiving, not proposing?"

"I guess we'll have to see who does it first. Now stop interrupting, you're getting me off topic, and this is something we need to talk about."

"Is it about having kids? Yes, I want them, preferably before I'm forty. Otherwise, everything else is negotiable."

She seemed startled for a second. "Everything? You mean you're okay with adopting? Dammit, you distracted me again! That's good to know, now *stop it*."

"Sorry, I'm nervous."

"Why?"

"Because I'm afraid you're about to spring something on me. Like 'Funny story, before we met I signed a contract to repair stuff on the space station for a year,' or 'Sorry, Titus, I just found out I'm being arrested for protesting police violence.'"

"Relax. And please stop talking." Her voice was gentle, and she soothed his nerves with a soft kiss. "This is nothing so dramatic. It's personal."

"Okay."

"Basically, we've never talked about our beliefs. If you're expecting me to attend First Presbyterian with you, that's never happening, and I probably won't be okay with sending our kids until they're old enough to decide for themselves."

"Oh." He nearly went boneless with relief. "Yeah, I can understand. Bible Belt-adjacent and all that, but I'm not big on organized religion either."

"That's good. Because the next thing is I'm basically a new age hippie type."

He blinked. "That's the big reveal? Like herb smudging, healing crystals, candles for luck, and...chakras? I don't know anything about that, but it's not a deal breaker. I can respect what you believe in without needing to understand or share your..." He hesitated "Faith? Is that the right word?"

"It works." From the brightness in her eyes, she was relieved by his casual reaction, and he mentally patted himself on the back. "When we move in together, eventually, you may catch me doing things that seem weird or pointless. Just take it that it's part of the new age stuff and be cool, all right?"

"Definitely. Were you seriously worried that I'd be judgmental about this?"

"Not worried, exactly. I just wanted to tell you who I am."

He kissed her temple, utterly charmed. "Thank you for trusting me. And for the record, I think I fell for you the first moment I saw you. The fact that we lived so close without meeting until now? It makes me wish my oven had broken sooner."

"Me too," she said. "That concludes the 'important talk' part of our evening. The only thing left is to get dressed and go see if our friends have wrecked the place without us."

It took ten more minutes to get their clothes on because Titus couldn't stop touching and kissing her, and he was half hard again by the time they ventured downstairs. Someone had moved the furniture against the walls and rolled up the area rug. Margie and Dante were dancing, and the quiet woman sure could move. Ethel was doing body shots off Calvin, and Trev had vanished with Leanne. Danica's cousin was making out in the kitchen with the big guy, locked onto his lips like she needed them to live.

"I Gotta Feeling" cycled up on the playlist, and holy shit, what a blast from the past. Titus had been—he did the math—so damn young when this song came out. But the tune fit the mood, and he offered his hand to Danica. She took it without a second of hesitation, not asking where they were going or why.

"Dance with me?"

Her neighbors might complain, but for now, he didn't give a damn. It was well past time for him to *live*, capture the precious moments that would never come again. Danica raised a brow, and then she slid into the Dougie, proceeding seamlessly into Gangnam Style, and he almost couldn't dance for laughing.

"It's on," he said.

His moves were no match for hers, as it was clear she had been a club kid back in the day. He looked forward to hearing all her stories. She apparently drew the line at twerking, and soon the music changed, shifting to a slower sound that gave him an excuse to get close to her. Danica wrapped her arms around his neck and made slow-dancing NC-17. Titus kissed her, not even caring who might be watching.

"Not tired of me yet?" she whispered, stroking a hand through his hair.

I probably have sex hair. Awesome.

He remembered hanging out with her in Arizona, where she fit in with his family and charmed everyone, made everyone happier, just by being there. "Never. It will never be enough." He said it differently than Olaf, all tenderness.

Titus saw the moment she realized what he was quoting. She grinned, clearly delighted to have an inside joke with him. "Play 'Jaja Ding Dong'?"

"We did that earlier, but I could be persuaded toward an encore."

Around midnight, Hazel Jeffords banged on the front door, orange cat draped over her shoulder. "If you keep it up, I'm calling the cops! Damn noisy kids."

Ethel knocked back the last of her drink and ambled to the front door. "Live a little, woman. Are you allergic to fun?"

The old women locked eyes, and they scowled at each other. Then Hazel said, "No, but I wasn't invited to have any, was I?"

"Come on in. I'm inviting your cranky ass."

Hazel seemed stunned. "But...I'm not dressed for a party."

"Whatever," Ethel said. "Get in here."

Somehow, Danica's crabby neighbor ended up teaching everyone how to play euchre while Goliath wandered the house like a religious pilgrim who was finally permitted to enter the promised land. The party ran late, ridiculously so. Titus probably wouldn't get any sleep before work in the morning.

Danica was laughing at something Dante said, trying to get to know all Titus's friends one-on-one. Miguel was too drunk to say much, as Ethel had a cast-iron liver, but Titus appreciated everything. Every look, every touch, every moment, every smile.

Maybe he'd eventually take Danica's time and love for granted, but he doubted it. Not when this relationship had been so hard-won that he'd almost lost all faith that somebody could return his devotion.

Never again. I believe in her, always. I believe in forever-love.

With every beat of his heart, he trusted that Danica was his future, and he was ready to see what awaited them on the far side of happily ever after.

ACKNOWLEDGMENTS

First, I must thank my amazing editor, Christa Désir. This book wouldn't exist without her, and that would be a shame because I adore Danica and Titus. Next, I extend heartfelt appreciation to the whole team at Sourcebooks. It's been such a pleasure collaborating with such talented and passionate booklovers, every step of the way.

Thanks to my wonderful agent, Lucienne Diver. Her drive and expertise make my life better in countless ways. I'm awed by her ability to multitask and count myself fortunate that she's always in my corner.

As ever, my deepest thanks to the wonderful readers who have been with me for over a decade. Your support means the world to me.

Thank you to the friends who offer encouragement when I'm struggling and never hesitate to lend an ear. I treasure you all, more than words can say—Bree, Donna, Courtney, Alyssa, Thea, Yasmine, Shawntelle, Lili—and the list goes on. I'm beyond blessed to have such phenomenal people in my life.

Finally, last but never least, thank you to my family. They always believe in me, even when my faith is flagging. I give special thanks to Alek, who always knows how to fix my plot problems. My books are better because my son is smart as heck. Indeed, he is a smart Alek.

I hope this story enchanted you.

ABOUT THE AUTHOR

New York Times and *USA Today* bestselling author Ann Aguirre has been a clown, a clerk, a savior of stray kittens, and a voice actress, not necessarily in that order. She grew up in a yellow house across from a cornfield, but now she lives in Mexico with her family. She writes all kinds of genre fiction, but she has an eternal soft spot for a happily ever after.

Discover the next enchanting Fix-it Witches installment with Boss Witch.

Ever-practical Clementine Waterhouse doesn't tumble headlong into love like her cousin, Danica. Rather, she weighs the pros and cons and decides if a relationship is worth pursuing. At least that's always been her modus operandi before. Peace is better than passion, as she learned from her parents' tempestuous and short-lived marriage. Clem prefers being the one in charge, always the first to walk away when the time is right.

Attraction has never struck her like lightning...until witch hunter Gavin Rhys rides into town.

Gavin Rhys is supposed to hate witches, and he's spent his whole life tracking them down. His family honor is on the line, and his father constantly demands proof that Gavin is nothing like his grandfather, a traitor who let everyone down. But things in St. Claire aren't what they seem, and Gavin is distracted from the job immediately by a bewitching brunette with a sexy smile and haunting secrets in her eyes.

Can the bossiest witch in town find true love with the guy committed to her downfall?